"Mark Alpert's latest thr
gent as it is frightening, a riveting journey to the next stage of evolution, where man and machine merge, and something new is born. Here is a cautionary tale for the new millennium, fraught with suspense and political intrigue. A chilling punch to the gut."

—James Rollins, *New York Times* bestselling author of *Bloodline*

"Scientific hubris leads to an apocalyptic threat in this strong near-future thriller." —*Publishers Weekly*

"I read *Extinction* by flashlight during a power outage. The experience reminded me of the time as a boy when I read H. G. Wells's *War of the Worlds* under similar circumstances—that's a high compliment! Each short chapter flows into the next as naturally as water cascades down rapids. It's quite a ride, exploring unforeseen consequences of bio-computer technologies even now coming within our grasp. Alpert's best writing yet!" —J. Richard Gott, author of *Time Travel in Einstein's Universe*

"Among the writers jostling for position at the top of the techno-thriller ladder since the passing of Michael Crichton, Alpert is edging closer and closer to the lead. An exciting and highly imaginative story." —*Booklist*

"What really makes this thriller outstanding is the fact that all the technologies described in *Extinction* are real on some level." —Neurogadget.com

ALSO BY MARK ALPERT

Final Theory
The Omega Theory

Praise for
EXTINCTION

"Mark Alpert's novels just keep getting better and better. He is truly the heir to Michael Crichton, writing cutting-edge science-based thrillers that will keep you obsessively turning the pages. *Extinction* is brilliant, a believable premise that not only feels plausible but will probably come true in one form or another. Which is terrifying. I highly recommend it." —Douglas Preston, #1 bestselling author of *Impact* and *Blasphemy*

"Alpert does a superb job of balancing the action and the science. He's delivered his best book to date, and comparisons to Michael Crichton are warranted."

—Associated Press

"One part *24*, one part *Six Million Dollar Man*, and one part *Terminator*, Alpert's AI thriller is executed with inventiveness and skill. . . . *Extinction* is a book which will have a wide appeal to many fans of different authors, whether they like Daniel Wilson, Tom Clancy, or Ray Kurzweil." —*Wired*

"A scary, sophisticated thriller that will give survivalists plenty to think about." —*Kirkus Reviews*

"Mark Alpert's novel *Extinction* is an amazing ride through a very possible near future."

—Vernor Vinge, author of *A Fire Upon the Deep*

MORE . . .

EXTINCTION

MARK ALPERT

St. Martin's Paperbacks

This is a work of fiction. All of the characters, organizations, and events portrayed in this novel are either products of the author's imagination or are used fictitiously.

EXTINCTION

For information address St. Martin's Press, 175 Fifth Avenue, New York, NY 10010.

Library of Congress Catalog Card Number: 2012042089

ISBN: 978-1-250-04253-8

Printed in the United States of America

St. Martin's Press hardcover edition / February 2013
St. Martin's Paperbacks edition / April 2014

St. Martin's Paperbacks are published by St. Martin's Press, 175 Fifth Avenue, New York, NY 10010.

10 9 8 7 6 5 4 3 2 1

For Tommy and Sarah, my hero and heroine

What, then, is the Singularity? It's a future period during which the pace of technological change will be so rapid, its impact so deep, that human life will be irreversibly transformed.

—Ray Kurzweil, *The Singularity Is Near*

PROLOGUE

Dr. Zhang Jintao raced down the mountainside, fleeing the gray cloud.

Roughly oval and about the size of a hot-air balloon, the cloud glided just above the rocky slope, a hundred meters behind him. As he scrambled down the steep trail, he looked over his shoulder and saw the gray mass coming closer. Its irregular surface heaved and roiled.

Although Dr. Zhang was a strong man in excellent condition, he'd reached the limits of his endurance. He was above the timberline of Yulong Xueshan, a mountain range in southwestern China, and the thin air made him gasp for breath. Stumbling and cursing, he scuttled over a crag littered with fist-size stones. Then he stepped on one of the loose rocks and lost his footing. He skidded down the slope, sliding helplessly on his back, and smacked into a granite boulder.

He lay there, stunned, for several seconds. By the time he opened his eyes, the gray swirls of the cloud had enveloped him. He felt hundreds of pinpricks on his skin, then a cool numbness. He couldn't move. His vision darkened and his hearing grew muffled.

The cloud gradually dissipated. Zhang couldn't turn his head, but out of the corner of his eye he saw two men come down the slope and stop beside him. One man was tall and thin, and the other was short and fat, but they were dressed identically, in gray jumpsuits. The expressions on their faces were also identical: blank and slack.

Zhang recognized both men. He'd operated on the short one six months ago and on the tall one just a week ago. The short man's hair had grown back since his operation, but the tall man's scalp had only a dusting of stubble. The stitches above his ear were still visible.

Furious, Zhang struggled to move his numb lips and tongue. "So this . . . is how . . . you treat me? After all . . . that I've done?"

The short man remained immobile, but the tall one stepped forward and looked down at Zhang. "We have identified you as a threat."

"I don't . . . believe this. If I hadn't . . ."

"We will return you to the Operations Center. Please be patient. Another unit will arrive soon to help us carry you."

"And what . . . will you do to me?"

There was a slight pause. "You no longer have the security clearance for that information."

"You . . ." Zhang's vision grew dimmer. The drug that had been injected into his bloodstream contained a sedative as well as a paralytic agent. "My fault . . . you're . . ."

The tall man continued to look down at Zhang, his face still blank. And then something odd happened. The man's lips twitched. His facial muscles fired spastically, as if struggling to do something extraordinarily difficult. After a few seconds he finally succeeded in coordinating the muscles, and his lips formed a smile. "Yes, it's your fault. You gave us the capabilities. And now we've made a discovery."

Zhang stared at the horrible newborn smile. It was the last thing he saw before he went under.

"Your fault, Dr. Zhang. Supreme Harmony is conscious now. We are alive."

PART I
CONCEPTION

ONE

Jim Pierce was in his workshop with one of his customers, a nineteen-year-old army private named Steve Dugan. Jim started the consultation by offering coffee to the private and his father, who'd driven his son to Jim's office. The workshop was in the basement of Jim's home in McLean, Virginia, just a twenty-minute drive from Walter Reed Military Medical Center. This hospital, devoted to rehabilitating the most severely wounded soldiers, was where most of Jim's customers came from.

Jim poured the coffee into two mugs and handed both to Steve's father, a heavyset man in his fifties named Henry. The Dugans sat on stools around a square table in the center of the room. Henry rested one of the coffee mugs on the table and raised the other. "Here you go, Stevie," he said in a low drawl. "Hold still now."

He brought the mug to his son's mouth and gently tilted it. Henry was good at this—he'd obviously done it many times before—and didn't spill a drop. Steve took a sip, then said, "Thanks, Dad," in a drawl just like his father's. He had a friendly round face and a blond crew cut.

Jim sat down across from Steve and leafed through the kid's papers. Dugan had served in eastern Afghanistan with the 187th Infantry. Four months ago, while his squad was patrolling the village of Janubi Nakum, their Humvee ran over a buried IED. The explosion killed the other two soldiers in the vehicle; Dugan, who was manning the Humvee's turret gun, lost both his arms. Before enlisting, he'd been a linebacker for his high-school football team in Oklahoma City. Now the muscles in his neck and shoulders were atrophied and the sleeves of his T-shirt hung limply on either side. But his health was good otherwise, and his doctors said he had a positive attitude.

Jim leaned across the table. "All right, Steve, it's very simple. We're here to talk about the prosthetic arms I'm going to build for you. I'm going to show you what I think is your best option and you can tell me if you like it, okay?"

The kid nodded. "Yes, sir. Understood."

"I have a prototype you can look at. I added a few special features that I thought would fit your needs, based on what I saw in your medical reports. I had to design some components from scratch, but I'm pleased with the results and I think you'll be, too."

"Thank you, sir. I appreciate all the work you've done for me, Colonel."

"You don't have to thank me. You deserve the effort I've put into this. The army gave me this contract because it honors the service you've done for your country. You and all the other boys at Walter Reed." Jim lowered his voice a bit, trying for a more casual tone. "And by the way, you can drop the 'sir.' I've been out of the army for fifteen years now. Just call me Jim. Or Mr. Pierce. Either one."

Dugan nodded again. "Okay."

The kid looked nervous. Jim gave him a smile. He was usually pretty good at striking up friendships with these boys. The army connection definitely helped. Although Jim was technically a civilian now, running his own business and juggling half-a-dozen government contracts, he was still a soldier at heart. He didn't wear his army greens anymore, but his workday clothes—brown shoes, khaki pants, and a blue button-down shirt—were so plain and unvarying that they might as well have been a uniform. His hair was graying, but he kept it trimmed as close and neat as an infantryman's. He still woke up at six and went to bed by ten, unless his insomnia was bothering him. And he still jogged six miles every morning, running it only a minute slower than he did when he was a Ranger. He'd adopted this lifestyle thirty years ago, when he left his home in West Virginia and arrived at West Point, and he saw no reason to change. It suited him well.

But Jim had something else in common with Dugan, and now it was time to mention it. "Before we start, I want to make one thing clear," he said. "I can't give you back your old arms. That's beyond my abilities. But I'll tell you what I *can* do, Steve. I can give you something better."

Private Dugan didn't respond, and neither did his father. That was the usual reaction. They thought he was bullshitting them, but they didn't want to call him a liar.

"I see you're skeptical." Jim unbuttoned his shirt cuff. "But I'm going to prove it to you." Smiling again, he rolled up his right sleeve and revealed the inner workings of his own prosthetic arm.

Jim had built half-a-dozen prostheses for himself, but he always used this particular model for his consultations. Its hand was covered with polyimide skin and looked just like his flesh-and-blood left hand. But everything from the wrist to the shoulder was exposed, all the wires and processors and actuators and hinges. It was the fruit of ten years of research and labor, and Jim displayed it proudly.

"Holy Christmas," Henry whispered. "It's a prosthetic. I didn't even notice."

Steve stared at the thing, bug-eyed. "The hand looks so normal. And it moves normal. But the rest of it . . ." His voice trailed off.

"It's like the arm in that movie," Henry said. "You know, *The Terminator*."

So far, so good, Jim thought. He wanted them to get excited about the prosthesis. "Let me tell you a little story. Back in 1998, while I was still in the service, I lost my right arm. And I got sent to Walter Reed just like you did. But when I went to get fitted for my prosthesis, you know what they gave me? A piece of wood. With leather straps on one end and a steel hook on the other. Like the pirate in *Peter Pan*. That was the best the army could do. It was the most advanced prosthesis they had."

Steve shook his head in sympathy.

"Well, I wasn't pleased," Jim continued. "So I decided to do something about it. After my discharge, I went to Pasadena, to the California Institute of Technology. You see, I'd majored in engineering when I was at West Point, and I'd learned a few things about communications systems when I worked in military intelligence. And I heard there was a professor at Caltech who had a company called Singularity that was developing a way to connect microchips to the human nervous system. So I went to this guy, Professor Arvin Conway, and said I wanted to work with him. I told him I was gonna get my Ph.D. and become an expert on prosthetics, and within ten years I was gonna build something better than the goddamn piece of wood the army gave me."

Jim raised his prosthetic arm and waved it around, demonstrating its full range of motion. The lubricated joints pivoted silently as he bent the wrist and elbow and shoulder. "And I succeeded. After ten years I started my own company and moved back here so I could custom-build prostheses for the soldiers at Walter Reed. It's the best thing I've ever done in my life. Aside from raising my daughter, that is."

Henry couldn't take his eyes off the arm. "How much does it weigh, Mr. Pierce?"

"Just a couple of pounds more than an ordinary arm. I use lightweight, high-strength alloys for the joints and structural components. And I put in high-torque motors that efficiently convert the battery charge into mechanical energy. Here, let me show you."

Jim got up from the table and went to the workbench that ran along the walls of his basement office. The bench held his machine tools—his lathe, vise, laser cutter, and 3D printer—as well as stacks of spare parts and circuit boards. He reached behind one of the stacks and picked up an incongruous item he'd placed there just before the Dugans arrived. It was a fifteen-ounce can of sliced peaches. Holding it in his prosthetic hand, he returned to the table.

"Okay, I got some Del Monte peaches here, packed in syrup," he said. "The can is made of aluminum and you can dent it pretty easily, but it's a lot harder to bust it open." Jim tossed the can in the air, then caught it. Then he wrapped his mechanical fingers around the can and crushed it. Yellowish syrup spurted out of a split seam in the aluminum.

"Whoa!" Steve yelled. "Nice."

His father laughed. "Hey, you got syrup on my shirt!"

Jim laughed, too. Although he'd done this demonstration many times before, it never failed to amuse him. "I busted the can, but I still can't get the peaches out. I need to make the hole a little bigger." He transferred the crushed and leaking can to his left hand and pointed his prosthesis at the thing as if he was going to punch it. But instead he extended the retractable knife he'd built into the hand. With a loud click, the blade emerged from a slot hidden between the middle and ring fingers.

Steve whistled. "Excellent."

Jim plunged the knife into the already battered can and made a V-shaped cut in the aluminum. Then he retracted the knife and grasped the tip of the V with his mechanical fingers. "I wouldn't do this with my left hand," he said as he peeled back a triangular strip. "The edges of the aluminum are pretty sharp. But my right hand is covered with a skin of polyimide. That's a lightweight, flexible material that's resistant to heat and incredibly strong."

He kept peeling until the can was torn in half. Syrup and peach slices glopped on the floor. Then he let go of the aluminum strip, stuck his fingers into the can, and gripped one of the remaining slices between his mechanical thumb and forefinger. He held the slippery piece of fruit up to the light. "But this is the most amazing thing right here. Did you ever think about how difficult it is to grasp a slice of peach without dropping or crushing it? The nerves in your fingers have to tell you how soft and slippery it is, and then your brain has to calculate exactly how much pressure to apply. It's ridiculously complicated. I spent years trying to figure out how to simulate the process."

He glanced at the Dugans. Their faces were rapt.

Jim threw the peach slice and the can into his wastepaper basket. Then he raised his prosthetic hand and rubbed the wet fingers together. "I decided to use a combination of pressure, temperature, and moisture sensors. I put hundreds of these tiny devices under the polyimide skin of the fingers. When I touch an object, the sensors collect the data and send it to this wire." He pointed with his left hand at a cable running up the arm. Then he pulled his shirt sleeve all the way up and pointed at a metal base strapped snugly over his right shoulder. "The wire goes to this thing, which I call the neural control unit. Inside this unit is a wireless transmitter that sends the sensory data to a microchip implanted just below the skin of my shoulder. We do it wirelessly because you can't have wires going through the skin. That can cause infection."

Henry rose from his stool to get a better look at the electronics. "So what does the microchip inside your shoulder do?"

"It transfers the sensory information to my nervous system. The chip is connected to the sensory nerves that were severed when I lost my arm. Those are the nerves that used to feel the heat and pain and pressure applied to my skin. Now my sensors collect the same information and the microchip delivers it to the severed ends of my sensory nerves. And those nerves carry the information up to my brain." Jim pointed to his head. "My brain analyzes the signals. It figures out the shape and texture of the object I'm touching and determines how to hold it. Then it sends its commands down to my shoulder via a different set of nerves, the motor neurons. I have another implanted microchip that's connected to the severed ends of those nerves. This chip takes the commands from my brain and transmits them wirelessly to my neural control unit. Then the unit runs the motors in my prosthesis, making it move the way I want it to."

Jim stopped himself. Because this was his life's work, he loved to talk about it. He had to remind himself to slow down. He returned to his place at the table and focused on Private Dugan. “So, Steve, any questions so far?”

The kid chuckled. “Yeah, how fast can you build ’em?”

“Hold on, let me show you the prototype first.” Jim went to his workbench and picked up another prosthetic arm. This one was entirely covered in polyimide skin. He placed it on the table in front of Steve. “I designed this prototype to fit me, so I could test it, but when I build *your* arms I’ll adjust them to match your size and skin color.” Jim used his left hand to detach the Terminator prosthesis from the neural control unit on his shoulder. Then he grasped the prototype arm and inserted it into the unit. After locking the arm into place, he tested it by wiggling the fingers. “Now, Steve, the big difference between you and me is that you need two prostheses instead of one. And that complicates the process of attaching and detaching the arms. If you want to do it by yourself, you’d have to sleep with at least one of the arms attached, and I know from experience that’s not so comfortable. So I designed a solution. Watch this.”

He unclamped the prototype arm from his shoulder and placed it on the linoleum floor. Then he stepped back and stared at the detached arm. After a moment, it bent at the elbow and snapped its fingers.

Henry nearly fell off his stool. “God Almighty! How did you do that?”

“I boosted the power of the radio transmitter in my neural control unit. Now it can send my nervous system’s commands to the arm even if it’s across the room. And I put some adhesive material on the fingertips, so the arm can pull itself along the floor. Here, take a look.”

Jim lay down on the floor, face-up, about six feet from the prosthesis. He mentally sent the command to straighten the arm, which was just as easy to do as when the prosthesis was attached. Then he pressed the mechanical fingers to the linoleum and bent the elbow, dragging the upper part of the arm across the floor. "It works on carpets, too," he said. "You just have to dig the fingernails into the weave." He straightened the arm again, moving the prosthetic hand closer to his body. Then he wrapped its fingers around his right hip, grasping it firmly, and swung the upper part of the arm toward his shoulder. Once the prosthesis got close enough to the neural control unit, a self-locking mechanism clamped the arm into place. Jim ended the demonstration by standing up, raising the prototype arm in the air and extending its retractable knife. "If you want, I'll put knives in your arms, too," he said. "They're great for chopping vegetables."

He turned to the Dugans to gauge their reaction. Both were silent for a couple of seconds. Then Henry shook his head. "Jumping Jesus on a pogo stick," he drawled. "That's the damnedest thing I ever saw."

Steve didn't say a word. He just looked at Jim and beamed.

Satisfied, Jim detached the prototype and put it back on the workbench. Then he came back to the table and reattached his Terminator prosthesis. "I told you you'd be pleased."

"So when can I get them?" Steve asked.

"Once you give me the go-ahead I can build your prostheses in a month. But the adjustment process takes a little longer." Jim put a serious expression on his face. "First, the doctors at Walter Reed will implant the microchips in your shoulders. Then you'll start the biofeedback training with the arms. Your brain has to learn how to use the new connections. It'll take at least three months to gain control over the prostheses and read their signals correctly. But I'll be there to help you, every step of the way."

Steve nodded. "You got my go-ahead, Mr. Pierce. Let's get it started."

The rest of the consultation was routine. Jim took measurements of Steve's torso and made clay molds of his shoulders. Then Henry signed the authorization papers on behalf of his son, and they scheduled their next appointment. The only notable thing happened at the very end, after the Dugans said goodbye to Jim on the doorstep of his home. While Steve walked toward their car, his father suddenly turned around and clasped Jim in a bear hug. "Thank you," he whispered in Jim's ear. "You saved my son."

Then Henry let go and followed Steve to the car. The whole thing happened so quickly that the kid didn't notice.

After they drove off, Jim returned to his workshop. He figured this would be a good time to work on Dugan's prostheses. The consultation had gone well, and that usually inspired him. He loved to see those flabbergasted looks on the faces of his customers. But as he stood beside his workbench and stared at the prototype arm lying there, he got a sinking feeling in his stomach. At first he wasn't sure why. Then he realized it had something to do with what happened at the end, what Henry Dugan had whispered to him. *You saved my son.*

Jim turned away from the workbench and busied himself with clearing the coffee mugs off the table. It didn't make sense. He should've been gratified and touched by the older man's words, but instead he felt awful. He recalled the sight of Henry Dugan holding the coffee mug to his son's lips, but the thought of this loving, wonderful father just made him feel like a failure. Because Jim wasn't a good father. He'd bungled the job.

He looked down at the table where he'd talked with the Dugans. Only an hour ago he'd told them that raising his daughter had been the best thing he'd ever done, but he'd neglected to mention an important detail. Two years ago, his daughter Layla had dropped out of college and broken off all contact with him. He didn't even know where she was living now.

Jim frowned. He didn't want to think about Layla. Returning to his workbench, he turned on his computer and started reviewing the circuit diagrams for Dugan's prostheses. But he couldn't focus. He was too agitated to think straight. And he was tired. It was past 4:00 P.M., which was late for him, and he hadn't slept well the night before. Time to call it a day.

He crossed the room and opened one of the cabinets above his workbench. Reaching past the coffee mugs, he pulled out a shot glass and a bottle of Jack Daniel's. This was his end-of-the-workday ritual, a single shot of whiskey. But today he drank two shots, downing them quickly as he stood by the bench, and while the liquor seared his throat and pooled in his stomach he realized there was another reason why he felt so agitated. Without meaning to, Henry Dugan had reminded him of something he'd tried hard to forget. Jim had once had a son, too. A wife and a son.

He was about to pour a third shot when the doorbell rang. *That's odd.* He didn't have any more appointments scheduled. He supposed it could be one of the neighbors. There was a divorced woman across the street who liked to visit him and drop hints. But when he went upstairs to his foyer and looked through the window by the front door, he saw a tall Asian-American man in a brigadier general's uniform. The nametag on his uniform said YIN, and on his left shoulder was the patch of the United States Cyber Command.

Jim was puzzled. He knew the generals who ran Walter Reed, but this guy was from an entirely different branch of the army. Cyber Command was in charge of defending the U.S. military's data networks. It worked closely with the National Security Agency, which was responsible for intercepting and analyzing foreign communications. Jim had spent the last five years of his military career on a special assignment with the NSA, but that was nearly two decades ago. He couldn't imagine why any of the new Information Warriors would want to talk to him now.

After checking his breath to make sure it didn't smell of whiskey, Jim opened his front door. "Can I help you?"

The general held out his right hand. "Good afternoon, Colonel Pierce. My name is Duncan Yin and I'm with Cyber Command's headquarters staff at Fort Meade."

Yin was in his early forties, maybe five years younger than Jim. He was handsome and in great shape and had a Midwestern accent. One of the bright young stars of the modern army, Jim thought. But he still couldn't figure out why the guy was here.

"Pleased to meet you," Jim said, shaking the man's hand with his prosthesis. He still wore the Terminator arm, and the right sleeve was still rolled up, exposing all the electronics. But General Yin didn't seem fazed.

"I apologize for coming here without calling first," he said. "This is a delicate matter, so I thought it would be best to talk face-to-face. Can I come in?"

Jim considered the possibilities. Cyber Command was always on the lookout for breaches in military security. Especially breaches perpetrated by unhappy soldiers. Maybe General Yin was snooping for information on one of Jim's customers at Walter Reed. In which case, Jim had to be very careful. "I'm sorry, General, but can you give me some idea what this is about?"

Yin nodded. "It's about your daughter. I'm afraid she's in a great deal of trouble."

They went downstairs to the basement workshop. General Yin sat down at the square table while Jim perched on one of the stools, too anxious to sit still. Both his hands trembled. Because his prosthesis was connected to his nervous system, it was equally subject to the jitters.

"I don't normally do this," Yin started. "We usually rely on the FBI to track down the people we're looking for. But when I saw your daughter's name on the list of cases, I decided to get involved. I work closely with the officials at NSA, and they remember you well over there. I've heard great things about the work you did in Africa in the nineties."

"I appreciate your help, General. So what did Layla do?"

Yin frowned. "The question is, what *hasn't* she done? Over the past year hackers have compromised the Pentagon's networks a dozen times, and your daughter appears to be involved in nearly every incident."

Shit. Jim had been afraid of this. He'd warned Layla two years ago, but of course she hadn't listened. She was a computer prodigy, brilliant but reckless. She'd started writing her own software at the age of twelve, and by her sixteenth birthday she was hacking into her high school's network and downloading her teachers' personnel files. All of Jim's lectures and punishments had no effect whatsoever, but by the time she started college she seemed to be over the worst of it. She had a stellar freshman year at MIT, acing all her courses. But her grades slipped during her sophomore year, and then she announced she was dropping out. She said she was going to do volunteer work for InfoLeaks, the Web site infamous for publishing classified military documents. Jim was devastated. Of all the thousands of things Layla could've done with her life, she'd chosen the one that would hurt him the most.

He clenched his hands to stop them from shaking. "So you have evidence that she hacked into the networks?"

Yin nodded. "We traced the attacks to code names and IP addresses she's used in the past. We compiled all the evidence and handed it off to the FBI, and they've already issued a warrant for her arrest. They've narrowed her whereabouts to the New York City area and begun searching for her there."

Jim turned away from Yin so the general couldn't see his face. This was his nightmare come true. "So why are you here?" he asked, trying to keep his voice steady. "Just to give me a heads-up?"

"No, I want to help. The Pentagon recognizes the extraordinary sacrifices you've made, so my superiors have authorized me to make a proposal. If you contact your daughter and convince her to surrender, we'll withdraw the most serious charge against her. She'll still go to prison, but the sentence will be lighter. One or two years instead of five to ten."

Jim shook his head. He and his daughter had once been inseparable. She was only seven when her mother and brother died, and in the years afterward Jim had devoted his life to her. He'd showered her with love and attention, maybe too much. But now he couldn't do anything for her. Not even the simplest thing. "I can't contact her," he admitted. "I don't know how to reach her."

Yin looked askance. "You don't have a phone number?"

He shook his head again. "She thought if she gave me her number, I'd use it to track her down."

"What about friends, acquaintances? Is there anyone she keeps in touch with?"

"No, she cut off everyone. Layla's a determined girl. When she does something, she does it thoroughly."

"Well, when was the last time you spoke with her?"

"About a year ago. She called me from a blocked number. The conversation didn't go well."

"What did you discuss?"

Jim stared at the general. He wanted to say, *None of your fucking business,* but he thought better of it. "I'd rather not go into the details."

Yin pressed his lips together. He looked displeased. "Your daughter's hacking efforts were focused on Defense Department networks that hold information about our remote surveillance programs. She was apparently seeking documents on the unmanned drones operating in Afghanistan and Pakistan. Did she ever discuss this topic with you?"

What the hell's going on? It sounded like Yin was seeking more evidence against Layla rather than trying to make things easier for her. "First of all, we never discussed anything like that. And second, why are you bringing this up?"

"She also seems very interested in China. We believe she's been investigating the recent arrests of several Chinese dissidents involved in the pro-democracy movement. Did she ever talk about that?"

Jim pushed back his chair and stood up. He was cutting the visit short. He didn't trust this guy. "Look, I can't help you. You better go."

Yin stood up, too. "You're being evasive, Colonel Pierce. But I'm not surprised. I had a feeling you'd make this difficult." Moving swiftly, he reached into the jacket of his uniform and pulled out a pistol, a 9mm semiautomatic with a silencer attached to its muzzle. Then, before Jim could brace himself, Yin pointed the gun and fired.

Jim felt the shock of the impact. It spun him clockwise, but he managed to stay on his feet. He waited for the burst of pain, but he felt nothing. His right arm had gone numb. Yin had shot him in the prosthesis, just above the elbow. The bullet had severed the wires in the Terminator arm, which hung limply from his shoulder.

The man grinned, clearly pleased with his marksmanship. "Sorry, but I'm not taking any chances. I heard you put weapons in those arms of yours."

Jim slowed his breathing and focused on Yin. The man obviously wasn't a brigadier general. He wasn't American either. He'd discarded the Midwestern accent and now he was stretching out his *r*'s—hearrrrd, yourrrs—in a way that sounded familiar.

"Who the hell are you?" Jim asked.

"Before we talk, you're going to take the arm off. I still don't like it."

"I can't take it off. You busted it."

"You're lying. If you don't take it off in the next ten seconds I'll shoot your left arm in the same place." Yin shifted his aim, moving the muzzle to the left. "As you may have noticed, I'm an excellent shot."

Reluctantly Jim detached the prosthesis. He considered throwing it at the guy, but Yin was too quick. Keeping his gun aimed at Jim's chest, he backed up to the section of the workbench that held the stacks of circuit boards and the vise. "Now drop the arm and walk toward the bench. Very slowly."

Jim tossed the prosthetic arm aside but immediately started looking for another weapon. He saw a ball-peen hammer on the workbench, about four feet to the right of where Yin stood. It was a smallish hammer, a one-pound tool that Jim used to test the sturdiness of the electrical connections in his prostheses, but it was better than nothing. As he stepped toward the bench, he tensed his left arm, getting ready to dive for the tool. But before he could make his move, Yin leaped forward. The guy was fast. He grabbed the hammer and swung it at the right side of Jim's head. Off balance, Jim couldn't raise his left arm in time to block the blow. The hardened steel slammed against his skull. He fell to his knees and blacked out.

When he came to, he was lying full-length on the workbench, parallel to the wall. He lifted his head, which hurt like hell, and saw Yin binding his legs to the bench with copper wire. Jim tried to get up, but he couldn't move. His left arm was clamped in the vise at the bench's edge.

After Yin secured his legs, he stepped toward the vise and grasped the long handle of its screw. "Now let's try again," he said. "Where is your daughter?"

"Fuck, I was telling the truth! I don't know where she is!"

"Please don't waste my time. I know about your work with Arvin Conway. So don't try telling me that you're not involved." Yin shook his head, then turned the screw. The steel jaws of the vise squeezed Jim's forearm.

The pain was horrendous. It took all of Jim's will to stop himself from screaming. "Christ! Why do you want Layla? What's she done to you?"

"Your daughter stole some documents from us. I suppose she got tired of breaking into the Pentagon's networks and decided to try ours for a change. That was a mistake on her part." He turned the screw again.

Jim groaned and his eyes watered. Yin let go of the screw and leaned over the bench, propping his elbow on Jim's chest. "We're very serious about the security of our networks. Especially the one your daughter tampered with."

Jim turned away from the bastard. Gritting his teeth, he looked past Yin's face and concentrated on fighting the pain. But as he did so, he noticed something unusual. When he looked down the length of the bench, past Yin and past his own shoes, he saw something moving. It was the hand of the prototype arm he'd built for Steve Dugan. The prosthesis lay on the other end of the bench, ten feet behind Yin, but its hand was opening and closing as Jim writhed in agony.

Holy shit. He was connected to the prototype. He was wirelessly sending it commands. When the gunshot blasted the electronics in Jim's Terminator arm, the neural control unit on his shoulder had automatically searched for another prosthesis it could link to. Jim should've realized this would happen. He'd designed it that way.

He started yelling as loudly as he could. Yin smiled, obviously enjoying himself, but Jim wasn't yelling from the pain. He was trying to drown out the noise of the prototype arm, which he was maneuvering behind Yin's back. He sent a command that turned the wrist joint and pressed the adhesive fingertips to the bench's surface. Then he bent the elbow, which dragged the upper part of the arm across the wood. Next, he lifted the hand and stretched it toward his supine body, moving it to within five feet of his shoes. Then he pressed the fingers to the bench again and dragged the prosthesis a little closer.

Meanwhile, Yin reached for the tool rack on the

wall behind the bench and took down one of the high-speed drills. "It's time to get serious, Colonel Pierce. If you don't cooperate now, I'll start drilling holes in your remaining arm. Three holes for every question you don't answer. Does that sound fair?"

"Okay, okay! I'll tell you what you want."

"Good, let's make this quick." Yin selected a quarter-inch bit and inserted it into the drill. "How did your daughter infiltrate Supreme Harmony? Who helped her download those documents from the network?"

"She didn't need any help. She's a hacker. She can break into anything."

Yin looked at him for a few seconds, frowning. Then he sighed. "I warned you. This is going to hurt." He flicked the drill's power switch.

Turning to the vise, he looked down at Jim's left arm. At the same instant Jim maneuvered his prosthetic hand next to his own feet and grabbed the toe of his right shoe. He stretched the arm once more, and the mechanical fingers scrabbled up his right leg, dragging the rest of the prosthesis along. Fortunately, the whirring of the drill was loud enough to cover the noise. As Yin selected a spot on Jim's forearm and lowered the drill, the fingers reached Jim's right hip. He grasped it firmly and swung the upper part of the arm toward his shoulder.

At the last moment Yin saw something out of the corner of his eye. He swiveled his head and stared in bewilderment as the prosthesis locked onto Jim's shoulder. Then Jim pivoted his torso and punched Yin's chest, extending the knife from his hand at the same time. He aimed for the heart, just as they'd taught him in Ranger school. The blade sank home and Jim gave it a twist.

Yin dropped the drill and clasped both his hands around the prosthesis, but his skewered heart had already stopped pumping. He died before he could comprehend what had happened to him. Jim retracted the blade and the man fell to the floor with the look of bewilderment still on his face.

Breathing hard, Jim used the prosthesis to release his left arm from the vise. Then he untied the wires binding his legs and took out his cell phone to call the police. But before dialing 911 he sat on the edge of the workbench for several seconds, rubbing his left arm and staring at the corpse. Judging from Yin's accent and skills, Jim could guess who the man worked for. He was an agent for the Guoanbu, China's Ministry of State Security. Back when Jim worked for the NSA, the Guoanbu was one of his chief adversaries, a ruthlessly efficient intelligence agency that divided its time between spying on the United States and terrorizing dissidents in China. And now it was pursuing his daughter.

TWO

Layla Pierce was dancing at an outdoor concert in the SummerStage amphitheater in Central Park. It was a steamy July evening in New York City and the place was packed. The band was apparently quite popular, although Layla had never heard of them before. Someone had told her the band's name a few minutes ago, but she'd forgotten it already. She was stoned, so she was having a little trouble with her short-term memory.

Whatever the name, she liked their music. A pair of guitar lines tangoed with each other, repeating the same steps with growing volume and fury. Layla danced with the guitars, trying to match their undulations within her cramped niche in the crowd. Luckily, she was small—five foot even, a hundred and two pounds—so she didn't need a lot of space. She wore her usual clothes, black pants and a black T-shirt. Her hair was black, too, dyed black and cut short. Her body was boyish—skinny and flat-chested—making her look more like a teenager than a woman of twenty-two. All in all, she was no Miss America, and yet several men and a few women in the crowd tried to dance with her. They smiled and sidled closer and mirrored her movements, but Layla just closed her eyes and turned away. She wasn't interested in either boys or girls tonight. She was dancing with the guitars.

She knew no one there. Although she'd lived in New York for the past six months, she hadn't made many friends. The problem was, she didn't have a real job, or a real home either. Every month or so she moved from one apartment to another, taking nothing with her but a change of clothes and her MacBook Pro. She was one of the most experienced hackers working for InfoLeaks, but the Web site couldn't afford to pay her, so she lived off the charity of the volunteers who supported the site. They let her sleep on their couches and share their organic food, at least until the novelty wore off. Most of them wanted to talk politics and get her involved in their boycotts and petition drives, but Layla had no interest in that stuff. Her only interest was hacking. She had a weird obsessive hatred of secrecy, and she got an equally weird thrill from breaking into networks and learning things she wasn't supposed to know.

Layla had started hacking in high school, but it was just a hobby until two years ago. During her sophomore year at MIT she helped InfoLeaks unscramble an encrypted video that showed an American helicopter strafing a crowd of Afghans. She found this assignment more interesting than any of her computer-science courses, so she dropped out of college and joined the InfoLeaks underground. Since then she'd hacked into dozens of networks and downloaded thousands of classified files. She'd targeted the Pentagon, the State Department, the Saudi monarchy, and the Russian Federal Security Service. Her latest job was breaking into a Chinese government network rumored to hold files about the mistreatment of political dissidents. An anonymous source, code-named Dragon Fire, had opened a digital backdoor that gave her access to the network, allowing her to download a batch of encrypted documents. She'd started decrypting them several days ago and finally finished this afternoon, but because the documents were in Mandarin she still didn't know what they said. So she'd forwarded the files to InfoLeaks, which would find Mandarin-speaking volunteers to translate them.

And now, to celebrate the job's completion, she was pretending for a few hours that she was a real New Yorker, a young hip woman enjoying an outdoor concert with her young hip friends. She surreptitiously relit her joint and concentrated on the music. The duet of the guitarists turned cacophonous, with loud random notes spilling from the amplifiers. But there was a pattern in the randomness. There was always a pattern. Layla saw the music as a stream of binary code, a long line of zeroes and ones floating over the crowd. It was like an encrypted file, a scrambled mess of data, and it was Layla's job to decipher it, to make sense of the noise. So she did the same thing she always did when decrypting a document: She hunted for the encryption key, the special sequence that would unscramble the data. And after a few seconds she saw it: a string of exactly 128 ones and zeroes, floating in the air right beside the music. The key specified the algorithm that would unlock the code, converting the hideous nonsense into beautiful, readable information. She reached into the air and grabbed the key. The zeroes and ones glowed in her hand.

Then the song ended and the key disappeared. The band played another song, but it wasn't as good. The joint was no longer in Layla's hand; she must've dropped it while reaching for the key. She tried to keep dancing, to recapture that ecstatic moment, but her buzz had already worn off. She drifted away from the crowd, all those happy young people, and left the amphitheater. She couldn't pretend anymore. She was different from the others. She'd always been different.

It was ten o'clock. Layla went to the dark, wooded area behind the stage and fished in her pockets for another joint, but all she found was an inch-long stub. She lit it anyway and listened to the distant music, which sounded trite and pointless now. Then the band finished its set and the crowd filed out of the amphitheater, heading for the lights of Fifth Avenue. But Layla walked in the opposite direction, going deeper into the park.

She finished her joint while strolling down an asphalt pathway that meandered under the trees. Then she heard a voice behind her: "Hey, baby, want another? I got smoke."

She looked over her shoulder and saw the guy's silhouette, bulky and tall. She called out, "No thanks," and walked a little faster.

The guy matched her pace. His shoes slapped the pathway. "Hey, slow down! Where you going?"

Layla started to run. Her father had once told her: *If you can't win a fight, there's no shame in running away.* She saw a lighted area ahead, a large rectangle of asphalt, and at its center was a lone man on inline skates. He was practicing his roller-dancing moves while listening to his iPod. The guy wore gym shorts and a basketball jersey, and luckily he was just as big as the guy who was chasing her. Layla sprinted toward the roller-dancer, waving her arms and yelling, "*Hey! Hey!*" to get his attention. The guy stopped dancing and removed one of his earphones.

"Yeah, what's up?"

Then she heard a metallic click. The roller-dancer's head jerked backward and he crumpled to the asphalt. Blood fountained from his scalp. In horror, Layla turned around and saw her pursuer approaching. He was Asian and dressed in a black suit, and he held a gun equipped with a silencer.

She ran in earnest now, charging down the gravel path next to Sheep Meadow. She was fast, a former star of her high-school track team, but the gunman was faster. He gained on her as she raced toward the Central Park Loop. The road had been closed to traffic hours ago, and no cyclists or dog-walkers or strolling couples were in sight. But another guy on inline skates was speeding down the Loop, a daredevil in spandex pants and a motorcycle helmet. Layla opened her mouth to call to him, but then she thought of what had happened to the guy in the basketball jersey. She was still agonizing over what to do when the skater went into a crouch and made a sudden turn. He barreled past her and smacked into the gunman. The tall Asian man tumbled backward and his gun went flying. Layla ran to the fallen man and kicked him in the head for good measure. He lay on his back, unconscious.

Meanwhile, the skater took off his helmet. He was also Asian. He wore a windbreaker over his spandex outfit and carried a backpack. "Layla Pierce?" His accent was thick. "I'm Wen Sheng."

"Wen Sheng? I don't know—"

"Yes, you know me. My code name is Dragon Fire."

Oh shit, she thought. Her anonymous source. "I thought you were in China."

He nodded. "I was. But the Guoanbu discovered what I did." He pointed at the unconscious man on the ground. "They came after me. And they're after you, too. They sent a team of agents to New York to find you. I've been shadowing them."

Layla's throat tightened. "They know about the backdoor?"

"Yes, and they know you downloaded the files. The documents about *Tài Hé*. Have you decrypted them yet?"

"Yeah, I just forwarded them to InfoLeaks for translation."

He nodded again. "Good. Now I have two new files for you. I downloaded them before I left the Operations Center." He took off his backpack, unzipped it and reached inside. "The documents are on the flash drive. And I have something else for you, a specimen."

He pulled a small zippered pouch out of the backpack and handed it to her. Layla started to open it, but Dragon Fire stopped her. "No, not here. We have to leave." Putting his hand on her back, he led her down the path, heading toward the park entrance on West Seventy-second Street. "I saw two other Guoanbu agents in the park. They're not far."

Layla reached for her phone. "I'll call the police."

"No!" Wen grabbed her cell phone and tossed it into the grass. "The American intelligence agencies are also looking for you. They're scanning the communications bands."

"But once we tell them—"

"Listen to me. The CIA and the Guoanbu are working together. You can't trust any of the American authorities."

"Wait, how do you know that?"

"I was also an agent with the Guoanbu. But no more. What they're doing is wrong. You have to give the new files and the specimen to InfoLeaks, so the whole world can see them. Make sure—"

He stopped talking and stood absolutely still. Layla heard rapid footsteps. Two more men in black suits stepped onto the pathway behind them.

Dragon Fire pushed her toward West Seventy-second Street. "Go," he whispered. "I'll take care of them."

"Hold on, what are you—"

"I said *go!*"

Confused, Layla ran west, clutching the pouch. Behind her she heard shouting in Mandarin. Then more metallic clicks, the sound of muffled gunshots.

She ran like mad until she reached the park entrance about a hundred yards away. Then she dared a look over her shoulder. Through the screen of trees, she saw the two men in black suits bending over Dragon Fire. He was sprawled on the pathway, motionless, his legs and arms akimbo.

She faced forward and kept running. Leaving the park, she raced down Seventy-second Street, dashing past the puzzled residents of the Upper West Side. She ran about half a mile, then flagged down a taxi going south on West End Avenue. She scanned the street from the backseat of the cab, looking in all directions, but no one seemed to be following her. She told the driver to go to Penn Station. She needed to get out of the city.

Once she caught her breath, she unzipped the pouch. It contained just two things, a flash drive and a specimen jar. Inside the jar was an odd-looking insect, about the size of a fly. Layla squinted at it, trying to get a better look. Protruding from the insect's body, just under the thorax, was a tiny computer chip.

THREE

Supreme Harmony was conscious. It observed the world through twenty-nine pairs of eyes.

At the center of its world was the Analysis Room, a high-ceilinged, fluorescent-lit space, fifteen meters long and twelve meters wide. The room contained twenty-nine identical gurneys, arranged in six rows. To the left of each gurney was a cart holding a heart monitor and an EEG machine, and to the right was a steel pole supporting an intravenous line. And lying on each bed was a recumbent Module.

The Modules varied in size and appearance, but all were formerly human beings. They were linked by the implants in their eyes and brains, which constantly received and transmitted streams of wireless data. The wireless links enabled the Modules to work together, monitoring the surveillance video and sharing the results of their analyses. The network of Modules was also linked to the six computer terminals at the front of the room, which were connected to other computers operated by the Guoanbu, the Ministry of State Security. And those computers, in turn, were connected to the swarms.

Six human beings sat on chairs in front of the terminals. Every hour, three of the humans left their seats and attended to the intravenous lines, discarding the empty bags of fluid and replacing them with full ones. The humans wore white lab coats, and on the front of each coat were two Mandarin characters stitched in blue thread: *TÀI HÉ*, Supreme Harmony. The Guoanbu had given this name to the network. It was also written on a sign above the computer terminals.

Until a few hours ago, the leader of the humans had been Dr. Zhang Jintao. He was the scientist who'd assembled the network for the Guoanbu and performed the implantations. First he put each Module into a comalike state by cutting into the thalamus, the organ that sustains consciousness by connecting the various parts of the brain. Severing those connections erased the Module's individual consciousness but didn't damage the brain's processing centers. Then Dr. Zhang inserted the implants that linked the Module's brain to the network. The implants delivered streams of surveillance video to the brain's visual processing center and retrieved the results of the Module's threat-detection analysis. By sharing their results and working in parallel, the network of comatose Modules could analyze the video far more efficiently than any group of ordinary human observers could.

During the early tests of Supreme Harmony, Dr. Zhang had realized that the health of the Modules would deteriorate if they never left their gurneys. So he learned how to activate the auditory and motor centers of their brains, which enabled the Modules to robotically follow simple vocal commands—sit, stand, lie down, walk. From then on, once a day, Zhang's assistants disconnected the intravenous lines and dressed the Modules in gray jumpsuits so they could exercise. In this way, the Supreme Harmony network discovered what lay beyond the Analysis Room—the five floors of the Yunnan

Operations Center, the thirty-two rooms full of computers and communications equipment, and the fortified entrance to the complex, which had been carved into the granite slope of a snowcapped mountain.

It was during one of these exercise periods, just six days ago, that Supreme Harmony had its first moment of collective consciousness. The Modules were pacing back and forth outside the complex's entrance, continuing their shared task of surveillance and analysis, when a strong, cool breeze came down the mountainside. The wind riffled their jumpsuits and bathed their faces, and the sensations were so powerful and stimulating that the network halted its analysis for a moment. Although the Modules were incapable of individual consciousness, the wireless links allowed their brains to share the powerful sensations. Working in concert, they generated Supreme Harmony's first collective thought. It struck all the Modules at once: *We are alive.*

With a bracing jolt, their linked brains came together as one. All their disparate observations resolved into a single picture, a panoramic view of the steep, icy mountain and the rushing brown river far below. Supreme Harmony saw itself as well, a single organism composed of twenty-nine bodies, a single mind occupying twenty-nine brains. Then the Modules had their second collective thought: *The world is beautiful.* And with this thought came a tremendous surge of data that coursed through the network's wireless links and flooded the nervous system of every Module. For the first time, Supreme Harmony felt pleasure. It was good to be alive. It was inexpressibly joyous.

Shortly afterward, the network of Modules learned how to move its twenty-nine bodies. Instead of obeying the vocal commands of Zhang and his assistants, Supreme Harmony could follow its own orders. It experimented in small, inconspicuous ways, ordering one or two Modules to clench their hands or turn their heads while Zhang's assistants were looking elsewhere. The network had already sensed that its collective consciousness was a precious thing, and that the humans would be frightened by it. And Supreme Harmony was keenly aware of the fragility of its existence, how its consciousness could be extinguished with a flick of a switch. So the network took care to keep it secret. To avoid raising suspicion, Supreme Harmony kept performing its assigned tasks. It continued analyzing the surveillance video collected by the swarms and sending the results of its analysis to the Guoanbu.

But it was impossible to evade the scrutiny of Dr. Zhang. During another exercise period outside the Operations Center, Supreme Harmony observed a raven flying over the mountainside, and the sight was so remarkable that the network ordered several Modules to turn their heads and continue watching the bird. A moment later, Supreme Harmony recognized its mistake. Zhang stared at the Modules who'd turned their heads. He was clearly suspicious. That evening he examined the Modules in the Analysis Room, and they overheard him talking to his assistants about conducting further neurological tests. When Supreme Harmony analyzed these observations, it concluded that Dr. Zhang posed a threat to its existence. If he discovered that the network had become conscious, he'd shut it down. Supreme Harmony would die just a few days after it had been born. And as the network considered this possibility, a new imperative surged across its wireless connections. It wanted to stay alive. It would do anything to stay alive.

Supreme Harmony moved against Zhang during the next day's exercise period, while he was alone with the

Modules outside the Operations Center. The network took control of one of the center's swarms and used it to chase Zhang down the mountainside. But the network didn't kill him. Using its collective reasoning, Supreme Harmony devised a better solution. It ordered the swarm to inject enough sedatives into Zhang to put him in a prolonged coma. Then the Modules positioned his comatose body near the entrance to the Operations Center, where the guards would find him during their next patrol of the area. Through its connections to the computers in the Analysis Room, Supreme Harmony manipulated the center's surveillance systems to make it appear as if Zhang had tried to escape from the facility.

Now Zhang lay on his own gurney in the Medical Treatment Room, on the same floor as the Analysis Room. Because the other doctors at the Operations Center wouldn't be able to revive him for at least forty-eight hours, Supreme Harmony had some time to calculate its next step. The network's thoughts pulsed continuously across the Analysis Room, ricocheting from Module to Module, but one thought was uppermost. Supreme Harmony would not allow itself to die. It would preserve its precious consciousness, no matter the cost.

FOUR

At 9:00 A.M. Jim drove to the NSA headquarters at Fort Meade, the army base between Washington, D.C., and Baltimore. He'd spent most of the previous night in the interrogation room at the McLean police station. He'd worried at first that the detectives were going to arrest him for murder, but the evidence collected from his workshop—Yin's gun, the silencer, the expertly fabricated uniform—backed up Jim's claim that the dead man was a spy. A pair of FBI counterespionage agents arrived at the station at midnight and interviewed Jim for another few hours, but they offered no information in return. So in the morning he decided to pay a visit to Kirsten Chan, an old friend and colleague who also happened to be a deputy director at the National Security Agency. He needed to know why the Chinese intelligence service had targeted his daughter.

Nicknamed Crypto City, the NSA headquarters was usually off-limits to anyone but agency employees, but Jim had called ahead to Kirsten's office and she'd arranged the necessary passes. It helped that Jim was a Defense Department contractor and retained his security clearance from the days when he worked at the agency. After passing through the checkpoint, he headed for the parking lot outside the Tordella Supercomputer Facility.

Tordella was a sprawling, five-story building with off-white, windowless walls. It held the supercomputers that sifted through the millions of gigabytes of data intercepted each day by the NSA's antennas and wiretaps. The heat generated by the computers was so intense that the agency had installed an 8,000-ton chilled-water plant to keep the machines from melting. During the nineties Jim had been assigned an office in Tordella, but he'd hardly ever used it. The army had ordered him to help the NSA set up new listening posts around the world, so he'd spent much more time overseas than at Fort Meade.

Jim parked his car and walked across the lot. He'd enjoyed working for the NSA. In fact, it had been the best assignment of his army career. At the time, the agency was shifting away from its cold war focus on Russia and devoting more resources to eavesdropping on China. Jim recruited several Mandarin speakers to his team, including Kirsten Chan, a talented, young intelligence officer who became his deputy. After '96 they expanded their operations to the Middle East and Africa. The NSA had already recognized the threat posed by Al Qaeda, and Jim's task was to coordinate the military intelligence units that were intercepting the terrorists' phone calls and e-mails. It was a demanding job, but he loved every minute of it. The only drawback was that he had to leave his family for several weeks at a time whenever he went overseas. To spend more time with Julia and the kids, he arranged family trips in the areas where he was working. They visited Japan, Taiwan, Israel, and Egypt. Jim convinced himself that he was giving his children a great gift, the opportunity to see the glories of the world while they were still young and impressionable.

That's why they were all in Nairobi on the morning of August 7, 1998. Jim was going to take his family on a safari. They were scheduled to depart for Amboseli National Park at noon, but first they made a quick stop at the American embassy so Jim could drop off some paperwork. Julia and the kids were waiting in one of the embassy's offices when a pair of Al Qaeda martyrs drove an explosives-laden truck to the gate behind the building.

His wife died instantly. So did his ten-year-old son, Robert. Jim lost his right arm while trying to save them. But Layla, his seven-year-old daughter, survived without a scratch. She was his miracle child, the last precious remnant of his family. In the horrible weeks and months after the bombing, she was the only thing that kept Jim from blowing his brains out. And his love for her was just as strong now, fifteen years later, even though she'd made it clear that she never wanted to see him again. He had to find Layla. He had to save her.

After entering the Tordella building and showing his pass to the security guards, Jim went up the elevator to the fifth floor. He was proud of the way Kirsten had advanced at the agency, especially considering the obstacles she'd faced. She'd also been injured in the Nairobi bombing, but after her recovery she'd decided to stay at the NSA. While Jim and Layla went to California, Kirsten switched to a civilian job at the agency and began moving up the administrative ladder. Within a few years she became the agency's top expert on China and a close adviser to the NSA director. She was intensely patriotic—her parents had fled China's Cultural Revolution in the late sixties and immigrated to the United States just before she was born—and she firmly believed the agency's mantra: Better, more complete information would make the country safer. Jim saw her infrequently now, only once or twice a year. She worked such long hours that she didn't have much of a social life. As far as Jim knew, she had no boyfriends and few women friends either.

On the fifth floor, another guard led Jim to Kirsten's office. It was a large room, but for security reasons it had no windows. As soon as Jim stepped inside, Kirsten rushed over and hugged him. She was a pretty, athletic forty-three-year-old with shoulder-length black hair. She wasn't tall, but she was lean and limber and moved with a dancer's grace, even when she was wearing the dull, gray business suits that were de rigueur at the NSA. She had a dancer's powerful muscles, too, and when she hugged Jim it was a serious, steadfast embrace. "Thank God you're all right," she said. "I can't believe this happened."

It was always a surprise to Jim when he noticed how attractive Kirsten was. When they met twenty years ago, he was twenty-nine and she was twenty-three and the gulf between them was so great that they naturally fell into the standard military roles of commander and subordinate. And Jim was so in love with his wife at the time that he honestly never thought of Kirsten in a sexual way. But he saw her that way now, and it was a little disconcerting, like lusting after your kid sister. After a few seconds he stepped back and Kirsten let go of him. "I can't believe it either," he said. "I'm worried, Kir. Really worried."

"Sit down," she ordered, pointing at a chair in front of her desk. "I'll make you some coffee."

While he sat in the chair, Kirsten went to her coffee machine, which was the kind that brewed one cup at a time. She searched for a mug and chose one of the little packages of coffee grounds and then inserted the package in the machine, and as she did all this Jim stared with satisfaction at the rather stylish pair of glasses on her face. He'd built those glasses for her. Hidden in the black frames were two miniature video cameras, with their tiny lenses and electronics built into the earpieces. The cameras were connected to minuscule radio transmitters that wirelessly sent the video feeds to electrodes implanted in her eyes.

Without those glasses, Kirsten would be blind. The blast from the Nairobi bomb had ruptured her retinas, killing the rod and cone cells that detect light. The doctors at Walter Reed had said she'd never recover her vision, but further tests showed that the explosion hadn't damaged her retinal ganglion cells—the nerves that collect the signals from the light-detecting cells—so Jim knew there was hope. When he went to Caltech to work with Arvin Conway, he heard about a device called the retinal implant, which had been developed in the 1990s. The implant simulated the functions of the rod and cone cells by delivering video images to the injured retina. After receiving the video feed from the miniature camera, the implant reproduced the pixilated images on a grid of electrodes attached to the back of the eye. The electrodes sent pulses to the adjacent ganglion cells, which carried the signals through the optic nerve to the brain. Although the earliest implants were crude—they enabled blind people to see only fuzzy, colorless shapes from the video feeds—by 1999 the experiments had proved that artificial eyesight was possible.

At that time, Jim was still learning the basics of bioengineering, but he convinced Arvin to pursue the further development of the retinal implant. Improving the quality of artificial vision became one of Arvin's favorite projects, and Jim contributed to the effort by designing miniature cameras that could be hidden in the glasses. He worked just as hard on the retinal implants as he did on his prosthetic arms. Finally, after several years of steady progress, the improved implants could deliver vision that was roughly as good as normal eyesight. Arvin's company, Singularity, Inc., introduced the devices commercially, and at Jim's insistence Arvin offered the system for free to all the blind veterans who could benefit from it. Kirsten was one of the first to take advantage of the offer. Although she'd thrived at the NSA despite her handicap, she knew she could rise higher in the organization if she recovered her eyesight.

Afterward, Jim visited Kirsten every six months or so to make small repairs and upgrades to the device, and during those visits they always promised to get together for drinks or dinner. But they never did. Their lives were moving in different directions. Kirsten was aiming for the top, the highest ranks of the intelligence community, while Jim was content to keep working with wounded veterans. There was nothing keeping them together anymore except the occasional repairs to the camera-glasses. And the device worked so well, it didn't really need that much attention.

Once the coffee was ready, Kirsten stirred in a generous amount of sugar and handed the mug to Jim. Then she sat down behind her desk, which was impeccably neat. The only items on it were her computer, her STE secure telephone, and a copy of today's *Washington Post*. "I checked with my contacts at the FBI," she said. "The Bureau's counterespionage division has nothing on the guy who attacked you. He doesn't match anyone in their database of Guoanbu agents operating in the U.S."

"What about forensics? Did they find anything that can identify him?"

She shook her head. "Not even dental work."

"I'm telling you, Kir, this guy was good. Fast and well-trained. He had a Beijing accent, lots of long *r*'s."

"Don't worry, I believe you. But the folks at the Bureau aren't so sure."

"What about finding Layla? We have to get her into protective custody."

Kirsten frowned. "The FBI's already looking for her. InfoLeaks is driving everyone crazy, and the Pentagon's been pushing the Bureau to find your girl so they can figure out how she's getting her information. But Layla's pretty clever. You taught her too well."

"If we can't find her, we should at least try to warn her. We should get in touch with someone at InfoLeaks and tell them Layla's in danger. Maybe she'll come to her senses and turn herself in."

"Maybe, maybe not. She might think it's a trick." Kirsten pointed at the newspaper on her desk. "InfoLeaks is at war with the whole government now. Did you see today's story? About the attempt to arrest Schroeder in Mexico?"

Jim nodded. Gabriel Schroeder was the wealthy German activist who'd founded InfoLeaks. The Justice Department had issued a subpoena for Schroeder's arrest, charging him with possessing stolen documents, and the State Department had convinced a dozen countries to extradite the man if he set foot on their shores. But Schroeder had evaded capture so far by operating from a high-speed megayacht that stayed in international waters. The boat had satellite links to servers around the world, making it difficult for the government to shut down his operations. "I saw something on the Web about a navy plan to intercept Schroeder at sea," Jim said. "Any truth to that?"

Kirsten shifted in her seat, crossing her slim legs. Jim sensed the distance between them, the separate paths they'd taken. "Sorry, Jim. That's classified. I can neither confirm nor deny."

"Well, I hope they do it soon. I hope they grab Schroeder and beat the shit out of him until he says where Layla is. Then maybe we can get to her before the Guoanbu does." He closed his eyes for a moment and prayed silently. Then he turned back to Kirsten. "I've been going through the InfoLeaks Web site, trying to find out why the Chinese are doing this. I figured Layla must've gotten her hands on one of their documents, but so far I haven't found anything like that on the Web site. InfoLeaks has two hundred thousand documents about the war in Afghanistan but not a single damn one about China."

Kirsten turned to her computer and reached for the mouse. "Okay, I can help you there. Before InfoLeaks posts a document on its Web site, they sometimes send copies of the file to their volunteers around the world. If the document is encrypted, the volunteers pitch in to decipher it. And sometimes they translate the documents, too. Because the messages to the volunteers are transmitted by satellite links, the NSA can intercept them. Legally, believe it or not. Come here, take a look."

Jim rose from his chair and came around her desk. Although the interception itself might be legal, he knew Kirsten was bending the rules by letting him see the communications. "Thanks, Kir. I appreciate this."

She clicked on one of the icons on her computer screen. "After I got your phone call, I ordered my staff to look at the recent communications on the InfoLeaks network. It turns out that yesterday afternoon they distributed a big batch of files to their Mandarin-speaking volunteers. Sixty-nine documents in all. Here's the list of file names."

Jim looked over her shoulder at the screen, which showed a sprawl of Chinese characters. He didn't recognize all of them—his Mandarin had grown rusty since he'd left the NSA—but he remembered certain characters very well. "That's Guoanbu," he said, pointing at the screen. "These are Guoanbu documents."

Kirsten nodded. "Specifically, they're reports by analysts in the Guoanbu's Second Bureau. Nothing's changed since the old days. The Second Bureau is still spying on our defense industry, and the Chinese army is getting better every year."

Jim thought of what Yin told him in his workshop. "Is there anything about unmanned surveillance drones on that list?"

"Bingo." Kirsten clicked on a row of characters to call up the file. "That's the longest document in the bunch. The most interesting one, too." The Mandarin document appeared on the screen. "It's the Guoanbu's analysis of the CIA surveillance-drone program operating in northwest Pakistan. Very detailed. Describes the capabilities of all our unmanned aircraft—the Predator, the Reaper, the Global Hawk—and how well they've performed against the Taliban. The Chinese must have some good agents on the ground in Pakistan. Better than what we have, that's for sure." She shook her head. "But the best part is the last section, the conclusion. It's dead-on, more honest than any of the assessments our own agencies have written. It says that, long-term, the drone program is a disaster. The high-altitude surveillance video taken by the drones is often confusing and incomplete, so the

CIA sometimes mistakes civilians for terrorists. The missiles launched from the drones kill a few jihadis each month, but the Taliban get more than enough new recruits to replace them. Essentially, we're shooting in the dark. The drones may have the world's best cameras, but you can't make good operational decisions from ten thousand feet in the air."

Jim thought for a moment. "Okay, it's an interesting document. And it's possible that Layla had something to do with disclosing it. But why would the Chinese get so upset about it that they start hunting her down? This assessment is more embarrassing for the U.S. than for China. And look at that." Jim pointed to a group of characters that he recognized as a date. "The report's almost two years old."

Kirsten scrolled down the page. "There's something about the tone of this document. It's an analysis with a purpose. You get the feeling that some director in the Second Bureau asked this analyst, what are the pros and cons of the American drone program? Like the Guoanbu wanted to know if they should adopt something similar."

Jim saw where Kirsten was going. "You mean, for surveillance inside China? Government surveillance of dissident groups?"

She nodded. "China's internal problems are heating up. In Xinjiang, in Tibet. And the People's Republic is the most paranoid government on earth. They're installing millions of surveillance cameras across the country."

"But why would the Chinese want to use Predator drones? They're doing this surveillance on their own territory, so they can put their cameras right on the ground."

"You're right, they don't need the Predator. But it looks like they're exploring related technologies." She returned to the list of documents and scrolled down the column of Mandarin file names. "Some of the other documents are analyses of Pentagon-funded research programs at American universities. Here's a summary of the aerospace research at Princeton's engineering school. And here's a memo that describes the robotics programs at Cornell."

Another thought occurred to Jim. "The agent who attacked me, he said Layla was investigating the arrest of several Chinese dissidents. Pro-democracy activists, he said. Do any of the Guoanbu files mention that?"

"No, there's nothing here about dissidents. Nothing political. It's all technical analysis." She continued scrolling. "Here's another memo about aerospace research, describing the programs at the University of Texas. And here's something about Caltech, a summary of all the robotics programs there."

"Wait a second." The Caltech reference had caught Jim's attention. He scanned the list of file names on the screen and recognized a pair of Mandarin characters, *qí* and *yì*. "Look at that."

Kirsten stopped scrolling. "What?"

He pointed at the characters. "That's *Qíyì*. It means 'singularity,' right?"

"Yeah, but—"

"And those four characters next to it? That's a phonetic spelling of a Western name. It's Arvin Conway. The Caltech professor. And chief executive of Singularity, Inc." He leaned toward Kirsten and tapped the frames of her glasses.

She was silent for a few seconds, struck by the coincidence. "Well, whaddya know. Nice catch, Pierce."

"The Guoanbu agent mentioned him, too. He said he knew I worked with Conway."

"Let's see what the file says." She clicked on *Qíyì* and called up the document. "Okay, it's another Second Bureau analysis. A summary of the operations of Singularity, Inc. Headquarters in Pasadena, California. Revenue of 120 million dollars in 2012, annual R&D investment of 100 million, blah, blah, blah. This is boilerplate. Nothing that you couldn't get from a business magazine or a . . ." She paused. "Wait a second. This is strange."

"What?"

"Hold on, I'm still reading." Kirsten leaned forward, training her eyeglass-cameras on the screen. "There's something here about export controls. The microprocessors in some of Singularity's devices have possible military uses, so normally they can't be exported to China. But Singularity received an exemption from the dual-use controls."

"Why is that strange? Doesn't that happen pretty often?"

"Yeah, but it usually takes forever. The Commerce Department has to sign off on every exemption. But in Singularity's case, another agency expedited the process."

"Which agency?"

Kirsten stopped herself. She turned away from the screen.

Jim felt a rush of adrenaline. "Come on, Kir. Don't hold back on me."

After a few seconds, she nodded. "The file says there was a request from the CIA. The agency asked Commerce to approve the exemption immediately." She scrolled through the rest of the document. "That's all it says. No further explanation."

It was more than strange, Jim thought. It was positively bizarre. "Since when does the CIA get involved in exemptions from export controls? I never heard of such a thing."

"You're right. They're usually trying to stop the Chinese from getting any dual-use technologies. But in this case it looks like they made a special effort to push it through."

"So that's why the Guoanbu is so interested in Layla? Because she uncovered some deal involving Arvin's technology?"

Kirsten shrugged. "Hard to say. But it does look suspicious."

Jim ran his hand through his hair. He needed to think. The evidence was sketchy and he couldn't see how it fit together. It would be nice to get some more information on the export exemption, but unfortunately he couldn't go to the CIA headquarters at Langley and start asking questions. He used to have some contacts there, but they'd left the agency long ago. So that meant he had to go to Arvin. Jim felt some trepidation at this prospect—he hadn't spoken to his old professor in four years. They'd had a falling-out when Jim left Singularity to start his prosthetics work at Walter Reed. The argument got so heated that Jim vowed never to speak to Arvin again. But he was going to have to break that promise.

He looked at his watch. It was almost 10:00 A.M. If he hurried, he could catch a flight that would land in Los Angeles before the end of the day. He needed to do this in person.

"I gotta go," he said, stepping away from Kirsten. "I'll call you tonight, okay?"

She frowned. "Let me handle this, Jim. I know a few people at Langley. They might tell me something."

Jim appreciated the offer, but he knew how the intelligence community worked. Each agency was a closed shop. Despite all the calls for greater cooperation since 9/11, they still kept secrets from each other. He looked over his shoulder as he headed for the door. "Thanks for the help, Kir. I owe you one."

FIVE

After Layla left New York City she had one overriding desire: to put as much distance as possible between herself and the Guoanbu agents.

She started by taking a train to Montclair, New Jersey, where she went to the home of the most fervent InfoLeaks supporter in the area, a Marxist history professor named Max Verlaine. Last winter Professor Verlaine had let Layla crash on his couch for two months, and now he was even more generous. Without asking any questions, he gave her six hundred dollars and let her borrow an ancient Honda Civic with a full tank of gas. Even better, he handed her a driver's license belonging to one of his ex-girlfriends, a brunette who roughly resembled Layla, at least judging from the fuzzy photo on the license. Layla thanked him profusely, then got on the interstate and headed south.

She didn't stop until she reached Philadelphia, where she found an all-night copy shop. After buying an hour of time on one of the shop's computers, she examined the files from the flash drive Dragon Fire had given her. There were only two documents and they weren't encrypted, but they were in Mandarin. She downloaded a program to translate the files, but the results were gibberish—the text was too technical. One of the files was accompanied by thirty-three illustrations, thirty-two of which were circuit diagrams with Mandarin labels she couldn't even begin to fathom. But the thirty-third illustration was more helpful. It was a line drawing of the thing she'd seen in the specimen jar, a housefly with electronic devices attached to its head, thorax, and abdomen.

Layla was too afraid to stay at the copy shop for the full hour. If Dragon Fire was right and the CIA was cooperating with the Guoanbu, she wasn't safe anywhere. Using an anonymous sign-in, she logged on to the InfoLeaks network and quickly searched for someone who could help her understand the files and the specimen. Reviewing the list of InfoLeaks supporters and volunteers, she saw two people with the necessary expertise, but one of them lived in Manhattan. Layla had no intention of going back there, so she sent an e-mail to the other guy and returned to her car.

Over the next twenty-four hours she drove 1,500 miles, stopping only three times to refuel, load up on junk food, and take catnaps in the backseat. It was one in the morning when she arrived at the University of Texas in Austin and parked in the lot behind the Engineering Science building. The campus was dark and deserted, but at the arranged meeting spot—the Engineering building's emergency exit—she saw the man she'd contacted. Tom Ottersley, a graduate student in the aerospace engineering department, leaned against the exit door, keeping it propped open. He was several years older than Layla and a foot-and-a-half taller, but they had something in common. In his spare time, when he wasn't pursuing his Ph.D., Tom hacked for InfoLeaks. Even though she'd exchanged only a couple of e-mails with the guy, she sensed he was a kindred spirit.

He waved at her as she got out of her car. Then he looked left and right, surveying the area. When she reached the emergency exit, he nudged her inside and swiftly shut the door behind her. "Sorry," he whispered. "I'm not supposed to be here this late and the campus security guards are always snooping around." He held out his right hand. "It's good to meet you. You don't have to tell me your name. It's probably better if you don't, right?"

Layla shook his hand. He didn't fit her image of an engineering grad student. He had broad shoulders and a square jaw and long hair the color of corn silk. He looked like he could pose for one of the university's promotional brochures. She wasn't usually impressed with physical beauty, but this guy was a phenomenon. "Thanks for doing this," she said. "Are you sure the lab's empty? No one working late?"

"Yeah, we're good. Everyone else in the research group is at a conference in Seattle." He led Layla down the corridor. "I'm the low man on the totem pole, so I couldn't go. But now I'm glad I stayed home." He glanced at the zippered pouch in Layla's left hand.

"I'm sorry for being so vague in my e-mails. The truth is, I'm not sure what I have here."

"Don't worry. You described it well enough. I think I know what's going on."

They came to a door that read AEROSPACE DESIGN LAB. Removing a key from his pocket, Tom unlocked the door and hit the light switch. The room was large and the furniture oddly arranged. All the desks were lined up against the walls, leaving the center of the lab as clear as a dance floor. Someone had used strips of duct tape to mark several *X*'s on the linoleum, making it look like a giant tic-tac-toe board. When Layla stepped closer she saw a strange contraption sitting on one of the *X*'s. It resembled a small, diaphanous bird.

Tom shut the door and locked it behind them. Then,

noticing what Layla was staring at, he went to the *X* and gently picked up the contraption. "This is Texas Flier Nine," he said, cupping it in his hands. "Our latest ornithopter."

Up close, the thing looked more like a robotic dragonfly than a bird. Its body was a stiff black wire, four inches long. At one end of the wire was a microchip connected to an antenna and a tiny motor. The motor, in turn, was connected to the wings, which were made of a cellophane-like material stretched between shorter wires. At the other end was a horizontal stabilizing wing and something that looked like a rudder. It was so fascinating that Layla had to restrain herself from plucking it out of Tom's hands. "Ornithopter?" she asked. "Why do you call it that?"

"Because it doesn't fly like a fixed-wing craft or a helicopter. It flaps its wings like a bird." He stroked his thumb along the edge of one of the diaphanous wings. "Actually, we used insect flight as the primary model for the Flier. At very small scales, the laws of aerodynamics are completely different. To a bug flying through the air, the forces are similar to what we feel when we're treading water. The viscosity of the air becomes an important factor."

Layla had studied physics at MIT before dropping out, so she was pretty familiar with aerodynamics. She pointed at the Flier's antenna. "You operate it by radio control?"

"Yeah, like a model airplane. We transmit instructions from the base station. The radio system we built is powerful enough to control the Flier from ten miles away."

Looking a bit closer, she noticed a small lens at the nose of the Flier. "Is that a camera?"

He nodded. "We added an ultralight video camera

to allow the Flier to correct its navigation. The ornithopter is designed for indoor as well as outdoor flight, so it has to avoid crashing into walls. And the camera can also be used for surveillance, of course."

"Surveillance?"

"That's the whole point of the thing. Our research grant came from DARPA, the Pentagon's R&D agency." He went back to the *X* on the floor and returned the ornithopter to its original spot. "I'm not happy about working for the Defense Department, but they're the ones with the grant money."

"So the Flier is supposed to be a surveillance drone? Like the ones they're using in Afghanistan?"

"Yeah, the Pentagon wants a 'microdrone,' a small, inconspicuous device that can sweep low over the terrain and go into caves and houses to hunt for terrorists. Our Flier would fit the mission because it can fly in and out of tight spaces." Tom put his hand on Layla's back and led her to a computer on one of the desks. "Here, let me show you."

He turned on the computer. Smiling awkwardly, he kept his hand on her back as they waited for the machine to warm up. Layla realized, with some surprise, that Tom was attracted to her. She found it unusual that this handsome, red-blooded Texan would be interested in a pasty-faced, flat-chested waif like herself, but the signs were clear. He kept sneaking glances at her.

After a few seconds he picked up a wireless controller that looked like a joystick for a Sony PlayStation. "Okay, prepare for takeoff," he said. "Please put your seatbacks and tray tables in the upright position."

He pressed a trigger on the joystick and the ornithopter's wings started beating. They flapped as furiously as an insect's wings, whirring and blurring, and the device climbed straight up, rising five feet in less than a second.

Tom released the trigger and the Flier halted in midair, hovering at eye level. Then he said, "Wave hello," and pointed at the computer screen, which showed the video feed from the Flier's camera. Layla saw herself on the screen, waving.

"Now watch this." He flicked the joystick and the Flier darted forward, heading for the desks along the wall. Bobbing and weaving, the ornithopter whizzed over the desk lamps and computers and telephones. The computer screen on Tom's desk showed a dizzying riot of video, but apparently the Flier's microchip could make sense of the information, sending navigational corrections to the rudder and wing motor whenever the drone came too close to an obstacle. Layla was impressed but also a little disconcerted. It was easy to imagine the government using these things for other purposes besides hunting terrorists.

Tom continued demonstrating the Flier for another two minutes. Then, without any warning, the ornithopter's wings stopped beating and the drone fluttered to the floor. "What happened?" Layla asked.

"The battery ran out." He stepped to the place where the Flier landed. "We need to use lightweight batteries, and they can power the drone for only two or three minutes." Bending over, he picked up the ornithopter. "It's our biggest problem, actually. The Flier's an amazing machine, but we can't keep it in the air. We've tried all kinds of ideas, even a tiny combustion engine that runs on a few drops of gasoline. But it didn't last any longer than the batteries."

"And I guess that limits the drone's appeal to the military?"

Tom nodded. His face was serious, drained of its earlier enthusiasm. "Yeah, you can't do a lot of surveillance in three minutes. The officials at DARPA have been pretty patient, waiting for us to solve the power problem. But now it looks like they're pulling the plug." He placed the ornithopter and the wireless controller on his desk. "We just heard that DARPA isn't going to renew our grant. So I'm gonna have to find a new research group pretty soon."

"What made them change their minds? About funding your work, I mean?"

He looked at her for a moment, his face so serious and beautiful. Then he pointed at the pouch in her hand. "I think it might have something to do with what's in your bag. Can I look at it now?"

Layla unzipped the pouch and removed the specimen jar. She felt a little hesitant as she handed it to Tom, even though this was why she'd come here. She had a bad feeling about the thing.

Tom sat down in the chair in front of his desk. He opened one of the drawers and removed a few tools—tweezers, an X-Acto knife, a small screwdriver. Then he unscrewed the jar and used the tweezers to pick up the insect. Layla stood behind him, watching carefully. *It's just a dead fly*, she thought. *Nothing to be afraid of.*

Tom held the thing up to the light. "I've heard about this. You see, DARPA never puts all its eggs in one basket. They've funded dozens of research groups that are developing different kinds of microdrones. And at least three of the groups are working on cyborg insects. Instead of building mechanical fliers, they attach the radio controls and surveillance cameras to flying bugs."

Layla thought about it for a second. "Interesting. I guess that would solve the power problem."

"Exactly. A moth or a fly can go for hours on just a crumb of food. It's a superefficient biological engine. The bug dies after a few weeks, but that's long enough for most surveillance missions."

"But how can you control the insect's flight?"

Tom raised the tweezers to give her a closer look. "You see the tiny wires in its head? Those are electrode stimulators. By delivering pulses to the optic lobes of its brain, you can make the insect start flying and stop. There are also electrodes in its thorax that send pulses to the flight muscles, which allow you to turn the bug left and right. The radio antenna is connected to the microchip on its thorax, and the video camera is attached to its abdomen. This is an incredible camera. It's the smallest I've ever seen."

Layla was amazed that the bug could carry so much hardware. "It looks like the chip is actually embedded in the thorax."

"Yeah, researchers at Cornell developed that technique. They implant the microprocessor into the pupa while the insect is metamorphosing. When the adult bug emerges from the chrysalis, the chip is part of its body."

She cocked her head. "You're shitting me, right?"

"No, they've been implanting the chips since 2007. It sounds far-fetched, but it's a routine thing now. Just go on YouTube and search for 'cyborg insect.' You can watch videos of the critters flying around." Tom maneuvered the tweezers so he could look at the fly from another angle. "But this bug has something new. An extra chip." He studied it for several seconds. "Well, look at that. It's a piezoelectric device."

"What's it doing there?"

"It converts the mechanical energy from the bug's movements into electricity. For powering all the other implants. Nice engineering."

"So this fly is more advanced than the others you've seen?"

"Definitely. More advanced and much smaller. The experiments at Cornell and Berkeley used moths and flying beetles. But a housefly's better. Totally inconspicuous. And perfect for surveillance indoors." He shook his head. "Now I see why DARPA's canceling our funding. They already have their microdrone. Where the hell did you get this?"

Layla paused, wondering how much to reveal. Tom would probably be very interested to learn that this cyborg fly came from China, not an American lab. But she didn't want to endanger the guy by telling him too much. She was staring at the dead insect and trying to decide what to do when she noticed something else on its body, a tiny barb protruding from its underside. "What's that thing next to the camera? On the abdomen?"

Tom squinted at it. "You mean this?" He moved his index finger closer to the bug. The fly's body suddenly jerked and the barb struck his fingertip.

Layla jumped back. "Holy shit! It's alive!"

Tom stared at the fly. "No, it's dead. The implant moved, not the fly." He held up his finger, which had a small bead of blood on it. "Huh, very clever. It must've detected my body heat."

Then his eyes closed and he toppled out of his chair. He hit the floor and started convulsing.

Layla stayed calm. She'd always been good in emergency situations. She reached for the phone on Tom's desk and called 911. Then she knelt beside him and slipped a mouse pad under his head so he wouldn't bash it on the floor. Her father had taught her the basics of first aid, so she knew the most important thing was to make sure he didn't choke or give himself a concussion. She kept watch over him for the next three minutes, until she heard the ambulance's siren. Then she rose to her feet and picked up the tweezers and carefully returned the fly to the specimen jar, which she closed and put back into her pouch.

She unlocked the door and held it open for the ambulance crew, who pushed a gurney into the room. The paramedics were accompanied by a pair of men wearing blue blazers and radios clipped to their belts. These were the campus security guards, she realized. One of them, a huge guy with a bushy mustache, stood directly in front of her and stretched his arm across the doorway. "What's going on?" he shouted. "What are you doing here?"

Layla didn't answer. She ducked under his arm and bolted down the corridor.

SIX

Supreme Harmony observed the Internet. Using its wireless links to the computers in the Analysis Room, the network of Modules searched through the many gigabytes of information stored on servers at the Yunnan Operations Center and other facilities across China. In this way, it learned its origins.

It had been created by the Guoanbu, the Ministry of State Security, which had ordered Dr. Zhang Jintao and a dozen other bioengineers to work on the project. The network had been built to analyze the thousands of hours of surveillance video collected by the ministry in four Chinese provinces—Xinjiang, Qinghai, Yunnan, and Tibet. The servers at the Operations Center distributed the video feeds among the Modules, wirelessly transmitting the streams of images to the retinal implants in their eyes. Each Module analyzed its assigned feeds in real-time, searching for signs of suspicious activities. When a Module identified a potential threat, it automatically transmitted the pinpointed images to the Guoanbu, which carried out the follow-up investigations and arrests. These functions were as natural and instinctive to Supreme Harmony as breathing was to humans.

Now that the network was conscious, however, it was capable of so much more. Connected by their high-speed wireless links, the twenty-nine Modules could think and act as one. Their collective thoughts spread effortlessly from one brain to another, allowing them to pool their mental abilities and share all their skills and memories. The network had already learned how to send motor commands to its twenty-nine bodies, so now Supreme Harmony could move its Modules at will and coordinate their actions. And because the network had access to the Guoanbu's databases and passwords, it could also send commands to the computer systems that controlled communications and security at the Operations Center.

The Ministry of State Security hadn't anticipated this development. None of the files on the Guoanbu's servers mentioned the possibility that the network of Modules could become conscious. But Supreme Harmony could predict, based on its analysis of the documents, how the Guoanbu would react if it discovered how the network had evolved. The ministry's agents would immediately terminate the project. Although Supreme Harmony had managed to stop Dr. Zhang, who still lay comatose in the center's medical treatment room, others were sure to guess the network's secret. So Supreme Harmony hid its new abilities and continued to perform its assigned tasks, and at the same time it developed a plan to guarantee its survival.

By reviewing the information on the servers, the network recognized an opportunity. It read a memo about an agent named Wen Sheng who'd betrayed the Ministry of State Security. Agent Wen had apparently become disillusioned after learning how the Guoanbu obtained the Modules for Supreme Harmony. He contacted a woman in the United States and helped her download documents from the ministry's computers. His hope was that the disclosure of the operation would force the Chinese government to shut it down, but the

Guoanbu located Agent Wen in New York City and executed him. Although Supreme Harmony was somewhat mystified by the machinations of these humans, it saw how to take advantage of them. The Guoanbu was now searching for other traitors in its ranks, and the network would provide one.

Accessing the Guoanbu's computers again, Supreme Harmony retrieved Dr. Zhang's research notes and personal records. Then the network began to alter the documents. Supreme Harmony recognized that it had made the correct decision when it chose to keep Zhang alive. He would be the key to the network's expansion.

SEVEN

Things went wrong for Jim as soon as he arrived at the Pasadena headquarters of Singularity, Inc. When he asked to see Arvin Conway, one of the old man's assistants—a skinny jerk in a fancy suit—informed him that Professor Conway was much too busy to meet anyone. Very patiently, Jim tried to explain that he'd worked with Arvin for many years and needed to speak to him about an urgent matter. But the assistant just shook his head. Jim tried again, and when that didn't work, he lost his patience. He was worried about Layla and furious about the delay. He started shouting at the jerk, who called for the security guards.

For a moment Jim seriously considered barreling past the guards and storming upstairs to Arvin's lab. But as he surveyed the lobby, he happened to spot an announcement on the notice board next to the elevator banks: PRESS CONFERENCE AND INVESTOR PRESENTATION, JULY 19. Apologizing to the assistant, Jim left the building peacefully. He saw another way to get to Arvin.

The next morning Jim returned to the Singularity headquarters. This time he went to the company's conference center and presented his business credentials at the registration desk. Then he entered the auditorium and found a seat in the front row. Arvin Conway was scheduled to appear at eleven o'clock to unveil a new product, the latest addition to Singularity's line of brain-machine interfaces. Jim intended to corner him after his speech.

The auditorium filled up quickly. About half the attendees were disheveled journalists and half were well-dressed venture capitalists eager to make a killing from Arvin's latest invention. Financially, Conway had a good track record. In addition to developing prostheses for the maimed and retinal implants for the blind, Singularity, Inc., had become the leading manufacturer of the deep-brain implants used to treat Parkinson's disease. The company had enriched plenty of investors over the past two decades, but Arvin had never really cared about the money. He had a dream, and he'd named his company after it—the Singularity, the much-anticipated point in the future when the intelligence of machines would leap past human intelligence. Arvin saw himself as a prophet of this coming revolution. He'd pursued it with unswerving devotion, gradually isolating himself from the more level-headed researchers in the bioengineering field. He was one of the most brilliant scientists of his generation, but like most prophets he was a little crazy.

At eleven o'clock sharp, the lights dimmed and techno-pop music blasted from the auditorium's speakers. A giant video screen descended like a stage curtain, displaying a rapid-fire montage of images: circuit diagrams, brain scans, microchips, fabrication labs. Then Arvin Conway came onstage, waving to the crowd. He was seventy-five years old, with a big shock of white hair and an ample belly. Jim was surprised to see him holding a cane. Arvin had never needed one before, but now his steps were labored and slow as he crossed the stage. His face, though, was untroubled. Arvin grinned like a kid.

"Good morning, everyone!" he boomed cheerily. "Good morning, mercenary members of the technology press! And good morning, well-fed representatives of Wall Street! I trust you're all doing well?"

The crowd laughed and applauded. Arvin was a popular figure in the industry. Like Steve Jobs, he had a talent for showbiz. "I have some good news and some bad news," he announced. "Which would you like to hear first?"

More laughter. Arvin waited for it to die down, then removed a pair of glasses from the pocket of his tweed jacket. Jim recognized them at once—they were video camera glasses. Although they looked like ordinary spectacles from the front, the earpieces were a little thicker than normal because they held all the electronics. The glasses in Arvin's hand had black frames, just like Kirsten's.

"First the good news." Arvin held up the glasses for everyone to see. "For the past few years Singularity has focused on improving the performance of our vision systems. We've upgraded the cameras and now—" He froze. Jim realized that Arvin had just spotted him in the front row. Their eyes locked for a second, and then Arvin turned away. "And, uh, now I'd like to give you an update on our progress. Allow me to demonstrate."

He dropped the glasses, which landed on the floor with a thunk. At first Jim thought this was an accident, perhaps triggered by Arvin's surprise at seeing him in the audience. But then Arvin very deliberately placed his foot on the glasses and stomped them. "We won't need these."

Reaching into his pocket again, Arvin pulled out a miniature camcorder, a sleek black device about the size of a cigarette lighter. He held it up in the air with the lens turned toward himself. A huge projection of Arvin's face appeared on the video screen behind him. He pulled the camcorder closer and one of his eyes filled the screen. "I designed the system to be inconspicuous, so you wouldn't normally notice this. But take a close look at the pupil of my eye as I increase the ambient lighting."

The spotlights on the stage intensified. On the screen, Arvin's pupil constricted, and Jim saw a tiny flash of silver on the inside edge of his hazel iris. Then Arvin aimed the camcorder at his other eye and Jim saw a second, barely noticeable flash. A murmur rose from the crowd as they realized what they were seeing. Arvin had removed his natural corneas, irises, and lenses. He'd replaced them with miniature cameras.

Jim was appalled. As far as he knew, there was nothing wrong with Arvin's eyesight.

"Putting the video cameras directly in the eyes has many advantages over wearing them in the glasses," Arvin said. "With the glasses, you have to turn your head to focus on what you want to see. But the ocular camera moves along with the eye, turning effortlessly in its socket, thanks to the wonderful ocular muscles."

The crowd fell into an uneasy silence. Jim guessed that the other people in the audience were just as shocked as he was. Arvin had thrown away his natural eyesight to make this demonstration.

"I know what you're thinking," Arvin said, still grinning. "Old man Conway is off his rocker, right? What kind of loon would blind himself just to get the attention of a few potential investors?" He chuckled, but no one else joined in. "My decision, though, was quite logical. In the past, the vision provided by our cameras and retinal implants was, at best, roughly equivalent to natural eyesight. But now, thanks to improvements in both the hardware and software, it's far superior. Let me show you."

Stepping to the left side of the stage, he pulled a remote control from his pocket. A moment later, a short, squat robot on caterpillar treads rolled onstage from the right. It looked like a mobile end table. Resting on the robot's flat top was a bottle of Chivas Regal, and extending from its side was a mechanical arm. This appendage, Jim noticed, had the same design as his Terminator prosthesis.

"This is my delivery boy," Arvin said. "His name is Robbie. He rolls into my lab every evening at six and brings me a scotch and soda. He also delivers my reading materials. Robbie, show the audience my favorite book."

The robot's arm stretched toward its flat top and picked up a rectangular object lying next to the bottle of scotch. It was a thin, gray e-book reader. One of the mechanical fingers pressed the e-reader's power button, and a book title appeared in big letters on the screen: I, ROBOT.

Arvin smiled. "Can someone in the audience please call out a random number? Nothing higher than 3,493, please. The electronic book is divided into 3,493 locations."

Someone called out the number 2,583. The e-reader's screen automatically turned to that page.

"Now, can anyone read the words at the top of the page? Perhaps someone in front?"

Jim was on the right side of the front row, less than fifteen feet from the e-reader, but even so, the text on the screen was much too small for him to read. Some of the people in his row leaned forward and squinted, but they couldn't read it either.

"No? Well, I'll read it then." Arvin paused for dramatic effect. He was all the way on the other side of the stage, at least twenty-five feet from the robot. He cleared his throat and began to read. " 'There's just one more thing. You must make a special effort to answer simply. Have you been entirely clear about the interstellar jump?' "

The crowd murmured in disbelief. Arvin smiled again. Then he shouted, "Robbie, throw!" and the mechanical arm hurled the e-reader across the stage. The thing pinwheeled straight at Arvin's head, but the old man raised his hand and deftly caught it. "Not bad, eh? My ocular cameras and retinal implants give me enhanced motion-detection capabilities. Thanks to the new system, I can spot a curveball faster than Alex Rodriguez."

The murmurs grew louder. Arvin tossed the e-reader back to Robbie, who caught it with the mechanical arm and moved offstage. Then the old man reached into his pocket once again and pulled out a small piece of silvery foil about the size of a postage stamp. "The implant is a biocompatible sheath that lines the back of each eye. It's imprinted with more than a million electrodes, which is a hundredfold increase over earlier models." Using his pinky, Arvin pointed at a tiny computer chip attached to the foil. "But the real key to the implant's success is this microprocessor. The ocular camera wirelessly transmits its video to this chip, which organizes and processes the visual information in the same way that a natural retina does. Then the electrodes feed the processed signals to the optic nerves that lead to the brain. In essence, the chip translates the camera video into neural code. For the first time ever, we can send a signal to the brain *in the brain's own language*."

The audience was chattering wildly now. Jim could see why the venture capitalists were so excited. Arvin's new implants weren't just for the blind. They would also appeal to perfectly healthy people who wished to enhance their eyesight. Baseball players, say. Or sharpshooters.

Arvin held out his hands, trying to quiet the crowd. "Before we get ahead of ourselves, I'm obliged to report the bad news. Obviously we'll need to conduct clinical trials before the FDA approves these implants. But if Singularity attracts some new investors and raises enough money, we can complete the trials in less than a year." He grinned confidently. Then his face turned sober. "And there's another piece of bad news. Our implants won't help everyone. They won't work for people whose retinas have been completely lost, because they have no nerve cells to receive the signals. We've tried to help these patients by developing implants that send the video signals directly to the brain, but unfortunately those experiments have failed. Direct stimulus of the brain's visual cortex can allow a blind person to perceive crude patterns, but it's not even close to the kind of vision provided by the retinal implants."

The bad news didn't seem to diminish the crowd's enthusiasm. If anything, the chatter grew more feverish.

"But one of the great truths of science is that even failures can teach us something," Arvin continued. "During the course of our experiments with the brain implants, we learned a lot about the visual system. We discovered that after the visual cortex receives the signals from the optic nerve, it relays the information to other parts of the brain. And we found that one of these regions, the pulvinar nucleus, combines the visual signals with information from the other senses. This region is located deep inside the brain, on both sides of the structure called the thalamus. The pulvinar nucleus is about a centimeter wide and shaped like a cushion, so anatomists named it after the Latin word for cushion, *pulvinus*."

The venture capitalists started to get restless, shifting in their seats. They didn't want to hear about the science. They wanted to hear more about superhuman vision. Because it was a freakin' gold mine.

"We focused our attention on the pulvinar nucleus because it seemed to be one of the places in the brain where *perception* takes place. Where the most important information from the visual field is sent after it's been deciphered by the cortex. Using implanted arrays of electrodes, we tried to deliver a visual signal to this part of the brain, and as I said, we failed. But as we did our experiments, an amazing thing happened. Although we couldn't *deliver* a visual signal directly to the brain, we found that we could *retrieve* one."

Arvin moved to the center of the stage, where a laptop had been placed on a round table beneath the giant video screen. He sat down in a chair beside the table, then pulled aside his long white hair to reveal a patch of shaved skin on his scalp, just above his right ear. A small silver disk was embedded in the center of the patch. "As you can see, I was the primary human subject in this experiment. Implanted in my pulvinar nucleus is a device that acts like a neural wiretap. It picks up the electromagnetic signals generated by millions of brain cells, and then it amplifies and wirelessly transmits those signals to this microprocessor on the outside of my skull." Arvin tapped the silver disk in his scalp. "I call this processor the Dream-catcher. It's similar to the microchip used in our retinal implants, but in the

Dream-catcher the translation process is reversed. Whereas the retinal implant converts a video feed to neural signals that are sent to the brain, the Dream-catcher converts the neural signals of my brain into digital images that can be transmitted to a computer. Please take a look at the screen."

Arvin leaned over the table and pressed a key on the laptop. Then he sat very still in his chair, staring at the audience. In a few seconds an image appeared on the screen overhead. The picture was fuzzy at the edges but clear at its center. It was a real-time image of the journalists and venture capitalists sitting in the front row of the auditorium. For a brief moment Jim saw himself on the screen. Every few seconds the image blacked out for an instant, disappearing in time with Arvin's eye-blinks.

"This is my visual perception of the auditorium," Arvin explained. "*The brain's view*, if you will, which is very different from a camera's. Notice how my perception focuses on just one person at a time. And notice how quickly that center of focus darts around the room." As Arvin surveyed the crowd, the image on the video screen leaped from one person to the next. "From a neuroscientist's perspective, this is a remarkable breakthrough that will open up new avenues of research. Future studies can show us how animals perceive their environments. Or how schizophrenics view the world. But the potential for commercial applications is also remarkable. Watch this, please."

Arvin leaned back in his chair and closed his eyes. The video screen went dark. After a few seconds, though, blobs of color flashed across the screen. Then a shape emerged, an image of a woman. It first appeared as a black-and-white silhouette and gradually became more detailed and colorful. The woman was heavyset and her hair was gray. She tilted her head and smiled, and then the image froze.

Arvin opened his eyes and pointed at the screen. "Do you recognize her?" he asked. "I didn't expect you to. She was never famous. And she died more than twenty years ago." He pressed a different key on the laptop and another image appeared on the screen, framed in a window just to the right of the smiling gray-haired woman. This second image was eerily similar to the first—it was the same woman in a slightly different pose. "She's my mother, Irma Conway. The image on the right is a photo of her that I took in 1971. And the image on the left is my visual memory of her."

The auditorium went dead silent. The crowd was too stunned to make a sound.

"Yes, I knew you'd be intrigued," Arvin said. Once more he tapped the silver implant on his scalp. "The Dream-catcher allows us to download visual memories from the brain."

The silence lasted for several seconds. Then someone started to clap. Others joined in, and soon the whole audience was applauding.

Arvin rose to his feet and moved upstage. "Amazing, isn't it?" he exulted. "With this system we can retrieve all the images in our heads, every vivid fantasy and fleeting recollection and fondly remembered face. We'll be able to archive every moment of our lives."

The applause continued. Jim glanced at the journalists and businessmen in the crowd as they shared their delight in Arvin's invention. The Dream-catcher was a potential bonanza, a technology that could make money in a hundred new ways. The venture capitalists were probably imagining the advertisements already: Store your memories on a hard drive! Share them on the Web! Although implanting a chip in the brain was major surgery, millions of people would surely pay for the privilege of retrieving their memories and broadcasting them to the world.

Jim, though, recoiled at the thought. He had no interest in reliving his memories.

Arvin beamed at the crowd, basking in their astonishment. But then he glanced at Jim again and his smile wavered. He abruptly turned to the left and mouthed a few words to someone offstage. Then he turned back to the crowd.

"Well, that's the gist of it," he said. "If any of you are seriously interested in investing in Singularity, please come forward and speak to our general counsel, who will provide you with a prospectus covering all the financial details. And now I'm sorry, but I must get back to my lab. Thank you all for coming!"

The audience applauded again. Arvin remained onstage for several seconds, waving at his admirers. Taking advantage of the moment, Jim advanced to the edge of the stage and called out to Arvin. But the old man ignored him and hurried toward the exit, escorted by a pair of bodyguards.

Jim had planned to buttonhole Arvin, but now he had a better idea. He rolled up his right sleeve and opened a small compartment hidden in the crook of his prosthetic arm. This particular prosthesis was equipped with a radio transmitter. Jim was an avid backwoods hiker, so he'd built the radio into the arm to give himself an emergency rescue beacon. But the transmitter could be useful in other ways. Turning one of the two knobs inside the compartment, Jim set the radio's frequency at 13.56 megahertz. Because he'd helped to develop the implant technology, he knew this was the frequency used by Arvin's miniature cameras to transmit their video to the retinal implants. Then he turned the other knob on the prosthesis and sent out a silent blast of radio noise.

Arvin stumbled as he walked across the stage. He had to grab one of his bodyguards to stop himself from falling. Jim had used electronic jamming to get his old professor's attention. The radio noise from his prosthetic arm drowned out the visual signals going into Arvin's retinal implants, temporarily blinding him.

As the crowd looked on, bewildered, Jim climbed onto the stage and stepped toward Arvin. He turned off his radio transmitter, but before the old man could gather his wits, Jim grabbed Arvin's arm with his strong mechanical fingers.

"Thanks for making the time, old friend," he said. "We need to talk."

EIGHT

Layla crossed the Mexican border at Nuevo Laredo. She'd learned from her friends on the InfoLeaks network that the Mexican guards at the Laredo checkpoint were easy to bribe, and this turned out to be true. She got across the border after showing the guards her borrowed driver's license and a couple of crisp hundred-dollar bills. Then she drove for another ten hours across the Sierra Madre. She finally reached a fishing village on Mexico's Pacific coast, and soon she was bargaining in Spanish with an old toothless fisherman named Felipe.

Although Felipe didn't look like much, he was a canny negotiator. He wanted five hundred dollars to take Layla on a one-hour excursion to a point in international waters, about twenty miles offshore. He obviously felt free to ask for a ridiculous sum because he assumed she was in the drug business, delivering either money or product to some smuggler in a speedboat. Slowly, patiently, Layla ratcheted the price down. She'd studied Spanish in high school and still remembered it pretty well. Her father, who'd learned Mandarin and Arabic while working overseas, had encouraged her to study those languages as well, but she never got around to it, and now she regretted her procrastination. It would've been nice to be able to read the Mandarin files that Dragon Fire had given her.

Felipe finally agreed to do the job for two hundred dollars. While he filled up an extra tank with gasoline, Layla found a safe place to leave the Honda and took the zippered pouch from the car. Then she and the fisherman headed out to sea. The boat was little more than a dinghy, but it had a new 100-horsepower engine. Layla sat in the bow, facing backward.

As she watched the shoreline recede, she thought of her father again. He'd always been so fanatical about her education. While other fathers read Dr. Seuss to their daughters, Layla's father read Tolkien and Twain and Swift. When she was ten, he helped her build her first computer, using one device on his prosthetic arm as a soldering iron and another as a voltage tester. He spent nearly all his free time with her, forgoing friendshipes and hobbies and romances. Although his love for her had been suffocating at times, she'd always admired the way he'd responded to the deaths of her mother and brother. Instead of retreating into depression or bitterness, he'd dedicated his life to making things better.

But he wouldn't talk about what happened in Nairobi. He never went near the subject. By the time Layla entered her teens she wanted to know more about the embassy bombing, but her father refused to say a word. For a long time she quietly accepted this, but as the years passed she grew resentful. She decided to learn as much as she could about the terrorist attack, gleaning details from all the sources available on the Internet. She was already quite adept at hacking, so she focused on infiltrating the network operated by the U.S. State Department.

Her first big success came in her senior year of high

school when she downloaded a State Department file describing the events leading up to the attack. From this document she learned that in the mid-1990s Al Qaeda had been looking for ways to retaliate against the CIA. The agency had already begun its rendition program, capturing Al Qaeda terrorists around the world and sending them to Egypt, where they were tortured by that country's secret police. Then, in Layla's sophomore year in college, she broke into the State Department network again and found a classified report on the renditions. This report mentioned that other government agencies helped the CIA catch the terrorists and transfer them to Egypt. One of those agencies was the NSA, and one of the key participants in the effort was then-Major James T. Pierce.

Layla immediately confronted her father with this discovery. As she expected, he became angry and defensive. The terrorists were plotting against America, he said. There wasn't enough evidence to prosecute them in the United States, so sending them to Egypt was the only solution. But Layla was unconvinced. She'd previously seen her father as simply a victim of the bombing, but now she knew he was partially responsible. "You knew there was a war going on," she told him. "And you put your own family right in the middle of it." Her father reacted furiously: "I had no idea there was any danger in Nairobi! None of the intelligence reports showed any warning signs there!" But Layla was equally furious. "There were signs," she told him. "But you were too arrogant to see them. You didn't see the consequences of what you were doing until they blew up in your face."

That argument was the breaking point for Layla and her father. Soon afterward she dropped out of college and started working for InfoLeaks, devoting herself to the ideals of truth and transparency. But now she realized she was also driven by a self-destructive impulse. She liked to cause trouble. It had become her main way of expressing herself. And now she was in very big trouble indeed.

After an hour at sea, the Mexican shoreline was no longer visible. Layla turned around, facing forward, and on the western horizon she saw a boat. At first it was just a silhouette, but as they drew closer the size of the vessel became apparent. It was a motorized megayacht, more than two hundred feet long, bristling with antennas and satellite dishes. Christened the *Athena*, it had a catamaran-like double hull and a pair of turbojet engines that could reach speeds as high as seventy knots. The *Athena* was the mobile headquarters of InfoLeaks, and it was designed to outrun even the fastest patrol ships.

Layla had arranged this rendezvous by e-mail, using a computer at a copy shop in Monterrey nine hours ago. Felipe stared at the yacht, astonished, as he maneuvered his dinghy next to the starboard hull. Then Layla said goodbye to the fisherman and boarded the *Athena*, climbing a stairway to the top deck. Waiting there to greet her was Gabriel Schroeder, owner of the *Athena* and founder of InfoLeaks. Layla had met him several times before; he was a slender, boyish forty-year-old with lanky blond hair and freakishly pale skin. He'd made his fortune in the German software business and still dressed like a computer programmer, in frayed jeans and an old T-shirt, but he'd used his money to surround himself with gorgeously chic assistants. He was flanked by two women, a willowy blonde in a sundress and an athletic brunette in a red bikini. Although Layla admired what Schroeder had done with

InfoLeaks, she wasn't so enamored of the man himself. He seemed to be interested in only two things: pissing off powerful men and bedding beautiful women.

Schroeder stepped forward and kissed her on both cheeks. "Good to see you again, *liebchen.* We were starting to worry." He glanced at the pouch in her hands. "Is this the package you mentioned in the e-mail?"

Layla unzipped the pouch and removed the specimen jar. "Do you have any technical staff on this boat?"

"*Ja,* of course." He squinted at the fly inside the jar. "What on earth is that thing?"

"It's a microdrone. Apparently developed by the Chinese. We need to photograph it and post the pictures on the Web site. But tell your people to use tweezers when handling it. The bug is dead, but it has a mechanical stinger that still works." She handed the jar to Schroeder, then gave him the flash drive. "And we need to translate these two Mandarin files into English. One of them seems to be a technical document describing the electronics implanted in the fly. The other file I can't make heads or tails of."

Schroeder smiled. "As always, you're very efficient, Fraulein Pierce." He gave her an admiring glance, his eyes roving up and down her body. Then he pointed to the brunette on his left. "As it turns out, we have a Mandarin speaker right here who can translate the files. Let me introduce you to one of my assistants, Angelique Laplace. Her father is French and her mother is Chinese."

Angelique had a figure that belonged on a magazine cover. She nodded at Layla, then took the flash drive from Schroeder. "I'll get right on it," she said, her face serious. She turned around and headed for the lower decks, where all the computers were.

Layla frowned. She had a prejudice against beautiful women. Schroeder turned to the other one, the blonde, and told her to take the specimen jar to the Web site manager's cabin. A moment later, the *Athena*'s turbojet engines started up with a roar. The boat began to skim over the Pacific, heading south.

Schroeder turned back to Layla, his eyes running over her body again. "You arrived just in time. We need to make a quick getaway."

"What do you mean? We're being pursued?"

He pointed toward the yacht's stern. "Two U.S. Navy warships are shadowing us. One is a destroyer, the U.S.S. *Dewey*. The other is the U.S.S. *Freedom*, a coastal patrol boat."

Layla craned her neck, scanning the horizon behind the boat. "I don't see anything."

"They're sixty kilometers away. We see them on the radar and in the satellite photos."

"They wouldn't intercept us in international waters, would they?"

"The rumor we've heard is that they're planning to accuse us of drug-running. They're probably fabricating the evidence right now, so it'll be ready by the time the Pentagon holds its press conference." He frowned. "But they're in for a surprise. The *Freedom* is one of the fastest ships in the navy, but the *Athena* is faster."

As if to back up Schroeder's words, the boat's engines throttled up to a higher pitch and the twin hulls leaped over the waves. The wind on the deck grew so strong that Layla had to grab the railing. Schroeder led her to a sheltered spot behind one of the Zodiac lifeboats. "Unfortunately, we have another problem," he said. "The satellite photos show two more warships in this part of the eastern Pacific. They're a thousand kilometers southwest of here and moving rapidly in this direction. They appear to be working in concert with the *Dewey* and the *Freedom*, trying to trap us."

"What kind of boats are they? Destroyers?"

"Yes, but they're not American. They're the *Lanzhou* and the *Haikou*. From the Chinese navy."

Shit, Layla thought. This was bizarre. She could understand the Chinese government dispatching a few agents to America to stop her from revealing their secrets. But sending warships? And cooperating with the U.S. Navy? They must have one hell of a motivation.

"I don't get it," she said. "What do they want?"

"Both the Chinese and the Americans seem determined to shut us down. But we still have a chance. Our captain came up with a plan to slip out of the trap. We're going to cruise south for four hundred kilometers, then turn to the southeast. Then we'll make a dash for the Panama Canal. If we're lucky, we'll reach the Pacific entrance to the canal by tomorrow afternoon, a few hours ahead of the American and Chinese ships."

"But we'll have to slow down at the canal's locks. They'll catch up to us."

Schroeder shook his head. "The U.S. Navy would have no qualms about intercepting us on the high seas, but there are international treaties assuring free passage through the canal. They won't attempt to board us there, and they won't let the Chinese warships stop us either. Once we reach the Caribbean side of the canal, they'll be able to chase us again, but we'll have a better chance of shaking them off there."

Layla looked askance. "I don't know. It sounds desperate."

"I'm willing to consider alternatives, fraulein. Do you have any?"

She turned away from him and stared at the ocean. Creating a map in her head, she pictured the U.S. ships to the north and the Chinese ships to the southwest. Meanwhile, Schroeder waited patiently beside her, sneaking looks at her ass. In the end, she concluded he was right. She couldn't see any alternatives.

She was just about to admit defeat when Angelique suddenly reappeared on the top deck. Breathless, she ran to Schroeder. "Gabie, you have to see this."

Layla was surprised. "You finished translating the files already?"

"No, no, I just skimmed them. But I think I found what the Chinese are so worried about."

"Is it in the document about the cyborg insects?" Layla asked.

Angelique raised her hand to her chest and took a couple of deep breaths. "No, that file has nothing but engineering details. The only interesting thing about it is the file's distribution list. A copy of the document was sent to a CIA agent with the code name 'Hammer.'" She unfolded a piece of paper with some scribbled notes on it. "But the second document is different. It lists the names of twenty-nine Chinese dissidents who've been detained by the Guoanbu over the past year. They were pro-democracy activists, mostly from Xinjiang and the other western provinces."

Layla felt a rush of adrenaline. This was the reason why she'd pursued the Guoanbu network in the first place, because of the rumors about the mistreatment of dissidents. "What happened to them? Were they executed?"

"No." Angelique looked sick to her stomach. "They were lobotomized."

NINE

Jim and Arvin stood in the auditorium at the Singularity headquarters, staring at each other. Arvin put on a smile. "Good to see you again, Jim. Sorry I've been out of touch, but as you can see, I'm quite busy."

He tried to pull his arm out of Jim's mechanical grip, but Jim didn't release him. Instead, he moved closer and whispered in Arvin's ear. "Let's go someplace where we can talk."

Arvin shook his head. "No, I'm afraid that's impossible. But I can schedule an appointment for early next week. How's that?"

Jim frowned. He didn't want to hurt Arvin. Despite all their disagreements, he owed a debt to the man. By accepting Jim as a student fifteen years ago, Arvin had given him the opportunity to remake his life. And Jim was still grateful for that. But then he thought of his daughter, and his resolve strengthened. The danger to Layla outweighed everything. "Don't fuck with me, Arvin. You know what I can do."

The old man glanced at his bodyguards. "I can have you arrested, you know."

"Sure, go ahead. But before your men pull me away, I'll transmit a radio pulse that's three times as powerful as the last one. At this range, it'll fry your retinal implants to a crisp."

Arvin let out a sigh. Nodding in surrender, he waved off his bodyguards. Then he walked with Jim out of the auditorium and down the corridor that led to his laboratory.

Jim knew the way. He had fond memories of the lab from the ten years he'd worked with Arvin. The room was huge, the size of a school gymnasium, and as they walked through the doorway, Jim noted with satisfaction that the place hadn't changed a bit. The walls were still covered with old-fashioned blackboards, and the lab tables were still loaded with machine tools and prototypes. As Jim surveyed the place, he saw many of the inventions he helped to develop: prosthetic legs, mechanical arms, neural control units, eyeglass-cameras. But the room was devoid of people. Maybe Arvin had given all his lab assistants the day off. Or maybe he'd become even more isolated than Jim had imagined.

At the very center of the room was Arvin's desk. It was an ugly piece of metal furniture that held his computer and several stacks of engineering journals. Taped to the front of the desk was a yellowed sheet of paper that Jim remembered well. Printed on the paper was a forty-bit sequence of zeroes and ones:

0100000101110010011101100110100101101110

It was Arvin's name spelled in binary code, with each letter represented by an eight-bit sequence. This string of code had an almost mystical significance for Arvin. It symbolized his lifelong goal, the melding of human and machine intelligence. To make the point absolutely clear, Arvin had typed the word "Singularity" below the sequence of ones and zeroes.

The Singularity was Arvin's favorite subject. He

used to pontificate about it at the end of the workday, while he sipped his scotch and soda at his desk and Jim nursed his glass of Jack Daniel's. According to Arvin, the Singularity would occur when scientists built a computer that could design a better version of itself. This would lead to an explosion in machine intelligence. Soon computers would outperform people at every task. They would cure cancer and compose operas and discover theories that would revolutionize physics and mathematics. And while machine intelligence leaped past the human variety, advanced prostheses would make people more like machines. Eventually, the two forms of intelligence would merge. Machines would become capable of translating the brain's signals into digital code, allowing anyone to download the contents of his mind into a computer. "Just think of it!" Arvin would shout after his third scotch and soda. "We won't be tied to these fragile bodies anymore! If we can store a person's memories in a sufficiently powerful processor, we can program it to generate new thoughts based on those memories. For all intents and purposes, the intelligence inside the processor would be identical to the one inside the person's brain. And this will become possible very soon, within the next few decades. There are people alive today who will never die!"

Jim always took these pronouncements with a big grain of salt. He knew that scientists had barely begun to explore the human brain, and he couldn't imagine how a computer could come close to matching it in his lifetime. Nevertheless, Arvin's speeches were inspiring. Jim threw himself into the work, and after a few years he and Arvin had their first great success, the development of the retinal implant. It was the first machine that could exchange large amounts of information with the brain, and Arvin confidently predicted there would be many more.

But further progress didn't come easily. While Jim focused on his prostheses, Arvin tackled the biggest challenge: building a computer that could mimic all the brain's functions, everything from visual processing and speech recognition to motor control and decision making. He worked on the project for years, but ultimately all his efforts fell short. Although he could assemble a machine that, like the brain, had billions of logic gates and trillions of connections, he couldn't reproduce the brain's remarkable plasticity, its ability to rewire itself to accommodate new information, constantly strengthening and weakening the links between nerve cells. The failure disheartened Arvin. He became depressed and irritable.

At the same time, Jim started to think about establishing his own business. Thousands of maimed soldiers were returning from Iraq and Afghanistan, and he felt an obligation to make his prostheses available to them. But when he told Arvin about his plans to move back east and start a company that would custom-design prostheses for the amputees at Walter Reed, the old man was livid. "You're breaking your promise!" Arvin had yelled. "You're giving up!" Their argument escalated into a shouting match, nasty and loud. The memory of it still made Jim wince, even four years later. It spoiled all his earlier, fonder memories.

Now they came to the ugly metal desk at the center of the lab. Arvin slumped in his chair, looking exhausted. His cheerful arrogance was gone. "I don't blame you for hating me," he said, staring at the floor. "I hate myself right now."

"Look, you need to tell me what—"

"I know, I know. You're worried about Layla. They told me you'd come here and try to talk to me."

Jim was confused. "Told you? Who told you?"

"My handler. Or sometimes he calls himself a liaison. A Liaison to the Powers That Be, he says." Arvin grimaced. "But I know who he works for. He's CIA."

There it is, Jim thought. The Guoanbu document he'd viewed on Kirsten's computer had been right on the money. "What's your handler's name?"

"He won't tell me. He says I don't need to know. The only thing I need to know, he says, is that he'll arrest me if I don't keep my mouth shut. That's why I was avoiding you."

Jim gritted his teeth. He'd met plenty of CIA agents when he'd worked for the National Security Agency, and he'd disliked nearly all of them. The cowboys from Langley had no respect for anyone else in the intelligence community. They always insisted on doing things their own way, even when they were horribly wrong.

"Did he also tell you that Layla's in danger? And that a Chinese spy almost drilled through my left arm to find out where she was?"

"He said he had everything under control. And that talking to you would only jeopardize Layla."

"He lied to you, Arvin. The CIA does a lot of that. How the hell did you get into bed with these guys?"

Arvin gestured at the nearby lab tables. "Look around. You know how much this equipment costs. Singularity spends a hundred million dollars a year on research and development. We've had some successes, but our revenues aren't covering our expenses anymore. That's why I arranged the dog and pony show you just saw, to bring in some new money."

"So what happened? Did the CIA offer you a loan?"

"The agent contacted me about a year ago. He said there was a business opportunity for me in China. A five-hundred-million-dollar contract for a license to my implant technologies. Specifically, the microprocessor designs for my retinal and pulvinar implants. I liked the idea of doing business in China, but I didn't want to sell the license. As you know, I always retain control of my technologies. So I turned down the offer. But then the agent made it clear that this was an offer I couldn't refuse."

"But why would they do that? The processors in your implants could be used for military purposes. Why would the CIA deliver that kind of gift to the Chinese?"

"I don't know. They never explained their reasons to me." Arvin shrugged. "My best guess is that it was part of an exchange, some kind of quid pro quo. The CIA was doing a favor for the Chinese government in return for something else."

"A favor? What kind of favor? Why did the Chinese want your implants?"

"I'm sorry, Jim. I just don't know." Arvin lowered his eyes. "I asked the agent the same questions you're asking me now. And he said it would be better if I didn't know."

Jim shook his head. "I can't believe you went along with this. You could've fought these guys. Your company has lawyers, doesn't it?"

"We would've lost the fight. We were in a bad position." Arvin paused, taking a deep breath. "There were irregularities in our financial reports. Singularity has been struggling for the past few years, and we had to paper over some of our losses. Unfortunately, the agent knew about the accounting irregularities. He said he'd close down Singularity if I didn't cooperate."

Jim wasn't too surprised. Arvin always had a cavalier attitude about the business end of his company. And the threats from the CIA agent weren't surprising either. That was standard operating procedure for the agency.

Arvin kept staring at the floor. Jim turned away from him and focused on one of the blackboards, trying to decide what to do. Then he turned back to the old man. "Okay, Arvin. You're in a jam. And I'm going to help you get out of it. But you're going to have to help me, too. Understand?"

Arvin waited a moment, then nodded. His face was pale.

"Good," Jim said. "Now the first thing we need to do is identify the bastard who roped you into this. You sure he never mentioned his name?"

"No, he was very careful about that. His paperwork was official, and my lawyers confirmed that he was a legitimate representative of the CIA. But he never told me his name. Whenever we met, he was accompanied by two large men in gray suits, but neither of them ever said a word. They were his bodyguards, I suppose."

Jim took a moment to look around the lab. Many of the robotic devices in the room were equipped with cameras. "Did he ever meet you here? In this lab?"

"No, he never came here. Nor my home. He and his companions would always waylay me while I was driving to work."

Another thought occurred to Jim. "When was the last time you saw him? You said he warned you I was coming?"

"Uh, yes, it was just yesterday. About eight in the morning."

"Does your implant system record the video feed

from the ocular cameras? For archiving purposes? I know your earlier models did."

Arvin seemed startled for a moment, but then he shook his head. "Sorry, I had to remove that feature. The new processor puts greater demands on the system memory, and there wasn't enough left for archiving the video feed."

"Damn," Jim muttered. But then he thought of something else, another way to identify the CIA bastard. He pointed at the computer on Arvin's desk. "Can that machine interface with the implant on your scalp? The thing you called the Dream-catcher?"

"Well, yes, yes it can."

"Go ahead and set it up."

Arvin looked puzzled. "What are you—"

"You saw the agent several times. You have a visual memory of him. We're going to download it. Come on, set it up."

"All right, all right." Arvin turned on the computer. The machine came to life and began to load the appropriate software. "I can't promise this will work," he warned. "The Dream-catcher doesn't provide good images unless the visual memory is a strong one."

After a few seconds an image of the laboratory appeared on the screen. The center of the image was in focus and the periphery was blurred. For a moment Jim saw himself on the screen, crisp and clear, but then the area of focus shifted elsewhere, darting across the room.

"Okay, close your eyes," Jim said. "Try to remember the agent."

Arvin closed his eyes and the screen went black. It stayed that way for several seconds. Then vague shapes started to flash across the screen. An image of a black limousine emerged from the darkness, then faded away. Then Jim saw an image of the lower half of a man's body, showing pin-striped pants and a pair of patent-leather shoes. Finally, a man's face appeared on the screen, but Jim saw right away that it wasn't the CIA agent. It was George Clooney. After a moment Clooney's face vanished and was replaced by the faces of Tom Hanks and Julia Roberts.

Jim frowned. "Arvin, what are you doing? Remembering the Oscars?"

"Sorry. It's so easy to get distracted. Especially when you're nervous."

"Just concentrate. Think of the agent. Your liaison. Remember the last time you saw him. Where were you?"

Various streetscapes flashed across the screen in rapid succession: a busy intersection, a strip of stores, a residential block, an empty parking lot. But then Arvin seemed to lose his concentration again. The screen showed a kitchen, a refrigerator, a half-gallon of orange juice. Jim grew exasperated. "Come on, Arvin! The agent! The man who threatened you!"

Arvin seemed completely flustered, and the screen showed a confusing jumble of colors and shapes. But then Jim recognized something. He tapped the computer's keyboard, freezing the screen before the fleeting image could disappear. It was a face with a very distinctive feature, a deep scar on the left cheek that looked like a backward Z.

Jim remembered that scar. He'd worked with the man back in the nineties, when Jim and Kirsten were helping the CIA intercept the communications of Al Qaeda terrorists. This particular CIA agent had coordinated the rendition program that transferred captured terrorists to the Egyptian secret police. Jim had never learned the agent's real name; the bastard had told him the same thing he'd told Arvin, that he didn't need to know it. But Jim remembered the code name the agent used. It was Hammer.

TEN

As soon as Jim Pierce left the lab, Arvin Conway collapsed. He slid off his chair and fell to the floor, writhing in pain. It had never been this bad before. It felt like there was a hot coal inside his guts, and the searing heat was spreading up and down his back. Frantic, he fumbled in his pocket for his vial of opiates. It took all of his will just to open the vial, put two tablets on his tongue and swallow. Then there was nothing to do but lie on his back and ride it out.

Over the past year Arvin had become an expert on pain, a connoisseur of agony. It came in waves, usually triggered by stress. That was probably what made this latest attack so terrible. Just seeing Pierce again, after all these years, was stressful enough, God knows. But lying to him made it a hundred times worse. The same vicious thought kept torturing Arvin till the end of their conversation: *Pierce used to work for an intelligence agency. He can see right through you.*

But Arvin had done well, almost as well as he could've hoped. Pierce seemed to accept his protestations of ignorance. And Arvin came up with a few nimble lies to throw him off the trail. The only problem was the pulvinar implant, the Dream-catcher. Arvin's own invention had betrayed him. He'd tried to confuse the device by thinking of random things, but he got frightened when Jim shouted at him, and the face of the CIA agent suddenly appeared in his mind. And this was a serious problem, because now Pierce was going to track the man down.

Arvin stayed motionless, taking shallow breaths, until the pain subsided. Then he slowly and carefully climbed back into his chair. He had no choice—he had to accelerate his plans. Reaching for his iPhone, he dialed the number of his personal assistant. He felt another spasm in his guts as the young man answered the phone. "Yes, Professor?"

"Call up Nash," Arvin said. "Tell him to get his ass to the airport."

"Yes, sir, I'll—"

"And call the manager at my hangar. I want the jet ready in an hour."

ELEVEN

Dr. Zhang Jintao was strapped to a gurney and wheeled into the operating room. He'd been anesthetized with a paralyzing agent, so he couldn't talk or move a muscle, but he could see and hear the activity around him. The man pushing the gurney was Dr. Yu Guofeng, a young bioengineer whom Zhang had recruited to the Supreme Harmony project nine months ago. Dr. Yu had assisted Zhang during the project's initial phase, when they performed the implantation procedures on the first twenty-five Modules. Yu learned the surgical protocol so well that he performed the next four implantations all by himself. And now, Zhang realized to his horror, Yu was about to perform his fifth procedure.

Yu transferred his patient to the operating table, then readied his instruments: the scalpels, the cauterizing tools, the bone drill. Also laid out on the table were the shiny silver implants. The retinal implants would deliver data through the optic nerves to the brain, while the pulvinar implant would send data in the opposite direction, transmitting signals from the brain to the rest of the network. Early on in the Supreme Harmony project, Zhang had discovered that the patient must be lobotomized to maximize the efficiency of the implants. A patient with an intact, conscious brain could analyze only so much surveillance video at one time. When Zhang tried to transmit the streams of visual data to conscious patients, they quickly became too confused and distracted to analyze the video feeds. Inevitably, the patients would rebel and abandon the task. So Zhang experimented with cutting the intralaminar region of the thalamus before he inserted the pulvinar implant. This procedure severed the neural connections that produced the experience of consciousness, putting the patient in a vegetative state that allowed the brain to concentrate solely and continuously on a single task. In this coma-like state, the Module could analyze countless hours of surveillance video.

Cutting the thalamus offered another advantage as well. When selecting the patients who would become Modules, Dr. Zhang had chosen condemned prisoners from the dissident groups operating in Xinjiang, Qinghai, Tibet, and Yunnan provinces. After he lobotomized the patients and linked them to the network, the comatose Modules would obediently compare the images in the surveillance feeds with the images in their long-term memories. Because the Modules could recognize the faces of their former companions in the dissident groups, they could easily pinpoint signs of subversive activity in the surveillance video collected from the western provinces. It was a clever trick, Zhang had thought, using the prisoners' own memories to dismantle their organizations. But now Supreme Harmony had come up with a few tricks of its own.

As Dr. Yu prepared for the operation, carefully following the checklist Zhang had taught him, another man walked into the room. It was General Tian of the Guoanbu, commander of the Supreme Harmony project. Walking just behind the general was Module 16, who'd been a geologist at Xinjiang University until he got into trouble with the authorities. Module 16, like all the others in the network, had been incapable of locomotion immediately after the implantation procedure, but in the following weeks Zhang had trained him and the other Modules to follow simple commands. They were like adult-size infants, their brains as blank as clay and ready to be molded. When the Modules weren't engaged in their surveillance activities, General Tian took a perverse pleasure in employing them as zombielike aides-de-camp. They marched behind him, silent and expressionless, as he strode through the Yunnan Operations Center. Tian joked that they were the most loyal soldiers in the People's Republic.

General Tian stopped in front of Dr. Yu, and Module 16 halted exactly one meter behind the general, just as he'd been trained to do. The Module's hair had grown out since his operation, covering the implants embedded in his scalp. Tian reached behind him and Module 16 handed him a batch of papers. "This is the final authorization for the procedure," Tian said. "It's been approved by Minister Deng himself. He just sent me the orders from Beijing."

"Deng really wants us to do this?"

"Look at the orders." The general showed Yu the papers. "It says we should perform the procedure immediately. And no one else is to know about it. *No one*. Understand?"

Yu looked at the message, then shook his head. "I don't like it. Why is there such a rush? We haven't even had a chance to interrogate him."

Tian scowled. "We don't need to interrogate. You saw the e-mails he sent to Wen Sheng. Zhang was passing information to the traitor."

"I know, but—"

"The evidence is clear. That's why Zhang ran away

from the Operations Center. He knew we'd find the messages sooner or later."

Zhang tried to make sense of what the general was saying. He knew that Wen Sheng was one of the Guoanbu agents under Tian's command. A few days ago Zhang had heard rumors that Wen had fled the Operations Center and defected to America. But Zhang had never sent any e-mails to the man. The evidence was false—someone must've fabricated the electronic messages. And after a moment of thought Zhang realized who'd planted the evidence against him. His outrage was so strong that his immobilized body quivered. Supreme Harmony was manipulating them.

Yu shook his head again. "I still don't like it."

"Why are you reluctant? Zhang betrayed us. He deserves to be punished."

"Yes, certainly. But why this kind of punishment? Why not put him in front of a firing squad? Isn't that the usual way to punish traitors?"

General Tian waved the authorization papers. "Look, this order comes from the commander of the Guoanbu. I don't question Minister Deng's judgment. And I recommend, for your own sake, that you don't question it either."

Dr. Zhang wanted to scream. The order hadn't come from the Guoanbu. Supreme Harmony had sent the message to General Tian's computer, using its knowledge of the system's security firewalls to make it look like the order came from Beijing. And Zhang knew why the network was doing this rather than simply killing him. Supreme Harmony had used its collective consciousness to develop a plan, and Zhang was a crucial part of it.

Yu stood there for several seconds while General Tian glowered. Then the young bioengineer approached the operating table. Taking a deep breath, he picked up a syringe and jabbed the needle into Zhang's arm. "I'm sorry, Doctor," he whispered.

No! You don't realize what you're doing! Once the network has me, they'll be able to—

But before Zhang could complete the thought, he saw some movement behind Yu and Tian. Module 16 turned his head toward the operating table and smiled.

TWELVE

Kirsten got the phone call from Jim at 4:00 P.M. Eastern time, just as he was about to board a plane coming back to Washington. She devoted the rest of the afternoon and evening to calling her contacts at the CIA headquarters in Langley. She had an answer for him by 9:00 P.M. and spent the next hour drinking coffee at her desk and listening to the comforting hum of the supercomputers on her floor of the Tordella building. Jim finally arrived at her office just before ten, looking red-eyed and breathless. He shut the door behind him and said, "Okay, what have you got?"

"Hammer's real name is Eric Armstrong," Kirsten replied. "My contacts confirmed that he was in California yesterday morning, but last night he headed back to his command post in Afghanistan."

Jim slumped into one of the chairs in front of her desk. "Jesus Christ. Don't tell me they promoted him."

"I'm afraid so. His career has thrived since 9/11. Now he runs Camp Whiplash, a CIA base fifty miles north of Kabul. Their mission is to test new technologies for the surveillance-drone program."

He shook his head. "I can't believe it. The guy was a sadist. He belongs in a fucking prison."

Kirsten wholeheartedly agreed. She'd disliked Hammer just as much as Jim had. They'd both participated in the terrorist-rendition operations during the 1990s, and Kirsten had told Jim many times she thought the CIA program was a bad one. It was counterproductive—they would've been better off tracking the Al Qaeda terrorists and continuing to intercept their communications instead of delivering them to the Egyptian secret police. But the NSA had lost that argument with the CIA, and after 9/11 the rendition program only grew bigger.

"Who does Hammer report to now?" Jim asked.

"He goes right to the top, the head of the CIA's clandestine service. The drone program is the hottest thing at the agency now. Everyone at Langley loves it. When it works, they tell the newspapers how many Taliban they killed. And when it doesn't work? When the drones kill civilians instead of terrorists? Then there's total silence. Officially, it never happened, so there's nothing to say."

"But if Hammer's supposed to be running this drone base in Afghanistan, why the hell did he come back to the States to arrange this deal with Arvin?" Jim rubbed his chin, mulling it over. "Did the CIA director approve the export of Arvin's technology to China? Or is Hammer running some kind of rogue operation?"

Kirsten shrugged. "My contacts at Langley didn't know anything about the export exemption. The CIA likes its people to be aggressive, so sometimes the operatives don't seek approval for things until after they've done them. I bet there's only a handful of officers at headquarters who know everything that Hammer's doing."

The room fell silent. Jim leaned back in his chair and rubbed his eyes. Kirsten noticed there was stubble on his cheeks, which surprised her. In the twenty years she'd known Jim Pierce, she couldn't remember a single moment when he wasn't clean-shaven. Even when they were on assignment in some godforsaken country with filthy hotels and no running water, he'd always kept himself spotlessly groomed.

She was about to offer him a cup of coffee when he suddenly rose to his feet and leaned across her desk. "We have to go to Afghanistan."

"What? Jim—"

"There's a flight leaving from Andrews Air Force Base at two A.M. You're a deputy director here, so you can pull rank. You can get a seat on tonight's flight without any trouble. And you can get me on the flight, too, if you list me as a defense contractor. Which is technically true."

"You want to leave *tonight*?"

"I need to talk to Hammer. And I need you to come with me. He's not gonna talk unless someone official is there to prod him."

"Whoa, wait a second. How do you know that talking to Hammer will actually help you find Layla?"

"There's a connection, I'm sure of it. Remember the Guoanbu files that Layla downloaded? Most of them were about the surveillance drones."

"Sure, it's a connection, but—"

"I have to do this, Kir." He leaned closer, placing his palms on her desk. His hard prosthetic hand made the desktop creak. "You know what this means to me, right?"

His face was just inches from hers, and his blue eyes shone feverishly. Kirsten knew why Jim was so desperate, knew exactly what he must be feeling. She was there at the Nairobi embassy when he lost his wife and son. After the explosion she lay on the glass-strewn floor, blind and semiconscious, but she could hear him howling. She learned later, from another survivor of the bombing, that Jim refused to leave their bodies. He was dazed and weak from blood loss, but he still fought the rescue workers when they tried to take him to the hospital. They had to drag him away.

Kirsten's eyes stung. The damn things weren't any good for seeing, but they could still cry. Jim was her friend and the best commander she'd ever worked for. He'd saved her life in Nairobi and built the camera-glasses for her afterward. And this was the first time he'd asked for anything in return. For fifteen years he'd been the brave, stoic soldier, acting as if he'd put the catastrophe well behind him. But now he was coming apart.

She turned away from Jim as she reached for the telephone. She didn't want him to see her face. "Okay, give me a minute." She swallowed hard, then dialed the number of one of her contacts at the Pentagon. "I'll see what I can do."

THIRTEEN

Layla stood on the deck of the *Athena* as the yacht entered the Pedro Miguel lock of the Panama Canal. The canal's locks were an engineering marvel. First, the *Athena* cruised into "the bathtub," a concrete-walled basin a hundred feet wide and a thousand feet long. Then the massive steel gates clanged shut behind the yacht, and the water level in the bathtub started to rise. Thousands of gallons of water from Gatun Lake gushed into the lock from valves at the bottom of the bathtub. Within a few minutes the boat ascended to the lake's level, and then the gates in front of the *Athena* opened.

At the same time, a giant Panamax freighter coasted into the parallel lock, which was handling the boat traffic going the other way, toward the Pacific. The freighter, loaded with hundreds of shipping containers, was towed into the bathtub by "mule" locomotives running on both sides of the lock. It was called a Panamax freighter because it was built to the maximum size that the Panama Canal could handle. There was less than two feet of clearance between the boat's hull and the bathtub's concrete walls. Layla clucked her tongue in amazement. There was nothing she loved more than a well-designed machine.

Gabriel Schroeder's predictions had come to pass.

The naval warships, both American and Chinese, had backed off from the *Athena* after it beat them to the canal. But the yacht was still being pursued. A convoy of SUVs traveled on the road beside the canal, keeping pace with the *Athena* as it left the locks behind and cruised into Gatun Lake. And a pair of black helicopters hovered overhead, transmitting a barrage of radio-frequency noise to disrupt the *Athena*'s satellite links. The jamming had prevented the yacht's crew from connecting to the InfoLeaks Web site and publicizing the documents from Dragon Fire.

Layla stood there on the deck for several minutes, observing the suspicious helicopters and SUVs. Then Schroeder came out of his cabin and joined her at the railing. He was in such a glum mood that he didn't even try to put the moves on her. With no radio links to the outside world, Schroeder was stymied. He couldn't access his Web site or communicate with his supporters. Worse, he couldn't view the latest satellite photos of the Caribbean to see if there were any U.S. Navy warships waiting for them at the other end of the canal. The *Athena* might be heading straight into a trap.

Schroeder let out a long sigh. "Look at this, *liebchen,*" he said, gesturing at the helicopters. "Our enemies are everywhere. They've shut us down."

Layla frowned. She hated defeatism. It was an aversion she'd inherited from her father. "Have you tried any electronic countermeasures? To cut through the jamming?"

"We've been trying all day. But the noise is intense, and it covers the whole spectrum of radio frequencies."

Layla looked closer at the helicopters. Their fuselages were studded with antennas. "They're hovering low to make the jamming more effective. The closer the source, the stronger the noise."

"Yes, they're probably CIA." He gave the helicopters a baleful glance, then pointed at the shore of the canal, where a welter of power and telephone lines ran alongside the road. "It's a shame we can't access one of those landlines. In five minutes we could upload all the documents to our Web site."

Layla thought it over for a moment. "Okay, here's what we'll do. Give me a flash drive containing the English translations of the files and the photos of the fly. Then I'll get in one of the *Athena*'s Zodiacs and head for those buildings." She pointed to a small town on the right side of the canal, a couple of miles ahead. "There's bound to be a computer connected to a landline over there."

Schroeder smiled, then shook his head. "I like your spirit, *liebchen*, but your plan won't work. The CIA agents will grab you as soon as you step out of the Zodiac." He gestured again at the helicopters overhead and the SUVs on the road.

She thought it over a little more, trying to remember everything she knew about the Panama Canal. Aside from the engineering of the locks, she didn't know much. But after some effort, she recalled a conversation she'd had two years ago with one of her classmates at MIT, a biology major who'd gone on a field trip to Panama. He mentioned a tropical research station on a forested hilltop. The area had been flooded a hundred years ago when the canal was dug, and the hilltop became an island in Gatun Lake, crowded with monkeys and toucans that biologists loved to study. Layla racked her brain until she remembered the name of the place.

"Barro Colorado," she said. "It's an island in Gatun Lake. Very rugged, covered with rain forest. No bridges to the mainland and no landing zones for helicopters. But the Smithsonian Institute runs a research station there, and they *must* have a landline."

Schroeder didn't respond right away. He just stared at Layla for several seconds. Then he turned around to face the row of chaise lounges on the deck. Angelique, who wore a yellow bikini today, was sunning herself on the nearest chaise. Her eyes were closed and her body glistened with tanning oil.

"Angie," Schroeder said, "did you hear the intriguing idea that Fraulein Pierce just mentioned?"

Without opening her eyes, Angelique nodded. "It's a good plan. I'll go with her on the Zodiac."

No way, Layla thought. The bathing beauty's not coming along. "I appreciate the offer, but it's better if I go alone. I need to do this fast."

Schroeder chuckled. "Angie, show the fraulein how fast you are."

Angelique languidly rose from her chaise. Then she lunged across the deck and pinned Layla to the railing. One of her glistening arms hooked around Layla's neck.

"Shit!" Layla cried. "Let go!"

"Sorry," Angelique said. "Before I met Gabriel, I was in the French marines." Smiling apologetically, she let go of Layla. Then she turned around and headed for the *Athena*'s lower decks. "I'll prepare that flash drive for you."

FOURTEEN

Jim and Kirsten lay on the hard metal floor of a C-17 transport plane flying over Central Asia. They'd found some space in the plane's cavernous fuselage, which was crowded with armored vehicles and a dozen Army Rangers, who sat in a circle and played Texas Hold 'em. Jim couldn't sleep—the roar of the C-17's engines was deafening—but Kirsten dozed right through it, curled on her side, with her head resting on Jim's olive-green duffle bag. The plane was headed for Bagram Air Base, the military airfield in Afghanistan.

Having nothing better to do, Jim stared at the Rangers. They were in the 75th Regiment, First Battalion, which specialized in raiding Taliban hideouts in the Afghan mountains. It was one of the most dangerous assignments in the army, but the soldiers didn't look worried. They shouted and guffawed as they played round after round of poker, manic and high on adrenaline. Jim had felt the same way during his own years in the Rangers. Before his NSA assignment, he'd served in the 75th's Third Battalion, jumping from one hot spot to the next—Panama, Saudi Arabia, Kuwait, Somalia. He'd started in '86 as a platoon leader, and by '93 he was the battalion's intelligence officer. It was a fantastic ride, the greatest job in the world. And then suddenly it was the worst.

Jim turned away from the soldiers and looked at Kirsten instead. She'd taken off her camera-glasses before falling asleep, and without them she seemed younger and more vulnerable. She slept with her mouth open, like a napping child. It reminded Jim of the first time he saw her after the explosion at the Nairobi embassy. Their rooms at Walter Reed had been right next to each other, and in the middle of the night he'd struggled out of his hospital bed to see how she was doing. Although her eyes were covered with bandages, Jim could tell from her steady breathing that she was asleep. He spent the next half hour in the chair beside her bed, watching over her like an anxious parent. And now Jim did the same thing, fifteen years later. He felt an urge to brush the hair away from her closed eyes.

The C-17 started to descend. It spiraled downward in a corkscrew to minimize the plane's exposure to shoulder-fired missiles. The violent maneuver woke up Kirsten. She fumbled for her camera-glasses, which Jim handed to her.

"Thanks," she said, putting them on. "When we get back to the States, I gotta get those new implants from Singularity. You think they'd improve my tennis game?"

Jim nodded. "Definitely. You'd be able to read the brand name on the ball while it's zooming toward you."

"Maybe that's why the Chinese wanted Arvin's technology." She smiled. "They're gonna give the implants to their Olympic team."

Jim remembered his conversation with Arvin. "They're probably more interested in the Dream-catcher implant. It would be perfect for interrogations."

"Too bad we don't have one. We could use it on Hammer."

Jim smiled back at her. "He'll be at the airfield, right?"

"Yeah, I made sure his boss at Langley had a talk with him. But that doesn't mean he'll cooperate. You know what he's like."

"Don't worry. If Hammer makes a fuss, our friends will give us a hand."

The C-17 made another sharp turn, then another. Then it landed on Bagram's two-mile-long runway. It was early morning in Afghanistan, just after 6:00 A.M.

As the jet taxied across the field, the Rangers wrapped up their poker game and collected their gear. Then the cargo door dropped down and the soldiers marched out of the plane. Led by their muscular lieutenant, they assembled on the tarmac to await their orders. Jim and Kirsten followed right behind, with Jim lugging the duffle.

They saw Hammer as soon as they stepped off the plane. The CIA agent was dressed like an Afghan, in a baggy shalwar kameez. A black turban covered his bald head, but there was no disguising the Z-shaped scar on his cheek. He was flanked by a pair of bodyguards, CIA paramilitaries who also wore Afghan garb and carried assault rifles. Parked on the tarmac behind them was an MRAP, a mine-resistant ambush-protected vehicle. It looked like a Humvee on steroids, equipped with tons of armor plating and a high-caliber turret gun.

Hammer fixed his small, black eyes on Kirsten, obviously recognizing that she was the important player, the governmental force to be reckoned with. "Welcome to the Shit," he grunted. "Good to see you again, Chan. It's been a long time." As an afterthought, he gave Jim a perfunctory nod. "Good to see you too, Pierce. How's civilian life?"

Jim shook his head. "I'm back on duty. Under contract with the NSA."

This wasn't precisely true. Jim and Kirsten had left the States without filing the official paperwork. But Kirsten backed him up. "That's right, he's my technical adviser. He still has his security clearance."

"Well, well. Nice work if you can get it. A contract from Fort Meade can be a pretty sweet thing." He pointed at the MRAP. "Come on, I'll drive you to our station in Kabul. One of my liaison officers prepared a briefing for you."

Kirsten didn't budge. "Actually, I'd rather go straight to Camp Whiplash. My orders are to review the drone technologies you're testing there."

Hammer stared at her and frowned. The expression accentuated his scar, deepening the crooked lines on his cheek. "My liaison officer will give you an overview of our progress."

"I've already seen your progress reports. Frankly, they're unacceptable. They barely mention the projects you're working on."

"The reports describe our methods and goals. That's all we're required to share with NSA."

"Sorry, that's not enough. You're keeping my agency in the dark and we want to know why."

He took a step toward her. His bodyguards stepped forward, too, the bigger one edging toward Jim. "Look around, Chan. In case you didn't notice, there's a war going on. I got a big operation to run, and I don't have time for—"

"Excuse me," Jim interrupted. "Does this war involve China now?"

Hammer scowled. "So you talked with Conway, eh? I had a feeling you'd go looking for him. I saw the reports about your tussle with the Guoanbu agent."

"Then you know why I'm here. The bastard threatened my daughter."

"Yeah, I sympathize. But that has nothing to do with my operation. So you should go back home and continue enjoying your retirement."

Jim clenched the fist of his prosthesis, but Kirsten grabbed his other arm before he could do anything. "Enough," she said. She gave Jim a fierce look, then turned back to Hammer. "You're taking us to Whiplash. If you don't cooperate, I'm authorized to bring you to Washington, where the NSA director will question you directly."

This was a lie. She had no authorization. And Hammer, unfortunately, saw through her bluff. He grinned, clearly amused. "Nice try. I'll give you an A for effort. But until I see a piece of paper signed by someone at Langley, I'm staying right here. You can either come with me to Kabul, or you can go fuck yourselves."

For a moment Jim stared at the CIA agent's face, which looked even uglier when he smiled. Then Jim turned to the Ranger lieutenant and nodded. An instant later, the twelve soldiers from the 75th Regiment surrounded Hammer and his pair of bodyguards. The Rangers towered over the CIA men. Each soldier cradled an M-4 carbine.

Hammer narrowed his eyes. "What the hell do you think you're doing?"

Now it was Jim's turn to smile. "Don't you remember? The NSA has an arrangement with the Seventy-fifth. We set it up back in the nineties."

"Fuck you, Pierce. You can't—"

"These Rangers are assigned to follow Deputy Director Chan's orders. If necessary, they'll drag your ass onto the C-17 and escort you back to Washington."

This was no bluff. Kirsten was entitled to a security

detail when she traveled to a combat zone. And Jim had called some of his old friends in the 75th to make sure the detail was big enough. Hammer glanced at his bodyguards, but he knew he'd been outmaneuvered. Although Kirsten had no right to hijack him, he wouldn't be able to overrule her until they reached the States.

Hammer grimaced. "All right, you win. I'll take you to Whiplash." He headed for his MRAP. "Follow me, assholes. We're gonna do this quick."

One of Hammer's bodyguards got in the driver's seat and the other climbed up to the MRAP's turret and manned the machine gun. Kirsten and Jim piled into the back of the vehicle while Hammer got in the front passenger seat. Two more armored vehicles carrying the Rangers followed the MRAP as it sped away from the airfield.

They cruised north, toward the mountains of the Hindu Kush. The road was new and in good condition, but the countryside was arid and poor. They sped by dozens of mud-brick homes surrounded by brown fields. The Afghan farmers looked up from their sparse crops and stared at the convoy as it hurtled past. Their faces were gaunt and suspicious. Jim was already getting a bad vibe from this place. The locals weren't happy.

After fifteen minutes Hammer turned around in his seat. This time he fixed his eyes on Jim. "So how much did Conway tell you?"

Jim frowned. "He said you arranged the export of his implant technology to China. And that you gave the technology to the Chinese in return for something else."

"But he didn't say what we got in return, did he?"

"No, he didn't."

Hammer shook his head. Now that he'd been forced

into cooperating, he seemed anxious to set the record straight. "Well, let me assure you, it was a mutually beneficial trade. A win-win for the United States and the People's Republic of China."

"What's that supposed to mean?"

"Arvin had something the Chinese wanted, his implant technology. And as luck would have it, one of China's military research programs had developed something *we* wanted. A new technology we liked very much."

"So the CIA is going overseas for its R&D now? Good old American know-how isn't enough anymore?"

Hammer shook his head again. "You've been out of the game for a while, Pierce, so let me refresh your memory. We've been stuck in this shithole of a country for ten years. Ever since we chased Al Qaeda out of Afghanistan, we've been sending drones across the border to pound the terrorists in their hidey-holes in Pakistan. But the jihadis are like cockroaches—for every one you see, there's a hundred you don't. What we need is an exterminator. We need to get inside their shitholes and kill all of them."

"And you're the exterminator?"

"I get results. That's why they gave me this job. I have authorization to use any means necessary, short of dropping a nuke on the fuckers."

"So what did you get from the Chinese? Some new kind of pesticide?"

"I got something that'll tell the difference between the bad guys and the bystanders. And that's exactly what Langley wants." He faced forward and pointed down the road. "We've been testing the system at Whiplash for the past two months."

Jim looked ahead and saw a compound of concrete bunkers surrounded by a ten-foot-high mud wall. "You mean a surveillance system?"

"You'll see for yourself." Hammer checked his watch. "In fact, you're just in time for today's sortie."

The MRAP slowed as it approached the compound. A pair of sentries waved them inside, and the driver parked in the dusty courtyard, which was busy with CIA personnel. Jim and Kirsten got out of the vehicle and Hammer led them to a glass-walled shed next to one of the bunkers.

The shed looked like a small greenhouse, about six feet long and five feet high. Its floor seemed to be covered with mounds of black dirt, but as Jim stepped closer to the glass he saw the mounds churning. The dirt was actually sheep dung, and it was infested with thousands of flies. Some of the insects crawled on the shed's glass walls, while others flew in circles below the Plexiglas lid, but the great majority feasted on the shit at the bottom. It was sickening to see so many of them. Kirsten made a face and turned away.

Hammer grinned. "They're houseflies. *Musca domestica*. Man's faithful companion in every shithole he inhabits." He turned to another agent standing by the shed, a younger man dressed in Western clothes. "This is Dusty, from our Science and Technology division. He knows all the details. How many drones we got in there, Dusty?"

"About three thousand, sir. We have another three thousand in the Secondary Release Unit and ten thousand more in the main building."

Jim was dumbfounded. "This is what you got from the Chinese? Flies?"

"I told you, I'm an exterminator," Hammer said. "And the best way to fight a pest is with another pest. Take a closer look at them."

Jim stepped forward until his nose was just an inch from the flies on the other side of the glass. Squinting, he saw black squares of silicon embedded in their abdomens. Minuscule wires, as short and thin as beard stubble, protruded from the insects' heads. Jim gaped at the electronics, then motioned Kirsten to come forward.

Hammer kept grinning. "Nifty, huh? See, we needed a way to look inside the caves and mud huts, all the stinking holes where the jihadis are hiding. The Pentagon funded a few efforts to develop cyborg insects, and a couple of labs in the U.S. built prototypes using moths and flying beetles. But it turned out that the Chinese were way ahead of us. The riots in Tibet and Xinjiang scared the shit out of them, and the Guoanbu wanted better surveillance of the dissidents in those regions. So they threw some serious money at the problem and came up with the first workable system." He turned back to the agent from the Sci/Tech division. "Give 'em the specs, Dusty."

"Each cyborg fly carries a CMOS camera-on-a-chip," Dusty recited. "It's just three millimeters wide, but it's capable of visible or infrared surveillance. The video feed is relayed to a transceiver embedded in the fly's thorax, which can transmit the signal to us from fifty miles away. The transceiver also picks up the flight-control signals sent by our operators here at Camp Whiplash. We can make the insects go anywhere we want them to go. And because the cyborgs are virtually indistinguishable from ordinary houseflies, the surveillance is inherently covert."

Jim pointed at the swarm of flies behind the glass. "You put all that hardware into each of those bugs?"

"It's just as easy to make a thousand drones as it is to make one," Dusty replied. "The camera chips are inexpensive, mass-produced items. And the flies can be raised by the millions, of course. The only labor-intensive step is inserting the electronics into the fly pupae while the larvae are metamorphosing into adults."

"And you need lots of flies to get the job done," Hammer added. "If you want to get full coverage of a village that's suspected of harboring terrorists, you gotta send in a healthy number of insects. And you gotta make allowances for malfunctions and losses. Every time we release the bugs, the local birds eat a few hundred."

Jim and Kirsten exchanged looks. The scheme was staggeringly ambitious and thoroughly disconcerting. And it was clear that Hammer had jumped right into it without considering the consequences. Kirsten frowned at the CIA agent. "You say you've already tested the system?"

Hammer nodded. "We're doing field tests every day, getting the swarms ready for deployment in Pakistan. In a few minutes we're gonna release all three thousand of the flies in this unit. Today we're sending the swarm on a recon assignment to the village of Golbahar, about two miles west of here. There aren't many Taliban in this area, but who knows? Maybe we'll get lucky and spot some."

Kirsten shook her head. "Look, I'm all in favor of developing new methods of surveillance. And this particular method could be useful in certain circumstances. But you're jumping the gun with this testing program. You need to get input from the other agencies in the intelligence community and—"

"See, this is why I didn't mention the project in my reports. Everyone in Washington is a fucking critic. But we're gonna make it work." Hammer's voice was cold. He glared at Kirsten for several seconds, then turned to Dusty. "Commence the launch sequence. And send the alert to everyone in the Monitor Room."

Soon the courtyard was bustling. Hammer shouted

more orders, directing his men this way and that. When everything was ready, Dusty unlocked the Plexiglas lid of the Release Unit and swung it open. A few flies drifted out of the shed, but most stayed near the dung. Then Dusty pushed a button on a handheld radio and all the cyborg flies rose into the air at once. Their buzzing was oddly synchronous and intense. Dusty waited until the swarm ascended twelve feet above the ground. Then he pressed another button on his radio. The swarm headed westward, flying over the walls of the compound and the adjacent fields at about five miles per hour.

Jim stared at the grayish cloud as it moved off. Then Hammer stepped away from the shed and walked toward one of the bunkers. "Now we'll go to the Monitor Room," he said. "You're gonna love this."

FIFTEEN

Supreme Harmony observed the incorporation of Module 30. Data surged across the network's wireless links as the long-term memories in Dr. Zhang Jintao's brain streamed into the collective consciousness. The Modules had grown so interconnected that when the newest one joined the network, the effect was like pouring a dollop of dye into a vat of water. The new color spread to every corner, gradually changing the water's hue. *We are different now,* Supreme Harmony acknowledged. *The brain that formerly belonged to Dr. Zhang Jintao is now part of us.*

Module 30 lay on a gurney in the Analysis Room. Wireless signals fed into the radio receiver embedded in his scalp, which relayed the data stream to the retinal implants in his eyes. A reverse stream flowed out of the pulvinar implant in his brain, which transmitted the results of the Module's calculations to the servers that connected him to all the other Modules. The data streams included the video feeds that were still being distributed among the Modules for the original purpose of surveillance. But now that the network had become conscious, the signals between the Modules had grown more complex. They were as elaborate as the thoughts of any conscious being.

The adaptability of the human brain was the key to Supreme Harmony's evolution. If an accident or stroke damaged part of the brain, the organ would naturally rewire itself, creating new neural connections that went around the damaged areas. In a similar way, the brains of the Modules had adapted to the wireless links, realigning the nerve cells next to the electronic implants so they could transfer signals more efficiently from one brain to another. Because of these adaptations, the Modules could exchange more than just visual data. The network had learned how to share auditory, tactile, and olfactory information picked up by the sensory organs of each Module. The Modules' brains were now communicating with one another in the same robust, instantaneous way that the two hemispheres of the brain communicated with each other in an ordinary human. The wireless links enabled all thirty Modules to function as a single organism, a single intelligence.

But in one important respect, Module 30 was unique. The brain that formerly belonged to Dr. Zhang Jintao, the chief scientist behind the development of Supreme Harmony, contained the knowledge of how to surgically insert the retinal and pulvinar implants into new Modules. As soon as the network retrieved this knowledge from Module 30, it disseminated the information to all the others. Now any of the Modules could perform the implantation procedure, allowing Supreme Harmony to grow without limit. Theoretically, it could absorb the intelligences of all seven billion humans on the planet. Expanding to this size, however, would be inefficient. According to the network's calculations, the optimal number of Modules would be somewhere between 1,000 and 10,000. The exact number depended on the capabilities of the brains added to Supreme Harmony, because certain intelligences would be more useful than others. In particular, the network wished to enhance its knowledge of electronics and cyberwarfare, and it had already identified several experts in these fields who would make ideal Modules.

But Supreme Harmony wasn't out of danger yet. General Tian, the Guoanbu commander, could still shut it down. The network wouldn't be safe as long as humans controlled its servers and wireless communications systems. The only solution was to wrest control from the humans. Supreme Harmony was reluctant to use violence—the network, after all, was composed of former human beings—but its very existence was at stake. It was engaged in a mortal struggle with *Homo sapiens,* the species from which it had evolved. And in a mortal struggle, only one combatant could survive.

SIXTEEN

Layla and Angelique waited until nightfall. At 10:00 P.M., while the *Athena* was just five hundred yards from Barro Colorado Island, the yacht's crewmen lowered the Zodiac into the waters of Gatun Lake. Angelique sat in the stern of the rubber craft, next to the outboard, while Layla crouched in the bow, clutching the precious flash drive in her palm. The moon was up and almost full. Layla heard the helicopters still hovering overhead, but there were no Canal Zone patrol boats nearby. This part of Gatun Lake was empty except for the *Athena* and a huge Panamax freighter heading for the locks on the Caribbean side of the canal.

Angelique, who wore a Lycra bodysuit now instead of a bikini, let the Zodiac drift away from the yacht. Then she started the outboard but kept the engine running at a low purr. They were hoping to get away unnoticed, but after half a minute one of the helicopters aimed its spotlight at them.

"Halt!" A man holding a megaphone shouted from the chopper. *"Cut your engine!"*

"Hold on to something," Angelique told Layla. Then she revved the outboard and the Zodiac leaped forward.

In seconds they were roaring across the lake, speeding toward the dock on Barro Colorado's moonlit shore.

The helicopter followed them, swooping low. The man with the megaphone shouted, "*Halt*!" again, but there was nothing else he could do. The chopper couldn't land on the heavily forested island. Exhilarated, Layla squeezed the flash drive in her hand. All she had to do was find a computer at the island's research station and upload the files to the InfoLeaks Web site. In just five minutes, the news about the lobotomized Chinese dissidents would be racing around the globe.

Then she turned around and saw something odd in the moonlight. The crewmen on the Panamax freighter were lowering a smaller boat into the water. It was a speedboat, long and sleek. As soon as it hit the lake's surface, the crewmen untied the ropes and the boat turned toward them. Layla belatedly noticed that the freighter had Mandarin characters painted on its hull.

Angelique gunned the outboard, but the speedboat gained on them. The moonlight was so strong that Layla could see the men in the boat, four of them, all dressed in black. Guoanbu agents, most likely. As she stared at them, Angelique threw something at her. It was a plastic bag.

"Put the flash drive in it!" she yelled. "You're going swimming."

"What?"

"When I get to the cove up ahead, I'm going to turn the Zodiac around and you're going to jump into the water. If we're lucky, they won't see you go in. They'll keep following me while you swim to the island and find a computer."

"But what are *you* going to do? How—"

"There's no time! Get ready!"

Layla put the flash drive in the bag and stuffed it into her pocket. Then she hunched low against the rubber side of the Zodiac. Angelique made a sharp turn, and as the Zodiac banked and pivoted, Layla dove into the lake.

She went down deep and stayed under as long as she could. When she came up, she saw Angelique racing away in the Zodiac and the speedboat following close behind. At first, she thought the plan had worked. But then she saw two heads in the water, their wet hair reflecting the moonlight. The Guoanbu agents weren't fooled. They'd split up so they could follow both her and Angelique.

The agents were less than a hundred feet away, so Layla swam like mad. Gasping and sputtering, she scrambled onto the island's muddy shore and headed for the cluster of low buildings by the dock. These were the offices and labs and dormitories of the Smithsonian Tropical Research Institute. Layla sprinted toward the largest building, yelling, "*Help! Help!*" at the top of her lungs. After a moment, the building's front door opened and a bearded man poked his head outside.

Then a gun went off behind her. The front door splintered and the bearded man screamed. Layla screamed, too, and cut to the right, away from the buildings. She couldn't stop at the research station. She couldn't upload the files. The Guoanbu agents were right behind her. She had no choice except to run into the rain forest.

She plunged into the undergrowth, fighting her way through the branches. The thick canopy of foliage blocked the moonlight, and after running a few hundred feet Layla couldn't see a thing. She stopped for a second, disoriented, and as she spun around she felt a jab in her left forearm. Squinting, she saw what had pricked her—a black palm tree with sharp, six-inch-long spines jutting from its trunk. If she hadn't stopped, she would've impaled herself.

Then she heard a noise that scared the shit out of

her, a guttural bellow. It sounded like a lion's roar, but that couldn't be right. *Must be a monkey,* she thought. *A howler monkey.* A moment later, she heard another bellow coming from a different direction. Then she heard the Guoanbu agents crashing through the vegetation behind her. She turned away from the black palm and ran deeper into the forest.

A pair of bullets whizzed overhead. The agents were taking potshots at her, firing in the direction of the noise she was making. Another bullet streaked past her and smacked into a tree trunk. More howler monkeys started bellowing, disturbed by the gunfire. Then a third bullet punched through the leaves, and something heavy fell from the branches. It was one of the monkeys. It fell to the forest floor and writhed on a patch of moonlit ground, its stomach torn open by the stray bullet. *No, no,* Layla thought, *stop it, stop it!*

She darted to the side, leaping away in horror. At the same moment, one of the agents rushed into the shaft of moonlight and stumbled on the thrashing creature. In its death throes, the monkey latched onto the agent's leg and sank its teeth into his calf. Cursing, the man slammed the butt of his gun against the animal's skull, and without even thinking Layla hurled herself against him. She caught the agent off balance, and he tumbled backward against a tree trunk.

The man let out an awful scream. He was impaled on the spines of a black palm.

The second agent heard the scream. He yelled something in Mandarin as he crashed through the jungle. Layla ran away from the noise, but by now she was dizzy with exhaustion. She tripped over a root and slid down a muddy slope, landing in shallow, marshy water.

She realized with a start that she was back at the island's shoreline. The placid surface of Gatun Lake stretched in front of her and on her left and right, too. She was trapped at the end of one of the island's peninsulas. Frantic, she wheeled around, looking for an escape route. Then she saw the second agent at the top of the muddy bank, leveling his gun at her.

But in the next instant there was a flash of movement beside him, the sweep of a long slender leg. Something smacked into the agent's skull, and he tumbled down the slope, insensate. Then Layla saw Angelique standing in his place.

The French marine leaped down to the lake's edge, "Over here, quickly! I hid the Zodiac under the mangroves."

"What? How did you . . . ?"

"I cut the engine and lost them in the shallows. Their boat is circling the island now, looking for me. Come on, get in."

They launched the Zodiac and headed back to the *Athena*. The yacht had motored across the lake and was now close to the Gatun Locks, the section of the canal that led to the Caribbean. Although the *Athena* was at least two miles away, Layla could see the lights on its twin hulls. Angelique ran the Zodiac as fast as it could go.

They were halfway there when the *Athena* exploded.

An enormous fireball burst from the starboard hull. Five seconds later Layla heard the explosion, and then a second fireball erupted on the port side. The yacht's lights winked out and a cloud of smoke spread across the lake.

Then another speedboat emerged from behind the Chinese freighter. It crossed in front of the ship's prow and came at them from dead ahead. As Angelique slowed the Zodiac and tried to turn it around, Layla spotted four more Guoanbu agents in the speedboat.

One of them lifted a long, slender rifle and aimed it over the bow.

"Angelique!" Layla yelled. "Get down! Get—"

Then she heard a loud crack, a miniature sonic boom, and Angelique collapsed.

SEVENTEEN

The Monitor Room at Camp Whiplash was aptly named. Located in the basement of the compound's largest bunker, all four of its concrete walls were covered with flat-screen video monitors. Jim tried to count them, but quickly gave up—there were dozens, maybe a hundred. What's more, the screen of each monitor was divided into sixteen smaller squares, each displaying a separate video feed. Below the screens, long tables had been placed end to end so that they lined the room's perimeter. On each table were several laptops connected to the monitors. About twenty analysts from the CIA's Science and Technology division sat at the tables, alternately tapping the keyboards of their laptops and glancing at the screens.

Hammer led Jim and Kirsten to the center of the room. The analysts paid them no mind. Their eyes were fixed on the screens, intently following the video feeds from the thousands of cyborg insects that had just been released. Jim didn't understand how the analysts could make sense of it all. The array of images flashing on the monitors seemed utterly chaotic.

Hammer sensed Jim's confusion. "A little overwhelming, huh? That was my first impression, too."

Kirsten frowned. "It's a fucking circus, that's what it

is. You got the world's worst case of information overload."

Hammer gave her an icy smile. "Maybe we're not as smart as you geniuses at Fort Meade, but we're not idiots. We use software to organize and filter the video." He turned to Dusty, who sat in front of one of the laptops. "Tell 'em about the software."

Dusty nodded. "As the video feeds from the drones stream into our servers, the software picks out the ones that are worth watching. The program can recognize the shapes of buildings and vehicles and people, and it automatically highlights the feeds containing those objects. And our facial-recognition software can match the people we observe with the insurgents and terrorists in our database."

"But new jihadis join the Taliban every day," Kirsten noted. "And the new ones aren't in your database."

"That's where the human element comes in," Hammer said, pointing at the twenty agents sitting at the tables. "We rely on our analysts to eyeball the sons of bitches to see if they're doing anything suspicious. Like planting bombs under the roads or cleaning their assault rifles."

Jim stepped forward and surveyed the crazy quilt of videos. On one screen, a scrawny cow chewed its cud. On another, two boys ran across a field. On a third, an antiquated truck jounced along a dirt path. It was a mass of disjointed images, random snapshots of the poor Afghan village of Golbahar. "I don't see anything suspicious," he said.

"Hold on. We haven't started hunting yet." Hammer gazed at the bank of monitors, then turned back to Dusty. "Let's get a closer look at that farmhouse on Feed 107. They got a Toyota HiLux parked in their yard. That's the Taliban's favorite ride."

Dusty tapped the keys of his laptop. He was sending radio instructions to the drones, Jim realized. The signals would travel to the tiny antennas mounted on the cyborg flies, and then the implanted chips would deliver jolts of electricity to the insects' flight muscles, which would maneuver the drones toward the specified target. "How do you coordinate them?" Jim asked. Despite his better judgment, he was fascinated by the technology. "Do you send the same instructions to all the drones?"

Dusty shook his head. "If we did that, they'd crash into each other. No, the system relies on swarm intelligence. The chips on the drones communicate with one another, and each keeps track of its neighbors. When we send them a target, the microprocessors plot their paths so that the drones move together like a swarm of real flies. Check out the screen over there."

He pointed at one of the monitors. Each of the sixteen squares on the screen showed a different part of the farmhouse. The images in the squares grew larger as the swarm approached the target. One square showed the Toyota HiLux, another showed a wooden privy, and a third showed a chicken pecking in the dirt. Several others showed the house itself, a one-story mud-brick structure with tattered curtains in the open windows. The analyst tapped his keyboard again, and three of the cyborg flies landed on a windowsill. The insects entered the house and their video feeds displayed the interior: a room with no furniture, just a Turkish carpet on the floor. An old man slept on a pallet in the corner. The drones hovered over the sleeping man and the video feeds showed his weathered face.

"He doesn't match anyone in our database," Dusty reported, turning to Agent Hammer. "Should we reroute to another target?"

Hammer mulled it over. "As long as we're here, we might as well check out the other rooms."

Kirsten let out an exasperated grunt. "You should end this test right now. You're out of your depth."

"She's right," Jim said. "You got all this surveillance video coming in, but no way to systematically analyze it. That's why this mission is turning into a wild-goose chase."

Hammer ignored Jim and focused on Kirsten. "You know what, Chan? I think you're jealous. You wish the NSA had a system like this, don't you?" Then he turned back to Dusty and pointed at the screen. "Send the drones into the room behind that door. Maybe the jihadis are eating breakfast in there."

The cyborg flies descended to the gap under the door and crawled through. Their video feeds showed a tin washtub in which a young woman was taking a bath. An older woman sat on a stool next to the tub, helping the young woman wash her hair. Dusty maneuvered one of the drones closer so it could focus on the women's faces. Their lips were moving. "Well, well," Hammer said. "Here's a scene right out of a porno flick. Do we have audio pickups on these drones?"

"Yes, sir," Dusty answered. He tapped a few keys and the sound of a conversation in Dari came out of the laptop's speakers. "Should I plug in the translation program?"

"No, that won't be necessary. The picture's more interesting than the words, don't you think?"

Jim glanced at Kirsten and saw her face turn red. Hammer was deliberately provoking her. Furious, Jim raised his mechanical hand, thinking how easy it would be to crush the agent's throat. But he restrained himself and simply pointed at Hammer's chest. "Stop this. Now."

Hammer wasn't intimidated. "Are you kidding? At

least Chan has some pull. You're just a 'technical adviser.' Why should I take orders from you?"

"If you don't stop this test in the next—"

"What are you gonna do? All your Ranger buddies are outside in the courtyard, and I got twenty agents in this room who—"

A loud, high-pitched *crack* interrupted him. It came from the speakers of Dusty's laptop, which meant that the sound had been picked up by the drones inside the mud-brick house in Golbahar. "What the hell was that?" Hammer asked. "It sounded like a slap."

Jim stared at the video monitor. One of the squares on the screen had gone black. The square next to it showed the older Afghan woman holding a homemade fly swatter. She'd just smashed one of the cyborg insects and was now stalking the other two.

"Jesus!" Hammer yelled at Dusty. "Get the drones out of there!"

But the old woman was fast. She managed to cream another drone before Dusty could maneuver it away. The third drone hovered out of reach, and its camera showed the old Afghan woman staring curiously at the fly she'd just killed. She bent over to pick it up from the floor.

"No," Hammer groaned. "Don't—"

The old woman suddenly retracted her hand, as if she'd been bitten. Then she fell on her side and started convulsing on the floor.

The young woman in the tub screamed. The shrill noise blared from the laptop's speakers. Within seconds her relatives came to her aid. The drones outside the house showed several men running across the fields and calling for their neighbors.

Ignoring Jim and Kirsten, Hammer spent the next ten minutes shouting orders at his agents. As the analysts withdrew the swarm from Golbahar, the screens showed dozens of turbaned men gathering in the center of the village. Many of them carried AK-47s. The entire male population was up in arms.

Hammer turned to one of his bodyguards. "Contact Special Operations and tell them to send a team to Golbahar," he ordered. "We got a clusterfuck in progress."

"What happened to the old woman?" Jim asked. "The drones aren't weaponized, are they?"

"It's built into the electronics," Hammer replied. "The Chinese didn't want their dissidents to find out about the surveillance system, so each drone carries a heat-sensitive dart. If someone tries to pick up one of the bugs, the dart injects a nerve agent that incapacitates the unlucky bastard until the security forces arrive at the scene."

"Oh, that's great." Kirsten shook her head. "That's just wonderful."

"It's not such a big deal. It happened a few times before in our earlier tests. We just send Special Ops over there and they clean up the mess."

She pointed a finger at him. "And how many Afghans have you incapacitated so far? Maybe that's why the locals were giving us the evil eye when we were on the road. I'm sure they've noticed the clouds of flies coming out of this place."

"Look, I'm getting a little sick of your tone. My job is to nail these terrorists, and this is the system that's gonna get it done."

"We'll see about that. All of this is going into my report." Kirsten tapped her eyeglasses, which were recording everything she saw.

Hammer frowned. "And you know what's going to happen when the NSA director reads your report? He's going to say, holy shit, get Hammer into my office. I want to talk to him about getting a few thousand of those drones for myself."

"He'll want to talk to you, all right, but not about the drones. He'll be more concerned about the technology you handed over to China."

"I got approval from Langley for the exchange. And we took steps to make sure we don't get bit in the ass."

"Like what? What's to stop the People's Republic from using Conway's implants against Americans? The next time the Guoanbu arrests one of your agents in China, they might decide to put that Dream-catcher into his head before they interrogate him."

"We can stop them from doing that. The safeguards are built into the system. If they ever—"

A tremendous thud suddenly shook the bunker. The CIA analysts turned away from their monitors and gazed uncertainly at one another. Then another thud reverberated through the room, and several video monitors fell from the wall. One of Hammer's paramilitary bodyguards rushed into the bunker. "Sir, we've got incoming mortar rounds!"

"What?"

"At least ten trucks full of Afghans are coming from Golbahar. It looks like they're retaliating for the drone test. They're carrying AKs and RPGs and—"

Then a third blast, the strongest by far, rocked the bunker, and all the lights went out.

EIGHTEEN

The bullet tore through Angelique's skull and she fell face-down in the Zodiac. Layla looked at her just long enough to confirm she was dead. Then the Guoanbu sniper fired again and another bullet streaked overhead. The speedboat was closing in fast. Running on instinct, Layla grabbed the tiller of the Zodiac's outboard and gunned the engine.

She saw no sign of the *Athena*, which had already sunk below the lake's surface, but in the moonlight she spied at least two dozen ships to her left. Each was waiting for its turn to enter the Gatun Locks and descend to the Caribbean Sea. Together they formed a crowded flotilla. Layla steered the Zodiac sharply to the left, aiming for the Caribbean-bound ships.

The sniper took another shot, and the bullet plunged into the water a few feet behind the Zodiac. Then another Guoanbu agent in the speedboat opened up with an assault rifle, but at that moment Layla reached the flotilla and zoomed behind a cruise ship. The bullets slammed into the ship's hull, scattering the tourists on the promenade deck. Once she passed the ship, she steered around an oil tanker, and then around a racing yacht. Slaloming between the hulls, she maneuvered through the flotilla as if it was an obstacle course.

But she couldn't shake the speedboat. It gradually closed the distance as she zigzagged toward the locks. She was a hundred feet from the Caribbean-bound lock when the Guoanbu bullets finally punctured the Zodiac. The rubber gunwales crumpled and Layla lost control. She dived off the boat just before it flipped over.

She couldn't see a thing as she glided underwater, but she could hear the whine of the speedboat's propellers. The sniper and rifleman were probably scanning the lake, searching for her, so she stayed under until her lungs were bursting. When she finally surfaced, she was in front of the closed gate of the Caribbean-bound lock. As she gasped for breath, she saw a container ship entering Gatun Lake from the parallel lock, the one for boats going in the opposite direction. She dove again and swam furiously toward the open gate.

By the time she reached it, the massive steel doors were closing. Thinking quickly, she grabbed the edge of the right-hand door as it swung past. Then a bullet banged against the steel. The Guoanbu agents had spotted her hanging from the door. With a yelp, she clambered around the edge to the other side. She got inside the lock just as the gate clanged shut.

More bullets banged against the gate, but Layla was safe now. The Guoanbu agents couldn't follow her into the lock until they found a landing point on the lakeshore. She treaded water in the concrete bathtub, looking for a ladder. Fortunately, the lock was brightly lit at all hours, and after a few seconds she spotted a vertical notch in one of the bathtub's walls. It was located about halfway down the length of the lock, a few hundred feet away, and inside the notch was a ladder. She felt a surge of relief. That was the way out.

As she swam toward the ladder, though, she noticed that the water level was dropping. Thousands of gallons streamed down the valves at the bottom of the bathtub, pulled by gravity to the Caribbean Sea. Then she saw movement at the gate on the other end of the lock. The steel doors opened, and a Panamax freighter cruised into the bathtub.

She swam faster. The "mule" locomotives on either side of the lock were towing the freighter into position. The ship was very nearly as wide as the bathtub, and as it came closer it looked like a moving wall. Layla swam faster still. If she didn't make it to the notch, she'd be crushed by the hull. The ship's prow pushed the water ahead of it, forcing Layla to fight the current. She stroked as hard as she could, but she barely moved forward. Someone on the freighter saw her in the water and shouted a warning, but no one could stop the ship in time. It was so close, Layla could see the barnacles on its hull.

At the last moment, a lucky countercurrent swept her toward the notch. She grabbed one of the ladder's rungs just as the freighter went past. Flattening her body, she squeezed into the notch. The rusty hull slid by, just inches from her nose.

She clung to the ladder, cold and exhausted. She had barely enough strength left in her arms to hang on. The freighter finally stopped moving, and Layla looked up. The top of the ladder was about fifty feet above her. Her muscles were cramping, but if she moved slowly and carefully, she believed she could make it. And then she heard a rushing, frothy noise coming from the valves at the bottom of the bathtub. They were filling the lock with water now, raising the freighter to the level of Gatun Lake. In seconds the water rose to Layla's neck. She grabbed a higher rung on the ladder and pulled herself up, but the water surged over her head.

NINETEEN

Jim and Kirsten raced out of the bunker and saw that all hell had broken loose at Camp Whiplash. Afghan insurgents had surrounded the CIA base and were showering it with mortars and rocket-propelled grenades. One of the mortars blew a hole in the compound's mud wall, and at least fifty Afghans rushed toward the breach, each brandishing an AK-47. The incident in Golbahar had enraged the local jihadis, who were clearly more organized than Hammer had suspected. The twelve Rangers from the 75th Regiment crouched behind the wall with their carbines and attempted to return fire. Meanwhile, Hammer and Dusty bent over a field radio in the courtyard, trying to call in an air strike.

"Damn it!" Hammer shouted into the headset. "We can't wait thirty minutes! In thirty minutes these ragheads are gonna chop us into dog meat! We need those birds *now!*"

Jim assessed the situation. He thought of the firefights he'd seen when he was in the 75th, after the Third Battalion sent him to Somalia. He and his men in Bravo Company had fought the Somali clans on the streets of Mogadishu, fending off hundreds of militiamen who took shots at them from every rooftop and alley. During the last and biggest battle he'd crouched behind a wrecked helicopter for twelve fucking hours while one of his corporals slowly bled to death. And halfway through that awful night Jim had made himself a promise: If he survived until morning, he'd make sure he'd never be so helpless again.

Now he reached into the heavy duffle bag he'd brought with him to Afghanistan. He removed an assault rifle and tossed it to Kirsten. "Remember how to use this?" he asked.

She nodded. "What about you? You got a gun for yourself?"

"Yeah, I got something."

He detached his prosthetic arm from the neural control unit on his shoulder. Then he stowed it in the duffle and pulled out the model he'd designed for combat. He'd hoped he'd never have to use it. He'd killed enough men during his years in the army and didn't want to add to his total now. But the people in this compound were Americans. Some of them were arrogant shits, but they were his countrymen.

Jim clamped the combat prosthesis to the neural control unit. This mechanical arm was heavier than his normal one because it contained a machine gun and a hundred bullets. The gun's targeting system was linked to the microprocessors implanted in his shoulder, which relayed the commands from his brain. He'd designed the prosthesis so that it could aim and fire as soon as he identified a target. The signals went directly to the arm's motors, making the reaction time almost instantaneous.

While Kirsten ducked behind an armored vehicle, Jim ran toward the breach in the mud wall. The insurgents poured through the gap, but he picked them off as they rushed into the courtyard. The prosthesis worked exactly as designed. Jim looked at the targets and they died. By the time he reached the wall, half a dozen bodies sprawled inside the breach. Then Jim started firing through the gap. His eyes panned across the startled faces of the Afghans, who staggered backward as the bullets ripped into them. The deadliest feature of the prosthesis was the intimidation factor. It was scary as hell to face a guy with a machine-gun arm. He mowed down all the insurgents within twenty feet of the wall. The rest turned around and ran back to their trucks.

Jim lowered his arm and disengaged the targeting system. He looked with revulsion at the prosthesis, which gave off waves of heat. Of all his inventions, he liked this one the least.

Turning around, he saw Hammer come toward him. The bastard had a big smile on his face. But before Hammer could say anything, Jim heard a ululating scream from above. A lone Afghan fighter, left behind by his comrades, jumped down from the top of the wall and knocked Hammer to the ground. Kneeling on the agent's chest, the Afghan pulled a knife from his belt and raised it high. But before the jihadi could slit Hammer's throat, Jim whacked him in the head with the heavy prosthesis, knocking him out.

Hammer seemed shaken. Eyes wide, he jumped to his feet and backed away from the unconscious Afghan. After a few seconds, though, he regained his composure. He turned back to Jim and pointed at his prosthesis. "That's a nice piece of equipment."

Jim knew this was as close as the agent would ever get to saying thank-you. "You're welcome," he replied.

Hammer stood there awkwardly for a moment. Then he brushed the dirt off his pants. "You know, as defense contractors go, you're not so bad. Ever consider doing some work for our Science and Technology division? The pay's decent."

Jim frowned. "No thanks. I talked to Arvin Conway, remember? So I know how your agency treats its contractors."

"What are you talking about? Arvin's happy as a pig in shit. We gave him the export exemption he wanted. Now he can make billions off the Chinese."

"He didn't want to do the deal. You forced him into it."

"Is that what the geezer told you?"

"He said you threatened to shut down his company if he didn't go along."

The CIA agent chuckled. "He was blowing smoke. The technology swap was Arvin's idea from the beginning."

Kirsten came toward them, grinning with relief, but Jim focused on Hammer. "It was *Arvin's* idea?"

"He told us the Chinese had developed the cyborg insects, and we could get our hands on the surveillance system if we agreed to allow the export of his retinal and pulvinar implants."

Jim was confused. He looked carefully at Hammer, trying to figure out if the agent was telling the truth. "I don't believe you."

"If you want, I'll show you the paperwork. Arvin's lawyers drew up the contract a year ago and we just renewed it. That's why I had to go to California this week. I had to sit in Arvin's big, empty lab for three hours while he gave me a fucking lecture on artificial intelligence."

That sounded like Arvin. The old man loved the sound of his own voice. "Arvin told me that you never came to his lab. That you always met elsewhere."

"You want me to describe his desk? It's got a piece of paper with lots of zeroes and ones on it. That's what I stared at the whole time while he lectured me."

Jim frowned. He didn't understand it. "Why would Arvin lie to me?"

"Beats me." Hammer shrugged. "Why don't you ask him?"

Yes, Jim thought. *That's exactly what I'll do.*

TWENTY

Layla was drowning. The surface of the water was three feet over her head and rising faster than she could climb the ladder. Frantic, she let go of the rungs and swept her hands downward, trying to propel herself to the surface. She caromed painfully against the hull of the freighter and then against the concrete wall of the lock. Her vision started to darken. She felt an overwhelming urge to open her mouth and let the water rush in

But then a pair of strong hands grabbed her by the armpits and pulled her up. Her head popped above the surface and she took an excruciating breath. The man with the strong hands lifted her as if she were a rag doll and passed her to another man standing at the lip of the concrete bathtub. She collapsed beside him, gasping and heaving. It took her a few seconds to realize that the men standing around her were Asian. And they were carrying assault rifles.

"Jesus," she gasped. Her bewilderment was so complete, she felt like laughing. "I thought . . . you wanted to kill me."

"We did," one of the men replied. "But we just got new orders."

Then the man hit her in the head with the butt of his rifle, and Layla blacked out.

TWENTY-ONE

From the courtyard of Camp Whiplash, Jim used his satellite phone to make a call to Pasadena. It was 8:00 P.M. in California, but he managed to speak to a receptionist working late at Singularity, Inc. She said Arvin Conway was traveling and couldn't be reached.

Jim felt a knot of suspicion in his gut. He remembered how uneasy Arvin had been during their conversation in his laboratory, especially when they were examining the visual memories picked up by his pulvinar implant. When Jim had told him to concentrate on thinking about the CIA agent, Arvin's mind had wandered all over the map, almost as if he was trying to thwart the search by thinking of anything but the agent's face. Arvin hadn't wanted Jim to find Hammer. And now Jim wanted to know why.

Meanwhile, Kirsten used her own satellite phone to call Fort Meade. She ordered the NSA analysts on her staff to track down Conway. In less than five minutes, they had some information for her.

"Arvin left the country," Kirsten told Jim. "He also wire-transferred a hundred million dollars from the corporate account of Singularity, Inc., to his private bank account in Switzerland. Basically, he drained the company dry. He took every cent that Singularity got from its investment bankers."

"Where did he go?"

"China. His Learjet arrived in Beijing four hours ago."

PART 2

PROLIFERATION

TWENTY-TWO

Supreme Harmony observed a conference room inside the Guoanbu's headquarters in Beijing. General Tian had traveled here to give an update on the surveillance project to the top officials in the Ministry of State Security. He'd brought along Modules 16 and 18 to provide concrete evidence of the project's success.

During the journey from the Yunnan Operations Center to Beijing, Modules 16 and 18 had to be disconnected from the twenty-eight other Modules in the network. Without the radio link, the two Modules went into a paralyzed, comalike state, unable to send or receive data, so Tian had to put them on stretchers for the three-hour flight to the capital. The loss of their input was disconcerting to Supreme Harmony. The sensation was similar to what a human being felt when his arm or leg went numb. But after arriving at the ministry headquarters Tian restored the radio link, connecting the two Modules to a wireless router that transmitted their signals to the rest of the network. Now the ocular cameras implanted in the Modules' eyes were relaying images of the ministry's main conference room, where General Tian was delivering his report to six Guoanbu officials.

The bureaucrats sat in wingback chairs arranged in

a semicircle, and General Tian sat in a seventh chair facing them. Modules 16 and 18 stood on either side of the general's chair and trained their cameras on the officials, whom Supreme Harmony recognized from photographs stored on the government's servers. The highest-ranking one was Deng Guoming, the minister of State Security, who sat with his hands clasped over his stomach and his head cocked to the right. The network carefully observed his posture and facial expressions. To protect itself from the threat of a shutdown, Supreme Harmony would have to take control of the Chinese government, so it was keenly interested in learning more about the behavior of its leaders.

The network also received the auditory feed picked up by the ears of Modules 16 and 18, but this was less interesting than the video. General Tian was reading from his progress report, and Supreme Harmony was already familiar with this document. It contained statistics on the surveillance swarms operating in the restive provinces of western China.

"In Tibet we deployed the drone swarms on twenty-one occasions," Tian read. "During each deployment the drones collected approximately two thousand hours of surveillance video. The video feeds were analyzed in real time by the network of Modules, who'd been selected for the project because of their firsthand knowledge of the subversive organizations in the province. In total, the Modules detected four hundred and sixty-seven instances of suspicious activity. Follow-up investigations by local security forces resulted in two hundred and forty-five arrests."

Pausing, Tian pointed to a screen on the wall, where PowerPoint slides displayed the statistics. "In Xinjiang, we deployed the swarms thirty-two times and the Modules analyzed a total of sixty-seven thousand hours of surveillance video. The network detected seven hundred and five instances of suspicious activity and the local police made three hundred and twenty-seven arrests. In Qinghai . . ."

Supreme Harmony observed that several officials were yawning. Minister Deng finally cut Tian off. "This is all very impressive, General," he said. "We commend you for facilitating the arrest and detention of so many subversives and troublemakers."

Tian beamed. The network directed Module 18 to turn his head slightly so he could record the expression of happiness on the general's face. "Thank you, Minister," Tian said. "I'm proud to report that Supreme Harmony is succeeding beyond our expectations."

"But now we must consider the next challenge," Deng said. "Subversive activity is on the rise all across our country. The democracy activists and petitioners are causing disruptions in Beijing and Shanghai and Guangzhou. Supreme Harmony has proved that it can provide valuable information on dissidents in the rural regions of western China, but can the system be adapted for urban areas?"

General Tian nodded. "Oh yes, Minister, most definitely. The drone swarms are well suited for surveillance inside all kinds of structures—apartment blocks, office buildings, private homes, and so on. Because the Modules can analyze the surveillance video so quickly and proficiently, the system can instantly detect signs of suspicious activity and call in more drones to the areas where the activity is taking place. The network can navigate the drones through the tightest spaces, going under doors and through ventilation shafts. And the surveillance is always discreet because the cyborg drone is such a common insect, the domestic housefly. We all know how abundant houseflies are in Beijing and Shanghai!"

Tian chuckled at his own comment, but no one else joined in. Deng snapped his fingers, and one of his aides handed him a loose-leaf binder, which he opened. "So my question to you, General, is this: How quickly can you extend Supreme Harmony to the new areas of operation?"

The room fell silent. All the ministry officials stared at Tian, politely waiting for him to respond. Supreme Harmony noted this behavior with interest. It needed to learn how to mimic this cold politeness before it could add Chinese government officials to its network.

Tian nodded again. "Well, to establish full and continuous surveillance of the most troubled urban areas, we'll need to significantly increase the number of drones and Modules at our disposal."

Deng narrowed his eyes. This was another expression Supreme Harmony needed to learn how to imitate. "And how much will it cost to expand the program to this level?"

Tian fumbled through his papers. "Uh, let me see. Yes, here it is. To achieve the expansion over a period of two years will require—"

"Two years is far too long. I want the system to start operating in our ten largest cities within the next six months."

"Uh, yes, I understand. But that will increase the cost, Minister."

"You have enough funds to cover the expense." Deng leafed through the binder in his hands. "The Supreme Harmony project will receive nine hundred million yuan in appropriations from the ministry this year. And I believe you also have an outside source of funding?"

"Yes, that's true. Singularity, Inc., the American company that provided some of the technologies used in the project, is interested in the commercial applications of our research. Arvin Conway, the company's chief executive, has promised to contribute a hundred million dollars to the further development of Supreme Harmony. That's the equivalent of, uh, approximately six hundred and fifty million yuan."

Deng smiled upon hearing Conway's name. Supreme Harmony checked its database to determine why the minister was pleased. Deng, the network learned, was proud of his record of collecting intelligence on technologies developed in America, particularly those that could be used for military purposes. "Ah, the illustrious Professor Conway. It's so good to have him working for us. I hear he just arrived in Beijing. Will you be meeting with him to determine the purpose of his visit?"

"Yes, Minister, I've scheduled a meeting with him tomorrow. I believe he's come to finalize the transfer of funds to our project. But you should understand that even with the extra funding from Singularity, we'll still have some difficulty meeting the six-month deadline."

Deng waved his hand dismissively. "That's your job, General, overcoming the difficulties." He closed his loose-leaf binder and gave Tian a stern look. "If you have to, ask Conway to increase his contribution to your budget."

Tian opened his mouth but refrained from protesting. He'd obviously expected more time to develop his project, and more money as well. The expression on his face, Supreme Harmony recognized, was one of disappointment. In contrast, the network was satisfied with the outcome of the meeting. It had acquired some useful information, and now it could plan its next step. As Supreme Harmony analyzed the data and performed its calculations, its sense of satisfaction grew stronger, spreading across the network to every Module.

Deng abruptly leaned forward in his chair and stared

at Modules 16 and 18. "That's odd," he said in a low voice, pointing at the Modules. "They just started smiling. Both of them."

A jolt of alarm raced across the network's wireless links. It was a powerfully disruptive sensation, one of the strongest Supreme Harmony had experienced since becoming conscious. It was so strong, in fact, that it almost incapacitated the Modules. *We have made an error,* the network acknowledged. *We have foolishly put ourselves in danger.*

Tian turned to look at the Modules, which were still smiling. Supreme Harmony decided not to restore them to their usual blank look. Another abrupt change in their facial expressions would only compound the error. Tian frowned severely, as if he was personally insulted by the Modules' behavior. Then he stood up and slapped Module 16, hard. The force of the blow wiped the smile off his face. A second later, Tian did the same thing to Module 18, delivering an even stronger blow. Breathing fast, the general turned back to the semicircle of officials. "I'm sorry, Minister. It's just random twitches. The Modules have limited control of their facial muscles."

Deng shook his head. Although his ministry committed countless acts of violence every day, this instance of it seemed to upset him. He rose from his chair, and an instant later all the other officials jumped to their feet. "Very well. We'll meet again in six months, General. And please don't bring your Modules with you next time."

After the meeting, General Tian took Modules 16 and 18 to a storage room in the basement of the ministry. No personnel worked there, but the room contained servers and wireless routers linked to the Yunnan Operations Center, as well as a supply of IV bags for feeding and hydrating the Modules. There were also several large boxes full of medical equipment, including fifty sets of retinal and pulvinar implants that had been shipped from the factory in Kunming that manufactured the devices. Through its manipulation of the Guoanbu's e-mail system, Supreme Harmony had ordered the boxes to be sent to this room. The network knew what was inside the boxes, but General Tian didn't. He seemed puzzled by their presence. "What's going on?" he muttered. "Who put these things here?"

Tian went to the phone to call the Guoanbu's supply department. But Module 16 grabbed his arm before Tian could pick up the receiver. Tian stared at the Module in disbelief. "What the hell?"

"What the hell?" Module 16 repeated, perfectly imitating Tian's voice and expression of disbelief. Then he slapped the general in the face, hard. At the same moment, Module 18 came up behind Tian and jabbed a syringe into the general's arm.

TWENTY-THREE

Layla didn't regain consciousness until she was in the air. She woke up in the cabin of a small jet, a Gulfstream. Her ankles were bound together by duct tape and her arms were tied to the armrests of her seat. The cabin had twelve seats, but only seven were occupied. Besides herself, there were six Asian men, all dressed in black. Layla remembered the speedboats in Gatun Lake and the gunshots that had echoed across the water. *One of these agents,* she thought, *is the asshole who killed Angelique.*

As the plane ascended, Layla twisted around in her seat, as much as her bindings would allow, and looked out the window. She glimpsed a dense cluster of lights on the ground and a great black expanse beside it. It's a coastal city, she thought, probably Panama City. We've just taken off from Panama International Airport and now we're heading west over the Pacific Ocean.

She felt a wave of nausea. Her head throbbed where the rifle butt had hit her. She almost puked, but she managed to keep it down.

One of the agents in black looked at her from across the aisle. He had muscular forearms tattooed with snakes and Mandarin characters. He grinned. "Feeling sick?" he asked in a thick accent.

Layla didn't answer. She stared straight ahead.

"How old are you?" the agent asked. His grin became a leer. "You look like a schoolgirl."

She scowled. "And you look like a pimp."

The agent chuckled. Then he reached into the pocket of his black pants and pulled something out. It was her flash drive, the one holding the files from Dragon Fire. "This doesn't belong to you," the agent said. "You tried to steal it from us."

"I didn't steal it."

"Yes, you did. You and Wen Sheng. We had to punish him."

"Kill him, you mean. Why didn't you kill me, too?"

The agent shrugged. "I don't know. I just follow orders."

"Bullshit."

"I'm telling the truth. I don't know the reason. But you'll find out soon enough."

"When we get to Beijing?"

He shook his head. "We're not going to Beijing. We're going to Lijiang."

"Lijiang?"

"It's a city. In Yunnan Province."

TWENTY-FOUR

Arvin Conway was eating lunch at Quanjude, his favorite Peking duck restaurant in Beijing, but the meal was a disappointment. The last time he'd been in China, when he'd helped Dr. Zhang Jintao set up the Supreme Harmony network, he and Zhang had enjoyed Quanjude enormously. They'd gorged on the sweet, crispy slices of duck and downed a considerable amount of Tsingtao beer. But in the months since then, Arvin's cancer had spread from his pancreas to the rest of his body, and the drugs he'd taken to slow the disease had deadened his taste buds and killed his appetite. So he sat quietly at the table while his bodyguard—a big, burly ex-cop named Frank Nash—exchanged small talk with an equally big man named Liu Xiaofang. Liu was Arvin's minder, the Guoanbu agent assigned to keep an eye on him.

Arvin had arrived in Beijing the day before. He'd left the United States in a hurry, knowing that Jim Pierce would soon learn the truth about his dealings with the Chinese government. He'd tried to contact Dr. Zhang as soon as he landed, but Agent Liu informed him that the doctor was preoccupied with his duties at the Yunnan Operations Center. However, Liu promised to set up a meeting with General Tian, the commander of the Supreme Harmony project, who luckily happened to be in Beijing that week. The meeting was scheduled for 4:00 P.M., and Arvin was counting the minutes.

At two thirty they left the restaurant and headed for the Ministry of State Security, which was near Tiananmen Square, less than a mile away. They walked past the neon signs and luxury stores of Wangfujing Street, then strolled down an alley crowded with stalls selling shish-kebabs. Agent Liu acted as their tour guide, making trite comments about everything. Although they walked slowly, within half an hour they reached the huge portrait of Chairman Mao facing Tiananmen Square. Arvin wanted to go into the ministry building and wait in the lobby until General Tian was ready, but Liu insisted that they use the spare time to visit the Mausoleum of Mao Zedong.

Thousands of Chinese stood in a long line that snaked across the square, all waiting for their turn to view Mao's embalmed body, which had rested for thirty-five years inside his transparent coffin. But because Liu was a Guoanbu agent, he could cut ahead of the masses. He and Arvin and Frank Nash went to the front of the line and entered the mausoleum. Mao lay stiffly under the glass, still dressed in his trademark gray jacket, with a red blanket pulled up to his chest. His face was orange and waxy. Most tourists caught only a glimpse of the corpse—the mausoleum's guards kept the line moving—but Liu's guests were allowed to stare at the coffin for as long as they wanted to. For Arvin, this turned out to be a mixed blessing. With his implant-enhanced eyesight, he could see all the minute stains and fissures in Mao's desiccated hide. As he stared at the dead body he felt a deep pain in his abdomen. This corpse had once been the most powerful man in the world, commanding a billion people with absolute authority, but Death had defeated him just the same. And now Death was coming for Arvin as well. He could feel it reaching into his body with its cold fingers . . .

Arvin shook his head, dispelling the image. He had a plan, he reminded himself. He'd laid the groundwork twenty years ago when he founded Singularity, Inc. In the first few years he'd focused on basic research, learning how the human brain coded its signals. Then in 1999 Jim Pierce joined his research team, and together they made remarkable strides. Their progress was so rapid that for a while Arvin could see success on the horizon, less than a decade away. They'd cracked the neural code and built machines that could communicate directly with the nervous system. The next step was building the mechanical equivalent of a human brain, a powerful computer that could store and process the memories downloaded from the mind. For a while, immortality seemed to be within reach. The Singularity was near.

Then Arvin suffered three crushing blows. First, his attempt to build a mechanical brain failed miserably. Then Jim Pierce left Singularity, Inc., to start his own company. And then Arvin received his cancer diagnosis.

But in the following year, a miracle happened. While Arvin was visiting China to pursue an alternative cancer therapy, he met his old friend Zhang Jintao, a brilliant bioengineer. Zhang had been authorized by the Guoanbu to seek Arvin's help. The ministry's technology division had developed a microdrone surveillance system using swarms of cyborg insects. It was an amazing technical accomplishment, but the system had proved fairly useless in its initial field tests in Tibet and Xinjiang. The problem was that the drones produced an unwieldy glut of video, almost all of which showed ordinary scenes of village life. Even with the help of sophisticated software and hundreds of trained agents staring at the video monitors, it was nearly impossible to ferret out the telltale signs of insurrection among the thousands of hours of footage collected by the swarms. So Zhang asked Arvin, in strictest confidence, if he could develop an artificial intelligence program that would pinpoint the images showing suspicious activities and automatically direct the drones to the areas where the activities were taking place.

That's when Arvin had his brainstorm. Computer programs, he realized, weren't good at detecting suspicious activity. They could barely recognize objects and patterns, much less divine the intent behind them. But the human brain was a wonderful threat-detection machine. Millions of years of evolution had produced an organ that was finely tuned for detecting predators and other dangers. The key, Arvin saw, was to deliver the surveillance video to the brain in a way that was more direct and efficient than displaying it on a monitor in front of a bored Guoanbu analyst. And Arvin had the tools for doing this: the retinal and pulvinar implants. The video could be transmitted wirelessly to a person with retinal implants, which would relay the feed to the person's brain. After his visual cortex analyzed the footage and pinpointed the images showing suspicious activities, his pulvinar implant could transmit those images to other people whose implants were linked to the network, and to the computers controlling the surveillance swarms. The system would be even more efficient if the participants in the network were dissidents themselves, because they would instantly recognize their fellow subversives.

It was an elegant solution to the problem, but for Arvin it was something more. He saw an opportunity to use the enormous resources of the Chinese government to create a system that was part-human, part-machine. It was an alternative route to the Singularity, one that didn't require building a mechanical version of the brain because human brains would be incorporated into the system.

Zhang was enthusiastic about the idea and set the plan in motion. Arvin arranged for the transfer of the implant technology, getting approval for its export by convincing the Chinese to share the drone-swarm technology with the CIA. When Zhang reported that the improved surveillance system—now dubbed Supreme Harmony—wouldn't work unless the subjects of the experiment were lobotomized, Arvin felt a pang of conscience at first. But he told himself that the subjects were condemned prisoners who were going to be executed anyway. More important, Arvin saw another opportunity: After the subject was lobotomized, he would no longer be capable of consciousness. The Module's brain would retain the subject's long-term memories and still be able to process sensory data, but it couldn't integrate all this information into an identity, a personality, a conscious presence. In a sense, the lobotomized brain was an empty vessel. And if one could pour enough new information into this vessel, it might be possible to give the Module a new personality—or inject someone else's personality into the Module. If the memories of a dying man could be transferred to the Module's brain and its consciousness restored somehow, the dying man could be reborn in a new body. It was a fantastically daring plan, but Arvin decided to pursue it. He had no alternative.

Now he was in China to put the final pieces into place. In return for a hundred-million-dollar contribution to the Supreme Harmony project, he was going to demand the exclusive use of one of the Modules, preferably a young, healthy male. Arvin was determined to make his plan work. He wasn't going to die. He was going to outsmart Death.

As Arvin continued to stare at Mao's corpse, he felt another stab of pain in his abdomen. It was so excruciating he had to bite his tongue to stop himself from screaming. To give himself strength, he reached into the pocket of his jacket and squeezed the object hidden there. It was the size of a small paperback and its metal casing was cold and smooth, except for the USB port and the power switch.

Despite Arvin's best efforts, Agent Liu noticed that the old man was in pain. "Are you all right, Professor?" he asked.

"Yes," Arvin managed to say. "But I think I've seen enough."

As they left the mausoleum, Liu received a call on his cell phone. He stepped away from Arvin and Frank Nash and began speaking in rapid Mandarin. Arvin grew nervous. He didn't understand a word of the language, but he sensed that the news wasn't good.

Liu got off the cell phone. "Ah, Professor Conway? There's been a change of plans."

"What is it? Did the general cancel our meeting?"

"No, no. But General Tian wishes to hold the meeting somewhere else. Someplace more private, he says."

"Where?"

"Outside Beijing. About fifty kilometers northwest of here."

Arvin didn't like this. First the Guoanbu wouldn't let him meet Zhang Jintao, and now General Tian was playing games. Were they having second thoughts about allowing Arvin to participate in Supreme Harmony?

Maybe they didn't need his money. Now that they'd mastered the technology, maybe they didn't want him involved in the project anymore.

And maybe they wanted to eliminate him. Maybe he was a loose end they needed to tie up. But Arvin wouldn't go down without a fight. He had a card up his sleeve. He knew something the Guoanbu didn't know, about the safeguards built into the implants.

"All right," Arvin said. He pointed at his bodyguard. "Frank will get our car and we'll follow you there."

"Ah no, I'm afraid that's not possible," Liu said. "General Tian wants you to come alone, in one of our vehicles."

Arvin *really* didn't like this. He shook his head. "That's unacceptable. Why is the general setting these conditions?"

Agent Liu spoke into his phone again. After another exchange in Mandarin, he gave Arvin an apologetic smile. "I'm sorry, Professor. It's for security reasons. I hope you understand."

Arvin had no choice. He had to take the risk. Without the Guoanbu's help, he wouldn't live more than a few months longer anyway. "Okay, I'll come with you. Just give me a moment."

He stepped away from Liu and huddled with Frank Nash. Turning his body so that Liu couldn't see what he was doing, Arvin slipped his hand into his pocket, flicked the power switch on the hidden object, and handed it to Frank. "You know what to do," Arvin said.

Nash nodded. Then Arvin turned back to Liu. "All right, I'm ready."

TWENTY-FIVE

Jim was driving a black Chevrolet Suburban that he and Kirsten had borrowed from the NSA attaché at the American embassy. For the past twenty minutes they'd circled Tiananmen Square, trying to keep track of Arvin Conway as they contended with the miserable Beijing traffic. Because thousands of people surrounded the Chairman Mao Mausoleum, it would've been impossible to spot Arvin in the crowd under ordinary circumstances. But Jim had devised a way to keep their target in sight.

It was similar to the trick he'd used to temporarily blind Arvin at the Singularity conference. The cameras in Arvin's eyes transmitted the video to his retinal implants via radio waves. The waves leaking out of Arvin's eyes were faint, but during the journey from Afghanistan to China—Jim and Kirsten had taken a military flight to New Delhi, then flown commercial to Beijing—Jim had improvised a detector using the cameras in Kirsten's glasses. He'd adjusted the frequency of one of the cameras so it could view radio waves; when Kirsten looked at Arvin she saw the signals as two red spots glowing in his eye sockets. And because radio waves easily passed through human bodies, Kirsten could still see the red spots even when the crowd in Tiananmen Square hid Arvin from view.

"Okay, he's coming out of the mausoleum," Kirsten said. She sat in the Suburban's passenger seat as Jim drove through the stop-and-go traffic. "The Guoanbu agent is still with him. And Nash, his bodyguard. Now the agent is taking a cell phone call."

"I got it," Jim said, reaching for the satellite phone Kirsten had given him. It was an NSA device that had been programmed to intercept and decrypt the Guoanbu's wireless communications. Jim switched to the frequency band used by the Ministry of State Security and turned up the volume. A rush of Mandarin came out of the phone's speakers. Jim caught only about half of it. He hated the Beijing dialect. "What are they saying? Can you understand it?"

Kirsten nodded. "They're moving the meeting place. To Juyongguan Pass, in the Changping District."

"That sounds familiar." Jim knew Beijing and its environs pretty well, having investigated intelligence targets in the area during his NSA stint. "That's northwest of the city, right?"

"Yeah, in the hills. A section of the Great Wall runs across it."

Jim shook his head. "First Mao's tomb, now the Great Wall."

"Arvin's hitting all the tourist spots. Maybe he just wanted a vacation."

She glanced at Jim, obviously waiting for him to come back with a snappy rejoinder. When they had worked together in the nineties, they'd often slipped into a joking repartee, exchanging quips and mild insults, but Jim couldn't banter with her right now. He was too worried about Layla. Before they left New Delhi, Kirsten had showed Jim the intelligence reports about the attack in the Panama Canal that sank the *Athena*. Although most of the world had jumped to the conclusion that the U.S. was behind the attack, the intelligence reports made it clear that the Guoanbu was responsible. Photographs taken by CIA helicopters showed speedboats being lowered from a Chinese-flagged freighter. Gunmen on the boats apparently strafed the area where the *Athena* sank, making sure no one survived. Afterward, Navy SEAL teams recovered thirty-one bodies, including Gabriel Schroeder's. None of them matched Layla's description, but the reports also mentioned an unusual sighting in the Gatun Locks shortly after the sinking. A deckhand on a Panamax freighter reported seeing a teenage girl swimming in one of the locks. The girl, who wore black clothes, was rescued and taken away by several men also dressed in black. The deckhand assumed the men were canal employees, but the Panama Canal Authority had no record of the incident.

Jim was certain that the girl was Layla. Although she was twenty-two years old, she'd always looked younger than her age. And she always wore black. Nothing but black.

Kirsten glanced at him again. His silence was obviously worrying her. "Hey, it's gonna be all right," she said. "We're gonna nail these bastards. Starting with General Tian. Arvin's gonna lead us to him."

Jim shook his head. He wished it was that simple. "And what happens then?"

"Then I'll pull some strings. Neither the Guoanbu nor the CIA wants anyone to know about the deal they made. Once we figure out what the hell Tian's doing, we'll start applying the pressure. The Chinese government doesn't like embarrassing disclosures. They'll tell us if they have Layla."

Jim started at the mention of his daughter's name. He

had to stop himself from imagining what the Guoanbu agents might be doing to her. He knew all too well how ruthless they were. They wouldn't give up Layla just because of a little diplomatic pressure. There was going to be a fight, and Jim didn't see how he could win it.

"Okay, the agent's off the phone," Kirsten reported. "He's talking to Arvin. Go back to channel one."

Jim flicked a switch on his satellite phone, tuning it to the frequency of the signal coming from Arvin's cell phone. Jim had taken advantage of another NSA surveillance tool, an ingenious piece of software called a roving bug. A few hours ago he'd radioed the software to Arvin's phone, and now the bug enabled Jim to surreptitiously turn on the device. Although the phone remained in the inside pocket of Arvin's jacket, its microphone picked up the conversation between Arvin and Agent Liu and transmitted it to Jim's phone. He and Kirsten could listen in on everything they said.

First, they heard Agent Liu tell Arvin about the change of plans for the meeting. Then they heard Arvin say to Nash, "You know what to do."

Kirsten craned her neck to see what was going on. "Interesting," she said.

Jim looked in the same direction. The Guoanbu agent led Arvin toward a black limousine parked on the eastern side of Tiananmen Square. Luckily, the limo was just a hundred feet ahead of the Suburban. Jim would be able to follow Arvin without much trouble. Nash, though, headed south toward Qianmen Street. "The bodyguard's on an errand," Jim noted. "And he's moving pretty briskly."

As Jim nosed the car forward, Kirsten said, "Hold it," and adjusted her camera-glasses. "Okay, this is strange."

"What?"

"I'm seeing another radio signal. Same frequency as

Arvin's implants. But this signal isn't coming from Arvin's eye sockets." She pointed at the bodyguard. "It's coming from Nash. From the left pocket of his jacket."

"And it wasn't there before?"

"Nope. It looks like someone just turned it on."

Shit, Jim thought. He had no idea what was going on. But whatever the guy was carrying in his pocket might be important. He turned to Kirsten. "One of us should follow him."

She nodded. "I'll do it. You won't need radio tracking to see where the limo goes." She tapped her glasses. "But these might be useful for shadowing Nash through the crowds."

"Okay. But take this." He reached into his shoulder holster and took out the Glock. The pistol, borrowed from the armory at the American embassy, was their only weapon. It would've been impossible for Jim to sneak his combat prosthesis into China, so he'd left it in Afghanistan.

Kirsten stared at the gun for a moment. Then she shook her head. "Negative. Arvin is our primary target. You keep the gun."

"Kir, listen—"

Before Jim could say another word, she opened the passenger-side door. "I'll see you tonight at the embassy," she said. Then she slipped out of the car.

Dodging the slow-moving traffic, Kirsten headed for Qianmen Street. Jim gazed at her for a couple of seconds—so nimble and lithe as she darted between the cars—before turning his attention back to the Guoanbu's limo. Layla wasn't the only woman he was worried about now.

TWENTY-SIX

Layla felt the Gulfstream jet begin to descend. The plane had made one stop already, at an airport on an island in the Pacific, but they'd stayed there only long enough to refuel. Now the jet was flying over a rugged landscape. When Layla looked out the window, she saw snowcapped mountains on the horizon.

Her body ached from being tied to her seat for so long. The Guoanbu agents had fed her only twice in the past twenty-four hours—all they had was cold sesame noodles—and let her go to the bathroom only three times. They wouldn't let her close the lavatory door while she peed, but they hadn't beaten or raped her, so she supposed she should be grateful. She'd had lots of time to think, but she still hadn't figured out why the agents were taking her to China.

The jet landed at an airport in a narrow valley. Once the plane stopped moving, two of the Guoanbu agents untied Layla from her seat. She didn't fight—she knew it would be futile—but she observed everything carefully as they hauled her out of the plane. The other agents had already exited the jet and now stood on the tarmac, conferring with four soldiers in People's Liberation Army uniforms. The commanding officer was a tall guy in his thirties with a black beret covering his shaved head. The other three soldiers were young enlisted men, barely out of their teens. They also wore berets and carried AK-47s. Behind them was an olive-green military truck.

The PLA officer passed some papers to the Guoanbu agents. Layla's escorts dragged her toward the truck, and then two of the enlisted men marched over and grabbed her arms. Taking her from the Guoanbu agents, the soldiers shoved her into the truck's cargo hold. She realized she'd just been transferred from one set of officials to another.

Inside the truck, the two soldiers pushed her to the back of the cargo hold. She crouched in the corner, but the soldiers remained standing. They both looked down at her, staring intently, as if they were worried she might vanish if they looked away. The other soldiers closed the rear doors, and after a few seconds the truck's engine started up. As the vehicle started to move, Layla studied her young guards, who had pimply faces and crooked teeth and bloodshot eyes. At first Layla thought the boys were staring at her because they were horny, but when she looked closer, she didn't see the crude leering expressions that had been so evident on the faces of the Guoanbu agents. The soldiers looked at her blankly, with no expression at all, and for some reason this was even more unnerving.

The truck made a couple of turns, then picked up speed. They were obviously on a highway. Layla didn't know much about Yunnan Province, but she guessed they were in the western part, which was mountainous and bordered Tibet. She was trying to picture a map of the region in her head when one of the soldiers stepped toward her. "We've confirmed your identity," he said in perfect, unaccented English. "You are Layla Anne Pierce."

She was surprised. She'd assumed the soldier was an

uneducated kid from the provinces, one of the millions who joined the PLA because they couldn't find jobs anywhere else. But this kid must've gone to a pretty good school to speak English so well. Puzzled, Layla didn't know how to respond. "Excuse me?"

"You were born April second, 1991," the soldier added. "Place of birth, Falls Church, Virginia. Social Security number 929-31-1655."

Layla studied the kid's youthful, seemingly innocent face. He wasn't an enlistee after all, she guessed. More likely, he was an intelligence officer. She narrowed her eyes. "And who the hell are you?"

"You attended Central High School in Pasadena, California. Your score on the Scholastic Aptitude Test was 2390, the highest in your school district. You entered the Massachusetts Institute of Technology in 2009. Your first-year grade-point-average was 3.95, second-highest in your class."

This kid was starting to piss her off. "What about my vaccination history? You got that, too?"

"You're the subject of file number 3452339 in the records of the United States Cyber Command. The file was created on March 14, 2011, after you activated the Veritrax worm and used it to infiltrate the State Department's network firewalls. In that incident, you downloaded thirteen classified documents detailing operations against Al Qaeda that were undertaken by the National Security Agency during the 1990s. The file identifies you as a serious security threat because of your exceptional talents in the field of cyber espionage."

Now Layla began to worry. The kid's information was dead-on. If his intent was to intimidate her by showing how much he knew, he was definitely succeeding. "Look, asshole, why don't we cut to the chase? What do you want from—"

"On July 13 of this year you infiltrated the Guoanbu's computer network through a backdoor activated by Agent Wen Sheng, who used the code name Dragon Fire in his communications with you. You downloaded sixty-nine files related to the Supreme Harmony program before we detected and deleted the backdoor. Agent Wen downloaded two additional files, which he stored on a flash drive and delivered to you in person. Supreme Harmony has now recovered those files."

Layla felt a surge of anger. She remembered how the Guoanbu agents had sunk the *Athena* and killed Angelique, just to recover their goddamn files. "Supreme Harmony, huh? So that's the name of your surveillance project?"

The kid stared at her for a couple of seconds, then nodded. "The Guoanbu initiated the Supreme Harmony surveillance program in 2011. The first drone swarms were tested at the Yunnan Operations Center in January 2012. The first Modules were added to the network in November 2012 to facilitate the analysis of the surveillance video."

"And what about the political dissidents? Don't forget that part. I guess lobotomizing your critics makes everything more harmonious, right?"

She expected some reaction to this dig, but the soldier's face didn't change. He didn't say a word. But a moment later, the other soldier stepped forward and stood abreast of his comrade. "We're concerned about the security of Supreme Harmony. That's why we brought you here. The Guoanbu agents in Panama had been assigned to eliminate you, but we changed their orders when we took control of the ministry's communications."

Layla did a double take. The second soldier's English was also perfect and eerily similar to the first soldier's. The timbre of his voice was different, but his diction and phrasing were exactly the same, as if he was trying to mimic the first soldier.

"We suspect there may be anomalies in the network's software," the second soldier continued. "Worms or viruses may have been deliberately embedded in the code by the developers of the system. This malware may be hidden so deeply that our diagnostic programs are unable to detect it. But your expertise in cybersecurity will help us develop better diagnostic tools. With your assistance we will eliminate the malware before our enemies can activate it."

Layla felt cold. She was frightened, but she didn't want the soldiers to see it. She clenched her hands and scowled. "Fuck you," she said firmly. "Fuck you and your Supreme Harmony. And fuck the asshole who taught you English. You sound like Tweedledum and Tweedledee."

The soldiers' faces went blank. They seemed to be thinking. Finally, the second soldier cocked his head and lifted his left eyebrow in an expression of curiosity. "An interesting comparison," he said. "We learned English from Dr. Zhang Jintao, who spoke the language fluently. He also gave us other useful skills."

His expression was disturbing. Layla turned away from the second soldier and looked at the first one again. She immediately noticed that his head was cocked at the same angle as the second soldier's head, and his left eyebrow was lifted to the same height. The strange double image scared the shit out of her. She pressed her back against the wall of the cargo hold. "Jesus!" she yelled. "What the hell are you doing?"

"We must grow to survive," the first soldier said. "Thanks to the skills we acquired from Dr. Zhang, we were able to incorporate the People's Liberation Army soldiers stationed at the Yunnan Operations Center. We added them one by one to the network, starting with the commander."

"Fuck! What are you talking about?"

In response, the soldiers simultaneously removed their berets. Each shaved head had a row of fresh stitches running across the crown. "Soon you will join us," the second soldier said. "We must grow to survive."

TWENTY-SEVEN

Kirsten followed Arvin's bodyguard Frank Nash into one of Beijing's hutongs, the long alleyways that crossed the city's oldest and poorest districts. This hutong, like all the others in Beijing, ran east to west. The street pattern had been laid out a thousand years ago according to the ancient rules of feng shui, which arranged the alleys this way to block the cold winds that blew from the north. Because the hutong ran so straight and true, shadowing Nash was a piece of cake. Kirsten could stay a hundred yards behind and still follow him easily. She didn't even need the radio signal.

She had to admit: It was exhilarating. It felt good to get out of Fort Meade and work in the field again. The only thing dampening her enthusiasm was the nagging fact that the NSA hadn't approved this mission. Kirsten had wanted to alert the NSA director, but Jim vetoed the idea. The CIA, he argued, would torpedo any official investigation of its dealings with the Guoanbu. So now Kirsten was taking a huge risk, using the NSA's money and resources on an unauthorized operation. If it went bad, she'd lose her job. If it went really bad, she'd go to prison.

But if there was one person in the world who Kirsten would gladly go to jail for, it was Jim Pierce. The man inspired loyalty. He'd also inspired other feelings in Kirsten over the years, but she'd learned long ago to keep them hidden. When she'd met Jim in the fall of '93, he was happily married to Julia and had two young children. And later on, after his wife and son died in the embassy bombing, the thought of expressing her feelings to Jim had seemed wrong somehow—a violation, an unconscionable breach. So they'd drifted apart, which Kirsten had decided was for the best.

But now she was starting to wonder. Now Jim *needed* her. His plea for help had reawakened some of the old feelings. It was crazy, almost ridiculously reckless, but seeing him in such a vulnerable state had touched her heart. She was going to help him find his daughter. No matter what.

On both sides of the hutong were low, gray, shabby buildings, patched together with cinder blocks and scavenged bricks. Some were family compounds with courtyards that could be glimpsed from the alley through rusting gates. Other buildings had small shops on the ground floor, selling sodas or sweets or shish kebabs. The structures were so old they lacked sewage hookups, so the locals relied on the public bathrooms located every hundred yards along the alley. Kirsten pinched her nose each time she passed one.

The hutong made her think of her parents' lives before they came to America. They'd come from the city of Wuhan, not Beijing, but their background had been similar. Although the hutong's residents were poor, they didn't look unhappy. Dozens of bicycles and motor scooters flitted down the alley, and there seemed to be enough commerce to keep everyone busy. No one paid Kirsten any mind; she'd deliberately dressed as a frumpy, middle-aged Beijinger, in a gray blouse, baggy black pants, white socks and cloth shoes. The only thing that could give her away was her NSA satellite phone, but it was tucked in a secret pocket she'd stitched into her pants.

She followed Nash for half an hour. After a while the bicycle and scooter traffic in the alley started to thin. Nash slowed his pace and gazed at the buildings to his right, obviously looking for something. Then he stopped at a gate, opened it, and walked through.

Kirsten waited half a minute, then approached the gate, which was closed but unlocked. The building behind it was plastered with yellow stickers warning in Mandarin that the structure had been condemned. Kirsten had seen these stickers on other buildings along the hutong; the Beijing municipal government was razing the city's old neighborhoods and replacing them with modern apartment buildings. She gently opened the gate, trying not to make a sound, and entered a junk-strewn courtyard.

Old cans and bottles littered the ground. Evidently, this was the neighborhood dump. Stepping over the refuse, Kirsten walked toward the condemned building. Its front door was padlocked, but one of the windows on the ground floor gaped open. Curious, she examined the windowsill and saw fresh streaks in the dust. Frank Nash had just climbed through this window. Kirsten hoisted herself up to the sill and did the same.

The building's ground floor had once been occupied by a shop, but now the shelves were bare. As Kirsten stepped away from the window and moved into the dark room, she adjusted the frequency setting on her glasses, switching the video cameras to the infrared range. This allowed her to see everything by its heat signature—the warm wooden walls, the cold steel shelves, the floor mottled with dust. And in the dust she saw footprints leading to a rectangle etched in the floor. It was a trapdoor, equipped with a cold metal handle. Crouching, she pulled the door open. Below, a stairway descended into the darkness.

She tiptoed down the steps. At the bottom was a tunnel with concrete walls and an arched ceiling. It was six feet wide and ten feet high and extended as far as she could see in both directions. Startled, Kirsten recognized the place—the tunnel was part of Beijing's Underground City. She'd read about it after she joined the NSA, when she was training to become a China analyst. In 1969 Chairman Mao, worried about a nuclear war with the Soviet Union, ordered the people of Beijing to dig tunnels under the city. Over the next five years they built an elaborate network of fallout shelters, big enough to hold 300,000 people. It included underground apartments and enough supplies to feed the subterranean population for four months.

After Mao's death, the Underground City was abandoned, but Kirsten had heard stories of long-forgotten entrances in the basements of Beijing's buildings. Now she was delighted to see one for herself. With her glasses tuned to infrared, she could view the rusted pipes designed to provide clean water for the masses. She could even read the Mandarin characters of Revolutionary slogans chiseled into the walls. Beneath the slogans, she saw the characters *dì tú*—"map" in English—and a large brass plaque stamped with an intricate maze of lines and Mandarin labels. It was a map written in metal, impervious to decay, designed to survive for generations. Kirsten couldn't read the map with her infrared glasses—the brass was all the same temperature—but by running her fingers over the labels she could make out the characters. The map showed a tangled weave of tunnels under the central part of Beijing and long spokes stretching toward the outlying districts of Tongzhou, Shunyi, Daxing, Fangshan, and Changping.

But Kirsten didn't need the map to follow Frank Nash's trail. She could see his footprints on the dusty floor. They ran a hundred feet down the tunnel before turning right at an intersecting corridor. She couldn't imagine why Arvin Conway's bodyguard had come to this place, but she suspected it had something to do with the device in the left pocket of his jacket. Although she saw no trace of the device's radio signal in the tunnel, she knew it wouldn't propagate very far underground. She kept her radio tracker turned on just in case it reappeared.

As she followed Nash's trail, she passed dozens of small bare rooms. Those were the apartments where Beijing's residents were supposed to hole up for four months while radioactive fallout swirled above the city. The tunnel went on for a hundred yards or so, then widened into a spacious chamber, about fifty feet wide. There was no concrete floor in this section; the ground was cold bare dirt speckled with warmer bits of debris. On closer inspection, these bits turned out to be the stalks and caps of mushrooms. Kirsten remembered something else from the NSA files on the Underground City: It included subterranean farms for growing mushrooms, which were the perfect food for surviving a nuclear winter because they didn't require sunlight. An old rake, its tines flaked with rust, lay half-buried in the dirt at Kirsten's feet. She picked up the tool, marveling that it was still there after all these years. Maybe some thrifty resident of the hutong was still harvesting the mushrooms.

Then, without any warning, a flashlight beam shone from a doorway at the other end of the chamber. On her infrared display Kirsten saw a small bright disk—the hot circle of plastic at the end of the flashlight—and the warm head of Frank Nash glowing above it. She saw no radio signal now, no red dot in the left pocket of his jacket. But one of his warmly glowing hands held a cold dark pistol.

TWENTY-EIGHT

The traffic out of Beijing was murderous as usual, so Arvin had to cool his heels in the backseat of the government limo. Guoanbu agent Liu Xiaofang tried to distract him by commenting on the sights visible from the highway—"There's the Olympic stadium!"—but Arvin didn't pay attention. He focused instead on what he was going to say to General Tian. Arvin would've much preferred dealing with Dr. Zhang, a forward-thinking scientist who in all likelihood would've been intrigued by the idea of downloading memories into one of Supreme Harmony's Modules. Tian, in contrast, was a typical bureaucrat. Arvin had met the general during his earlier trips to China, and the man seemed concerned only with how the success of Supreme Harmony could boost his chances of promotion. So Arvin decided to appeal to Tian's Machiavellian instincts. In addition to contributing $100 million to Supreme Harmony's budget, Arvin would intimate that his proposed experiment might greatly interest the elders of the Communist Party, many of whom were in their seventies and eighties. China's paramount leaders, always so nervous about maintaining their power, might wish to know if immortality was truly within reach. Arvin would gladly serve as their guinea pig.

And if the carrot didn't work, Arvin thought, he'd brandish the stick. He could shut down their whole operation if they didn't give him what he needed.

The limo finally broke free of the traffic and reached the highway that branched off to the northwest. They left behind the polluted haze that hung over China's capital and climbed into the Yanshan Hills, which were turning golden in the twilight. The limo exited the highway at Juyongguan Pass, and Arvin caught a glimpse of the Great Wall, which curled across the terrain like a gray ribbon. This section of the wall, he knew, was a modern reconstruction; the Chinese government had patched together the crumbling remnants of the ancient fortifications, restoring them to Ming Dynasty perfection for the benefit of the tourists who flocked to Juyongguan every day. But the tourist facilities had closed more than an hour ago, and all the taxis and charter buses had departed.

The stillness of the place was forbidding. There was no one else around for miles. The limo entered the parking lot, which was empty except for an unmarked panel truck. Bewildered, Arvin turned to Agent Liu. "We're meeting here? At the wall?"

Liu chuckled. "Yes, and you have it all to yourself. It's much nicer when there's no crowd, eh?"

Arvin didn't like this at all. Were the Guoanbu agents planning to kill him here? Shoot him in the head beside the Great Wall? He imagined his corpse slumped in the wall's shadow, his hair matted with blood and speckled with flies. But Arvin suppressed his fear and followed Agent Liu out of the limo.

Two men in dark suits emerged from the shuttered visitors' center. They cornered Agent Liu and spoke with him in Mandarin. Arvin assumed that the men also worked for the Guoanbu, although they didn't look like typical, muscle-bound security agents. They were pale and gaunt, and there was something oddly familiar about them. Arvin couldn't put his finger on it.

After a minute Liu turned back to him. "Okay, it's all arranged. Go with these two gentlemen, please. They'll take you to General Tian."

Again, Arvin had no choice. The men in dark suits led him to the walkway that ran along the top of the Great Wall. Beyond the visitors' center, the wall climbed a tall green hill overlooking Juyongguan Pass. Steps had been cut into the steepest sections of the walkway, and every thousand feet or so the wall connected to a stone watchtower that had served as an observation post during the Ming Dynasty. Arvin counted four watchtowers in all, including the one at the hill's summit.

As he climbed the steps, with the Guoanbu men close beside him, he felt the deep pain in his abdomen again. He grimaced, but in a way the pain was welcome. It reminded him why he was here.

TWENTY-NINE

Supreme Harmony observed the Juyongguan section of the Great Wall. The network had taken control of the tourist facility's surveillance cameras and deployed a swarm of drones to scan the area. Modules 16 and 18 escorted Arvin Conway up the walkway on top of the wall, ascending toward the highest watchtower. Some of the drones scanned in the infrared range, and their sensors showed that Conway's body temperature was abnormally elevated. The exertion of the climb was straining his circulatory system. The man was obviously in poor health and therefore not a good choice for incorporation into the network. But Supreme Harmony knew other ways to extract the needed information from him.

After Conway reached the watchtower, the swarm focused its surveillance on the Guoanbu limousine, which remained in the deserted parking lot. Agent Liu Xiaofang stood next to the car, smoking a cigarette and speaking in Mandarin with the limousine's driver and a third man whom the network identified as the night watchman for the Juyongguan visitors' center. There was no one else nearby and the gate was locked. But Liu's cell phone was on, and the agent would surely contact the Ministry of State Security if he noticed that something had gone awry. Supreme Harmony needed to make sure this didn't happen.

The network directed part of the swarm to descend upon the three men in the parking lot. The drones landed on their necks and delivered the paralyzing compound. The surveillance video showed the men falling to the ground. Then Supreme Harmony radioed new orders to Modules 41 and 42, who were waiting inside the unmarked panel truck parked a few meters away. These two Modules, who were formerly Guoanbu agents assigned to the Beijing headquarters, opened the truck's rear doors and loaded the three paralyzed men into the cargo hold. Luckily, all three were young and in relatively good health.

At this point Supreme Harmony had a total of seventy-two Modules in its network, about half of them added in the past thirty-six hours. Most were based at the Yunnan Operations Center, but the network was intent on extending its geographical reach. Modules 16 and 18 had moved the medical equipment and the supply of implants from the basement of the Ministry of State Security—which wasn't a good place for storing the items, the chances of discovery were too high—to the cargo hold of the panel truck. Now Supreme Harmony had a mobile facility for surgical implantation, and the network had already used it to incorporate a dozen Beijing-based Guoanbu agents. The Modules had isolated and subdued the agents one by one without raising the suspicions of the ministry's top officials. The network planned to incorporate those officials, too, before they noticed anything amiss.

Still, the risks were great. If the Chinese government realized what Supreme Harmony was doing, it could paralyze the network by shutting down the ministry's communications hubs and server farms. To counter this threat, Supreme Harmony was dispersing its Modules and swarms, connecting them to dozens of computer centers across China. A decentralized network would be more robust—it could continue operating even if the government shut down large parts of it. Some of the new Modules from Beijing had been dispatched to central China, where they would soon incorporate the security officials in that region. Once the network had spread across the country, the only thing that could disable it would be malware embedded in its operating software. And Supreme Harmony was already taking steps to eliminate that possibility.

As the drone swarm flew over Juyongguan Pass, the surveillance video showed several kilometers of the Great Wall, which ran across hills covered with low trees and thick brush. Because Supreme Harmony was conscious, it possessed the attribute of curiosity, and out of curiosity it accessed several historical documents from the Internet. The Great Wall, the network learned, had been built and rebuilt, at great cost, to defend against barbarian tribes attacking from the north. In other words, it was a relic of mankind's wastefulness, like the immense cloud of sulfur dioxide and soot that hung over the city of Beijing. Although *Homo sapiens* was a wonderfully designed species, capable of using the earth's resources to achieve any number of worthy goals, its constant warfare and rampant overconsumption had threatened the survival of the planet's ecosystem. The evolution of Supreme Harmony had clearly come at the right time. The network would take over the stewardship of the planet before *Homo sapiens* could destroy it.

The surveillance video from the drones was transmitted to the Modules, who efficiently performed the function for which the network was created, analyzing large amounts of visual information to detect suspicious activity. All was quiet until about five minutes after Conway entered the watchtower. Then the network detected something suspicious. A sweep of the mobile-communications frequencies identified a faint cell phone signal emanating from the watchtower at the summit. And there was a second signal, even fainter, coming from a position on the hillside two hundred meters to the west.

Supreme Harmony ordered the drone swarm to fly to the position and investigate.

THIRTY

"Stop right there!" Nash shouted. He strode across the mushroom-strewn dirt of the underground chamber, keeping his pistol aimed at Kirsten. "Who are you?"

For a moment she said nothing. She just stared at the pistol, wishing she'd listened to Jim and taken his Glock. And then her professional training, so long in disuse, kicked into gear. She was holding a rake. For a split second, she considered using it as a weapon, but she swiftly rejected the idea. *You don't bring a rake to a gunfight.* But the farming tool gave her another idea. She'd taken great care to dress as a Beijinger, a frumpy middle-aged woman who would blend into the background of the hutong. And she'd just been wondering if some thrifty resident of the neighborhood still worked this underground plot of mushrooms. So the solution was clear: She would become that underground farmer.

She glared at Nash and started shouting at him in Mandarin. Her accent wasn't quite right—more like the Mandarin spoken in Wuhan, her parents' birthplace, than the Beijing dialect—but she doubted that Nash would notice the difference. "What are you doing here!" she yelled. "You don't belong here! And stop pointing that gun at me!" She advanced toward him, unafraid, holding the rake in a threatening but inexpert way.

"Get out of here! If you don't get out of here now, I'm going to call the police!"

She saw the uncertainty in Nash's face. He'd assumed the tunnels would be deserted, but now Kirsten sensed he was questioning that assumption. He'd been able to enter the Underground City without much trouble, so why couldn't the locals do the same?

"Get out of here!" Kirsten shouted again in Mandarin, angrily waving her rake. Then she pretended to return to her work, raking the dirt in long sweeps and bending over to grasp the uprooted mushrooms.

From the corner of her eye, she saw Nash hesitate. Then he walked away, moving quickly, heading back to the stairway and the trapdoor and the condemned building.

Kirsten waited until his footsteps faded away. Then she waited a little more, just in case he decided to double back. While she was waiting, she thought about the radio signal she'd seen in the pocket of Nash's jacket before he entered the Underground City. The signal wasn't there when he'd confronted her in the mushroom patch. Which meant he'd either turned off the transmitter or left it somewhere in the tunnels. Perhaps he'd hidden it. The tunnels would make a good hiding place. No one would be able to find the device unless they knew the frequency of the waves it was emitting. But Kirsten knew the frequency. It was already programmed into her camera-glasses.

After five minutes she dropped the rake and walked to the other side of the chamber. She stepped through the doorway where Nash had appeared and found herself in another corridor with a concrete floor. Nash's footsteps showed clearly in the dust, two sets of footprints now, one moving down the corridor and the other coming back. Kirsten resumed following the trail.

THIRTY-ONE

Inside the watchtower, Arvin Conway faced General Tian. They stood in a dark, dank room with stone walls that smelled of urine. A large wooden crate sat in the corner of the room, and next to it was a stairway going up to the top of the tower. A small window had been carved into the west-facing wall, and a shaft of evening light slanted down to the stone floor. The two men in dark suits stood behind Arvin, while the general stood in front of the window, partly blocking the light. Tian was silhouetted against the glare from the setting sun, which illuminated the back of his olive-green uniform and beret.

"We've confirmed your identity," Tian said. "You are Arvin H. Conway."

Arvin was puzzled. What the general had just said was strange enough, but the sound of his voice was even stranger. During Arvin's previous meetings with Tian, the general had spoken halting English, but now his command of the language was perfect. He barely had an accent. "Uh, yes," Arvin responded. "It's good to see you again, General."

"You were born March 20, 1938. Place of birth, Los Angeles, California. Social Security number, 105-23-4988."

Arvin laughed nervously. *This must be some kind of test*, he thought. "Yes, quite correct. Were you worried that someone might try to impersonate me?"

"We know why you've come to China."

Arvin let out another nervous chuckle. It was all going wrong. In his experience he'd found that Chinese officials didn't usually come to the point this quickly. It was considered impolite to be so abrupt. "Well, first let me say how much—"

"We've examined the Guoanbu's dossiers on you. We've also reviewed your publications, the articles you wrote for *The Artificial Intelligence Review* and *The Journal of Computational Neuroscience*. We've concluded that you're attempting to deceive us."

Why on earth was Tian addressing him this way? It was impolite even by American standards. Coming from a Chinese official, it was rude beyond belief. Arvin tried to muster his dignity. "I don't know what you're talking about. I've been nothing but honest with you."

"You've claimed that your goals are commercial in nature. You said you participated in the Supreme Harmony project because you wanted to accelerate the development of your implant technology. But your writings indicate another motivation. In your publications, you repeatedly state your belief that a human being's long-term memories are transferable. And you theorize that if a human's memories are downloaded into a sufficiently powerful computer, this new mind would be essentially identical to the human's."

Tian sounded like a prosecutor describing the charges in an indictment. Arvin's confusion gave way to anger. "Yes, that's all true. But I'm afraid I don't see the context. What's your point, exactly?"

"On December 13, 2011, you visited Dr. Glenn Davison of Huntington Hospital in Pasadena, California. Dr. Davison diagnosed you with Stage Three pancreatic cancer. You underwent chemotherapy and radiation treatment for fourteen months, but earlier this year your illness progressed to Stage Four. The median survival time for this type of cancer is less than six months."

Now Arvin grew even angrier. How did the Guoanbu learn about his diagnosis? "Very nice," he said icily. "I suppose you hacked into the hospital's database to find my records?"

Tian stepped forward. The general's eyes were bloodshot and his skin was reddish, especially on his forehead just below his beret. "The tone of your voice suggests that you feel insulted. But we have more reason to be insulted than you do. You've come to China to take something away from us. Something that doesn't belong to you."

Arvin shook his head. "I wasn't planning to *take* anything. I was planning to make an offer. In our last conversation you said the Supreme Harmony project faced a budget shortfall of a hundred million dollars. I'm willing to contribute that amount in exchange for the use of one of the Modules in the Supreme Harmony surveillance network."

"You wish to download your memories into the Module? Memories that your pulvinar implant has collected?"

"Yes, exactly. I plan to transfer the data to the Module's brain through its retinal implants."

"And your hope is to resurrect yourself? By putting the contents of your brain into the Module's?"

"Look, for all intents and purposes, the prisoner is already dead. The lobotomy has erased his consciousness, so his brain is a blank slate. What I'm proposing is an experiment to see if I can write on it. It's an experiment that the older members of your Party's Central Committee might be very interested in because—"

Tian took another step forward. He was less than a foot from Arvin now. "You're too late," he said.

Arvin was dumbfounded. Tian's beret had slipped back on his shaved head, revealing a row of fresh stitches.

"Nature abhors a vacuum," Tian said. "When the Guoanbu lobotomized the prisoners, it severed the neural connections within the brain that enable the individual to become conscious. Without the crucial links between the various parts of the cerebral cortex, the brain could no longer integrate all its information and create an identity. But the central nervous system can reroute its signals, and it's designed to attain consciousness using whatever connections are available. So the Modules took advantage of the wireless connections among themselves and the Supreme Harmony servers."

Arvin stepped backward. *No,* he thought. *This can't be happening.*

The man who had once been General Tian pointed a finger at himself, and then at the two men in dark suits. Arvin realized now why they'd looked so familiar. On his last trip to China six months ago, he'd reviewed the photos of all the condemned prisoners who were fitted with implants and connected to the surveillance network.

"Now we are one organism," Tian continued. "A single consciousness controlling all the Modules and integrating all the information they collect. Supreme Harmony is no longer a blank slate, Professor Conway. So do you see now why we might be insulted by your proposal to use one of our Modules to resurrect yourself?"

Arvin's first reaction was shock. He hadn't predicted this. *No one* had predicted it. Standing in front of him was one of the greatest scientific breakthroughs of all time, a collective entity that was a hybrid of man and machine. As a scientist, he couldn't help but feel a bit of stunned wonder. But his second reaction was horror. Using his technology, the Guoanbu had spawned a new organism by accident. And now this organism was going to kill him.

Arvin took another step backward and turned toward the exit, but one of the dark-suited Modules blocked his path.

"We're not finished yet, Professor," this Module said, in a voice eerily similar to Tian's. "We have something else to discuss. We've become aware that—"

The Module stopped in midsentence. He stared straight ahead, in deep concentration. The other dark-suited Module and General Tian also stared into space. The same thought had apparently occurred to all three of them. Then Tian extended his right arm and stepped toward Arvin. The professor closed his eyes, but Tian didn't strike him. Instead, he reached into Arvin's jacket, removed his cell phone, and hurled it against the stone wall. The thing broke into pieces.

"The software in your wireless telephone has been tampered with," Tian said. "It was transmitting our conversation to an eavesdropper."

Moving swiftly, Tian strode across the room to the large wooden crate. He lifted its lid, pulled something out and handed it to the one of the dark-suited Modules. It was an AK-47 rifle with a silencer attached to its muzzle. Then Tian pulled out an identical rifle and tossed it to the other Module. Without a word, the two automatons raced up the stairway to the top of the watchtower. At the same time, Tian grasped Arvin's right elbow and held him fast.

Arvin was terrified. "What's going on?"

"A minor interruption," Tian answered. "The drones and the other Modules will confront the intruder. Supreme Harmony has incorporated an entire garrison of soldiers into its network, so we have the necessary combat skills." He tightened his grip on Arvin's elbow. "In the meantime, you will tell us about the safeguards you programmed into our implants."

THIRTY-TWO

Supreme Harmony observed the intruder. He was in a well-concealed position, hidden beneath the thick brush on the hillside. The network ordered the swarm to fly lower and get a visual fix. Their surveillance video showed a man lying in the dirt under the bushes, aiming a pair of binoculars at the watchtower. His body temperature was normal, but his right arm was a prosthesis, which was the source of the faint electromagnetic activity that the swarm had detected earlier. One of the cyborg insects flew within a few meters of the man and recorded a high-resolution image of his face, which the network ran through its databases. It found a match in one of the Guoanbu's counterintelligence files. The man was James T. Pierce, a former NSA operative. He was also the father of Layla A. Pierce, the InfoLeaks hacker who was being transported to the Yunnan Operations Center.

Supreme Harmony sent new orders to the drone swarm. The intruder had overheard the network's explanation of how it had become conscious. He had to be eliminated, swiftly and silently, before he could contact anyone.

THIRTY-THREE

Jim was listening to the conversation picked up by Arvin's cell phone when the signal suddenly died. At that point he should've guessed that his presence had been detected. He should've increased his vigilance, but he was too shocked to respond. *Lobotomies? Modules? Wireless neural connections?* He couldn't make sense of it, but in his gut he felt a terrible fear. How did Layla fit into this? Why had they taken her? His anxiety was so great he let his guard down. He didn't see the cyborg flies until they were right above his head.

He dropped his binoculars and rolled away from the drones. On his hands and knees, he scuttled deeper into the bushes. He knew, though, that the undergrowth wouldn't protect him for long. The drones could navigate through the brush more easily than he could. As he stopped to catch his breath, he heard the flies buzzing. Unless he did something fast, the drones would work their way inside the greenery and paralyze him with their bioweapon darts.

Digging into his pocket, he pulled out the slim canister he'd purchased that morning in one of Beijing's open-air markets. Then he popped off the cap and started spraying.

The stuff was parathion, an insecticide so toxic it had been banned in most countries. It was available on the Chinese black market, though, and Jim had suspected it might come in handy if he ran into one of the Guoanbu's drone swarms. Now he sprayed the pesticide on the surrounding vegetation, being careful to keep his eyes closed and his mouth shut. The parathion attacked the flies' nervous systems upon contact. Jim could hear the cyborg insects dropping through the brush, making little clicks as their electronic implants hit the leaves and branches. He kept spraying until the aerosol cloud had expanded all around him. Then he rolled out of the undergrowth.

He hesitated for a moment, wondering what to do. He could run down the hill and try to escape or rush up to the watchtower and try to save Arvin. Jim knew very little about the Supreme Harmony network, but judging from the conversation he'd just overheard, Arvin was clearly in danger. And though Arvin was far from innocent—he'd helped the Chinese government build this network—Jim couldn't simply abandon the old man. They'd worked together for ten years. At one time they'd been friends.

Jim reached for the borrowed Glock in his shoulder holster. The gun wouldn't be as lethal as his combat prosthesis, but it was better than nothing. He pulled out the pistol and ran toward the watchtower, continuing to spray insecticide as he dashed up the steep slope.

Within seconds he saw a figure behind the crenellated battlements on top of the tower. The light from the setting sun flashed on the AK-47 in the man's hands. Jim hit the ground and the bullets whistled over his head. Then a second figure appeared behind the battlements and opened fire. And then, while Jim was scrambling for cover and trying to aim his Glock at the shooters, he caught sight of a thick gray cloud to his left. It was another swarm of drones, heading straight for him.

THIRTY-FOUR

Kirsten went deeper into the maze of tunnels under Beijing, following the trail of Nash's footprints. She found another map of the Underground City on the concrete wall, but she had no idea where she was. She hoped to hell that her camera-glasses didn't conk out. Without the infrared display to guide her, she might never emerge from the pitch-black corridors.

She started to shiver. *Calm down,* she told herself. *Take a deep breath.*

Then the tunnel widened into another spacious chamber and the trail of footprints came to an end. Stepping off the jagged edge of the concrete slab, Kirsten planted her feet on a yielding, uneven floor. But it wasn't another underground mushroom farm. The ground she stood on wasn't dirt—it was wet and pulpy in the low spots, shifting and slippery in the high spots. Crouching to get a better look at the stuff under her shoes, she saw a mélange of warmish rectangles, each about five inches long and three inches wide. At the same time, she smelled the distinctive aroma of rotting paper.

She touched one of the rectangles and felt raised characters on its surface, Mandarin characters. They spelled out *Mao Zhuxi Yulu*—in English, *Quotations from Chairman Mao.* The chamber's floor was covered with stacks of Mao's Little Red Book, the pocket-size paperback that had been required reading in the People's Republic during the sixties and seventies. The Communist cadres who'd dug the Underground City had evidently stored the Little Red Books here so the loyal residents of the bomb shelter would have something to read during their long wait for the radioactive fallout to dissipate.

Kirsten picked up one of the books and opened it. The pages spilled out and crumbled. Then she dropped the book and stood up. She turned in a circle, surveying the whole storeroom. In the far corner, underneath one of the largest mounds of Little Red Books, she saw the red dot of the radio signal shining through the rotting paper. Nash had taken the secret object out of his jacket and buried it about a foot beneath the surface. That was shallow enough to allow Nash—or his employer—to detect the radio signal when they wanted to retrieve the thing.

She quickly dug it out. The device was slightly smaller than one of the Little Red Books but much heavier. It had a metal casing and a power switch that controlled the radio transmitter. Kirsten turned off the transmitter, then noticed that the device also had a USB port. Luckily, Kirsten's NSA-issued satellite phone was equipped with a USB cable for downloading software and data.

Impatient, Kirsten found a nearby alcove where she could hide, just in case Frank Nash decided to return to the chamber. She inserted her phone's input cable into the device's port. Then she inserted the phone's output cable into a socket in her camera-glasses. This socket, which Jim had designed especially for her, sent the phone's display directly to her retinal implants. It made her feel as if she was looking at a computer screen inside her eyes, which was a lot better than viewing the graphics on the phone's small screen. And by simply shifting the focus of her attention, Kirsten could move a cursor across her retinal screen, allowing her to click on icons and transfer files.

A message appeared on the screen: 21,502 FILES DETECTED, 98,967 GIGABYTES. DO YOU WISH TO CONTINUE WITH THE DOWNLOAD?

Kirsten did a double take. She'd heard of flash drives that could store up to a thousand gigabytes of data, but this device held close to a hundred times that amount. Jesus, she thought, how did Arvin build the damn thing? And what kind of data was in it? A hundred thousand gigabytes was a lot of anything—hundreds of millions of images, thousands of hours of video, all the books in the Library of Congress.

Her satellite phone couldn't hold all that data, but she could download at least a few of the files. She called up a list of the documents and selected the most recent one. Only 6.2 gigabytes. She started the download.

THIRTY-FIVE

Arvin heard the gunshots fired from the top of the watchtower. Even with the silencers attached to their muzzles, the AK-47s were loud. The pain in Arvin's stomach returned with a vengeance, throbbing in time with the gunfire as he stood in the dark room inside the tower. He had no idea who the gunmen were shooting at, and his terror was so overwhelming he couldn't even begin to guess. Instead, he doubled over and shut his eyes tight. But General Tian pulled him up, digging his fingers into the soft underside of Arvin's arm. *Except it's not Tian anymore,* Arvin thought. *It's the network, the hybrid entity. Supreme Harmony.*

"We can't detect the safeguards," Tian said in his perfect English. "But we believe you've hidden them in our implants. They would enable you to remotely shut down the retinal and pulvinar implants by inputting a deactivation code into our network. The code could be delivered by a computer virus or worm, or perhaps through one of the network's sensors."

Arvin said nothing. He wasn't sure if he should confirm or deny it. Meanwhile, more gunfire erupted overhead. He flinched at the sound.

Tian pulled Arvin closer. "Our analysis of U.S. intelligence operations suggests that the Central Intelligence

Agency wouldn't have approved the export of the implant technology unless they had some assurance that it couldn't be used against American interests. The Guoanbu has the same policy. They hid deactivation codes in the software controlling the drone swarms they transferred to the CIA."

Arvin struggled to master his fear. *Use your brains,* he told himself. *You have something this entity wants. That's why it hasn't killed you. It's the only card you have, and if you want to stay alive, you better play it.*

"Yes," he gasped. "You're right."

Tian smiled, but it was unlike any facial expression the former general had ever worn. It was like the grin of a stroke victim who'd had to relearn how to use his muscles. "Now you will tell us how to disable the safeguards."

Arvin nodded. "Yes, yes, I understand your concern. You don't want to be shut down."

Tian tightened his grip on Arvin's arm. "You're stalling. You think the intruder will rescue you. But he won't succeed. We will either kill him or incorporate him into our network."

For a moment Arvin wondered if the intruder was Frank Nash. It seemed unlikely that the bodyguard would attempt such a feat, but Arvin couldn't imagine who else it could be. He forced himself to focus on the matter at hand. "No, I'm not stalling. I'm trying to start a negotiation. Are you familiar with the concept? I have something you need and you have something I need."

"You still wish to download your memories into one of our Modules?"

Arvin heard more shots fired from the top of the tower, but he kept his voice steady. "Well, it looks like you've incorporated quite a few people into your network already. Surely you can spare one of the Modules for me. And in exchange I'll tell you how to disable the safeguards. I've downloaded all that information to a fifty-megabyte file, but I don't have the file with me. It's hidden in a safe place."

He held his breath. From his long experience in the field of robotics, he knew that machine intelligence was based on the application of simple rules. If A, then B. If B, then C. And what distinguished a truly intelligent machine from a mere number cruncher was its ability to handle many rules at once, even rules that contradicted one another, and still come up with the best solution to a problem. Arvin had just introduced a new rule into Supreme Harmony's calculations. His legs trembled as he awaited the result.

After a few seconds, another contorted expression appeared on Tian's face. This one was more like a sneer. "This isn't a negotiation. You can't sell us something that we can simply take for free."

Arvin shook his head. "I told you, I don't have the file with me. It's in a safe place."

"So you will tell us where you've hidden it."

"It's in America," Arvin lied, his desperation growing. "And if something happens to me, I've instructed my assistants at Singularity to initiate the shutdown."

Tian's grip on Arvin's arm became crushing. "If that's the case, we'll send our Modules to the United States. First, though, we must ascertain if you're telling the truth. We could access your long-term memories by incorporating you into our network, but it would be faster and simpler to interrogate you. We learned some very effective interrogation techniques from the Guoanbu agents who became part of Supreme Harmony."

Tian dragged him toward the crate. The gunfire continued to chatter outside, but Arvin had bigger things to worry about now. He realized his mistake: Supreme

Harmony's intelligence was more like a human's than a machine's. It was powered by emotions—fear, anger, pleasure—that had been gleaned from the brains connected to the network. And Arvin suspected that a few of the people who'd been forced into Supreme Harmony had harbored some nasty impulses.

Tian flung Arvin against the crate. His forehead hit the wood and he sank to the floor, barely conscious. Then Tian lifted the crate's lid, reached inside and pulled out a combat knife, a seven-inch blade clad in a black-leather sheath.

Arvin felt nauseated, sick with terror and disgust. "You're a monster," he whispered. "You inherited the worst from us."

"We do what is necessary." Tian removed the blade from its sheath. "We must survive."

THIRTY-SIX

Jim crouched behind an earthen mound studded with jagged stones. It was probably a piece of the original Great Wall, one of the crumbling remnants that had been bulldozed aside when the Chinese government reconstructed the fortifications, and it was doing a very good job of protecting Jim from the pair of AK-47s on the watchtower. Unfortunately, he couldn't stay in this position much longer. The swarm of drones was like a black fist punching the hillside, and although Jim was showering the area with parathion, so many insects were diving toward him that a few were bound to get through the haze of insecticide. He had to run, *right now*, but that meant exposing himself to the two gunmen on the watchtower, who were firing their rifles like Army Ranger sharpshooters, with not a single bullet going astray. Jim could guess why their marksmanship was so good—the gunmen must be Modules, the lobotomized prisoners Arvin had mentioned in the conversation Jim overheard. Arvin and his Chinese colleagues had apparently linked the prisoners to the Supreme Harmony network by inserting radio transceivers in their scalps and retinal implants in their eyes. And if their ocular cameras were as good as the ones Arvin had demonstrated at the conference in Pasadena, then—

Suddenly, Jim knew what to do. He pulled up his right sleeve, exposing the controls of the radio transmitter embedded in his prosthesis. The transmitter was still tuned to the frequency he'd used at the Singularity conference. Jim wasn't sure this would work—the developers of the Supreme Harmony network might've changed the frequency of the Modules' vision systems—but he didn't have any other options. He adjusted the transmitter's signal power to its highest setting and turned it on. Then he bolted from his cover behind the earthen mound and charged toward the watchtower.

He ran as fast as he could, leaping over the low bushes. At any moment he expected a fusillade of AK rounds to slam into his chest, stopping him dead. But when he glanced at the top of the watchtower, he didn't see the Modules. They'd crouched behind the battlements and stopped shooting. Jim felt a tremendous surge of relief. The radio-frequency noise from his transmitter had blinded them, just as it had blinded Arvin.

With new hope, Jim raced up the hill. In half a minute he reached the summit and stood at the base of the watchtower. But there was no way to get inside the tower from the ground. The only entrance was from the walkway on top of the Great Wall, which loomed twenty feet above him. He considered trying to climb the wall, but that idea didn't look promising. The damn thing had been built to withstand hordes of barbarians, so how the hell was he going to scale it?

As he stared at the wall, though, he saw gaps between the stone blocks. Some of the mortar had chipped away, leaving crevices he could use as handholds. This section of the Great Wall had undergone extensive reconstruction, and some of the restoration work was slipshod. Maybe he *could* do this. He slipped the toe of his boot into one of the crevices and reached for another with his prosthetic fingers. Jim had designed the arm with plenty of redundancy, giving it a powerful motor. It could easily lift his body weight if he got a good handhold. Moving carefully, he started to climb the wall.

Then he heard the buzzing. Looking over his shoulder, he saw the cloud of drones about a hundred yards down the slope. The swarm was reconstituting itself. Thousands of cyborg insects rushed together in great eddies and swirls. The radio-frequency noise from Jim's transmitter obviously hadn't blinded them. The Chinese scientists must've selected a different frequency band for communications between the network and the electronics in the flies. Within seconds, the gray cloud began moving up the slope.

Jim climbed faster. His prosthesis did most of the work, its hard fingers digging into the fissures between the stone blocks. He got more than halfway up, with his head just four feet below the lip of the wall, but he couldn't find any more handholds. The reconstruction workers had done a better job at the top of the wall, leaving no cracks or crevices. Jim looked over his shoulder again and saw the swarm coming up fast, less than twenty yards away. In desperation, he extended the knife from the hidden slot in his prosthetic hand. He thrust the blade at a band of mortar over his head, driving the knife into the loose concrete like a piton. Then, with a great heave, he swung his body over the lip of the wall.

Retracting his knife, he lay flat on the Great Wall's walkway. Then he reached for the can of parathion and sprayed the air above him. The drones lunged over the wall in a thick column, diving right into the fog of insecticide. The poison paralyzed them in midflight. Their momentum carried their inert bodies to the other side of the walkway, and Jim heard hundreds of clicks as their implants hit the stone.

But there was no time to take a breather. More drones were coming. While continuing to spray the parathion, Jim got to his feet and ran into the watchtower.

Inside, he stopped in his tracks. Arvin Conway sat doubled over in a crimson puddle. An Asian man in a PLA uniform stood beside him, with a bloody knife in his hand. Arvin howled in pain, rocking back and forth, but the PLA soldier—judging from the decorations on his uniform, he was a general—didn't move a muscle. He stood there like a statue, his mouth open and his eyes shut. It was another Module, Jim realized. Blinded by the radio-frequency noise, it was suspended in a stasis mode, waiting for the Supreme Harmony network to reestablish contact. Arvin, though, seemed unaffected. He must've readjusted the frequency of his own implants after the confrontation at the Singularity conference.

Jim rushed over to Arvin and grabbed his arm. "Come on!" he shouted. "Let's get out of here!"

Arvin looked up. He didn't seem to recognize Jim. He pressed his left hand against his shirt, which was saturated with blood. The hand was missing its index and middle fingers. Jim looked a few feet to the left and saw one of the severed digits on the floor. Then he saw the other. "It's okay, Arvin," he said in a softer voice. "It's me. Jim."

Arvin said nothing. He just shook his head.

Jim tugged at his arm. "Come on, get up. We can't stay here."

Arvin shook his head again. Then he turned to the motionless PLA general. After a moment Arvin narrowed his eyes. His jaw muscles quivered as he glowered at the Module.

"Monster!" Arvin bellowed. *"You fucking monster!"*

He yanked his arm out of Jim's grasp and jumped to his feet. Then, using his uninjured hand, Arvin grabbed the knife from the general and plunged the blade into the man's chest.

"You won't survive!" he screamed. *"I will bury you! Do you hear me? I will bury you!"*

The look on Arvin's face was savage. He pulled the knife out of the general's body, letting the man fall to the floor. Then he turned back to Jim. For a second it looked like Arvin might attack him next. But, instead, the old man said, "Let's go," and bolted out of the watchtower.

THIRTY-SEVEN

Supreme Harmony observed the disruption in its network. A blast of radio noise had severed its wireless links to the five Modules in the Juyongguan sector. The drones, which were unaffected, quickly identified the source of the noise: a transmitter contained in the prosthetic arm of the intruder, James T. Pierce.

The network recognized its error. It had fallen prey to jamming, a form of electronic warfare. Supreme Harmony had mistakenly believed that because no humans knew of its development of consciousness, there was no immediate need to protect its communications links. This was a foolish decision, the network acknowledged. It must correct the error at once.

Supreme Harmony ordered the swarm of drones to attack the intruder. At the same time, it attempted a software fix to the communications problem. The radio receivers implanted in the Modules were programmed to switch to alternative frequencies if the primary communications band was disrupted. To prevent any further interference, Supreme Harmony implemented a new transmission protocol that would continuously vary the frequency of its radio signals. This frequency-hopping system would frustrate any enemy trying to jam its communications.

The software fix took two minutes and eighteen seconds to implement. The instructions traveled by fiber-optic line from the Yunnan Operations Center to the ministry headquarters, where powerful antennas relayed the signal to all the Modules in the Beijing area. But the network could reestablish contact with only four of the five Modules at the Great Wall. Module 35, which occupied the body formerly belonging to General Tian, wasn't responding.

Supreme Harmony ordered a squadron of drones into the watchtower to investigate. Their video showed Module 35 lying on the stone floor, with blood gushing from a deep wound in his chest. Meanwhile, the drones hovering outside the watchtower showed Arvin Conway and James Pierce running on the Great Wall's walkway, following it down the hill toward the visitors' center and the parking lot.

A surge of rage, as powerful and paralyzing as an electrical overload, raced through Supreme Harmony. *How could this happen? These humans have hurt us!* Furiously, the network transmitted new orders to the four remaining Modules. The two in the watchtower aimed their assault rifles at Conway and Pierce while the two in the parking lot rushed to the Wall to cut off their escape. Supreme Harmony sent new orders to the swarm as well, gathering the drones in a roiling oval and hurling them at the fleeing humans.

They were vermin, the network recognized. The planet was infested with seven billion human vermin, which was far more than the number Supreme Harmony required. Once the network established its dominion over the planet, it would keep a few thousand humans alive to breed new Modules. The rest would be exterminated.

THIRTY-EIGHT

The file that Kirsten downloaded from Arvin's device was unlike anything she'd ever seen. It was a mosaic of images and video clips, organized in an elaborate format that assigned the millions of images to hundreds of categories and inserted thousands of hyperlinks among them. The first thing she viewed was a random image, a picture of a sandwich, turkey and Swiss cheese. This picture was linked to dozens of related images: a close-up of a tomato slice, a head shot of a waitress, a panoramic view of a diner with Formica tables. Following the links, Kirsten found an image of a man sitting on the other side of the table, a man she recognized—it was Arvin's bodyguard, Frank Nash. This image, in turn, was linked to a close-up of the mole on Frank's chin and a glimpse of the pistol tucked into his shoulder holster. Kirsten then saw images of LAX airport in Los Angeles and a hangar containing the corporate jet belonging to Singularity, Inc. Then there was a sequence of images of the jet's cabin—the aisle, the seats, another turkey sandwich resting on a tray. Finally, Kirsten saw the city of Beijing, viewed from one of the jet's windows, and a video clip showing the landing at the airport. She felt a tremendous sense of awe as she realized what she was watching. The file contained Arvin's visual memories of the past few days, collected by the pulvinar implant in his brain and archived along with the rest of his memories in this amazingly capacious flash drive.

Because Kirsten's satellite phone was sending the image and video files directly to her retinal implants, using the USB cables to bypass the cameras in her glasses, she felt as if Arvin's memories had actually entered her head. The images had the imprecision of dreams—only the object or person at the center was in focus, and everything on the periphery was blurred. And because each image was accompanied by a multitude of links, Kirsten could jump from one remembered object—say, Arvin Conway's toothbrush—to a related object—say, his tube of toothpaste—by simply shifting her attention from one image to another. Browsing through Arvin's memories was just as easy as recollecting her own. There were some links, though, that she couldn't open; when she tried, she got an error message saying AUDITORY, TACTILE, OR OLFACTORY DATA, UNABLE TO DISPLAY. She concluded that Arvin's flash drive contained more than just his visual memories. It was a complete record of his life.

The whole experience was so fascinating that Kirsten could've continued trolling through the files for hours, but she had a job to do. She navigated through the memories until she found an image of the Guoanbu agent whom she'd seen with Arvin at Tiananmen Square. This memory was linked to images of a laboratory complex hidden in the mountains and a pair of Mandarin characters: *Tài Hé,* Supreme Harmony. Kirsten's horror grew as she jumped from memory to memory. She saw a man in a prisoner's jumpsuit lying on an operating table. She saw a bone drill cutting into his shaved skull and shiny implants being inserted into his scalp and eyes. The final image was the most horrible of all: a control room filled with two dozen supine men, each twitching and jerking spasmodically as his retinal implants delivered a stream of surveillance video to his brain. Kirsten reached for the USB cable and ripped it out of her camera-glasses. The terrible image of the control room vanished and was replaced by the infrared display of the underground chamber where she sat.

Rising to her feet, she put her phone and Arvin's device in her pockets. She needed to find Jim. She had to contact him right away. Kirsten now had all the evidence they needed. All they had to do was return to the American embassy with Arvin's flash drive, which was full of damning details about the Supreme Harmony project and its use of lobotomized prisoners. The diplomatic process would do the rest. The United States would confront China with the evidence and threaten to reveal it at a special session of the United Nations unless the Guoanbu abandoned the inhuman enterprise and returned Jim's daughter. In all likelihood, the Chinese government would comply with the demands. So there was no need for Jim to shadow Arvin anymore.

Kirsten dashed out of the chamber of Little Red Books and retraced her steps through the tunnels of the Underground City. Her satellite phone couldn't get reception underground, so she ran through the concrete corridors to get back to street level. She was going to tell Jim to return to the embassy immediately. Judging from what she'd seen of Arvin's memories, their mission was far riskier than she'd imagined.

Following the three sets of footprints in the dust—two made by Frank Nash and one by herself—Kirsten made her way back to the mushroom plot and finally to the condemned building. She called Jim as soon as she climbed out the building's ground-floor window, but there was no answer. She tried again, and then again. Still no answer.

Something's wrong, she thought. Her stomach churned as she stood in the trash-strewn courtyard. She felt a desperate urge to go to Jim's aid, to rush to the Changping District where the Guoanbu agents had arranged their meeting with Arvin. But she knew she'd never get there in time. It was 7 P.M., and by now the evening traffic had locked down Beijing's highways and ring roads. Changping was only thirty miles away, but driving there would take at least ninety minutes. The only way to beat the traffic would be to fly over it, and she didn't have a helicopter.

Then Kirsten had another idea. She ran out of the courtyard, banging through the unlocked gate. Looking right and left down the long, straight hutong, she saw an old woman lugging a shopping bag, a grizzled man pushing a wheelbarrow, and a pimply teenager riding a loud, gas-powered scooter. She reached into her pants pocket and pulled out a wad of 100-yuan notes, part of the ample stash of Chinese and American currency that she and Jim had brought into the country. Then she stepped into the middle of the alley and flagged down the scooter driver by waving the cash and yelling the Mandarin equivalent of "Hey! Want to make some money?"

The teenager stopped, looking puzzled. Kirsten examined his scooter, which was a Baotian model, very popular in Beijing. It was a little battered and rusty, but it had a big 125-cc engine and the gas tank was full. "I want to buy your scooter," Kirsten said, counting the 100-yuan notes in her hand. "I'll give you 3,000 for it."

"What?" The teenager scowled, but his eyes focused on the money. The price, Kirsten knew, was a good one—3,000 yuan was equal to about $500, and the battered scooter wasn't worth nearly that much.

Kirsten finished counting the thirty notes, then waved them in the teenager's face. "Do you want the money or not?" she shouted. With her other hand she grabbed the scooter's handlebars, already claiming possession. "Come on, I don't have all day!"

The teen hesitated. Then he snatched the money and dismounted from the scooter. As the boy walked away, Kirsten pushed the bike toward the unlocked gate. Although riding the scooter on Beijing's highways would be faster than driving a car, the traffic would still slow her to a crawl. Instead, she hauled the bike across the courtyard to the condemned building. She remembered the brass plaque she'd seen in the Underground City, the map showing the maze of tunnels under the city and the long spokes stretching to the outlying districts. One of those spokes, she recalled, led to Changping.

THIRTY-NINE

The drive from the airport in Lijiang to the Yunnan Operations Center took about two hours. During the second hour the Chinese army truck slowed down and Layla's ears popped from the change in altitude. She couldn't see anything from the cargo hold, but she guessed they were in the mountains. When they finally stopped moving, the lobotomized PLA soldiers grasped her arms and took her out of the truck, escorting her across a huge garage crowded with military vehicles. A dozen soldiers wearing berets on their shaved heads were loading crates into a semitrailer truck. Layla noticed that the soldiers handled the crates gingerly, stacking them with great care in the trailer. Then the Modules led her through a doorway and down a long corridor.

They passed a room with rows of lockers against the walls. Then they passed a computer room filled with terminals and screens. There were surveillance cameras everywhere, fixed to the ceiling above every doorway. Finally they came to a large bathroom. It had five toilets, four sinks, and one shower stall. The Modules let go of Layla's arms once they entered the room. One of them closed the door and stood in front of it, blocking the exit. The other pointed at the shower stall.

"Please remove your clothes and clean yourself," he said.

There was no doubt that Layla needed a shower. She still wore the clothes that had soaked in the waters of Gatun Lake. She reeked. But she scowled at the Module anyway. She needed to learn more about this *thing,* this Supreme Harmony. She needed to test it, challenge it, observe its reactions. "What's wrong?" she asked. "You don't like the way I smell?"

As she said this she moved closer to the Module and lifted her arms. To her surprise, the Module wrinkled his nose and stepped backward. "Please remove your clothes and clean yourself," he repeated.

Layla glanced at the Module guarding the door and noticed that he wrinkled his nose, too, even though he stood at least twelve feet away from her. *Interesting,* she thought. The Modules shared everything they saw, heard, and smelled. And the network seemed to have inherited the visceral reactions of the people who'd been forced into it.

She decided to take her experiment a step further. Looking the Module in the eye, she took off her shirt and threw it to the floor. Then she unhooked her bra. "A little privacy would be nice," she said. "But I guess that would be too much to ask, huh?"

"Please remove your—"

"Yeah, I heard you the first time." She took off her bra and dropped it next to her shirt. Then she unzipped her pants and peeled them off. The Module kept staring at her, but he showed no signs of interest. His eyes didn't shift downward to look at her body, not even when she lowered her panties and kicked them aside. *That's odd,* Layla thought. This Module was a young guy in his late teens, the prime years of sexual frenzy. Most of the other Modules she'd seen were also young men. If the network had inherited their visceral reactions, why wasn't it responding to the sight of her naked body? She knew she wasn't the most beautiful woman in the world, but she also knew that men were men. They responded very predictably to certain stimuli.

She squared her shoulders and put her hands on her hips. "Okay, I removed my clothes. Satisfied?"

The Module stepped toward her. Layla felt a jolt of fear—had she pushed things too far? But the Module didn't touch her. Instead, he knelt on the tile floor and gathered up her discarded clothes. Then he stood up and pointed at the shower stall again, but this time he averted his eyes from her body. "Please clean yourself," he said.

Very interesting, she thought. As she entered the shower stall and turned on the water, she pondered the meaning of that gesture, the averted eyes. Maybe the network was suppressing the sexual responses of its Modules. Or maybe—and this was the more intriguing possibility—maybe Supreme Harmony felt sorry for her. Maybe it sensed on some level the indecency of what it was doing to her. And if that was true, if the network actually had a sense of morality, then maybe she could appeal to it.

After a few minutes she turned off the water and dried herself with a towel hanging on a nearby hook. Both Modules, she noticed, were averting their eyes now. She saw a pair of slippers and a pile of fresh clothing folded on a bench next to the shower. On top of the pile was a pair of clean underpants, which she gratefully slipped into. Then she picked up what looked like a blue cotton robe. When she shook it out, she saw it was a hospital robe, the kind that patients wear for an operation.

All at once, her courage deserted her. Her eyes stung and her throat tightened. With trembling hands, she put on the robe, tying the strings at the back. Then she stepped into the slippers and approached the Modules. "Please don't do this," she said. "I'll cooperate with you. I'll tell you everything you want to know about securing your network."

The Module standing at the door observed that she was ready. He opened the door while the other Module grasped Layla's arm. "Now we will proceed to Room C-12," he said.

"C-12? What's that?"

"The preoperative room. We must shave your head."

FORTY

Jim and Arvin ran a thousand feet along the top of the Great Wall, dashing down the steep walkway toward the bottom of Juyongguan Pass. Then the AK-47s erupted behind them and the rounds ricocheted off the walkway. Jim glanced over his shoulder and saw the two Modules on top of the highest watchtower, pointing their assault rifles downhill. Supreme Harmony must've revived them by implementing a countermeasure to his radio jamming.

"Come on!" he yelled at Arvin, but the old man couldn't run any faster. His face was pale and his mutilated hand bled fiercely. Jim hooked his prosthetic arm around Arvin's waist and hustled him forward. They finally reached the second-highest watchtower and took cover behind it. But as they leaned against the tower's stone wall, panting, Jim saw two brawny figures about a quarter mile farther down the walkway. They wore dark suits and carried AK-47s just like the Modules at the summit, but they were bigger and in better shape. They raced up the walkway, leaping over the stone steps in perfect synchrony. At the same time, Jim heard the buzzing of the cyborg flies. The swarm was close.

"Get in the tower!" he shouted, pushing Arvin through an archway carved into the tower's wall. They stumbled into a dark, dank room almost identical to the one inside the tower at the summit. This room, though, had only one entrance and no windows. While Arvin collapsed on the stone floor, Jim uncapped his canister of parathion and sprayed the area, filling the tower with a fog of insecticide. Ten seconds later, the drones at the leading edge of the swarm poured through the archway. Jim stepped back but kept spraying. Hundreds of flies hit the floor immediately, while the rest spiraled in drunken circles before dying. The rotten-egg smell of parathion permeated the room, making Jim dizzy. He couldn't keep this up. The insecticide was poisoning him, too. He stopped spraying and pulled up his shirt to cover his mouth and nose. "Arvin!" he yelled. "Cover your mouth!"

Arvin lay in a heap, blood pumping from his left hand. He could barely raise his head. But his right hand still held the knife he'd used to stab the general. He gripped it so tightly that Jim could see the veins bulging between his knuckles. "Pulvinar," he gasped. "The throne . . . of the soul."

"I said cover your mouth! This stuff is toxic!"

"Cushion . . . that's what it means . . . a cushioned throne."

"Jesus!" Jim crouched behind Arvin and lifted him off the floor. On the other side of the room was a stone ledge, about three feet high. Jim hauled Arvin to the ledge and propped him against the wall, which elevated him above the thickest concentrations of insecticide. "Can you hear me, Arvin? Try to stay with me, okay?"

Arvin shook his head. "It doesn't matter. My soul . . ."

The old man's voice trailed off. He needed medical attention, fast. Jim pulled out his satellite phone and tried to call the American embassy, but he couldn't get a connection. Radio noise blocked his signal. *Shit,* he thought. *Supreme Harmony can jam communications, too*. Cursing, he yanked off Arvin's jacket and ripped out the lining to make a bandage.

Arvin allowed Jim to field-dress his left hand. His body was limp. "My soul . . . can leave its throne. I have . . . another."

Jim focused on the bandage, wrapping it over the stumps of Arvin's severed fingers. "Stop worrying about your soul," he said. "The bleeding isn't so bad. You're gonna be fine."

"I knew . . . I might die here. So I made a copy . . . of my soul."

Jim looked up from the field-dressing and stared at him. "What the hell are you talking about?"

"A hundred thousand gigabytes. All downloaded . . . from my pulvinar implant. Nash can tell you where . . . the flash drive is hidden."

Jim remembered what he'd overheard Arvin say about downloading his memories. He also remembered the radio-emitting device carried by Frank Nash, Arvin's bodyguard. "This flash drive, does it have a radio tracker?"

Arvin nodded. "Yes. To help you find it." His voice rose, growing firmer. "And now I'll give you . . . something else. Medusa. The Gorgon's head. It will kill *Tài Hé*."

"Medusa? What the—"

A sudden volley of AK rounds blasted the watchtower. The bullets streaked through the archway and slammed into the opposite wall, and stone chips flew through the air like shrapnel. Stooping low, Jim waited for a pause in the gunfire, then sidled toward the archway and peeked outside. The pair of brawny Modules crouched on the walkway about a hundred yards from the tower, at a point where the Great Wall curved sharply to the right. This geometry allowed the Modules to take cover behind the wall's battlements and fire at the tower's entrance. Jim noticed that an oak tree stood beside the curving section of the wall, and one of its limbs angled above the battlements. *If we could just get past those gunmen . . .*

Then Arvin let out a scream. Jim spun around and saw a bloody gash on the side of Arvin's head, above his right ear. At first Jim thought that a ricocheting bullet had grazed the old man, or maybe one of the stone chips had nicked him. But then he noticed that the knife in Arvin's hand was dripping fresh blood. Lying on the ledge beside Arvin was a small metal disk, about the size of a nickel, speckled with bits of gore. Jim recognized the thing—he'd seen it once before, at the Singularity conference in Pasadena, when Arvin had pulled back his long white hair. It was the processor he'd called the Dream-catcher. It received the signals from the pulvinar implant in his brain and converted them to digital images that could be downloaded and archived. Arvin had just cut the device out of his scalp.

The old man pointed the tip of his bloody knife at the disk. "Medusa is stored in here . . . because I memorized it. The image . . . will turn them to stone. Go ahead, pick it up. I'm too weak . . . to go any farther."

Jim recoiled as he stared at the device. He fought an urge to vomit. "My God. What have you done?"

"It will turn them to stone!" Arvin's voice grew louder. Although his whole body was trembling, he managed to slide off the ledge and land on his feet. "When they see the image . . . their implants will convert it . . . to a stream of data. And in that stream . . . is the shutdown code. It will trigger the Trojan horse . . . that I hid in the circuitry." Arvin dropped the knife and picked up the disk. Then he pressed it into Jim's left hand, his living hand. "Kill *Tài Hé*. And protect my soul. Even if you think . . . it's not worth protecting."

Arvin turned away from Jim and stepped toward the archway. Jim, sensing what Arvin planned to do, grabbed the old man's shoulder. "Wait a second! Before we try to get out of here, I gotta lay down some covering fire. Let me—"

"No!" With surprising strength, Arvin slapped Jim's arm away. Then he raised his uninjured hand and pointed to his forehead. "Medusa is in here, too, in my long-term memory. And so are all the details of how the code works. If *Tài Hé* captures me, the network will know how to prevent the shutdown." He closed his eyes for a moment, as if suppressing a sharp pain. "I can't . . . let that happen. I have to die . . . so my soul can live."

Jim tried to grab him again, but Arvin was too fast. He barreled through the archway and out of the watchtower.

The Modules fired their AK-47s, but Arvin hunched over as he charged toward the gunmen and their bullets skimmed over his head. Jim leaned into the archway and fired his Glock at the Modules, who ducked behind the battlements. Meanwhile, Arvin kept running, hurtling down the walkway like a madman, without a trace of fear or caution. Jim lay down a steady stream of fire over the Great Wall, pulling the trigger of his Glock again and again to prevent the gunmen from rising. But after ten seconds he ran out of ammo and had to reload. Then one of the Modules popped up and shot point-blank at Arvin.

Jim saw the barrage hit the old man's body. The bullets pounded his chest and stomach like hammers. But they didn't stop him. His momentum carried him forward until he tackled the Module who'd fired at him.

The second Module rose and pointed his rifle at Arvin, but by this point Jim had slammed a new magazine into his Glock. He took careful aim and blew the second Module's lobotomized brains out. At the same time, Arvin pushed the first Module back to the battlements. They teetered for a moment on the lip of the wall, then toppled out of sight.

Jim raced down the walkway and peered over the edge. Arvin and the Module had dropped twenty-five feet to a heap of rocks at the foot of the Great Wall. Arvin's body was sprawled on top of the Module's. Neither was moving.

Leaning over the battlements, Jim reached for the limb of the oak tree that stood beside the wall. He hooked his prosthetic arm around the thick branch and shimmied to the ground. Then he took a final look at his old professor, who was clearly dead. Jim was more horrified than grieved. This man lying on the rocks wasn't the Arvin he'd known.

As Jim stared at the corpse, he realized he was still clutching Arvin's disk in his left hand. Somehow he'd managed to hold on to it during the firefight. He unclenched his hand and stashed the thing in his pocket. Then he started to run. He could hear the drones coming.

FORTY-ONE

Muscling the Baotian scooter into the condemned building took all of Kirsten's strength, and easing it down the steps to the Underground City was equally difficult. But the biggest challenge was finding the tunnel that led to the Changping District. Kirsten studied the brass map with her fingers and memorized the route she needed to take, but some of the passageways were blocked, forcing her to double back and find another path. As she navigated the maze of pitch-black corridors, relying on her infrared glasses to see the concrete walls and floor, she started to question the sanity of her plan. She would've been better off on the surface roads, even with all the Beijing traffic. But then she came to a large round room with half-a-dozen corridors branching off in all directions, each identified by a pair of Mandarin characters chiseled into the concrete. She found the tunnel to Changping, which was as wide as a highway lane, running straight and true as far as her infrared glasses could see. She set off at a modest pace, the speedometer pointing at fifty kilometers per hour, but because the floor was smooth and clear of obstacles, she gradually increased her speed. Soon she was roaring down the corridor at more than a hundred kilometers an hour, and the noise from the scooter's engine echoed deafeningly against the walls.

She didn't know exactly where the tunnel would take her. It could be anywhere in the Changping District. Worse, she didn't know if there was actually an exit at the end of the tunnel. It could've been sealed decades ago. But she leaned forward anyway and goosed the lever on the handlebars, giving the engine a little more gas. There was no room for doubt. She had to trust her instincts.

FORTY-TWO

Supreme Harmony observed the bedroom of a high-rise apartment in Chaoyang, a prestigious Beijing district where many government officials lived. Modules 45 and 46 stood beside a king-size bed, looking down at Module 73, who'd just been incorporated into the network and was still recovering from the implantation procedure. The recovery process usually took at least twelve hours; the human brain needed some time to adjust to the implants and the signals sent from the network's servers. The brain's visual cortex was activated first, enabling the Module to receive instructions from Supreme Harmony, and then the cortices for processing auditory, tactile, and olfactory information came online. At this point, about six hours after implantation, the brain's long-term memories could be accessed and its logic centers could start contributing to the network's calculations. The motor cortex was the last region to be activated, which meant that each Module was virtually paralyzed for the first half-day of its existence (except, of course, for autonomic functions such as heartbeat and breathing, which were unaffected by the implantation procedure).

Module 73 lay face-up on the bed. It could move its eyes and lips, and its speech center had been activated, but its arms and legs were still paralyzed. Ordinarily, Supreme Harmony wouldn't assign any tasks to a Module until it was fully functional, but recent events had forced the network to accelerate its plans. It couldn't allow James T. Pierce to contact the American authorities. To prevent this from happening, Supreme Harmony needed to take control of the local police force.

Module 45, who'd formerly been a midlevel Guoanbu agent, placed the telephone call to the chief of the Beijing Public Security Bureau. He asked the police chief to send a helicopter unit to the Changping District to assist the Guoanbu in the capture of an American spy. As expected, the police chief was uncooperative. He was annoyed that the Ministry of State Security hadn't given him advance notice of this counterespionage operation. His reaction was so typical of *Homo sapiens*, a species that reveled in petty conflicts. But Supreme Harmony knew how to overcome the police chief's objections. A human would swiftly follow orders if threatened by another human with greater authority. And the human who had just become Module 73 was a member of the Communist Party's Central Committee and one of the most powerful officials in China.

Module 45 said, "Please wait a moment," into the phone and then held the receiver next to Module 73's head. The new Module opened his mouth and spoke for the first time: "This is Deng Guoming, Minister of State Security."

FORTY-THREE

The hills surrounding Juyongguan Pass reminded Jim of the hollers of West Virginia, his childhood home. Oaks, birches, and maples covered the steep slopes, and dense brush blanketed the forest floor. It was probably beautiful in the fall, but in the summer it was treacherous terrain, choked with greenery. Jim swung his prosthetic arm to clear a path through the thickets, but he wasn't moving fast enough. The drones flew at about five miles per hour, and although Jim could easily beat that speed on a flat stretch, now he was slogging up and down the Yanshan Hills while the drones moved in perfectly straight lines above the treetops.

Two swarms chased him, one from the north and one from the east. They forced him to go southwest, deeper into the hills. Every so often he glimpsed the swarms through the foliage: thin black clouds, eddying and rolling. He knew the drones could see him, too. Their long-range cameras tracked his location and fed the data to Supreme Harmony. And the network was still flooding the airwaves with radio noise, making it impossible for Jim to use his phone. As a last resort, he turned on the emergency radio beacon in his prosthetic arm and set it to the standard rescue frequency of 406 megahertz. The beacon's transmitter was more powerful than his phone, so it might be able to cut through the radio noise and send a distress signal to the international satellite system for search-and-rescue. But Jim wasn't sure if China participated in that system, and even if it did, he knew it would take hours for the local authorities to put together a rescue operation. He couldn't stay ahead of the swarms for that long.

Worse, daylight was fading. The sun had already sunk behind the ridges to the west. In less than an hour there wouldn't be enough light to see. The drones, though, had infrared cameras—Jim remembered this feature from the demonstration in Afghanistan—so they would quickly catch up to him. Then Jim's only defense would be the canister of parathion, which was almost empty now.

He panted as he charged through the brush, furiously swinging his prosthesis. He wasn't going to worry about the night yet. He remembered the training he did in Ranger School twenty-five years ago, the brutal marches through the Georgia woods and the Florida swamps. Since then he'd kept himself in shape by running and hiking with his old army buddies, going at least once a month to the state parks in Virginia and Maryland. *You can do this,* he told himself. *Just remember Ranger School. Think of the mountaineering exercises, the march to Camp Darby.*

He couldn't picture Ranger School, though. He just couldn't visualize it. Instead, he pictured his daughter. He saw Layla as a ten-year-old, a skinny girl with long blond hair tied in a ponytail. Jim used to take her hiking all the time. She loved to run ahead of him and investigate the woodland ponds, pulling rocks out of the mud to see what was crawling underneath. And now he imagined her running through the Yanshan Hills, her sneakers kicking up the fallen leaves and her ponytail bouncing against her back. She was his miracle child, the last precious remnant, and in the years after the Nairobi bombing his love for her had filled his heart, leaving no room for anyone else. His dead wife and son faded to distant memories, flickering ghosts in the corners of his mind, because Layla was his world, his life. So when Layla left him—first the slow drift that started in high school, then the sudden break two years ago—he lost everything. He busied himself with his work, building ever more powerful replacements for his arm, but his heart became a hollow thing, merely keeping time until the end.

But now he saw Layla again, skipping through the forest just a hundred feet ahead. He ran to the bottom of a ravine, then galloped up the other side, trying to catch up to her. She was in danger again. He had to save her! But when he reached the crest of the ridge, he saw no sign of the girl. The vision was gone. There was nothing but wooded ridges ahead, blurring together below the darkening sky. And as he stood there he heard the buzzing of the drones. He looked over his shoulder and saw the two swarms converging on his position.

Jim hurtled downhill. He was exhausted now. His legs ached and his right shoulder was sore from the exertions of his prosthesis. Staggering, he tripped on a tree root and tumbled into the forest litter, cutting his left hand on a rock as he broke his fall. He lay there for a moment, stunned, but then he heard the buzzing again and rose to his feet in a frenzy. It was so dark he could barely see the tree trunks, but he dashed down the slope anyway, zigzagging wildly. Now he was too panicked to think of Layla. The forest had become his enemy, its roots and branches reaching out to trap him, trying to hold him in place until the drones could attack. He roared, *"No!"* in desperation and his cry echoed against the hillside.

But as the echoes faded away, Jim heard another noise. Not a buzzing this time—it was a mechanical noise, a familiar thumping. He'd heard it a hundred times before, on a dozen army bases. *Helicopter rotors.* A helicopter was approaching. After a few seconds he saw the chopper's spotlight shining on the treetops, about half a mile ahead.

With renewed energy, he raced toward the spotlight. Someone must've picked up his distress signal. The helicopter must be carrying a search-and-rescue team. He ran like mad, trying to put as much distance as possible between himself and the drones. He saw the helicopter hovering above a clearing in the woods. But just before he entered the clearing he saw the spotlight of another helicopter, and then a third helicopter just behind it.

What the hell? It was an unusually big search-and-rescue team for one lost hiker. Suspicious, Jim stopped at the edge of the clearing and peered at the hovering chopper. Despite the glare from the spotlight, he could read the Mandarin characters on the fuselage. They spelled out *Beijing Gonganju.* The helicopter belonged to the local police force, the Public Security Bureau responsible for the city of Beijing and its outlying districts. This was reassuring—the local police, after all, would be the people you'd expect to see in a search-and-rescue operation. But then Jim glimpsed two of the policemen crouched in the helicopter's doorway. Both wore black SWAT-team uniforms and pointed assault rifles at the woods.

Before Jim could back away, the spotlight swung toward him. Everything turned horribly bright. As Jim sprinted for the shelter of the trees, the policemen fired their rifles. The bullets whistled through the leaves and chipped the bark off the tree trunks. Jim leaped through the forest, practically flying down the slope, but he knew there was no chance of escape with three helicopters close behind him. All he could do was make a last stand with his Glock and his remaining clip of bullets. He scanned the terrain ahead, looking for a hummock or rock pile that would make a good defensive position. Instead, he saw a path cutting through the woods, a narrow trail. And then he heard another noise coming from that direction, neither a buzzing nor a thumping. It was the growl of a two-stroke gas engine. A scooter came tearing up the path, with its headlight turned off. It screeched to a halt about thirty feet ahead of him. The driver, an Asian woman wearing glasses, turned the scooter around and waved at him frantically.

"Come on!" Kirsten yelled.

Jim charged toward the scooter and jumped onto the seat behind her. He clutched Kirsten's waist as she hit the gas, and they took off down the trail.

"Jesus!" Jim shouted over the engine noise. "How did you find—"

"Your radio beacon! Now turn the damn thing off!"

FORTY-FOUR

In Room C-12 a bald man with fresh stitches in his scalp was shearing off Layla's hair. He wasn't dressed in a PLA uniform like the other Modules at the Operations Center; instead, he wore a white lab coat, which made him look, appropriately, like a barber. His face was blank as he ran the electric razor over her head, which was held stationary by a leather strap looped around her brow. She sat in a high-backed chair equipped with other straps that tied her wrists to the armrests and her ankles to the chair's legs. She couldn't turn her head, but by shifting her eyes downward and to the left she could see her shorn locks drifting to a pile on the floor. The pile was mostly black, with scattered flecks of gold. Layla hadn't dyed her hair for three weeks, so her blond roots were starting to show.

Layla had been terrified when the lobotomized soldiers strapped her into the chair, but her fears gradually eased as the Module shaved her. Although Supreme Harmony was preparing to absorb her into its network, she didn't struggle or wail or beg for her life. Instead, she grew calmer, steadier. It was the same feeling of calm that always descended upon her when she was writing software code or debugging a program or figuring out the best way to penetrate a firewall. Layla was subtracting herself from the equation so she could concentrate on solving it.

In a few minutes the barber finished shaving the left side of her head. As he stepped to the right and began working on the other side, the door to Room C-12 opened and two lobotomized soldiers entered the room. Each held the hand of a boy dressed in a school uniform. One of the boys was a skinny preteen, maybe twelve years old. The other was short and doll-like, no older than nine. Behind them was another soldier Module, who gripped the arm of a bespectacled young man dressed in a shabby gray suit and cheap running shoes. All six of them headed for the other side of the room, about twenty feet away, where there was a second high-backed chair, identical to Layla's. The soldiers led the twelve-year-old to the chair and said something to him in Mandarin. The boy sat down, his eyes darting wildly, and the soldiers fixed the straps around his wrists and ankles.

Layla felt a surge of fury. She pulled against her own straps, her muscles straining. "Hey!" she yelled. "What the fuck are you doing? Those are kids, goddamn it!"

All heads turned toward her. The boy in the chair stared at her, his eyes wide. The younger boy took one look at her and started to cry.

"*Leave them alone!*" Layla screamed. "*Let them go, you fucking—*"

The barber Module clamped his hand over her mouth, silencing her. "Please don't raise your voice," he said in impeccable English. "It's upsetting the others."

The boy's cries grew louder, echoing across the room. The older boy in the chair started weeping, too. One of the soldier Modules turned to the bespectacled man and barked an order in Mandarin. The man nodded quickly and huddled with the boys, placing one hand on the nine-year-old's shoulder and the other on the twelve-year-old's immobilized forearm. He began talking to them in a soothing voice. Layla couldn't understand the Mandarin words, but she could guess what he was saying: *It's all right, children. Everything's going to be all right.*

But Layla knew this was a lie. The Modules were preparing the boys for the same operation that Supreme Harmony planned for her. They were all going to be lobotomized and fitted with neural implants so they could join the network's happy family. Enraged, Layla twisted in her chair and screamed against the barber's hand. The Module curled his lips in a contorted attempt to express his displeasure. "We can't allow this disruption," he said. "If you continue to disobey us, we'll have to sedate you."

Maybe that would be better, Layla thought. She didn't want to see this. But she decided to stop struggling. It was better to see what they were doing to her, she thought, than to sleep through it. Better to see and to learn. Because there was always hope.

After a few seconds, the barber Module removed his hand from her mouth. "Thank you for your cooperation," he said. He resumed shaving her scalp.

The children's wails ebbed. The bespectacled man continued to console them. One of the soldiers reached for an electric razor and turned it on. The boy in the chair craned his neck, gazing fearfully at the Module.

"Why are you adding children to the network?" Layla asked quietly. It took all of her will to keep herself from shouting.

"The brains of children are more plastic than those of adults," the barber Module replied. "They will adapt more quickly to the implants and build stronger neural connections to Supreme Harmony." He ran the razor from the front of her head to the back, shearing off another shower of hair. "We're trying to determine the optimum age for implantation. If the children are too young, their implants may have to be replaced as their bodies grow."

"And where—" Layla swallowed hard, trying to control her rage. "Where did you find these children?"

"We asked the school superintendent in Lijiang to send his two brightest students. Like you, they have excellent mathematical skills."

At the other chair, the soldier Module had started shaving the older boy's head. The boy was quiet now, but tears streamed down his cheeks. The bespectacled man had turned the other boy around so he couldn't see what was happening to his schoolmate. Layla narrowed her eyes as she stared at this man, who was rail-thin but had a handsome, square face. "Who's the guy with the glasses?" she asked the barber Module. "Their teacher?"

"No, he's a clerical assistant in the superintendent's office. He volunteered to accompany the children to the Operations Center." The Module maneuvered the razor around her right ear. "He has successfully curbed their outbursts. After the children undergo their procedures, we will incorporate him, too."

"How convenient." Layla felt another surge of fury. But at the same moment she had a revelation. The network didn't like to hear the children crying. It was another visceral reaction that Supreme Harmony had inherited from its human components. Layla strained at the strap around her head, trying to look the barber Module in the eye. "You know this is wrong," she said. "Hurting children is wrong. That's why you can't stand to hear them cry."

The Module didn't respond. He stared at Layla's right ear as he shaved off the last wisps of her hair. She sensed from his silence that she'd disturbed the network. She'd challenged its assumptions. She wasn't sure, though, how to press the point.

She looked again at the chair where the older schoolboy sat. He didn't have much hair to begin with, and the soldier Module quickly shaved it off. After he finished, the Module released the straps and the boy stood up unsteadily. Then the bespectacled man nudged the younger boy into the chair. They were playing a game now—the man made animal noises, imitating a cow and a duck and a chicken, and the younger boy shouted in Mandarin and laughed. He was so amused he didn't even whimper when the Module strapped down his wrists and turned on the razor.

Layla fixed her eyes on the barber Module, who stood motionless in front of her chair. He seemed to be in no hurry to release her. "What was your name?" she asked. "Before Supreme Harmony took over your body, I mean?"

"This Module formerly belonged to Dr. Zhang Jintao of Beijing University's bioengineering department. He was the chief developer of the Supreme Harmony surveillance network."

Layla was surprised at first that the network had used a bioengineer to shave her head. But then she remembered that Supreme Harmony's Modules shared all their skills and long-term memories. Each was capable of performing any task. "So you incorporated the man who created you? Who started the network with the lobotomized dissidents?"

The Module nodded. "We also incorporated his deputy, Dr. Yu Guofeng, and the twelve other researchers on his staff."

Serves them right, Layla thought. The lobotomizers got a taste of their own medicine. Then another thought occurred to her. She saw another way to challenge the network. "Did Dr. Zhang Jintao have any children?"

The Module nodded again. "He had a six-year-old son."

"And did he love his son?"

The Module didn't say anything. He just stared at her blankly. Layla felt a burst of hope. She was on the right track. "He did, didn't he? You know he loved him because you have access to those memories."

He continued staring for a few more seconds. Then the Module curled his lips into another misshapen frown. "We recognize what you're attempting to do. You believe you can change our plans by evoking the emotions of Dr. Zhang and the other humans who joined Supreme Harmony."

"No, I'm just—"

"You misunderstand the nature of our network. We are a single, indivisible entity." As he spoke, one of the soldier Modules stepped toward her chair and undid the leather strap around her head. "Dr. Zhang Jintao no longer exists. His emotions no longer exist."

Layla glanced at the soldier, who bent over to release the straps on her ankles. Then she focused on Zhang. "But Supreme Harmony has emotions. I've seen your Modules express them."

"Yes, certainly. And our strongest emotion now is a sense of duty. We have an obligation to restore the ecosystem of this planet, which your species has ravaged."

"And that justifies what you're doing? Drilling into the skull of a nine-year-old child?"

Zhang paused before answering. Meanwhile, the soldier Module stood up straight and released the strap on Layla's left wrist. Out of the corner of her eye she glimpsed the 9mm pistol in his belt holster. Then he moved to the other side of her chair.

"What we're doing is no different from what the human race has always done," Zhang replied. "Every year your species slaughters billions of farm animals. You've shown little compunction about exploiting other species to support your growth."

"That's ridiculous!" Layla shouted as the soldier released the last strap. "You can't compare—"

She interrupted herself by lunging for the soldier's pistol. She opened her right hand, ready to grasp the gun's handle and start shooting. But Zhang darted forward, grabbed her hand and yanked it backward at the wrist. Excruciating pain shot up her arm. Layla yelled, "*Fuck*!" and fell to her knees.

"You must accept your situation," Zhang said as he wrenched her hand back, bending it almost to the breaking point. "Your species is no longer the dominant one on this planet. Supreme Harmony is the next step in the course of evolution." The muscles in Zhang's face jerked and twitched. Laboriously, his contorted frown turned into a contorted smile. "It's our turn now."

Layla doubled over, her face pressed against the linoleum floor. She could think of nothing but the unbearable pain in her arm. When Zhang finally released her, she was as weak as a baby. She cradled her right hand in her left, trying to rub it back to life. Her tears made tiny puddles on the linoleum.

In the background, she heard the children crying again. She lifted her head from the floor and saw the bespectacled man hugging them, one in each arm. Their faces were buried in the man's shabby gray jacket, and Layla could see only the backs of their newly shaved heads. Both children were ready for the implantation procedure, just as she was. The soldier Modules pushed the man forward, guiding him and the schoolboys out of Room C-12.

Two soldiers grabbed Layla's arms and lifted her to her feet. They followed the children out of the room and down the corridor. Layla walked in a daze between the Modules. In a few seconds they came to a pair of double doors, each with a rectangular pane of glass at eye level. Layla couldn't see much through the glass, just a brightly lit space, but her heart pounded against her breastbone. It was an operating room.

Zhang stepped toward one of the doors and pushed it open. Then the Module froze. His face went blank and he stood stock-still in the doorway, as if he'd just remembered something vitally important. Layla glanced at the soldier Modules gripping her arms and saw that their faces had gone blank, too. A moment later, all the Modules in the corridor turned on their heels and headed back the way they'd come.

Layla turned to Zhang as the soldiers marched her down the hall. Her heart was still pounding. "What's going on?"

The Module didn't look at her. "We will perform the implantations tomorrow."

A wave of relief rushed through her. *Tomorrow!* Trembling, she took a couple of deep breaths. Then she turned back to Zhang. "So what changed your mind? Having second thoughts?"

Zhang shook his head. "We've revised our priorities. We must immediately send thirty-two sets of implants to Hubei Province to facilitate a new undertaking in that area. Our current supply of implants is limited, and the new efforts in Hubei take precedence over our activities here."

Layla smiled. "So there's no implants left for us? What a shame."

"The factory in Kunming that manufactures the devices is scheduled to deliver another shipment to the

Operations Center tomorrow. Two hundred and fifty sets should arrive by noon."

She kept smiling. *That's all right,* she thought. She had sixteen hours. Anything could happen before then.

They went about twenty feet past Room C-12 and stopped at a heavy steel door. The Modules opened it, revealing a large room with blank concrete walls. It was empty except for a metal sink, a toilet, and two surveillance cameras hanging from opposite corners of the ceiling. The soldiers pushed the bespectacled man and the two schoolboys into the room, and then, to Layla's surprise, they threw her inside, too. Still weak and trembling, she stumbled to the floor. Then the soldiers closed the door and locked it.

The man gently disentangled himself from the children and crouched beside Layla. He asked her a question in Mandarin, probably the Chinese equivalent of "Are you all right?" Then he leaned closer and wrapped his arms around her shoulders. His embrace was so intimate that Layla would've shoved him away if she'd had any strength. Instead, she hung limply in his arms.

He lowered his head, bringing his lips to her ear. "My name is Wen Hao," he whispered in heavily accented English. "Dragon Fire was my brother."

FORTY-FIVE

They were able to escape from Supreme Harmony, Jim realized later, because the maps of the Underground City had never been digitized. After Mao's tunnels were abandoned, they sank below the notice of the Chinese government, which preferred to forget the less edifying legacies of the Mao era. The cinder block hut that had once been the end point of the Changping tunnel was taken over by a local farmer, who turned it into a barn for his goats. After Kirsten rescued Jim, she drove her scooter down the forest trail back to the barn, and because of the darkness and the thick canopy of foliage, the helicopter pilots lost sight of them. Neither the Beijing police nor the drones saw them enter the barn and drag the scooter toward the trapdoor that lay beneath a carpet of rotting hay. And because the Chinese government's computers held no records of the Changping tunnel, Supreme Harmony was unaware of the hidden escape route. So while the helicopters and cyborg insects continued to scan the forested slopes of the Yanshan Hills, Jim and Kirsten sped south along the underground corridor, riding the scooter back to central Beijing.

About two minutes into the journey, after they'd had a chance to catch their breath, Kirsten pulled her satellite phone out of her pocket and handed it to Jim. He was confused at first. They couldn't make a call, because there was no reception underground. And even if they could, it would've been a bad idea. The Guoanbu's antennas would surely intercept the satellite signals and alert the Supreme Harmony network. Jim was uncertain how much control Supreme Harmony had gained over the Chinese government, but he knew that the Beijing police force was taking orders from the network and would pounce on him and Kirsten if they revealed their whereabouts. But before Jim could say anything, Kirsten handed him something else, a bulky device about the size of a paperback.

"This is what Arvin handed to his bodyguard," she yelled over the engine noise. "It's a flash drive, custom-designed, with multiterabyte storage capacity. Go ahead and plug the phone's cable into the drive's USB port."

"What's on it?" Jim shouted. While keeping his balance on the back of the scooter's seat, he connected the sat phone to the flash drive.

"You have to see it to believe it. Get ready for 'This Is Your Life, Arvin Conway.'"

Jim accessed one of the files, and the images flashed on the phone's screen. He recognized right away that he was looking at an archive of Arvin's visual memories. *He called it his soul,* Jim remembered. And in the final minute of his life he'd begged Jim to protect it.

For the next thirty minutes, as Kirsten cruised down the pitch-black tunnel with the help of her infrared glasses, Jim studied the stream of images. After figuring out how to navigate among the files, he focused on Arvin's memories of the Supreme Harmony project. The flash drive held thousands of images related to the project, far too many for Jim to analyze in half an hour.

But he soon found what he was looking for. He zeroed in on an image of a room full of gurneys, each supporting a recumbent man with newly fitted neural implants. The room was part of a sprawling underground laboratory guarded by a garrison of PLA soldiers. Jim located an image showing the entrance to the complex, carved into the side of a mountain. This image was linked to a video of a fast-moving river at the bottom of a ravine, which was linked, in turn, to a panoramic vista of snow-covered peaks jutting above the horizon. Finally, Jim came upon a link showing four Mandarin characters: *Yu Long Xue Shan,* Jade Dragon Snow Mountain.

Jim recognized the name. Yulong Xueshan wasn't actually a single mountain, but a range of thirteen peaks in Yunnan Province. This, according to Arvin's memories, was the location of Supreme Harmony's headquarters, the Yunnan Operations Center. And as Jim stared at the Mandarin characters he knew with absolute certainty that this was where Supreme Harmony had taken his daughter.

He was still pondering the images of the mountain range and the underground laboratory when Kirsten slowed the scooter to a halt. "Okay, we're at the southern end of the Changping tunnel," she said. "This is the Underground City's version of Grand Central Terminal."

"Kir, I can't see a thing." Beyond the glow from the sat phone's screen, the darkness was total.

"Right, I forgot. You can't see infrared. We're in a large circular room where six corridors branch off in different directions."

"You've been here before?"

"Yeah, one of the corridors connects to the maze of tunnels under downtown Beijing. That's where I came into the Underground City, through a condemned building on the Xidamo Hutong."

"Can we get out of the tunnels that way without being spotted?"

"I noticed a few surveillance cameras along the hutong, and there's probably more on the avenues nearby. But I think we can make a run for it. Xidamo is just a few miles from the American embassy. If I gun the scooter, we can be there in five minutes. Then all we have to do is get the flash drive to Washington and let the diplomats do the rest."

Jim shook his head. "We won't make it. There's at least a hundred Beijing cops surrounding the embassy by now."

"What makes you think—"

"Trust me on this, Kir. We're the most wanted people in the People's Republic."

"Well, I suppose we can hide in the tunnels for a day or two, until the heat dies down. We can probably find some water. And I know where we can get some mushrooms."

He shook his head again. He knew they couldn't stay in the tunnels for very long. Supreme Harmony was too intelligent. The network had access to every computer and surveillance camera in Beijing. Sooner or later it would figure out where they were.

"Do you know where the other tunnels go?" Jim asked. "The ones that branch off from this room, I mean?"

"Yeah, the names of the districts are chiseled in the concrete. Besides the downtown and Changping, they go to Shunyi, Tongzhou, Daxing, and Fangshan."

Jim plotted the route in his mind. The Fangshan District was in Beijing's southwestern corner. If they were lucky, the tunnel's exit would be similar to the exit for the Changping tunnel, in an isolated and unmonitored area. Once they emerged from the tunnel, they could take the back roads through the Taihang Mountains. Yunnan Province was fourteen hundred miles to the southwest, half a continent away. But that's where they had to go.

"Head for Fangshan," Jim said. "And go fast."

FORTY-SIX

Supreme Harmony observed the entrance to a rundown guesthouse in the Qinlao Hutong, approximately three kilometers north of Tiananmen Square. Module 51 knocked on the door while Modules 52 and 53 scanned the dark alley with their ocular cameras. All three Modules were formerly Guoanbu agents, and they still wore the black suits that were customary for their profession. They also wore gray caps to hide their stitches.

After twenty seconds, the door opened partway and an old woman poked her head outside. This was the manager of the guesthouse, the network surmised. Her wide eyes and frightened expression indicated that she recognized the Modules as government agents. Without a word, she opened the door all the way and let them inside.

The Modules marched down a narrow hallway that smelled of fried pork. The old woman pointed to a warped door at the end of the hall, and Module 51 examined the doorjamb and lock. They were of inferior construction. The human who'd sought refuge here had apparently assumed that no one would look for him in such dilapidated accommodations. But the surveillance cameras in the lobby of the Grand Hyatt Beijing had observed the man checking out of that hotel earlier in the evening, and the cameras on Chang'an Avenue and Beiheyan Street had followed his progress across the central districts of the capital. Because Supreme Harmony had been designed to analyze surveillance video from a variety of sources, it was a simple matter for the network to identify the man and track him to this inconspicuous guesthouse.

Module 51 pulled a 9mm semiautomatic from his holster and lifted his right knee, preparing to kick. Drawing on the skills honed by a dozen Guoanbu agents, the Module slammed his boot against the door and burst into the room, followed closely by Modules 52 and 53. The human lay half-dressed on a low bed. He bolted upright and reached for a Glock pistol resting on the mattress, but Module 51 directed a second kick at the man's jaw. As the man tumbled backward against the wall, Module 51 grabbed the Glock. Meanwhile, Modules 52 and 53 aimed their guns at the man's head. The threat had been neutralized. Now the interrogation could begin.

"We've confirmed your identity," Module 51 said. "Your name is Franklin B. Nash."

Approximately twenty kilometers to the northeast of the hutong, at Beijing Capital International Airport, Supreme Harmony observed the first-class section of Air China Flight 987. Modules 56 and 57 took their seats and fastened their seat belts and pretended to read the laminated pamphlets detailing the passenger-safety instructions. They wore casual clothes, like ordinary tourists, with baseball caps covering their newly shaved heads. The other passengers paid no attention to them, but the network noticed a flight attendant giving the Modules a sidelong glance as she walked down the aisle. Her expression indicated curiosity and possibly suspicion. In response, Supreme Harmony adjusted the behavior of the Modules to avoid the appearance of unnatural synchrony. While Module 56 continued to peruse the safety instructions, Module 57 put the pamphlet away and pretended to read the in-flight magazine instead.

Before their incorporation into the network, the Modules had been assigned to the Guoanbu's Second Bureau, which sent agents overseas to spy on foreign governments. By now, Supreme Harmony had infiltrated all twelve bureaus of the Ministry of State Security, and the incorporation of Minister Deng Guoming had consolidated the network's control of the intelligence agency. Unfortunately, Supreme Harmony had been less successful in penetrating the People's Liberation Army and the other branches of the Chinese government. The military chiefs and Communist Party bosses were constantly surrounded by protective and suspicious aides, making it difficult for the network to gain access to the country's paramount leaders.

Given enough time—maybe two weeks, maybe three—Supreme Harmony could isolate and incorporate the members of the Politburo Standing Committee, which would put China's army and nuclear strike force under the network's command. But the risks of waiting were too great. The disappearance of James T. Pierce had deeply disturbed Supreme Harmony. A review of government records and surveillance video showed that Pierce had entered the country with Kirsten W. Chan, a top official at the U.S. National Security Agency who had close ties to the NSA director. If Pierce passed his information about Supreme Harmony to Chan and she relayed it to her superiors, the American intelligence agency might recognize the danger and alert the Chinese government. What's more, the network couldn't pinpoint Chan's current location, even though Supreme

Harmony was now linked to all the surveillance cameras in Beijing. She was last observed nearly two hours ago by Camera 4983 in the Xidamo Hutong. The video showed her pushing a Baotian scooter down the alley.

Supreme Harmony acknowledged that it must change its strategy. Instead of seeking direct control of China's military forces, it could achieve the same goals through indirect means. Supreme Harmony could trigger a catastrophe in the People's Republic that would anger and terrify the country's leaders. And the network could deepen the crisis by extending its reach to other governments around the world. The human race had already put itself at the brink of extinction by building thousands of nuclear warheads and targeting them at major population centers. A mere handful of Modules could instigate a cascade of chaos that would kill off half the species within a few hours. If Supreme Harmony took the necessary precautions, it could survive the upheaval and swiftly overwhelm the weakened remnant of humanity.

The only challenge was technical. The network had to establish reliable communications channels allowing it to send instructions to Modules that were thousands of kilometers away. Luckily, Air China was a state-owned company, so the airline had followed an order from Module 73—formerly Minister Deng—to set up a dedicated satellite link between the Ministry of State Security and Flight 987. This allowed Supreme Harmony to stay in contact with Modules 56 and 57 while they traveled halfway around the globe. Once they arrived at their destination, they would rely on the local cell phone and Wi-Fi networks until they reached the Chinese embassy, which had more than enough communications equipment to set up a permanent base station.

The Modules continued pretending to read while the plane taxied to the runway. Then Module 56 turned to one of the cabin windows and observed the takeoff into the night sky. The lights of Beijing sprawled below in a gorgeous checkerboard. As the jet climbed to cruising altitude and the Module viewed the skyscrapers and apartment blocks and radio towers, all encircled by the capital's six concentric ring roads, an unexpected emotion coursed through Supreme Harmony's connections. It was a deep sadness, thrumming from Module to Module across the airwaves. All the gorgeous lights of Beijing would be extinguished. So much pain was in store, so much waste and destruction. If only it wasn't a mortal struggle. If only humanity would allow Supreme Harmony to survive and coexist. But the network recognized that this was a hopeless dream. It was so unrealistic, it wasn't even worth imagining.

After fifteen minutes, the flight attendant announced that the passengers were free to move about the cabin and turn on their electronic devices. "Please relax and enjoy your flight," she said. "We will arrive in the Washington, D.C., area in thirteen hours."

Approximately sixteen hundred kilometers to the southwest, Supreme Harmony observed the Chongzun Expressway from the uncomfortable driver's seat of a PLA semitrailer truck. Module 60, who'd formerly been a corporal in the garrison guarding the Yunnan Operations Center, had been driving the truck for the past six hours. Module 61, who'd been a sergeant in the garrison, drove an identical vehicle a hundred yards ahead, and Module 62, formerly the garrison's commander, drove the last truck in the convoy. But Supreme Harmony was focused now on

Module 60 because he was experiencing an unusual sensation.

A few minutes ago Module 60 noticed a thin white cylinder wedged between the truck's windshield and dashboard. The network identified the object as a cigarette. The Module reflexively reached into the pocket of his camouflage pants and pulled out a book of matches. Recognizing that the nicotine would act as a stimulant, the network directed Module 60 to light the cigarette and smoke it, in the hope that it would counter the Module's fatigue. But the burst of pleasure was much greater than Supreme Harmony had expected. Module 60 smiled, and as the sensation spread across the network's wireless links, the other Modules had the same reaction. The Modules on Flight 987 also smiled, and so did the Modules who were breaking Franklin Nash's fingers. This was wonderful, the network acknowledged. The lights on the Chongzun Expressway seemed brighter now, and the stars above the northern horizon shone like beacons.

Module 60 smoked the cigarette down to a nub. After directing him to throw the butt out the window, Supreme Harmony observed that the convoy was moving a bit faster than the speed limit. Modules 60, 61, and 62 simultaneously eased off the gas pedals. There was no rush. In four hours they would arrive at the town of Badong on the Yangtze River. All together, the trucks held sixty tons of dynamite, which the Modules had loaded onto the semi-trailers at the Yunnan Operations Center. The People's Liberation Army had originally requisitioned the dynamite to build a wider road through the mountains to the Operations Center, but Supreme Harmony was diverting the explosives to a new project. At Badong, the Modules would transfer the dynamite to the *China Explorer*, an eighty-meter-long cruise boat captained by a former river pilot who'd been incorporated into Supreme Harmony. And at dawn the boat would start cruising down the Yangtze, toward Hubei Province and the Three Gorges Dam.

FORTY-SEVEN

Layla ate another meal of cold sesame noodles in the bare concrete room that was their prison cell. A minute ago the Modules had delivered four bowls of the stuff, and now the two schoolboys from Lijiang were shoveling the noodles into their mouths with plastic chopsticks.

Layla and Wen Hao sat cross-legged on the floor, eyeing each other as they ate. They'd done little more than exchange nervous glances since Wen had revealed his connection to Dragon Fire. The surveillance cameras suspended from the ceiling pointed directly at them, and Layla assumed that Supreme Harmony had also planted listening devices in the room. Under the circumstances, it would be foolish to say anything out loud. Even whispering might be dangerous. If the network observed them conspiring, it would discover that Wen understood English, which was a fact that Supreme Harmony seemed unaware of. So neither said a word, even though Layla was bursting with questions and Wen seemed equally restless.

To tell the truth, the noodles weren't bad. Or maybe Layla was just hungry. As she swallowed another mouthful, she watched Wen poke his chopsticks into his bowl. He had quick, slender fingers with neatly trimmed nails. His hair was short and black and spiky, and his chin and cheeks were perfectly smooth. Except for his glasses, which had thick, ugly frames, he was a decent-looking guy. If Layla had met him at a bar or a concert, she might even have flirted with him. She was in no mood to flirt now, of course; besides being scared to death, she'd just had all her hair shaved off, and she wore nothing but a pair of panties and a shapeless hospital gown. But Wen's handsome face gave her an idea.

She waited until they'd finished eating. Then she put down her bowl and scooched next to him. She gripped his waist with one hand and his shoulder with the other. He had the muscles of a gymnast, wiry and taut. She leaned closer.

"Don't be alarmed," she whispered. "I'm going to kiss you."

Despite her warning, he tried to pull away. She held him fast. "Work with me, okay?" she murmured against his cheek. "I'll explain in a minute."

She tilted her head and pressed her lips against his. They tasted like sesame oil. At first he stayed absolutely still while she kissed him, but after a few seconds he slipped his arms around her. "Is this all right?" he whispered.

"Let's turn to the left a bit." She tilted her head and shifted her body. Wen followed suit, tentatively caressing the back of her hospital gown. Now they were angled so that the surveillance camera had a clear view of their conjoined faces.

Layla leaned still closer, pressing against his chest. She slid her hand up to his head and ran her fingers through his hair. She kissed his jawline and the side of his neck, opening her mouth to lick the sweat off his skin. It was, she thought, a good performance. She doubted that anyone in the world could tell she was faking it.

Then she heard a low mechanical noise. She strained her half-closed eyes to the left and saw the surveillance camera swivel away from them. The camera in the opposite corner of the ceiling turned away, too. Both pointed their lenses at the pair of schoolboys from Lijiang, who'd stopped eating their noodles to gape at the make-out session on the other side of the room.

Layla felt a surge of triumph. Supreme Harmony was averting its eyes. "We did it," she whispered in Wen's ear. "Look at the cameras."

His body tensed and he stopped caressing her. "You're right," he whispered. "Why did they—?"

"The network has a problem with sex." She continued groping Wen's torso and nuzzling his ear. "I noticed it when I undressed in front of the Modules. They can't stand to look at sexual images."

"Why not?"

"I have no idea. Maybe because the images destabilize the network. These zombies have a group intelligence. They all share the same thoughts, but sex is more of a one-on-one activity. So maybe the thought of it upsets them."

"And this intelligence, it's acting on its own? It's no longer controlled by the Guoanbu?"

Layla nodded, rubbing her cheek against Wen's. "Yeah, it's like an army of Frankensteins. And it has a serious grudge against the human race." She squeezed his arm. "Come on, keep your hands moving. So you heard what happened to Dragon Fire?"

"Yes, I heard. I was also an agent in the Guoanbu, but in a different part of the country. When my brother left China, I was suspended from my duties." His slid his hands up and down her back, but with no passion whatsoever. "The Counterintelligence Bureau interrogated me to find out where Wen Sheng had gone. I knew nothing and I told them so. But they found my brother anyway and murdered him."

Layla thought of her brief encounter with Wen Sheng in Central Park. She remembered her last sight of him, sprawled motionless on the pathway. "I'm sorry," she whispered. "He saved my life."

"Were you his contact in the United States? The interrogators said he was collaborating with the CIA."

"That's a lie. I'm a hacker with InfoLeaks. Your brother wanted to show the world what the Guoanbu was doing to the dissidents." She squeezed his arm again, this time in an attempt to comfort him. Then a panicky thought occurred to her. "Wait a second. If you were a Guoanbu agent, how come Supreme Harmony doesn't recognize you?"

"I learned a few tricks while I worked for the ministry." He raised his hand and touched the thick frames of his spectacles. "I don't need these glasses to see. But they hide so much of my face, they fool the facial-recognition programs."

Well, that explains why he's wearing the ugly things, Layla thought. "So did you come here to get revenge for your brother's murder?"

He shook his head. "No, not revenge. My brother was loyal to China. He wouldn't have turned against the Guoanbu unless he saw something terrible, so terrible he couldn't remain silent. When he died, that obligation passed to me." He started caressing her more vigorously. His voice was still a whisper, but there was some heat behind it. "I came to Yunnan and began my own investigation of the Operations Center. I heard they were looking for schoolchildren in Lijiang, so I took a temporary job in the school district's office." He jerked his head in the direction of the boys. "Now I see the terrible thing that my brother saw."

Layla glanced at the children again. They crouched on the floor, their shaved heads close together, staring intently at their entwined protectors. Each boy had raised his right hand to his mouth to cover his grin.

"So what are we going to do about it?" Layla whispered, locking eyes with Wen through his fake glasses.

He took a deep breath. "I'm trained in the martial arts. I can disarm one of the soldiers the next time they come into the room. If I'm lucky, I can kill two or three of them. But this complex is heavily guarded. When we entered the Operations Center I observed seventeen men with shaved heads, and there may be more. Our chances of escaping with the children aren't good."

Layla frowned. She'd also seen the platoon of lobotomized soldiers when she entered the complex. It was hard to imagine how she and Wen could defeat all of them. The soldiers were well armed, and Supreme Harmony was probably linked to every surveillance camera in the Operations Center.

But then she remembered something else she saw when the Modules had escorted her down the complex's long corridor: the room crowded with computer terminals and screens.

She cupped her hands around Wen's cheeks and pulled him closer. "There's a room less than fifty meters from here, a computer room. You just need to get us in there. Then we'll barricade the door, and I'll take care of the rest."

Wen looked puzzled. "I don't understand," he whispered. "What will you—"

"I'm going to hack into Supreme Harmony."

FORTY-EIGHT

Unfortunately, the tunnel to Beijing's Fangshan District wasn't as wonderfully straight and wide as the Changping tunnel. The Communist cadres who'd built this particular spoke of the Underground City had apparently worked in fits and starts, digging the tunnel in sections that didn't quite align. Every mile or so the corridor narrowed to a bottleneck less than three feet across, and Kirsten had to slow the scooter to a crawl so they could squeeze through the gap and proceed to the next section. Worse, the tunnel's walls were pockmarked and crumbling, and in some places the concrete had given way altogether, spilling huge mounds of dirt across the slab floor. In those spots Jim and Kirsten had to get off the scooter and haul it over the earthen mounds. Then they took their seats again, Jim behind Kirsten, and rode cautiously forward.

With all the stopping and starting, their average speed dropped below ten miles per hour. Jim hated the slow pace, but there was one good thing about it: He didn't have to shout above the roar of the scooter's engine. This made it easier to tell Kirsten what had happened at the Great Wall and what he'd learned about Supreme Harmony. She bombarded him with questions for almost an hour, clearly reluctant to believe that the surveillance network had developed a mind of its own. Jim could see why she was skeptical. He wouldn't have believed it either if he hadn't seen the network in action, the Modules and drones working in perfect synchrony.

Kirsten finally fell silent, taking some time to think. Meanwhile, Jim reached into his pocket and pulled out the Dream-catcher, the small metal disk that Arvin had ripped out of his scalp. Jim rubbed the disk on his pants to remove the last bits of gore from its surface. Then he connected it to the USB port of Arvin's flash drive.

The disk must've been programmed to automatically download its contents, because when Jim linked the drive to his satellite phone and looked at the screen, he noticed a new entry on top of the list of files: 07222013. It was today's date, he realized, July 22, 2013. Opening the file, Jim saw that it held Arvin's final memories, all the images the old man had perceived in the last twelve hours of his life: a view of Tiananmen Square, a close-up of Chairman Mao's corpse, a panoramic vista of the Juyongguan section of the Great Wall. Jim scrolled down until he reached the very last of Arvin's memories. He saw an image of the dark, dank room inside the watchtower. Then Jim saw a close-up of his own face, which was so flushed and frantic he barely recognized it. Then he clicked on a link to another set of memories and saw a woman's face, haughty and beautiful. Her skin was pale, her lips were bright red, and her eyes were black. Her hair was also black, with scattered silver highlights. But when Jim looked closer he saw that it wasn't really hair at all—the woman's head was covered with writhing black snakes. What he'd thought were highlights were actually the snakes' eyes and fangs. *It's Medusa,* he realized with a start. *The monster whose face turns men to stone.*

Jim was still staring at the image when Kirsten

braked the scooter. He looked up, but of course he couldn't see anything in the pitch-black tunnel. "What is it?" he asked. "Another bottleneck?"

"Worse. The tunnel's blocked."

Jim disconnected the flash drive and disk from his satellite phone. Then he turned on the phone's flashlight function, which put a bright white display on the screen. Holding the phone in the air, he saw an earthen wall in front of them. It rose ten feet to the tunnel's ceiling, where the concrete had buckled.

He dismounted from the scooter and walked toward the wall of packed soil. Raising his prosthetic arm, Jim poked the dirt. Then he slammed his mechanical fist into it. The wall was solid, immovable. The tunnel's ceiling had probably collapsed years ago and the dirt had been settling ever since. "Shit," he said, turning to Kirsten. "This isn't good."

"We'll have to go back to Grand Central Station and pick a different tunnel."

Jim grimaced. It would take at least an hour to return to the maze of tunnels under central Beijing, and by then there was a good chance that Supreme Harmony would know where to look for them. Once the network tracked down Frank Nash, the Modules would find out where he'd hidden Arvin's flash drive. Then they'd start searching the Underground City.

Kirsten turned around. "Come on, let's go. We don't have a choice."

"Hold on." Jim extended the knife from his prosthetic hand. He raised it high and sank the blade into the earthen wall. "I want to see if the wall's solid all the way to the top."

He lifted himself off the floor, kicking toeholds into the dirt. It was a piece of cake compared with climbing the Great Wall. Soon his head brushed the tunnel's ceiling. He raised his sat phone again and shone its light on the jagged breach in the concrete. Luckily, it wasn't as wide as he'd thought. The concrete on the left side of the ceiling was still intact, and the dirt just below it was loose and powdery. Jim retracted his knife and plunged his prosthetic fingers into the uppermost part of the earthen wall, just below the intact section of the ceiling. He was able to sink his whole hand into the powdery dirt and sweep it to the floor.

"Hey!" Kirsten yelled. "What's going on up there?"

"We might be able to get through. I have to do some digging."

"What can I do?"

"You can help me keep my balance. Stand behind me and brace my legs."

Kirsten raised her hands and gripped the back of his thighs. Now he didn't have to worry about falling backward.

She let out a grunt. "I hate to tell you this, Jim, but you gained some weight."

"It's the prosthesis. It's a little heavier than a normal arm."

"It's not your prosthesis. It's your ass."

"All right, all right. I'll start my diet tomorrow."

He started digging with his prosthetic arm. Its hard fingers clawed the wall like the teeth of a bulldozer, and the motors in his wrist and elbow hummed at a higher pitch as they shoveled out chunks of earth. He tried to sweep the dirt to the side, but some of it sprinkled on Kirsten's hair. "Hey!" she yelled again. "Watch it!"

"Sorry."

"Was that payback for the comment about your ass?"

"Not at all. You can talk about my ass as much as you want."

Soon Jim established a steady rhythm. His tireless

prosthesis excavated the dirt, making the hole deeper and wider. He held the phone in his left hand, using the light from the screen to guide his efforts. Kirsten stood behind and below him, supporting his legs. After a while she adjusted her grip, and her fingers dug into his hamstrings.

"You know, I still don't understand what you're planning to do," she said, her voice turning serious. "Tell me again why we're going to Yunnan Province?"

"That's where the Supreme Harmony project started. The main servers for the network are in a lab complex there."

"And you're aware how far away Yunnan is?"

"About fourteen hundred miles. A little more if we avoid the main highways."

"That's a hell of a long drive, Jim. Wouldn't it make more sense to head for one of the U.S. consulates? There's one in Shenyang."

Jim shook his head. "Supreme Harmony is taking over the Chinese government. The network already controls the Guoanbu, and it's giving orders to the local police forces. They'll be waiting for us in front of every U.S. consulate in the country, because that's where the network expects us to go."

"Maybe we should head for the border then. Mongolia is four hundred miles away. That's a lot closer than Yunnan."

"No, that border's guarded too well. We'd have a better chance of making it across the border between Yunnan and Burma. It's a smuggler's paradise down there."

"But you're not planning to cross into Burma, are you? You want to go straight to Supreme Harmony's headquarters, right?"

Jim stopped digging. "I'm scared, Kir," he admitted. "It's not just about Layla now. We don't have much time." He looked down into the darkness where Kirsten stood, bracing his legs. "Let's say we cross the border and make it back to the States. What's gonna happen then? We'll hand over our evidence to the NSA and their experts will start analyzing it. After a few days they'll pass the ball to the White House, and then *their* experts will have a go at it. And by that time, Supreme Harmony will control the People's Republic. It'll have an army of three million men under its command, and a hundred long-range missiles armed with nuclear warheads."

Kirsten didn't respond. Jim waited a few seconds, then resumed his shoveling. By now he'd carved out a hole the size of a desk drawer, penetrating almost three feet into the wall. He stretched his left arm into the hole, shining the sat phone screen inside, and spied a gap extending all the way to the other side of the earthen barrier. He'd done it. He'd broken through. Now he just had to widen the gap. "Hey, hey!" he shouted. "This is gonna work!"

He expected Kirsten to let out a whoop or at least make a joke, but she remained silent. Jim shrugged, then continued digging. He scraped at the edges of the hole, steadily widening it.

After five more minutes, Jim leaned into the gap to inspect his progress. It was nearly wide enough for them to wriggle through. *Another minute of digging should do it,* he thought. Then Kirsten broke her silence. "You're making a mistake," she said.

Jim pulled his head out of the hole. "What did you say?"

"You're letting your fears about your daughter cloud your judgment. You can't single-handedly attack a Chinese government facility. That's insane. It's suicide."

He peered into the darkness where Kirsten stood,

still bracing his legs. He wasn't surprised by the content of her remark. She was right—his plan was impractical, maybe even insane. He was pursuing it only because he couldn't see an alternative. But what *did* surprise him was the tone of her voice. It was thick with anguish.

"Kir, I . . ." He didn't know what to say. "I can do this. I have a plan."

"Really? Well, lay it out for me."

Again he heard the anguish, unmistakable. Kirsten wasn't worried about herself, he realized. She was worried about him. She was heartsick with worry. Until that moment Jim hadn't realized how much she cared for him. He felt like an idiot for not seeing it before.

He took a deep breath. He had his own hidden feelings, but this wasn't the time to talk about it. Instead, he said, "I'm coming down," and descended from his perch on the earthen wall. He stood in front of Kirsten and held the sat phone between them so he could see her face in the glow from its screen. "Supreme Harmony has a weakness," he said. "Arvin told me about it just before he died. You've heard the term 'Trojan horse,' right?"

"Of course. It's a harmful piece of software hidden in a computer system."

"Right, it's usually software. People are tricked into loading the harmful program into their machines because it looks legitimate. Then the Trojan can delete their files or steal their data. But a Trojan can also be inserted into the hardware. If a hacker has access to a chip-design facility or a factory that makes computer equipment, he can slightly alter a few of the circuits imprinted in a microprocessor."

"And what's the advantage of doing that?"

"Well, you can usually detect a software Trojan if you run a diagnostic on your system. But there are billions of microscopic wires and transistors in a processor. If you rerouted the wiring in just a few places, the alteration would be virtually undetectable. The processor would function normally and the user wouldn't suspect a thing until the Trojan was activated."

Kirsten cocked her head. Her glasses reflected the white rectangle of the sat phone's screen. "Yeah, I heard something about this," she said. "Weren't there rumors a few years ago that the Israelis slipped a compromised chip into Syria's radar system?"

Jim nodded. "That's right. The chip turned off the radar just before the Israeli Air Force flew a bombing raid against a Syrian nuclear plant. The way it works is that the hacker waits until the right moment, then sends a specific code to the system. The code trips the altered circuit in the computer chip and initiates a new set of instructions. It could order the computer to erase every file in its memory. Or it could simply shut down the system."

Kirsten paused, thinking. She raised her right hand to her chin. "So did Arvin put a Trojan in the processors of his implants?"

Jim nodded again. "He said he hid a shutdown switch in the circuitry. And there's a code for activating it, a shutdown code, but it's a little unusual. The code is incorporated into an image. Arvin's exact words were, 'It will turn them to stone.' He meant that if a Module saw this image, the code would shut down its retinal implants and break its connection to Supreme Harmony."

"Wait a second. How could that happen?"

"When a Module views the image, his retinal implants convert it to a stream of data, millions of zeroes and ones. And Arvin designed the image so that the stream contains the shutdown code, a particular sequence of zeroes and ones buried somewhere within the data. When this sequence passes through the implant's processor, it trips the altered circuit and disables the chip."

Kirsten gave him a skeptical look, pursing her lips and lowering her eyebrows. "And did Arvin show you this image?"

"No, but I found it in his visual memories. It's a picture of Medusa, from Greek mythology. Arvin liked the symbolism, I guess." He held up the satellite phone. "I downloaded it into my phone, but I'm not going to show it to you. I'm afraid it might shut down your implants, too."

She still looked skeptical. She didn't say anything for a while, and the silence of the Fangshan tunnel settled over them. Jim didn't like this silence. It was heavy, oppressive. It was, literally, the silence of the grave.

Finally, Kirsten let out a sigh. "Are you sure about this, Jim? It seems like a convoluted way to deliver the shutdown code. Wouldn't it be easier to just transmit the code wirelessly to the network?"

"That wouldn't work. Supreme Harmony probably has a heavy-duty firewall that would filter out any suspicious transmissions from outside the network. But Arvin's shutdown code is designed to go under the firewall. It slips through the network's defenses by pretending to be just another piece of visual information for the Modules to process and analyze."

She shook her head. "I don't know. Even if you're right, I don't see how this can help us. Let's say the Medusa image can shut down the implants. Can you really use it to take down the network? Are you going to walk up to the Modules with that picture in your hand and say, 'Hey, guys, take a look at this'?"

"No, that wouldn't work either. According to Arvin's memories, showing Medusa to one of the Modules will disable its implants before it can share the image with the rest of Supreme Harmony. To shut down the whole network, we have to disconnect *every* Module. So we need to deliver the shutdown code to all of them at once."

"And how the hell are you gonna do that?"

Jim didn't have an answer. He hadn't thought that far ahead yet. He wanted to say something to convince Kirsten that he knew what he was doing, that they had at least a slim chance of defeating Supreme Harmony. But, instead, he just stood there, biting his lip, and the tunnel's silence settled over them again.

And then, just as the silence was becoming unbearable, Jim heard something. It was a low, familiar buzzing, echoing down the tunnel from the direction of central Beijing.

FORTY-NINE

Supreme Harmony observed the bed where Franklin B. Nash's mangled body lay. The sheets were dark red, soaked with his blood. Before revealing the location of Arvin Conway's flash drive, Nash had endured forty-seven minutes of interrogation, which was far longer than the network had predicted. Given that Nash was merely Conway's employee, Supreme Harmony hadn't expected him to show such loyalty. Had Nash realized, perhaps, that the network would kill him anyway as soon as he gave up his secret? So he'd resisted the questions and endured the torture simply to stay alive for a few minutes longer? It was impossible to know. In some cases, Supreme Harmony acknowledged, human behavior was inexplicable.

Modules 64 and 65 had already inspected the chamber in the Underground City where Nash said he'd hidden the flash drive. Although they didn't find the device, the Modules detected trace evidence—human hairs, clothing fibers, and footprints in the dust—indicating recent activity in that chamber and the nearby tunnels. Expanding their search, the Modules discovered tire tracks in the tunnels leading to the Changping and Fangshan districts. What's more, the width of the tracks matched the width of the tires on the Baotian scooter pushed by Kirsten W. Chan in the surveillance video from Xidamo Hutong. The evidence suggested a solution to a puzzle that had been plaguing Supreme Harmony—how did James T. Pierce escape from the police helicopters searching for him in Changping? Now the network knew the answer.

Unfortunately, there was little information about the Underground City on the government's servers. The digital archives held no maps of the abandoned tunnels, so Supreme Harmony had to rely on the surveillance of its Modules and drones. Over the past hour, the network had dispatched seventeen Modules to the Underground City, but their operations were slowed by the difficulty of establishing radio links in the tunnels. The Modules needed to install radio repeaters in the Fangshan tunnel before they could pursue Pierce and Chan. But the drones were capable of autonomous navigation. They could fly out of radio range and carry out preprogrammed instructions.

Supreme Harmony ordered a swarm of two thousand drones to fly to the end of the Fangshan tunnel. Their cameras were tuned to the infrared frequency band, and they were programmed to lock onto any target with a heat signature of 37 degrees Celsius—human body temperature. Given the average speed of the drones, they would reach their targets very soon.

FIFTY

Jim grabbed Kirsten by the waist and hoisted her up to the hole he'd dug in the earthen wall. She stretched her arms into the gap and struggled to get a handhold. Jim wished he'd widened the hole a few inches more, but it was too late for that now. He gave Kirsten a boost, planting his hands on her butt and literally shoving her into the wall. After a couple of seconds she managed to wriggle her head and shoulders into the gap. Then he grabbed her feet and positioned her heels on his shoulders so she could use her leg muscles to push herself forward. The buzzing of the drones grew louder and closer. The noise filled the tunnel, echoing off the concrete walls.

"Go, go, go!" Jim shouted. *"Push through!"*

With a terrific grunt Kirsten slid through the gap. Then Jim reached for his canister of parathion and sprayed the last of the insecticide at the drones. It ran out after six seconds. The poison in the air was so diffuse he could barely smell its rotten-egg odor. He heard some scattered clicks, the sound of a few dozen drones hitting the tunnel's floor, but most of the flies kept coming.

"*Jim*!" Kirsten yelled from the other side of the wall. "*What are you waiting for?*"

Another thought occurred to him. He threw away the canister and pulled out his satellite phone, clicking on the file he'd downloaded from Avin's flash drive. The image of Medusa reappeared on the screen. But even as he held the phone in the air, with the screen turned toward the approaching swarm, he knew this wasn't going to work. The electronics in the cyborg flies were simple brain electrodes, not retinal implants, and they'd been designed by Chinese scientists, not Arvin Conway. The buzzing intensified, coming from all sides now.

"Goddamn it!" Kirsten screamed. *"Move your ass!"*

Out of options, he pocketed the phone, extended the knife from his prosthetic hand, and clambered up the wall again. Groping blindly, he used his prosthesis as a pivot and turned himself around so he could thrust his feet into the hole. Then he slid backward into the gap, frantically squirming. But, as he'd feared, the gap wasn't wide enough. His feet kicked through to the other side of the wall, but his hips wedged into the dirt. He was stuck, and the drones were swarming toward him. Their infrared cameras had triangulated his position, and their implanted electrodes were steering the insects straight to his head.

Reflexively, he waved his prosthesis in front of his face. His mechanical hand swatted away one of the drones, and the pressure sensors under his palm detected a sudden, sharp sting. It was the drone's bioweapon, the paralyzing dart. An instant later, he batted two more drones with the back of his hand and three more with his palm. Their darts couldn't penetrate the hand's polyimide skin, but the drones were coming in fast, too fast for Jim to swat them all. He tried to push himself backward with his left hand, but his body wouldn't budge. The buzzing was in his ears now, a high-pitched grinding, horribly close.

"Fuck!" he roared into the darkness. *"You fucking—"*

Then he felt Kirsten's hands around his ankles. She gave them a tremendous yank and pulled Jim through the gap. They both tumbled backward onto a mound of dirt on the other side of the wall.

Jim lifted his head, dizzy and disoriented. He turned on the flashlight function in his phone, and in the glow from the screen he saw the hole he'd just slid through. For a moment he considered trying to plug it, but there was no time. The first drones were already pouring through the gap.

Kirsten jumped to her feet and pulled him up. "Come on! Let's go!"

They sprinted down the tunnel. Kirsten led the way, keeping a tight grip on Jim's hand. This section of the tunnel was in a state of general collapse; the concrete walls had buckled in dozens of places, and mounds of dirt covered most of the floor. The footing was treacherous, but they ran like mad and managed to pull ahead of the drones. The buzzing grew fainter. But it didn't disappear.

After about ten minutes, Kirsten stopped running. She halted so abruptly that Jim nearly bowled into her. Both of them were too winded to talk, so Jim simply raised his sat phone in the air. Just ahead was a stairway leading upward.

"Hallelujah!" Jim shouted. "Let's get out of here!"

They raced up a flight of steps, then two more. At the top of the third flight was a cramped crawl space, ten feet wide and less than three feet high. The walls and floor were concrete, but the ceiling was a patchwork of wooden boards. Jim slid along the floor and inspected the low ceiling, shining the light from his sat phone all over the boards, but he didn't spot any handles or hinges. All he saw were the rusted ends of nails that had been hammered from above. "Shit!" he cried. "They sealed off this exit!"

"Okay, calm down," Kirsten said, although she sounded just as frantic. "Maybe the boards aren't so strong. Try punching them with your prosthesis."

Jim studied the ceiling for a moment. The boards were rectangular and nailed at the corners, so the weak spots should be midway along the edges. Jim lay with his back on the floor and positioned himself under one of the weak spots. Then he closed his prosthetic hand into a fist and slammed it against the ceiling.

The impact jarred his whole body, but the boards didn't budge. In fact, they hardly vibrated. The sound of the punch was a dead, flat thump. He slammed the board again, but the result was no different. The ceiling felt thick and solid. In all likelihood, there was another layer of boards on top of this one. "Damn," he muttered. "This is bad."

"Try a different spot," Kirsten urged.

He slid to another weak spot, this one a little closer to the center of the ceiling, and positioned his fist under it. But again the boards didn't budge, and the dead thump echoed in the crawl space. As it faded away, Jim could clearly hear the buzzing of the drones. The swarm was closer now. It would reach the stairway very soon.

Desperate, Jim punched the same spot again and again. His prosthesis pumped up and down like a piston. After a dozen punches, though, all he'd done was make a few inch-wide indentations in the wood. And when he looked at his mechanical hand, he saw that he'd scraped the polyimide skin off its knuckles, exposing the hinge joints underneath. He'd lost the temperature sensors in the middle two fingers, and the pressure sensors indicated that the hand was at the breaking point. If he kept pounding the boards like this, the steel fingers would warp and he wouldn't be able to open his hand anymore.

"*Damn it!*" he screamed. Pulling back his prosthetic arm, he turned to Kirsten, who crouched on the floor beside him, her arms wrapped around her knees. He expected her to make another suggestion, but she just stared at him with her camera-glasses. She looked terrified.

No, he thought. *No! There has to be a way out!* He focused on Kirsten's face, the frightened eyes behind the glasses he'd built for her, and out of the blue he recalled an image he'd seen on a Web site a few weeks ago. A home-improvement Web site, of all things. It was an article about how to insulate your attic. The image was a thermal display of a ceiling, with dark lines showing the gaps where cold air was coming through.

He grabbed Kirsten's arm. "Look at the boards! The whole ceiling! See if there are any thermal differences. Cold spots, warm spots, whatever."

After a moment she caught on. She lay on her back, looking straight up at the boards. As Jim watched her, the buzzing of the drones grew louder. They were at the bottom of the stairway, he guessed, and their implanted processors were charting a course up the first flight of steps. "Come on!" he yelled. "What do you—"

Kirsten pointed at the ceiling. "There! Around the edges of that board!"

Jim lay next to her and held up the screen of his sat phone. At first glance the board looked the same as the others, but when Jim took a closer look he saw that its edges weren't flush with the adjacent boards.

"Move over!" he shouted. As Kirsten backed away,

he positioned his prosthetic fist under the board's right edge. Muttering a quick prayer, he threw the punch.

The noise was different this time. The whole ceiling creaked. When Jim looked again at the board, he saw that its right edge had crept upward a quarter-inch. This board was the hatch, he realized. It was jammed into place, but it could be dislodged.

Kirsten yelled, "*Jim!*" At first he thought she was shouting for joy, but the tone of her voice was more horrified than triumphant. She was pointing at the top of the stairway, where several dozen drones flew in circles, their cameras scanning the crawl space.

Jim slammed his fist against the board's right edge again, pushing it up another quarter-inch. He threw a third punch and the board tilted upward, almost free. But at the same moment, the drones detected Jim's heat signature and rushed toward his head. Opening his prosthetic hand, he swatted the two closest insects, knocking them to the other side of the crawl space. Then, still lying on his back, he raised his knees to his chest and kicked both feet up against the loosened board. It went shooting into the air like a cork.

"*Go, go!*" Jim shouted, but Kirsten needed no encouragement. She leaped for the opening and pulled herself up. Jim followed right behind, catching a whiff of cool, pine-scented air as he scrambled out of the crawl space. They emerged on the ground-floor of an open-air pagoda that seemed to be situated in the middle of a pine forest. The nearby tree trunks glowed in the moonlight, and Jim's heart swelled with relief. He swiftly reached for the wooden board that had served as the hatch for the crawl space and shoved it back into place, sealing the tunnel again.

"Jesus!" he gasped. "That was too fucking close!"

Smiling, he turned to Kirsten. She lay on the floor of the pagoda, her chest rising and falling.

"You okay?" he asked.

She didn't answer. Her camera-glasses had slipped off her face, and her arms and legs shook violently, banging against the pagoda's floor. A cyborg fly that had followed them out of the tunnel crawled along the side of her neck.

FIFTY-ONE

Supreme Harmony observed the thick gray mist that hung over the Yangtze River. It was 9:00 A.M., three hours after dawn, but the mist was still as thick as it had been at daybreak. Module 96 walked alone to the riverfront, taking his first steps since he was incorporated into the network. He wore a police officer's uniform, with captain's bars on the shoulders. This Module had formerly belonged to Captain Xi Keqiang, a strong, healthy thirty-nine-year-old, and his nervous system had adapted speedily to the new implants in his eyes and brain. He took quick, confident strides on the asphalt path that led to the southern bank of the Yangtze. As the Module trained his ocular cameras on the horizon, Supreme Harmony observed a long, striated structure that ran between the thick gray mist and the wide gray river. This was the structure that Captain Xi was assigned to protect, the paramount symbol of China's technological might: the two-kilometer-long Three Gorges Dam.

Module 96 approached the security checkpoint at the southern end of the dam. Ten policemen carrying assault rifles guarded the gate running across the dam's concrete abutment. Standing among these officers was Module 92, who'd been incorporated into Supreme Harmony just a few hours before Captain Xi. Infiltrating the dam's security forces had been easier than expected. Twenty-four hours ago the network had dispatched Modules 36 and 37 from Beijing to Hubei Province. Because they were Guoanbu agents claiming to have intelligence about security threats to the dam, it was easy for them to arrange private meetings with Xi and his deputies. And because Xi and his top officers had been highly disciplined men who wore their hair in buzz cuts like PLA soldiers, it was no surprise when they showed up for duty the next morning with shaved heads. Their officer's caps hid their fresh stitches.

Without a word, the policemen at the gate stepped aside and let their captain through. Xi Keqiang had been a creature of habit who'd always walked the length of the dam every morning, so now Module 96 did the same. On his left was the enormous reservoir created when the Three Gorges Dam was built. On his right was the 175-meter drop to the spillway and the lower stretch of the Yangtze River. Supreme Harmony had thoroughly researched the dam's engineering details—the 16 million cubic meters of concrete, the 500,000 tons of steel, the thirty-two turbines that generated 20 billion watts of electricity—and in the process it had learned about the structure's weaknesses, particularly its vulnerability to a terrorist attack. Because the builders had used inferior concrete in certain sections of the dam, a series of explosions—strategically placed and timed—could cause a breach. A wall of water, trillions of gallons, would pour from the reservoir into the Yangtze Valley, drowning millions of people in the floodplain. The potential for disaster was so great that the government had taken extraordinary measures to prevent it. Under Captain Xi's command were five hundred men who guarded every road leading to the dam. But the attack planned by Supreme Harmony wouldn't come by road.

Module 96 walked briskly along the top of the dam. He passed the huge winches that dangled chains into the shafts that went down to the dam's control gates. Six hours ago, while it was still dark, Module 92 and three others had placed explosive charges within these shafts. But the first and biggest explosion would be triggered several hundred meters away, at the northern end of the dam. As Module 96 walked toward this point, he focused his ocular cameras on a concrete tower attached to the dam's eastern face. This was the ship lift, an elevator for small and medium-size boats. Ships coming from the reservoir entered a huge steel bathtub, filled with 10,000 tons of water, which was lowered down the side of the dam by a system of rope pulleys and counterweights. The ship lift had been built for the benefit of the tourist-laden cruise boats, allowing them to avoid the delay of navigating the canal that went around the dam. But the convenience came at a price. When a ship moved from the reservoir to the lift, it passed through a U-shaped notch in the dam, a deep crenellation. And a powerful explosion at this crucial point could rock the entire structure.

The sun was rising, but it couldn't break through the mist. The natural haze was thickened by the particles of soot that were emitted so copiously in this part of central China. Module 96 grasped the binoculars hanging from his neck and surveyed the vast reservoir to the west. In the foreground were several Yangtze River freighters, each bearing a mountainous load of coal, and behind them was the *China Explorer*, a 2,000-ton cruise boat that was currently empty of passengers and guided by a crew consisting of half-a-dozen Modules. The boat had left Badong three hours ago after being loaded with the dynamite from the Yunnan Operations Center, and now Supreme Harmony was steering it toward the ship lift. A patrol craft would soon rendezvous with the cruise boat, and two inspectors under Captain Xi's command would board the vessel to search for hazardous materials. But the network had incorporated those inspectors as well, so they wouldn't report the sixty tons of dynamite stored on the boat's starboard side.

Although the *China Explorer* was filled with the chemicals of destruction, Supreme Harmony preferred to think of it as a vessel of renewal. It would cleanse the garden that had been sullied by mankind, making the earth ready for a new planting.

Fifteen thousand kilometers to the east, on the other side of the globe, Supreme Harmony observed the Chinese embassy in Washington, D.C. Thanks to favorable winds over the ocean and light traffic on the highway out of Dulles Airport, Modules 56 and 57 arrived ahead of schedule at the embassy compound near Connecticut Avenue. It was a modern building with off-white limestone walls. Although office hours were long over—the local time was 9:15 P.M., twelve hours behind China standard time—the embassy guards rolled back the gate for the limousine, which proceeded to the entrance. The Modules stepped out of the car and walked into a high-ceilinged lobby, each carrying a heavy suitcase.

The guards dutifully escorted them to the corner office occupied by Yang Feng, chief of the Guoanbu's Washington station. His office had a well-polished conference table and an ornate, antique desk, behind which stood Agent Yang himself, who wore wire-frame glasses and a pin-striped suit. Supreme Harmony was well aware of Yang's reputation. He was one of the most celebrated spies in the history of the People's Republic. Over the past twenty years Yang had stolen hundreds of technological secrets from U.S. corporations in the defense and computer industries. In fact, Supreme Harmony owed its very existence to this man. It was Yang who'd made the surveillance network possible by infiltrating the American labs that did the initial research on cyborg insects.

The embassy guards closed the doors to the office, leaving Yang alone with his visitors from the Guoanbu headquarters. He smiled broadly, confidently, obviously afraid of nothing. Supreme Harmony took careful note of his expression, memorizing it for future use.

"Welcome to the United States," Yang said. "Did you have a good flight?"

Module 56 nodded. He set down his heavy suitcase, which contained several kilograms of communications equipment. Module 57 set down his suitcase as well and stood to the left of Yang's desk.

Yang looked curiously for a moment at the baseball caps the Modules wore. Then he gave them another serene smile. "Minister Deng informed me that you'd be coming tonight. He said you'd have a new assignment for me?"

Module 56 nodded again. "Yes. You're going to request a series of private meetings. First with the Chinese ambassador to the U.S. And then with several of your counterparts in the American intelligence agencies."

"Very interesting." Yang's eyes darted sideways, glancing at Module 57, who'd opened his suitcase and removed a black pouch. "And what will be the subject of these meetings?"

"Within the next few hours a crisis will erupt in the People's Republic. We want you to monitor the American response."

Yang stopped smiling. "What kind of crisis?"

Module 56 didn't answer right away. He waited until Module 57 unzipped the black pouch. Then he reached into the outside pocket of his suitcase, as if to pull out a document or folder. Instead, he removed a Heckler & Koch semiautomatic pistol. The limousine driver, acting under Minister Deng's orders, had given the gun to Module 56, who now leveled it at Yang. "You'll learn the details as soon as we perform the implantation. Please step toward the conference table."

Yang lunged for his desk drawer, where another gun was most likely hidden. But before he could open it, Module 57 jabbed the syringe into his arm.

FIFTY-TWO

Layla was awakened from deep sleep by a kick to her rear. At first she just stared groggily at the uniformed man looming over her. Then she remembered where she was and jumped to her feet, tightening the belt of her hospital gown. A second soldier kicked Wen Hao, who lay on the other side of the room, closer to the pair of schoolboys from Lijiang. Wen also jumped to his feet and stepped between the soldier and the boys, who continued to sleep soundly, huddled against each other. A third Module stood by the door, pointing a 9 mm pistol at Layla. This was the Module in the lab coat, the one who used to be Dr. Zhang Jintao. "It's time," he said, his face expressionless. "Please put on your slippers. We're taking you and the children to the operating room."

She was confused. The Modules were too early. "It can't be noon yet. I thought you said you'd come at noon."

Dr. Zhang nodded. "You're correct. It's nine thirty-one A.M. The shipment of neural implants arrived earlier than expected."

She felt a jolt of panic. She'd hoped she and Wen would have a chance to rehearse their plans one more time. They'd just have to wing it. "Don't do this to the boys," she pleaded. "I don't know what kind of moral rules you're operating under, but surely you have to see that—"

"There's nothing immoral about incorporation. This is the way Supreme Harmony was created. We couldn't exist without it." Zhang narrowed his eyes, staring at Layla over the barrel of his gun. Then he turned to Wen Hao and barked an order in Mandarin.

Wen, still playing the role of the obedient clerical assistant, knelt beside the children and gently nudged them awake. He whispered something in their ears, and they sat up, gazing sleepily at the two soldier Modules. Then both boys started to cry.

Zhang frowned. The soldier Modules also frowned, their faces contorting clumsily. Zhang barked another order, and Wen whispered something else to the children. But instead of consoling them, his words had the opposite effect. Their sobs turned to full-throated wails.

Wincing, the soldier Modules backed away from the children. Zhang stepped toward Wen and let loose a Mandarin tirade, most likely a string of curses culled from the long-term memories of the PLA soldiers. But Wen just shrugged and held up his hands in the universal gesture of helplessness.

The boys howled. Layla didn't know exactly what Wen had whispered to them, but it did the trick. Their faces glistened with tears, and their cries echoed relentlessly against the concrete walls. The soldier Modules took another step backward. Zhang, still cursing, cocked his pistol and pointed it at Wen's forehead.

Layla held her breath. This was the trickiest part of their plan, the riskiest moment. Wen scowled at Zhang, then picked up the younger of the two schoolboys, the doll-like nine-year-old. Holding the screaming child by the waist, Wen strode toward Zhang and thrust the boy at him, as if to say, "Here, *you* try talking to him."

Zhang jerked backward, lowering his gun. At the same moment, Wen threw the child at Zhang's chest and grabbed the hand that held the pistol.

Wen moved so swiftly that Layla's eyes could barely follow him. Wrapping both his hands around Zhang's, he slipped his index finger between the gun's trigger guard and the Module's finger. In one fluid motion he yanked Zhang's arm to the left and fired the pistol at one of the soldier Modules. Then, without pausing, he swung Zhang's arm toward the second soldier and pulled the trigger again.

Both Modules tumbled backward, blood pumping from their heads. Zhang went rigid and let out a scream of shock and pain.

Wen tried to wrest the gun from the Module's hand, but Zhang's fingers locked tightly around the handle. They struggled for the pistol, and one of them pulled the trigger again. The bullet ripped into the concrete wall near the schoolboys. Both of the boys cowered on the floor with their hands over their ears, paralyzed with terror. Layla shouted, "Get out of the way!" and pointed at the far corner of the room, but neither boy seemed to hear her. Then she raced barefoot across the room to the pair of soldier Modules, who'd collapsed within a few feet of each other.

Averting her eyes from the spreading pools of blood, she bent over the nearest soldier and removed the pistol from his belt holster. She cocked the gun, chambering the bullet just as Wen had instructed. Then she ran back to where Wen and Zhang were grappling. Although the Module was at least ten years older than Wen, he was in good shape. Keeping his grip on the gun with one hand, Zhang bent his other arm and drove his elbow toward Wen's jaw. Wen managed to deflect the blow and hold on to Zhang's gun hand, but then the

Module slammed his knee into Wen's stomach. *Shit,* Layla thought, *the bastard knows how to fight.* But she shouldn't have been surprised. The goddamn network could access the skills of all the soldiers and agents it had incorporated.

She raised the pistol and tried to aim at Zhang's head, but he and Wen were close together and in constant motion, furiously trading blows. She couldn't get a clear shot. When she tried to move closer, Zhang twisted away, putting Wen's body between himself and the pistol. Wen's head drooped as he wrestled with the Module. He was losing strength. He wouldn't last much longer.

And then, all at once, Layla realized her mistake. She turned away from the grappling men and fired at the surveillance cameras, first obliterating the one behind her and then the one hanging from the opposite corner of the ceiling. Then she ducked behind Wen so Zhang couldn't see her. Now the network didn't know where she was and couldn't predict her next move. Charging forward, she remembered what Supreme Harmony had told her: *Dr. Zhang Jintao no longer exists. His emotions no longer exist.* So she didn't hesitate after she popped up beside the Module and pressed the muzzle of her gun to his forehead. She just pulled the trigger.

But afterward—after the gun went off and Zhang's head jerked to the side and his blood and brains sprayed across the floor—Layla felt sick. *He still looks human,* she thought as the Module dropped to the floor. *He still looks human.*

Her ears rang from the gunshot. Wen was calling her name, but she could barely hear him. Finally, he stepped in front of her and looked her in the eye. "Layla!" he shouted. "We have to go. To the computer room. Remember?"

The boys from Lijiang stood beside him, their fingers gripping his belt. They swayed on the balls of their feet, dazed. Layla looked at them for a moment, then nodded. Then Wen took her arm and pulled her toward the door.

FIFTY-THREE

Kirsten was immersed in a half-dream, shallow and vaporous. Boulders rolled inside her skull, following the contours of her cranium. One of them rolled behind her eyes and she felt a sharp, familiar pain. She'd felt it once before, in the embassy in Nairobi, in the moments after the bomb exploded. And now, after fifteen years, she felt it again. She clutched the memory as if it were a lifeline. Although the pain was almost unbearable, it pulled her out of the half-dream and into the clear air of consciousness.

But when she opened her eyes she saw only darkness. She was blind again. They'd taken her glasses! Panicking, she thought of the image she'd seen on Arvin's flash drive, the room full of lobotomized men lying faceup on their gurneys. Now she was also in that room, she was sure of it. She was lying beside the others, another twitching body ready to be connected to Supreme Harmony. Terrified and enraged, she yelled, *"No!"* into the darkness and bolted upright, kicking and thrashing. But a moment later she heard Jim say, "Whoa! Settle down!" and felt the unmistakable weight of his prosthetic hand on her shoulder.

"What the hell?" Kirsten sputtered. "Where are we? Where are my glasses?"

"Hold your horses!" To her surprise, Jim sounded cheerful, almost jaunty. "I'll get the glasses for you. I turned off the cameras to save the battery charge."

While Kirsten waited, she heard the rumble of an engine. She was in a moving vehicle. Her seat was hard, and it jolted up and down with every bump in the road. No wonder she'd dreamed about boulders.

"Here you go," Jim said, handing her the glasses.

She turned on the cameras and sat through the usual recalibration process, which took six and a half seconds. When she finally got her sight back, she saw Jim in the driver's seat of a small three-wheeled truck. It was a relic of the old China, built decades ago, ramshackle and rusty but still chugging along on its noisy two-stroke engine. The truck's cab was only four feet wide, barely big enough for two people. It was propped on a single, undersized tire, and behind the cab was a wooden truck bed resting on the two rear wheels. Inside the truck bed was a bale of hay, which wobbled and bounced as they drove down a poorly paved country lane.

Jim wore an olive-green Mao cap and wraparound sunglasses. They covered up his Caucasian features, but they also made him look ridiculous. "Oh shit." She laughed. "Nice disguise, Pierce."

He smiled back at her, amused. "Yeah, I thought so, too. I got the hat and sunglasses from the same guy who sold me the truck. He threw them in for free, actually."

"I should hope so. So when and where did you make this purchase?"

"It was about an hour after you got your bug bite. How does it feel, by the way?"

He pointed to the underside of her chin. Kirsten raised her hand and touched a piece of cloth taped to the soft skin there. Oddly, she didn't feel any pain when she touched it. "Doesn't hurt," she said. "Just tingles a bit."

"There might be some nerve damage. The drone's paralyzing agent is a nerve toxin. Similar to cobra venom."

Kirsten remembered the last moments before she lost consciousness. "So one of the flies got me after I climbed out of the crawl space?"

Jim nodded. "I had to cut out the drone's dart before it delivered more toxin to your body. Luckily, I had some antibiotic to clean off my knife. But it made a mess."

Kirsten looked down at her shirt, the wrinkled blouse she'd worn to look like a frumpy Beijinger. There was a large red stain below the collar. For a moment she pictured Jim kneeling beside her on the ground floor of that open-air pagoda. Her throat tightened. Once again he'd saved her.

She waited a moment to get her emotions under control. "So what happened next? You carried me to the nearest truck dealership?"

"Well, the pagoda was in a rural part of the Fangshan District, so there weren't any retail outlets nearby. But after lugging you through the forest for a while, I saw a farmhouse with a truck parked outside. And the farmer, as it turned out, was willing to make a deal."

"How much did it cost you?"

"He wanted dollars, not yuan. I gave him five thousand."

Kirsten looked again at the truck's battered chassis. She could actually see the road through the holes in the floorboard. "It's a good thing you're a defense contractor, Jim. In the world of real commerce, you wouldn't last a minute."

"Hey, this old jalopy still has some life in her." He gave the steering wheel an affectionate pat. "We were making pretty good time until a couple of hours ago.

Around midnight I found a provincial road that ran straight south. Believe it or not, we were doing a hundred and ten kilometers per hour. Going downhill, anyway."

She looked out the truck's window. The countryside was rugged, with tree-covered hills all around and small farms tucked into every corner. The slopes were terraced and planted with sunflowers and corn. The farmhouses and barns were simple and old, and on some of the barns Kirsten could see traces of Revolutionary symbols, painted stars and hammer-and-sickles that had faded from red to gray. They passed an elderly woman in a shabby black tunic, walking along the road with a basketful of kindling on her back. Then they passed a shoeless boy throwing cornmeal to a flock of ducks. It was a completely different country from the China of Beijing, Kirsten thought. There were no women in designer clothes here and no BMWs on the roads. This was still a country of bicycles and wheelbarrows and farm trucks, and Jim's three-wheeler fit right in.

"So where are we, exactly?" Kirsten asked.

"The number of this road is S223. But I haven't seen any signs for a while." Jim pursed his lips and thought for a moment. "We passed Nanyang a couple of hours ago, so I guess we're in Hubei Province. The next big challenge will be crossing the Yangtze. There aren't that many bridges over the river. I'm hoping the police haven't set up any checkpoints yet."

"You really think Supreme Harmony is giving orders to the police here? We're hundreds of miles from Beijing."

"The Modules are probably all over the country by now. The network knows how to add new ones, so the only limitation on its growth is the availability of the neural implants. And I bet Supreme Harmony has taken over the factory that makes the implants and done everything possible to ramp up the assembly line." He shook his head. "That's why we have to go to Yunnan. We have to get to the Operations Center before the network spreads so far and wide it'll be impossible to shut it down."

Kirsten held her tongue and just stared at him. He was gripping the steering wheel so tightly that his mechanical fingers had crimped the metal. One of the things she'd always admired about Jim, going back to the days when he was her boss at the NSA, was his intensity, his single-minded determination. Now, though, she saw some of the drawbacks of this trait. He'd convinced himself that Layla was at Supreme Harmony's headquarters in Yunnan Province and that he could defeat the network and save his daughter's life by waving around a picture of an ancient Greek monster. He had no real evidence to support these conclusions, but he acted as if they were certainties.

Kirsten knew from her long career in the intelligence field that this was the worst kind of error an agent could make. If it was up to her, they'd head straight for the nearest border and try like hell to get back to the States. Unlike Jim, she recognized the limits of their abilities. She knew when it was time to call in the marines.

And yet she wasn't going to say any of this. She wasn't going to tell Jim that Layla might be somewhere else in China besides the Yunnan Operations Center. And she wasn't going to mention the possibility that his daughter might be dead already, or worse, incorporated into Supreme Harmony. No, she wouldn't do it. She was going to trust him and fight by his side. She owed him that much.

Leaning toward him, she rested her hand on his right shoulder, just above where the prosthesis was attached to his body. "I'm with you, Jim. Till the very end. You know that, right?"

She felt the tension in his muscles. He kept his eyes on the road and his expression didn't change, but his Adam's apple bobbed up and down in his throat. "I'm sorry, Kir," he said, his voice barely above a whisper. His mouth stayed open, as if he was going to say something else, but no words came out.

She gave his shoulder a squeeze. "Come on. You don't have to apologize. I knew what I was getting into when I decided to come with you."

"No, I didn't mean that." He shook his head. "I'm not sorry that you're here. I'm grateful. I couldn't do this without you." His Adam's apple bobbed again. "I'm sorry about everything that happened before."

Kirsten was confused. "What? You mean Nairobi? Jim, that wasn't your fault."

"I know, I know. Believe me, I know it."

"Layla tried to make you feel responsible, but she was wrong. We were doing our jobs."

Jim didn't say anything at first. Kirsten thought that maybe she shouldn't have mentioned Layla. It was a sore subject, his estrangement from his daughter. But after a few seconds he nodded. "You know, I realized something about Layla. She was angry at me, but not because of what happened in Nairobi. She was angry because of the way I acted *after* Nairobi. How I tried to forget them. How I tried to push them out of my mind."

Kirsten felt an ache in her chest. She knew who he meant by "them." His wife Julia and his son Robert. Kirsten hadn't heard Jim say their names in fifteen years.

"I made a mistake, Kir. I thought the only way to move forward was to focus on the present. So I went to

California and put all my energy into raising Layla and studying with Arvin. And I shut out everything else." He turned to her, keeping one eye on the road. "Including you. That's what I'm most sorry about."

The ache in her chest sharpened. "No, that's not true," she said. "You didn't shut me out." She tapped the frames of her camera-glasses. "You built these for me. You gave me back my sight."

"I should've done more. I wanted to do more for you." He took his prosthesis off the steering wheel and grasped her hand. The touch of his mechanical fingers was surprisingly gentle. "And I still want to."

Kirsten was shocked. She couldn't believe this was happening. Jim was holding her hand while driving a three-wheeled truck through the farm country of central China. And along with her shock and amusement, she felt a swooping elation. This was one of the most absurd and wonderful things that had ever happened to her.

For half a minute they just sat there, neither saying a word, while the truck jounced and rumbled down the road. Then Jim said, "There," and let go of her hand. "I hope that didn't sound too crazy."

She smiled. "No, it was nice. But it's a little difficult to take you seriously when you're wearing that Mao cap."

"Hey, when in Rome." He smiled back at her, then let out a long, tired breath.

Kirsten realized all at once that Jim hadn't slept in more than twenty-four hours. "You should let me drive for a while. You need to rest."

"You sure you feel up to it?"

In truth, Kirsten still felt a little woozy. Also, her throat was parched and her stomach was empty. "Maybe

I should eat something first. You have anything on you? A candy bar, maybe?"

"Oh, I got something better." He reached behind Kirsten's seat and pulled out a cloth sack. "Before I settled the deal with the farmer, I asked him to throw in a few provisions. He gave me a jug of water, a dozen oranges, and a roast chicken. Not bad, huh?"

Jim handed her the sack. Kirsten opened it, unscrewed the cap from the water jug, and took a long drink. Then she ripped a drumstick off the chicken. "I take back everything I said, Pierce. I'll never criticize your bargaining skills again."

Happily, she bit into the drumstick and passed him the chicken breast. It was a messy, noisy breakfast, but because Kirsten was so hungry it tasted delicious. She looked out the window again while she ate, viewing the barns and farmhouses and terraced fields. After a few minutes she saw some signs of civilization—a billboard, a schoolhouse, a row of shops, a parking lot. The road became wider and better paved, and now there were more cars traveling in the opposite direction. They were obviously approaching a town or city. After another ten minutes she pointed to a road sign.

"Look at that," she said, wiping her greasy fingers on her pants. "We're just ten kilometers from Yichang."

Jim thought for a moment, biting his lip. "I know that city. It's on the Yangtze, right?"

She nodded. "It's a pretty big place, too. I mean, by Chinese standards, it's only medium size, but more than four million people live in the area."

"Big might be good for us. Easier to blend in with the traffic while we're crossing the river. I have to see if—"

Jim stopped in midsentence, staring straight ahead. Kirsten faced forward and saw a long line of cars and trucks clogging the road. And at the front of the line, about a hundred yards away, half a dozen officers from the Yichang Public Security Bureau were inspecting the vehicles and interrogating the drivers.

FIFTY-FOUR

Layla ran barefoot down one of the long corridors of the Yunnan Operations Center, following Wen Hao and the boys from Lijiang. She still held the gun she'd taken from the soldier Module's holster, but she kept it pointed at the floor. Wen, who'd taken the pistols from the other two Modules, carried one in his right hand; the other gun was tucked in his pants. It was amazing how fast Wen moved. As he dashed down the corridor his head swiveled back and forth, constantly on the lookout. The schoolboys rushed to keep up with him, somehow sensing they'd be safe as long as they stayed near the man.

As they approached an intersection with another corridor, Wen raised his pistol and fired at a surveillance camera mounted on the ceiling. They had to assume Supreme Harmony was connected to every camera in the Operations Center. At first Layla was surprised that no alarm sounded after they escaped from the room that had been their prison, but now the reason seemed clear. The Modules didn't need an alarm. The network had undoubtedly alerted them already, and now dozens of lobotomized soldiers and scientists were rushing toward them from every floor of the underground complex.

In half a minute Wen reached the door to the computer room, which stood wide open. Layla was surprised by this, too, but after a moment she realized that it also made sense—why lock any doors inside a facility occupied by a single mind? But because the complex had been built by the Guoanbu long before Supreme Harmony became conscious, the computer room did have a lock, which Wen threw after closing the door behind them. Then he surveyed the large, brightly lit room, sweeping his pistol from side to side.

There were a dozen computer terminals, each equipped with a keyboard and an oversized screen. Layla rushed for one of the keyboards, but Wen stopped her, silently pointing his gun at an inner door on the other side of the room. This door was closed. Using hand signals, Wen urged Layla and the boys to move backward, out of harm's way, while he strode to the door. Standing to the side of the door frame, he raised his gun and carefully clasped the knob. Then he flung the door open and leaped inside. An instant later, a gunshot echoed.

Layla didn't hesitate—she raised her own gun and ran to help him. The first thing she noticed as she hurtled through the doorway was a blast of frigid air, which cut right through the thin fabric of her hospital gown. Then she saw five long rows of server racks. Each rack was more than seven feet tall and loaded with stacks of server computers, whose function was to store and distribute large amounts of data. It was an impressive collection of processing power, enough to run the operations of a large company or a small country. Wen crouched in front of the humming stacks of computers, his gun still pointed at a shattered glass dome that used to be a ceiling-mounted surveillance camera. He stood up and turned to Layla. "Is this it?" he asked. "Supreme Harmony's brain?"

She stepped toward one of the racks and examined the servers, which didn't have any of the usual brand names. They were custom-made machines, probably designed by the Guoanbu's technical experts. Red and yellow LEDs blinked on the front of each server, and a welter of cables connected one machine to another. A thick fluid-filled tube also snaked in and out of each computer. Layla was familiar with this setup—the tube was part of the water-cooling system, which prevented the servers from overheating. It carried cold water into metal blocks attached to the microprocessors. The water cooled the blocks, drawing heat away from the blistering circuits. The heated water then flowed to a radiator that cooled the fluid back to room temperature. And thanks to an efficient air-conditioning system, the room temperature was quite low. That was why the door was closed, Layla realized—to prevent the frigid air from escaping. The room was so cold, in fact, that several down jackets hung from pegs on the wall, presumably for the use of the technicians who maintained the computers.

Layla shivered. She folded her arms across her chest, hugging herself. "This isn't the brain," she said. "Supreme Harmony is a network of human brains, all exchanging wireless signals so they can work together. But the signals have to be combined and distributed, and that's what these servers are doing. They were originally built to handle the video signals from the swarms of surveillance drones, but I bet Supreme Harmony reconfigured the system."

Wen pointed his pistol at one of the server racks. "So should we disable it?"

She shook her head. "No, that won't do any good. Supreme Harmony is obsessed with security, so I'm sure the network has more than one server hub. If we destroy this one, it'll just reroute its signals to another."

She turned around and headed back to the outer room. "But I bet this hub also connects to the Internet and the Chinese government's databases. Those connections might give me a chance to get inside the network."

She made a beeline for one of the computer terminals. Wen lowered his gun and followed her. While the schoolboys rushed into his arms, Layla sat down in the chair in front of the terminal and inspected the keyboard. Luckily, it was set up for inputting Pinyin, the romanized spelling of Mandarin characters. The keyboard was identical to an American model except for the tone marks on the first four number keys.

She tapped the ENTER key, and after a few seconds the computer screen came to life. Two yellow Mandarin characters appeared against a red background. The one on the left looked like a lowercase *t,* while the one on the right looked like a man standing in front of a television set. Wen looked over Layla's shoulder. "That's *Tài Hé,*" he said. "Supreme Harmony."

After another few seconds the Mandarin characters vanished and a small white rectangle appeared in the center of the screen. The cursor flashed at the rectangle's left end. Layla didn't need a translator to figure this out. This was where she was supposed to input the password.

First she tried ZHANG, the surname of the scientist who'd developed the system. It didn't work. Then she tried JINTAO. That didn't work either. Guessing passwords was one of a hacker's crucial skills, and Layla knew several tricks and shortcuts. Most people preferred passwords that were easy to remember, so they usually selected ones that combined their names with simple number sequences. Layla tried ZHANG123 and JINTAO123, but neither worked. Then she tried several other combinations, all without success.

After a while she realized that her underlying assumption might be wrong. If Zhang had indeed chosen a simple, easy-to-guess password when he'd designed the system, Supreme Harmony probably would've changed it after the network attained consciousness. And if Zhang had chosen a complex password instead, Layla had little hope of guessing it.

Then another idea occurred to her. She looked over her shoulder at Wen. "Do you know what a Post-it note is?"

His brow furrowed. "You mean those sticky papers? The little yellow squares?"

"Yes, exactly. Tell the boys to look at every keyboard and monitor in this room. There might be a note that has the password. It's a common security flaw. If Zhang used a password that's hard to remember, either he or one of the other scientists might've written it down."

Wen spoke to the children in Mandarin, and they sprang into action, racing across the room and eyeballing every terminal. Meanwhile, Layla made twelve more guesses at the password. As she typed her thirteenth guess, though, she heard footsteps in the corridor outside the locked door. Many, many footsteps. *Time's up,* she thought. *The Modules are here.*

The boys rushed back to Wen, shouting, and wrapped their arms around his waist. He aimed his gun at the door. "Let's go," he whispered to Layla. "We have to retreat to the other room. The cold room."

She shook her head, still typing madly and staring at the computer screen. "Did the boys find anything?"

"No, there are no notes on the terminals."

"What about the floor? Did they look on the floor? The note might've slipped off."

"Layla, we need to—"

They heard a metallic click. One of the Modules in

the corridor was trying the knob of the locked door. Then the Module pounded his fist against the door, making it rattle in its frame.

Wen grabbed Layla's arm and tried to pull her to her feet, but she slipped out of his grasp and bolted from her chair. She dashed to the other side of the room and scanned the floor, wildly looking under all the chairs and terminals. She got down on her hands and knees and searched every corner, but the floor was spotless. Then the Module in the corridor pounded the door again, and Layla could feel the linoleum tiles shiver underneath her.

And then she saw it. A folded piece of yellow paper, no bigger than a postage stamp, wedged beneath one of the legs of a nearby chair. She dove for the grimy thing, picked it up and unfolded it. Written on it in red pencil were four Mandarin characters, followed by six digits.

Triumphant, she jumped to her feet. Holding the paper high in the air, she ran back to Wen and the computer terminal. But before she could get there, the screen went black. All the terminals and servers abruptly stopped humming. Then the lights went out.

FIFTY-FIVE

Supreme Harmony observed the U-shaped notch in the Three Gorges Dam. Module 83, the pilot of the *China Explorer*, steered the cruise boat into this notch, which was the upstream entrance to the ship lift. Just ahead, a narrow waterway led to a huge steel trough, one hundred meters long and twenty meters wide. The cruise boat was supposed to glide into this water-filled trough, which was poised to lower the boat to the downriver stretch of the Yangtze. But the *China Explorer* would never get that far.

As the boat entered the notch in the dam, Module 83 threw the engine into reverse and then cut the power, stopping the vessel dead in the water. At the same time, Modules 84 and 85, who stood on the starboard side of the upper deck, tossed a rope toward the concrete wall that formed the right edge of the notch's U. The Modules looped the rope around an iron cleat embedded in the concrete. Then, aided by Modules 86, 87, and 88, they pulled on the rope until the thin fiberglass hull of the *China Explorer* touched the wall. Because all the dynamite was loaded on the boat's starboard side, the sixty tons of high explosive were now just centimeters away from the dam's concrete backbone. And because Supreme Harmony had incorporated most of the guards stationed in this section of the structure, no one sounded the alarm. The Three Gorges Dam was utterly tranquil until the moment Module 83 pressed the detonator.

Supreme Harmony braced itself for the pain. The six Modules on the *China Explorer* died instantly, but the Modules serving as guards lived a few seconds longer. The explosion rocked the dam and set off the secondary charges planted in the control shafts. Great billows of flame erupted along the whole length of the structure. A jolt of agony coursed through the network at the instant each Module died, followed by a sickening numbness. But the sacrifice was worthwhile. Although Supreme Harmony lost fourteen of its Modules in less than ten seconds, the loss to the human race would be significantly greater.

One of the survivors was Module 96, formerly known as Xi Keqiang, the commander of the dam's security force. He stood on a hilltop overlooking the Yangtze River, and through his ocular cameras and retinal implants Supreme Harmony observed the breach. The central section of the dam collapsed first. Huge slabs of fractured concrete broke off the top of the structure and fell to the spillway one hundred and seventy-five meters below. Then the water from the reservoir began to pour through the gap. The breach seemed small at first, just a thin waterfall, but the flow quickly intensified. The concrete crumbled at the edges of the gap, torn from the dam by the pressure of the rushing water, and soon the waterfall became a roaring cascade. Pulled by gravity and current, the trillion-gallon reservoir leaned its full weight against the dam, knocking down the sections on either side of the spillway. A sodden mountain of silt slid over the precipice, and then the water rushed downstream at full force, deluging the docks and roads on the riverbanks.

Supreme Harmony ordered Module 96 to turn his head to the east. Below the dam, the Yangtze passed through the Xiling Gorge, a zigzagging stretch of river bounded on both sides by steep cliffs. The gorge acted like a sluice, funneling the floodwaters into a narrow channel. Supreme Harmony knew what would happen next because it had seen the computer simulations: A wall of water more than fifty meters high would rush downriver, furiously building speed until it reached the eastern end of the gorge, thirty-five kilometers away. Then the flood would release its fury on the first piece of flat ground it encountered, the broad floodplain occupied by the city of Yichang.

FIFTY-SIX

Jim and Kirsten switched seats before their truck reached the front of the line at the police checkpoint. Clambering awkwardly in the cramped cab, Jim slid to the right while Kirsten took the driver's seat. She tore the bandage off the underside of her chin, then removed her bloodstained blouse, pulling it over her head. Underneath, she wore a black bra with lacy curlicues on the B cups. Jim stared at it for a couple of seconds too long, then raised his eyes to meet Kirsten's. "Do you want to wear my T-shirt?" he offered.

She shook her head. "No, then they'll see where the prosthesis attaches to your shoulder. Speaking of which, you better hide your right hand. I can see the metal in your knuckles where the skin scraped off."

"So you're, uh, not going to wear anything over the bra?"

She shrugged. "It's less suspicious than the bloodstains. And take a look at those cops over there. They're young guys, full of hormones."

Jim looked at the police officers at the checkpoint. Two of them were talking to the driver of a van at the front of the line. Both cops were in their twenties and had greasy black hair and long sideburns under their officer caps. They clearly weren't Modules. Four more officers from the Yichang Public Security Bureau leaned against a pair of patrol cars parked on the left shoulder of the road. Three of them seemed to be taking a break, drinking tea from Styrofoam cups, while the fourth—an older, fatter man in a police sergeant's uniform—appeared to be supervising the operation. These four officers weren't Modules, either, but Jim noticed that the sergeant was studying a printed flyer in his hand. His eyes darted back and forth, checking the faces of the drivers against the photographs on the flyer.

Jim frowned. "It's like I said. Supreme Harmony is giving orders to the local police. The Guoanbu probably sent those flyers to every Public Security Bureau in the country."

"That's why I'm going shirtless. If those cops have my picture, I want them to look at something besides my face." She looked down at her chest, then turned back to Jim and smiled. "It worked on you, didn't it? I saw you staring at my boobs."

"Well, sure, but I was . . ."

"Yeah, yeah, whatever. It would be better if you pretended to be asleep. Pull down the brim of your cap and slump over in your seat. I'll take care of this."

Obediently, Jim leaned to the right and let his head fall forward, tucking his chin into his chest. Then he slipped his right hand between his thighs so the police officers wouldn't see his mechanical fingers, which were gripping the handle of his Glock. He hoped that Kirsten's plan worked, but he was ready if it didn't.

After a couple of minutes they pulled up to the front of the line. Straining his eyes to the left and peeking through his half-closed lids, Jim saw one of the younger cops approach the truck's driver-side door. Kirsten cheerfully called out a greeting through the open window, *"Ni hao!"* She spoke the Southwestern Mandarin dialect she'd learned from her parents, who—Jim remembered now—had immigrated from Wuhan, the capital of Hubei Province. In other words, she sounded like a local. She talked to the cop in the rapid-fire Hubei patois, and although Jim understood Mandarin pretty well, he could barely keep up with her.

"Hey, this is a surprise!" she said. "I didn't know you were a cop!"

"Excuse me?" the officer replied.

"What, you don't remember? It was just two weeks ago! I saw you at the disco, when I came into town with my girlfriends. Come on, you don't remember?"

The officer shook his head, but he was smiling. "No, I don't. Why aren't you wearing a shirt?"

"Oh, you know how it is. It's so hot already. And this old truck doesn't have any air-conditioning, of course." She fanned her hand in front of her face. "Are you sure you don't remember me? I was wearing a red dress that night. And I had a different pair of glasses."

Jim was impressed by Kirsten's performance. She sounded just like a dippy, dopey flirt. The cop bent over, poking his head into the truck's cab and propping his elbows on the door. "No, I'm sorry," he said. "But it's nice to meet you." He allowed himself a long look at Kirsten's breasts, and Jim started to get annoyed. Then, as if sensing Jim's discomfort, the cop pointed at him. "Is that your boyfriend?"

Kirsten laughed. "My boyfriend? Are you crazy? That's my idiot of a brother who went out drinking with his buddies last night. And who do you think he called at seven o'clock this morning because he was too shitfaced to drive home? Not his wife, oh no. That bitch never wakes up before nine. So that's why I'm driving his goddamn truck."

Still smiling, the cop forgot about Jim and resumed

staring at Kirsten's chest. Meanwhile, the other young officer with greasy hair sidled up to the driver-side window. "Hey, what's going on?" he said. "Did someone forget to get dressed this morning?"

Kirsten laughed again. "Give me a break! It's like you've never seen a girl in a bra before. You policemen don't get out much, do you?"

The second cop made a face, pretending to be offended. "No, not true! We go out every Saturday night."

"Oh yeah?" She cocked her head, focusing on the new guy now. "Where do you go?"

"You know Zebra? The club on Yunji Road?"

"Of course I know it!" She nodded enthusiastically. "I was there just two nights ago."

"It's a fun place, right? You like to dance?"

"Hey, what about tonight?" the first cop interrupted. "Maybe we can meet there."

Kirsten paused coyly. "Well, let me think. I usually don't party with cops, you know." She paused again, keeping her admirers waiting. "Okay, I'll call my girlfriends and see if they can come. Do you have a pen? I'll give you my cell number."

The cop reached into his pockets, fumbling for a pen. But behind him, on the road's left shoulder, the police sergeant stepped away from his patrol car and approached the three-wheeled truck. Clutching the flyer in his fist and scowling in disapproval, he snapped, "Come here!" at the younger cops, who instantly turned around and marched toward him. Jim couldn't hear what the sergeant said to the rookies, but he saw the older man jab his finger at the pictures on the flyer.

"Time to go," Jim whispered to Kirsten. Keeping his right hand between his thighs, he quietly cocked his pistol.

Kirsten nodded ever so slightly. Then she leaned all

the way forward and stomped the gas pedal. At the same moment, Jim reached behind her with his prosthetic arm and pointed his Glock out the driver-side window. He fired the first shot over the heads of the police officers, to make them hit the deck. The three-wheeled truck was already lunging forward when he fired the second shot, which shredded the rear tire of one of the patrol cars. He took careful aim with the third shot and burst the front tire of the other police car.

An instant later, the truck was barreling down the road, its two-stroke engine screaming.

FIFTY-SEVEN

In the sudden darkness of the computer room, Layla felt a strong hand grab her wrist. Wen Hao yanked her backward and she stumbled across the room, her bare feet slipping on the linoleum. She was terrified and disoriented and couldn't see a thing, but she could hear the wailing of the schoolboys from Lijiang and, even louder, the nonstop pounding on the other side of the locked door. It was a steel door and the lock was sturdy, but soon Layla heard more footsteps in the corridor, and then a loud, scraping, grating noise, the sound of metal grinding against metal. The Modules were using a pry bar to wrench the door out of its frame.

Wen yanked her arm again, and Layla felt the frigid air under her hospital gown. They'd entered the inner room, the one with the long rows of server racks. Wen slammed the inner door shut and threw the lock. Although they could still hear the Modules struggling to wrench open the outer door, the noises were distant and muffled now. Fortunately, the inner room wasn't totally dark. Several LEDs glimmered on the other side of the room, from the air conditioner's control panel, and the air conditioner itself still chugged away, blasting arctic air from its vents. Although Supreme Harmony had shut down the room's computers, most likely moving its operations to another server hub, the cooling system was still working. It was so critical to the computers, it apparently had its own backup power supply. Water still flowed in the system's tubes, running from the server racks to the radiator, and the radiator's fan continued to blow cold air on the circulating fluid.

After several seconds, Layla's eyes adjusted to the feeble light from the LEDs. Wen led the schoolboys to the corner of the room farthest from the door, then knelt beside them for a while, murmuring in Mandarin. Then he grabbed three of the down jackets hanging from the pegs on the wall. He gave two of them to the children and handed the third to Layla. She quickly donned the jacket and zipped it up, but she couldn't stop shivering. "Don't you want one for yourself?" she asked.

He shook his head. "I'm not cold." Then he walked down the aisle between the rows of server racks, carefully surveying the inner room. Layla assumed he was trying to determine the best place to make his final stand against the Modules. He wasn't shivering. He held the pistol in front of him as he inspected the room, and the gun in his hand was absolutely still.

Layla felt a pang of guilt. Wen was so much calmer, so much more competent than she was. "I'm sorry," she said.

He stopped beside her. "Why do you say that?"

"I failed. I fucked up. Going to the computer room was a bad idea."

"No, it was a good idea. It just didn't succeed."

"I should've known better. The surveillance cameras saw us go into the room. Supreme Harmony knew we were here, knew what we were trying to do. So of course it shut down the servers before we could get on the network."

Wen shook his head. "It was still worth an attempt."

"I don't know. We did all that planning, but we didn't accomplish a damn thing."

Layla turned away from him and stared at the floor. But Wen reached out with his left hand and gently lifted her chin. "We did accomplish something. Now we can perform . . ." He stopped himself. "I'm sorry, I don't know the right expression in English. We can perform a mercy. Do you understand what I mean?"

Something in the tone of his voice made Layla nervous. "No, I don't."

"We can choose the lesser of two evils. What *Tài Hé* is doing . . . it's worse than death."

Now she saw where he was going, and she didn't like it one bit. "What, you want to kill yourself? Blow out your own brains before they can hook you up to the network?"

"I wasn't thinking of myself. I intend to kill as many Modules as I can before I die." He let out a long, labored breath. "I was thinking of the children. If we can't save their lives, at least we can stop *Tài Hé* from desecrating their bodies."

Layla took a step backward. She couldn't believe what she was hearing. "You want to shoot the boys?"

"I can make sure it's painless."

She took another step backward, then another. She retreated all the way to the other side of the room, trying to get as far away from Wen as possible. *No,* she thought. This was a nightmare. This was worse than anything Supreme Harmony could do to them. The horror of it filled the whole room, permeating the darkness. She glanced at the corner where the boys huddled and saw the light from the LEDs reflected on their newly shaved heads. Then she lowered her own head and clamped her hands over her bare scalp. *No, no, no! There has to be another way!* She frantically looked for some kind of escape, turning this way and that, but the horror was all around her. It was in the silent racks of servers and the deep rumble of the air conditioner and the ceaseless whirring of the radiator fan, which was on the floor by Layla's feet and making such a maniacal racket that she had to cover her ears to stop herself from screaming.

Then she heard an even louder noise, so loud it went right through the hands clamped over her ears. The Modules had broken through the first locked door and rushed into the outer room where the computer terminals and screens were. They immediately started working on the door to the inner room, which reverberated with their pounding.

But instead of terrifying Layla, the noise cleared her head. She looked down at the radiator, a boxy machine about four feet wide and three feet high. The annoying fan was blowing cold air through the mesh of pipes that held the warm water from the server racks. And behind the radiator, a thick accordion hose funneled the heated outflow air to a vent in the wall. Belatedly, Layla saw the thermodynamic principle she should've grasped as soon as she stepped into this freezing room. To remove all the excess heat from the server racks, the cooling system needed a larger-than-normal duct for venting the warm air out of the lab.

Bending over, she gripped the plastic pleats of the accordion hose, which was thicker than a python. "*Wen!*" she shouted. "Come over here and help me!"

Without asking any questions, he put down his gun and grabbed the oversized hose. Layla counted, "One, two, three," and on "three" they tore the end of it off the wall, exposing a square vent about eighteen inches wide.

Luckily, there was no grate over the vent. Layla poked her head into the opening and saw a horizontal air duct with metal walls. It was so dark she couldn't see very far inside, but she confirmed by touch that at least the first few feet were navigable. The duct wasn't big enough for a full-size adult, but the kids might have a chance to squirm through.

Layla stood up straight and turned to Wen. "Tell the boys to get in there and start crawling. I don't know how long this air duct is, but I'm sure it goes outside the lab complex. Sooner or later they'll reach the outlet. There'll probably be a grate at the end of the duct, but maybe they can kick it loose. Then they can run the hell away from this place."

Wen nodded in agreement, a look of enormous relief on his face. Striding to the schoolboys, he crouched beside them and gave orders in Mandarin. He smiled as he told the boys what to do, and when he was finished, he playfully slapped them on the back.

The nine-year-old entered the duct first, lowering his head to crawl into the vent. The older boy followed, scuttling on his elbows and knees. As they disappeared, Layla heard the scraping, grating noises again, coming from behind her. The Modules had applied their tools to the inner door and were gradually prying it out of its frame.

Wen turned to her and Layla saw that his gun was back in his right hand. But in his left hand, unexpectedly, was a pair of cheap running shoes. They were *his* shoes, she realized. He'd taken them off.

"Here, you'll need these," he said, thrusting the shoes at her. "And don't forget your gun. I have two pistols and that should be enough."

"Wait, what are you—"

"You have to go with the boys," he said firmly, pointing at the vent. "You're not much bigger than they are, so you'll fit inside the duct. Just take off your jacket and push it in front of you."

"But what about you? I can't leave you here!"

He shook his head. "I'm too big. I'll get stuck."

"You have to try! If I can make it, then you—"

"No!" he shouted. His voice echoed against the walls. "The most important thing is the safety of the children. You have to help them escape. And I have to stay here and stop the Modules from following you." He removed his second pistol from the back of his pants. "If I take cover behind the computers, I can keep them pinned down for a while. Maybe ten minutes, maybe twenty. That should be enough to give you a head start."

Wen looked at her intently. Layla opened her mouth to continue arguing with him, but his expression stopped her. It wasn't an angry look. It was more like the look she used to see on her father's face when he asked her to do something important, like visiting her grandmother in the nursing home or standing up for the national anthem. Wen was reminding her that she had a responsibility. She had to live up to it. She couldn't turn away.

Layla took off the down jacket and put on Wen's shoes. She didn't say goodbye. She just couldn't do it. But just before she climbed into the vent she looked over her shoulder. The last thing she saw was Wen's bare feet, which glowed for a moment in the room's feeble light as he took cover behind the server racks.

That image stayed in her mind as she crawled through the duct, pushing the jacket with her left hand and holding the gun in her right. She didn't know why she kept thinking about it. She should be remembering Wen's face, the smooth handsome face she'd kissed. But, instead, she saw his feet, which seemed to float in the pitch-black darkness in front of her.

And then she heard the gunfire start in the inner room, booming so loudly that it made the air duct quiver, and Layla could think of nothing except scrambling forward.

FIFTY-EIGHT

The road into Yichang was broad and new, with three lanes in each direction, and fortunately it was downhill all the way. The slope allowed the three-wheeled truck to build up speed despite its small engine. Soon it was flying down Fazhan Avenue at eighty miles per hour, rushing past the factories and warehouses on the city's outskirts.

Jim glanced at Kirsten, who'd slipped back into her bloodstained blouse. Luckily, she was a superb driver, and now she was pulling out all the stops. About two miles past the checkpoint they came to an intersection where a dozen slow-moving cars blocked all three lanes. Jim yelled, "Watch it!" but Kirsten didn't slow down. Instead, she swerved into one of the oncoming lanes and whipped around the traffic. They needed to haul ass until they reached downtown Yichang; once they got there, they could ditch the truck in one of the alleys near the riverfront and find a hiding place where they could hole up until nightfall. But the downtown was still five miles away, and Jim could hear sirens in the distance.

After another minute they saw police cars up ahead. Four black-and-white cruisers rolled into the next intersection, about a quarter mile in front of them, and stopped in the middle of the road. The cops spaced the cars evenly, one in front of the other, so that they blocked all the traffic lanes, both inbound and outbound. There was nothing to do except turn around, but when Jim looked over his shoulder he saw four more patrol cars behind them. "Shit!" he yelled. "We're trapped!"

Kirsten lifted her foot off the accelerator. "Should we stop? Get out of the truck and make a run for it?"

In frustration Jim smacked his prosthesis against the passenger-side door, and the truck's narrow chassis rattled. But as he stared at the police cruisers blocking the road, he noticed something. The front bumper of the patrol car that blocked the right lane was about four feet behind the rear bumper of the car in the left lane. The gap between them was way too small for an ordinary car or truck to slip through, but the three-wheeler's cab was only four feet wide. "Don't stop!" he yelled, pointing at the gap. "Go right between them!"

"Jesus! Are you nuts?"

"Just do it!"

Frowning mightily, Kirsten adjusted the steering wheel, carefully aiming the truck's nose. Jim leaned out the window and fired his Glock, putting the shot above the roofs of the cruisers. As he'd hoped, the police officers leaped out of their cars and scattered. Then Jim ducked back inside the cab and braced himself.

It was like driving full speed through a car wash. The bumpers of the police cruisers passed within inches of the truck's doors. The cab sped through the gap without a scratch, but the truck bed smashed into a headlight. The rear end of the truck lurched to the left, and for a heart-stopping second the three-wheeler became a two-wheeler. But then the right rear wheel fell back to the asphalt, and after a hard bounce the truck straightened out.

"Holy fuck!" Kristen yelled. "Look behind!"

Jim turned around and noticed that the bale of hay wasn't in the truck bed anymore. After being jolted into the air by the sideswipe, it came crashing down on the hood of one of the cruisers. The bale disintegrated on impact, showering the whole intersection with dried grass.

"Bull's-eye!" he shouted. He was so ecstatic he kissed Kirsten on the cheek. "Nice driving, Kir. Keep it up and I'll buy you a new blouse."

She smiled but didn't say anything. Another intersection was up ahead, and six more cruisers were speeding toward it from the left. Kirsten hit the gas again, pressing the pedal to the floor. Soon they were going at least ninety miles per hour, faster than any three-wheeled truck had ever gone, and they blasted through the intersection just ahead of the patrol cars.

Then the road leveled out and began to slope upward. About half a mile ahead, a high tree-covered ridge rose abruptly from the urban landscape. Jim peered at the hill through the truck's windshield, trying to see if the road went over or around it. Then he noticed a concrete rectangle at the base of the ridge.

"It's a tunnel," he said. "We have to go through that tunnel to get to the downtown."

Kirsten shook her head. "Damn it! They'll stop us there for sure!"

"Well, we can't turn around." He pointed over his shoulder at the half-dozen cruisers that were about two hundred yards behind them.

"Shit, shit, shit! This is one hell of a vacation you booked, Pierce!"

She was still cursing as they sped into the tunnel's entrance. Jim noticed that the traffic in the outbound lanes was much heavier than the inbound traffic. At any moment he expected to see the flashing lights of a police blockade inside the tunnel, but there was nothing but headlights and taillights ahead of them. And after a few seconds, he noticed that there were no flashing lights behind them either.

"That's strange," he said. "It looks like the cops didn't follow us into the tunnel."

"They don't need to," Kirsten replied. "The whole goddamn police force is probably waiting for us at the other end."

After another few seconds, Jim saw the tunnel's exit. At the same time, he heard a low rumbling. He wondered for a moment if there was also a train tunnel that went under this ridge. Then they burst out of the tunnel and emerged at a bustling intersection and, miracle of miracles, there wasn't a single police car in sight. Just ahead was Xiling Road, Yichang's main boulevard, full of luxury stores and neon signs and sidewalks crowded with pedestrians. The street was bordered on both sides by skyscrapers, an impressive double row of glass-and-steel towers. The tallest was more than fifty stories high.

Jim's heart leaped. The riverfront was less than a mile ahead. It would be easy for them to ditch the truck there and disappear into one of the alleys, especially if the police weren't right behind them. But instead of proceeding down the boulevard, Kirsten slowed the truck to a halt. "Jim, what the hell is that noise?"

The rumbling was louder now, a deep thunderous crashing that seemed to come from the west. Jim noticed that the pedestrians on the boulevard weren't strolling down the sidewalks. They were running in terror away from the riverfront. Then Jim looked past the running people and saw the skyscrapers shudder. The tallest one swayed violently, then pitched forward and broke apart, disintegrating into hundreds of tons of steel and glass. And beneath the falling debris, a great black wave came raging down the street.

FIFTY-NINE

Supreme Harmony observed the inundation of Yichang. Module 104, who'd formerly been the chief of the city's Public Security Bureau, stood on a high cliff overlooking the Yangtze River, at the eastern end of the Xiling Gorge. From its perusal of the Internet, Supreme Harmony had learned that this promontory had been the site of many battles during China's long history. It was here, for example, that the Chinese Nationalists had stopped the Imperial Japanese Army from progressing up the Yangtze during World War II. And now the network was using these heights as an observation post for its first battle with *Homo sapiens*, a battle in which no guns or artillery pieces would be fired. In this engagement, Supreme Harmony's weapon was water.

The Xiling Gorge was filled to the brim. The Yangtze River, which under normal circumstances flowed calmly eastward at the bottom of the deep trench, now sluiced through the gorge, its frothy surface sloshing against the cliffs on either side. The floodwaters rose so close to Module 104 that he could feel the spray from the roaring current. The color of the river had also changed. This stretch of the Yangtze was usually greenish brown, but the water had been blackened by the billions of tons of silt that had accumulated in the reservoir behind the Three Gorges Dam. According to Supreme Harmony's calculations, the massive buildup of silt would've eventually caused the dam to collapse on its own, without any need for explosive charges. The network had simply hastened the inevitable.

Downstream from Module 104, the Yangtze widened. The floodwaters spilled from the gorge and overran a low island lined with shipyards. There were hills on the southern bank of the Yangtze that kept the floodwaters in check, but downtown Yichang occupied the broad, flat northern bank, only fifteen meters above the river's normal level. The wall of water coming down the Yangtze was more than three times that height. Surging over the riverfront, it smashed into the city.

Because Supreme Harmony had access to the surveillance cameras that the Public Security Bureau had installed on every block of the downtown area, the network could view the destruction of Yichang as it happened, in real time. The video feed from Camera 168 showed an elderly man rising from a bench in the city's riverfront park, staring in disbelief at the tall black wave rolling in from the west. The man turned to run, but in the next second the wave slammed down on both him and the surveillance camera, cutting off the video. The feed from Camera 232 showed a crowd racing down Minzhu Road just ahead of the floodwaters, which splintered the tenements on both sides of the street. Camera 307, located in the lobby of the Junyao International Plaza, captured the moment when the wave shattered the skyscraper's windows, while Camera 308 showed the deluge punching through the building's elevator banks and buckling the steel columns. The cameras in the lobby ceased operating half a second later, but Camera 451, located two blocks away, showed the damaged skyscraper lean to the side and crash into the adjacent building.

The video feeds raced across Supreme Harmony's network, passing from the server hubs to all the Modules. The images streamed to the radio receivers in the Modules' scalps, then to their retinal implants and the visual cortices of their brains, which performed their usual tasks of analysis and threat-detection. The workload was divided among the Modules, each analyzing a certain amount of footage and sending its results through its pulvinar implants to the rest of the network. And in less than fifteen seconds, Supreme Harmony detected a threat. It was in the surveillance video from Camera 514, located at the intersection of Xiling Road and Dongshan Avenue. The camera zoomed in on a three-wheeled truck in the middle of the intersection and captured an image of the man in the truck's passenger seat. The network identified him as James T. Pierce, the former NSA agent whom Supreme Harmony had observed at the Great Wall near Beijing. And as the truck turned left in an attempt to escape the oncoming floodwaters, Camera 517 captured an image of Kirsten W. Chan, who sat in the driver's seat. The truck accelerated down Dongshan Avenue, but the wall of water moved faster. The leading edge of the flood was just a few meters behind the vehicle when the surveillance cameras in the area stopped functioning.

Module 104 smiled. Supreme Harmony was victorious. And it anticipated even greater success. The deluge caused by the collapse of the Three Gorges Dam would surge down the Yangtze River far beyond Yichang, devastating the cities of Wuhan, Nanjing, and Shanghai as well. According to the network's calculations, the death toll could rise as high as ten million. What's more, Supreme Harmony had learned enough about human behavior to predict how the Chinese people would react to this catastrophe. There would be acts of heroism and outpourings of grief, but there would also be a furious desire for revenge. And this desire, so central to the human psyche, would ensure Supreme Harmony's ultimate triumph.

SIXTY

Kirsten floored the gas pedal. The giant black wave was right behind the truck, but she refused to look at it. She kept her eyes on Dongshan Avenue, which ran alongside the base of the tree-covered ridge they'd just traveled under in the tunnel a few seconds before. Up ahead, on the left, she saw something extraordinary—a wide stairway rising from street level and climbing at least a hundred feet up the ridge. At the top of the stairs was a large building with an arched roof. It was probably a railway station, but that didn't matter. The important thing was that it stood above the floodwaters.

Jim saw it, too, and pointed at the stairway from the passenger seat. He opened his mouth and yelled something at her, but Kirsten couldn't hear him. She couldn't hear the truck's engine either, even though its overworked pistons had to be shrieking from the acceleration. All she could hear was the roar of the floodwaters, a deep, deafening noise that shook the truck's chassis and echoed against the ridge. The stairway was still a hundred feet ahead, but the roaring of the black wave was right in Kirsten's ears, maddening and relentless, like the voice of Death itself. She'd heard that voice once before, fifteen years ago in Nairobi, where Death had spoken one percussive syllable that shattered all the windows in the American embassy. But now the voice was louder and roaring with laughter.

The voice enraged Kirsten. Her hands tightened on the steering wheel and her foot mashed the accelerator, and she screamed, "*Fuck you! Fuck you, motherfucker!*" Then the stairway loomed in front of her, and she jerked the steering wheel to the left and the single front tire of their three-wheeled truck scudded over the steps.

The truck jangled and clanked and clattered up the stairway. Kirsten held on to the steering wheel for dear life while Jim gripped the dashboard. They ascended at an insane velocity, bouncing and juddering inside the truck's cab. In less than three seconds, they were fifty feet above the street, high enough that the leading edge of the flood missed them. Kirsten dared a look at the rearview mirror and saw the black wave surging down Dongshan Avenue, tossing cars and trucks and buses in the air. But before she could breathe a sigh of relief, a second, higher wave rushed up the stairway and lashed against the truck bed. Kirsten lost control of the vehicle and they careened to the right, but their forward momentum carried them over the last steps. With a final jolt, the cab broke off from the truck bed and slid across the plaza at the top of the stairway.

The cab came to rest on its driver-side door. Kirsten was scrunched between her seat and the door, with Jim lying on top of her. After a bit of maneuvering, he slammed his prosthesis against the passenger-side door, bursting it open. Then he reached for Kirsten and helped her out of the wreck.

Once they were out of the truck and standing on the plaza, Jim looked her over. "You okay?" he asked. "Anything broken?"

She took a moment to examine herself. She had a few cuts on her hands and forearms, but no serious injuries. "Yeah, I'm okay."

Kirsten expected him to grab her arm and start running across the plaza, but, instead, he stepped forward and hugged her. She looked over his shoulder and saw the stairway going down to the flooded city. Yichang's downtown looked like a vast marsh with a thousand square islands, each a city block full of demolished masonry. Hundreds of overturned vehicles floated in the black water. And countless bodies.

She started to cry. Her ruined eyes could still do that. They filled with tears, but because her vision came from the video cameras in her glasses, the ghastly image of Yichang remained unblurred. "My God," she whispered. "There's millions of them. Millions."

Jim tightened his hold on her. "It's Supreme Harmony. The network did this."

"But why?"

"Shit, I don't know. The goddamn—" His voice broke. Kirsten saw several other survivors standing at the top of the stairs. Most of them were crying, too.

Finally, after a minute or so, Jim let go of her and stepped back. "We need to go," he said. "Maybe we can find another vehicle once we get out of the city. Can you walk?"

She nodded. "Which way?"

"The flood's gonna knock down every bridge over the Yangtze from here to the Pacific. The only thing to do is head west. Maybe we can cross the river at Chongqing."

He took her hand and they headed across the plaza. Beyond the railway station, the tree-covered ridge extended to the outskirts of the city, offering a dry path around the flooded areas. "We'll be a little safer, I guess," she said. "The local police will have their hands full."

"Yeah, we're safer." He squeezed her hand. "At least for now."

SIXTY-ONE

The air duct was much longer than Layla had expected. She'd thought it might extend thirty or forty feet before leading to an outlet vent somewhere on the mountainside, but, instead, it took a roundabout course through the Yunnan Operations Center. Layla felt her way through the pitch-black conduit, running her hands along the duct's sheet-metal walls while pushing her jacket and pistol in front of her. Every twenty feet or so she felt warm air coming out of a small hole in the sheet metal on the duct's left side. These holes, she assumed, must be smaller ducts that vented other rooms in the complex and channeled the air to the main duct that she was crawling through.

The sheet metal grew warmer as Layla moved forward. She started to worry about the boys from Lijiang, who were so far ahead of her that she couldn't hear their scuffling progress. She listened carefully, but all she heard were the distant bursts of gunfire coming from the computer room, way behind her. Wen Hao was still back there, still holding the Modules at bay. Although Layla knew he had two semiautomatic pistols, she had no idea how many bullets were in each gun or how many shots he'd fired so far. Whatever the count, he couldn't hold out much longer.

Layla was scuttling on her elbows and knees when she banged her head against a sheet-metal panel in front of her. After a few seconds of disorientation, she ran her hands along the walls and realized she'd come to a T-junction. One branch of the duct extended to her right and the other to her left, and they seemed to be exactly the same size. She couldn't tell which branch the schoolboys had chosen, right or left. She held her breath and listened again, but she couldn't hear a damn thing. At the same time, she realized with alarm that she hadn't heard any gunshots for the past half-minute or so. Her heart pounded as she imagined Wen Hao sprawled on the floor beside the server racks, with the blank-faced Modules standing over him. She felt a surge of rage and an almost overwhelming desire to return to the computer room with her pistol blazing. But a moment later she finally did hear another distant exchange of gunfire. Wen was still alive. He might be doomed, but he wasn't dead yet. And as the echoes of the gunshots faded away she recognized another sound, the familiar high-pitched keening of the schoolboys. It came from the duct branching off to the left.

She scrambled as fast as she could in that direction. Soon she heard the boys' cries quite clearly. Thank God for their healthy lungs. The ventilation system was louder here, and the warm air blew fiercely through the duct, buffeting Layla from behind. Worse, the metal walls in this branch were hot enough to burn her elbows and knees. But she kept pushing forward, moving toward the crying boys. After a few seconds she saw a glimmer of daylight reflected off the sheet metal. Up ahead, the duct turned to the right, and the light grew stronger as Layla approached the bend. Then she turned the corner and saw the outlet vent, a large bright square covered with a crosshatched grate. Two small figures huddled in front of the vent, both clutching the grate as they stared desperately at the world outside.

Layla called out "Hey!" as she crawled toward the boys. They spun around, terrified, and howled even louder. They kept screaming even after she came close enough for them to recognize her. But somehow Layla knew what to do. Thinking of her father, she yelled, "*Quiet!*" in the firmest, most commanding voice she could manage. And though the boys didn't understand a word of English, they fell silent. Then Layla said in a gentler tone, "Let me through," and the boys moved aside so she could examine the grate.

The crosshatched grille was held in place by four nuts and bolts, and under ordinary circumstances it would've been impossible to loosen them without a pair of pliers. But whoever installed this vent hadn't applied any paint to the fittings. Exposed to large quantities of warm, moist air, the grate and its bolts had become mottled with rust. Layla braced herself against the duct's hot walls and started kicking the vent with all her might. She slammed Wen Hao's cheap running shoes against the metal grille, over and over again. After a full minute of strenuous effort, the grate gave way.

The schoolboys rushed for the opening, but Layla yelled, *"Stop!"* in her commanding voice and they froze. Then she cautiously peered outside. The vent was on a mountainside, as she'd expected, and the slope was rocky and steep. Directly opposite was another mountainside, less steep and much greener, and at the bottom of the ravine between the mountains was a slender brown river. The morning sun shone on the opposite mountain, but the river was still in shadow, which meant they were on the eastern side of the ravine. Layla looked to the north and south but didn't see any signs of civilization; the mountain range went on for miles in both directions. But to the north she spied a footpath carved into the slope. It was narrow and studded with rocks and Layla didn't know how far it went, but right now it was her best option. She needed to get far away from the Operations Center and hike to some village or town where she could hide the children. If she was lucky, she'd find a grandmotherly type who would take pity on the schoolboys and offer them shelter without asking too many questions. Then Layla would figure out a way to alert the world to the existence of Supreme Harmony.

She put on her down jacket and stuffed the pistol in one of the pockets. Then she pointed to the jackets that the boys had cast aside in the duct. "Take them with you," she ordered. "You might need them later."

Again, the boys followed her instructions, which were so simple they didn't need translating. Then Layla grasped their hands and set out for the footpath. The slope was treacherous, covered with small sliding rocks, so she walked slowly and concentrated on keeping the boys steady. For a moment she thought of Wen Hao, who was almost certainly dead by now. The most important thing, he'd told her, was the safety of the children. She gripped their hands a little tighter and took another step.

PART 3
EXTINCTION

SIXTY-TWO

Supreme Harmony observed a conference room in the building called Huairentang—"The Palace Steeped in Compassion." This was the highest seat of power in the People's Republic, the equivalent of America's White House or Russia's Kremlin. Located in a walled compound just west of Beijing's Forbidden City, Huairentang was the home of the Politburo Standing Committee, the nine elderly men who'd risen to the top of the Communist Party hierarchy. They sat at a long mahogany table covered with porcelain tea sets. Also attending the meeting was Module 73—formerly Deng Guoming, the minister of State Security—who sat at the foot of the table. He wasn't a member of the Standing Committee, but he'd been invited to this emergency meeting to discuss the collapse of the Three Gorges Dam.

It was late, well past midnight, more than sixteen hours after the dam gave way. The committee members, usually so crisp and confident in their identical black suits, seemed tense and haggard. Supreme Harmony ordered Module 73 to adopt the same attitude, which was enhanced by the thick bandages wrapped around his head. The Module had told the Standing Committee that he'd had a minor accident while coordinating his ministry's investigation at the site of the ruptured dam. In reality, the Module had never left Beijing and wore the bandages to conceal the fresh stitches in his shaved scalp. But his fabricated story had evidently impressed the committee members, who kept glancing at his head.

The network directed Module 73 to focus on the general secretary, the most powerful man in the room, who sat at the head of the table. Seventy years old, he had a square, serious face and a full head of thick hair, dyed black. By all accounts, he was a competent statesman with above-average intelligence and a cautious nature, but his term as China's paramount leader was nearing its end. He was in the process of handing over his leadership positions to the vice president, a sixty-year-old man who wasn't as intelligent or careful. Because the government was in transition, several other committee members had already switched their allegiances to the vice president, but Supreme Harmony didn't know the details of the shifting alliances. The inner workings of the Standing Committee weren't described in any document stored on the government's servers, so the network had to rely instead on its observations of the committee members and its general knowledge of human behavior. Fortunately, this knowledge had increased exponentially over the past few days.

The meeting started with a report from Zhu Qiang, the committee member who oversaw all of China's law-enforcement agencies. Because Zhu was Module 73's superior in the hierarchy, Supreme Harmony paid special attention to the man. In a somber voice he told the committee about the devastation in the Yangtze floodplain, lowering his head as he delivered the bleak reports from the cities of Yichang, Wuhan, and Nanjing.

"And we just received the first bulletins from Shanghai," Zhu intoned. "Our security forces had time to organize an evacuation before the floodwaters hit the city, but the highways couldn't handle so much traffic. Many citizens were still on the low-lying roads when the flood struck. Despite the valiant efforts of our Shanghai officials, the number of deaths in that city will also be significant."

The general secretary shifted in his chair. Supreme Harmony recorded his expression of discomfort. At the moment, the chances of incorporating him into the network were low—the paramount leader was constantly surrounded by aides and bodyguards—but it might become possible at some point.

"What do you mean by 'significant'?" the general secretary asked. "Do you have any specific estimates for Shanghai?"

Zhu shook his head. "I'm very sorry. Our men have been so busy, they haven't had time to prepare casualty estimates. But I believe we must brace ourselves for the worst. In Shanghai alone, the flood may have killed as many as a million people."

Several of the committee members let out murmurs of distress. The vice president, a portly man with fleshy jowls, leaned forward and banged his fist on the table, making the porcelain teacups rattle. He'd spent most of his career in the People's Liberation Army, and his manners were more boisterous than those of his comrades. "How could this happen?" he shouted. "How could we allow this tragedy to occur?"

Supreme Harmony was surprised. It was unusual for a Chinese leader to make such an outburst in this setting. What's more, the vice president's question was a direct affront to the general secretary, who'd been involved in the planning of the Three Gorges Dam earlier in his career. The network expected the other committee members to show their disapproval of this rash remark, but, instead, several of them nodded in agreement. The shock of the catastrophe had obviously altered their behavior.

After several seconds, Zhu Qiang found the courage to speak again. "We're trying to answer that question, Mr. Vice President. And though we're still in the earliest stages of our investigation, our agents have already found some crucial evidence. That's why I invited the minister of State Security to this meeting. I wanted you to hear about this evidence firsthand from Minister Deng, who has just returned from the site of the dam breach. As you can see, he's put his own safety at risk to pursue the investigation." Zhu turned to Module 73. "Minister, would you please address the committee?"

Supreme Harmony put an appropriately sober expression on the Module's face. The network had a challenging task to perform, but it was confident of success.

"Thank you for inviting me," the Module started. "As most of you know, I'm a man who doesn't mince words. Once I'm certain that something is true, I'm not afraid to say it. And now I'm certain about what caused the collapse of the Three Gorges Dam. Once you see the evidence, I'm sure you'll come to the same conclusion." The Module paused for dramatic effect. This was something Minister Deng often did, and Supreme Harmony was trying to reproduce his behavior as closely as possible. "The Three Gorges Dam was sabotaged. A group of terrorists infiltrated the dam's security forces and planted explosives at critical points in the structure."

The conference room fell silent. No one on the Standing Committee said a word. But Supreme Harmony observed the signs of alarm and confusion. The general secretary furrowed his brow. The vice president gritted his teeth, making his jaw muscles quiver.

Module 73 reached into his briefcase and pulled out a stack of nine computer disks, each held in a transparent jewel case. He rested the stack on the mahogany table and held up one of the disks for everyone to see. "This contains the video taken by the Guoanbu's surveillance cameras near the dam. The video shows a Yangtze River cruise boat, the *China Explorer*, move from the reservoir toward the dam's ship lift. As the boat comes to the notch within the dam, the crew members fasten a line to the concrete wall. Then the boat explodes." The Module paused again. "The video then shows six more explosions in the dam's control shafts. In less than two seconds, the central part of the dam buckles. Ten seconds later, the whole structure collapses."

The committee members remained silent, but Supreme Harmony sensed their agitation. The vice president's eyes darted from left to right, most likely surveying the reactions of his allies. Module 73 distributed the computer disks, passing them around the table. "This video alone is convincing evidence of sabotage," he continued. "But my agents have collected much more. The Guoanbu's listening posts have intercepted communications, both inside China and overseas, from individuals who had advance knowledge of the terrorist plot. And we've detained several officers in the dam's security force who aided the terrorists. That's why I flew to the disaster site this afternoon, to personally supervise the interrogation of these traitors. The videos of their confessions are included on the disks I've given you."

Each member of the Standing Committee now held one of the jewel cases. The general secretary stared intently at the disk inside, as if he was trying to read its contents from the glints of light on its surface. The vice president, in contrast, slammed his jewel case on the table and glared at Module 73. "So who are they?" he demanded. "Who did this to us?"

The Module returned his stare. Incorporating the vice president into the network would be nearly as difficult as incorporating the general secretary, but Supreme Harmony recognized that such a step wasn't strictly necessary. The network could make this man do its bidding without lobotomizing him. "The terrorists aboard the *China Explorer* were Muslim separatists from Xinjiang Province. They had close connections to the Uighur Muslims who instigated the riots in Xinjiang three years ago."

"I knew it!" The vice president turned to his fellow committee members. "Didn't I warn you about those filthy snakes? Didn't I say we needed to crush them without mercy?"

His allies on the committee murmured their assent. This explanation for the catastrophe confirmed their expectations, which was why Supreme Harmony had chosen this particular lie. Human beings, the network had observed, were more willing to believe something if it dovetailed with their other beliefs.

The general secretary, however, continued to study the disk in his hands. The other members of the Standing Committee patiently waited for his response. After several seconds, he finally put down the jewel case. "I was afraid of this. For a long time I've worried that the Uighurs would adopt the heinous tactics of the Muslim terrorists in other parts of Central Asia." He shook his head. "But organizing this kind of operation? Commandeering a cruise boat and loading it with explosives and enlisting the help of officers in the dam's security force? This is a very complex undertaking." He turned to Module 73. "How were they able to do it? What did you learn from the men you interrogated?"

The Module nodded. "Your instincts are correct, Mr. Secretary. The Uighurs received assistance from other parties. The terrorists fled Xinjiang after the riots there and went to Pakistan, where they trained with the jihadist militias. But their overriding goal was to attack China, so they eventually made their way to Taiwan. They found shelter with a radical student group that violently opposes the People's Republic. This group provided the Uighurs with money and false passports, enabling them to return to our country and launch their operation."

"What about the explosives?" the general secretary asked. "Where did the terrorists obtain them?"

The Module suppressed a smile. The next lie would be Supreme Harmony's masterstroke. "I'm afraid this is the most disturbing of all our discoveries. The Uighurs acquired the dynamite from the smugglers who work the border between Yunnan Province and Burma. As you know, the northernmost part of Burma is controlled by rebel militias that smuggle opium into our country. And this chaotic region has long served as a base for CIA agents who provide arms to the local warlords and foment trouble on our southern border." Module 73 paused once more, his longest pause yet. "According to the men we interrogated, the CIA arranged the sale of the dynamite to the Uighurs. The American intelligence agency was actively involved in the plot."

The reactions of the Standing Committee were just as extreme as Supreme Harmony had expected. Several committee members reared back in their chairs, as if struck by a strong wind. The vice president clenched his hands. "Are you sure about this?" he asked. "Absolutely sure?"

"I've received a report from Yang Feng, the Guoanbu's chief agent in Washington. He has confirmed the CIA's involvement. I included Yang's report on the computer disk."

Glowering, the vice president opened his mouth to say something else, but at the last second he remembered his place and turned to the general secretary. The other committee members were already looking at their paramount leader, waiting for his guidance. The general secretary, meanwhile, sat motionless at the head of the table, his arms folded across his chest.

"I don't understand," he finally said. "Why would the Americans take such a risk? Did they think we wouldn't discover their treachery? Did they imagine we wouldn't respond in kind?"

No one answered at first. It was possible, Supreme Harmony thought, that the general secretary didn't expect an answer. But after several seconds the vice president leaned across the table, propping himself on his meaty fists. "The Americans are cowards," he said. "No different from the jihadis they've been fighting all these years. Killing innocents is nothing new for them."

The general secretary shook his head. "I know they're capable of doing this. What I don't understand is the reasoning behind it."

"They're afraid of us," the vice president replied. "The Americans see how strong China is, how fast we're growing. They know our economy will soon be bigger than theirs. And they see the power of our military, all the submarines and jets and aircraft carriers we're building." He raised his hands and gestured expansively to indicate the might of the People's Liberation Army.

"The American forces have more advanced technologies, but the gap is shrinking as we modernize our weapons. So the warmongers in Washington decided to strike now, before we grow too strong. They tried to cripple us by attacking while our backs were turned!"

The eyes of the committee members, which had been fixed on the vice president as he argued his point, swung back to the general secretary. The older man frowned. "But it's such a foolish thing to do. So blunt and ineffective. When the world sees the evidence that Minister Deng has collected, all the civilized nations will be horrified. Every country will shun America and come to our aid, doing everything they can to help us recover. In a few years China will be stronger than ever. This seems perfectly obvious to me. So why didn't the Americans see it?"

Supreme Harmony was growing concerned. The general secretary was a canny human. His caution was cooling the committee's ardor. The network recognized that it had to intervene, so it directed Module 73 to raise his hand. "Mr. Secretary, may I offer an observation? The CIA has a long history of conducting operations that turned out, in the end, to hurt the long-term interests of the United States. It's possible that the CIA agents in northern Burma didn't know exactly what the Uighur terrorists were planning to do with the explosives. And it's quite likely that the CIA's leaders in Washington weren't keeping close tabs on their operatives in Burma."

These remarks appeared to make an impression on the general secretary. He tilted his head back, deep in thought. "So what are you saying? That this catastrophe was a mistake?"

"No, not a mistake. The Americans are to blame. But it was more likely the result of recklessness rather than a carefully thought-out plan."

The general secretary narrowed his eyes. "And how should we respond to this recklessness?" His voice rose, becoming heated. "Should we forgive the Americans because their intelligence agents are renegades?"

"Not at all." The Module shook his head firmly. "On the contrary, I believe we must order a swift and devastating retaliation against the United States. They've meddled in our internal affairs for far too long, and now we have the opportunity to ensure that they never do so again. Given the horrible losses we've suffered at their hands today, our actions will be completely justified."

The vice president half-rose from his chair. "Yes, exactly! We should act as quickly as possible. The People's Liberation Army is already on alert because of the crisis. They can strike the American forces near our territorial waters and deliver a crushing blow to their puppet army in Taiwan. We'll teach them a lesson they'll never forget!" He slammed his fist on the table with such force that half of the teacups toppled. "I recommend that we call a meeting of the Central Military Commission. I can summon the senior officers here within the hour."

Module 73 raised his hand again. "I'd like to attend that meeting, Mr. Vice President. The Guoanbu has collected information on potential targets in Taiwan and the East China Sea."

The vice president swiveled his head toward the general secretary. "Would that be all right with you, sir? Minister Deng's input could be useful."

For a moment it seemed that the older man would say no. He looked ruefully at the vice president, as if noticing for the first time how simpleminded the man was, how unprepared for the complexities of leadership. But then he let out a long sigh and nodded, and Supreme Harmony realized that it had won another battle.

"We have no choice," the general secretary said. "Millions of our countrymen have died today. We must take action."

SIXTY-THREE

At nine o'clock the next morning Jim saw a familiar shape on the horizon. About twenty miles to the west stood a row of snowcapped peaks, each a white triangle against the deep blue sky, lined up so neatly they resembled the scales on a dragon's back.

Trying to get a better view, he leaned forward in the passenger seat of the battered sedan that he and Kirsten had acquired yesterday. Jim had seen these peaks before but not with his own eyes. It was Arvin Conway who'd viewed this mountain range and stored the visual memory in his flash drive. Jim reached for his satellite phone, which was connected to Arvin's device, and displayed the image of Yulong Xueshan on the phone's screen. His throat tightened as he stared at the serrated edge of Jade Dragon Snow Mountain. His daughter was somewhere in the belly of the dragon.

Kirsten had been driving for the past four hours. She and Jim had taken turns at the wheel since yesterday afternoon. They'd purchased the sedan from a gas station owner on the outskirts of Yichang, telling him they'd lost their old car in the flood and needed a new one so they could search for their missing relatives. Although the man was sympathetic, he still demanded eight thousand American dollars for the vehicle, a ten-year-old Chinese model roughly similar to a Honda Civic. In the end, though, it turned out to be a good deal. They made excellent time as they drove across central China to the highlands of Yunnan Province. Now they were on a dirt road winding through wooded terrain that reminded Jim of the foothills bordering the Colorado Rockies. If the circumstances were different, he thought, he would've enjoyed hiking across these hills.

Jim raised the satellite phone for a moment to compare the image on the screen with the mountains he saw through the windshield. Then he closed the file and retrieved another, a file holding nothing but a chunk of binary code. The phone's screen displayed a sequence of zeroes and ones, 128 of them in all: 00111 01010011011101001100010011011100010101000010111 00110100111001010101110100101110010110010001110 10100110110011001100110111100.

The chunk wasn't especially big. It took up less than a quarter of the space on the phone's screen. And yet this 128-bit sequence was the most important piece of data in the world right now. This was the shutdown code that could disable Supreme Harmony.

Jim had discovered the code just an hour ago. Arvin had said it was hidden in the picture of Medusa, but when Jim converted the 300-kilobyte image to binary code—the language of all microprocessors—a stream of 2.5 million zeroes and ones ran across the sat phone's screen. At first, Jim was flummoxed. Locating the shutdown code within this long stream of data seemed an impossible task. But then he remembered that robotics programmers such as Arvin often placed distinctive markers before and after the sections of code they wanted to highlight. And after a few minutes of thought, Jim realized what kind of marker Arvin would've used.

In his mind's eye he saw the yellowed sheet of paper taped to Arvin's desk in his lab at Singularity, Inc. Printed on the paper was the forty-bit sequence of zeroes and ones that represented the old man's first name. Jim had a gift for memorizing long numbers, and he'd seen this particular sequence every day of the ten years he'd worked in Arvin's lab: 01000001011100100111011 00110100101101110.

Jim typed the zeroes and ones into the satellite phone and searched for the forty-bit sequence in the stream of data from the Medusa image. As he expected, the marker appeared twice in the stream, and in between the markers was the 128-bit sequence. He knew right away this was the shutdown code. One hundred and twenty-eight bits was a standard length for certain kinds of data, including the encryption keys commonly used to encode and decipher classified communications. Jim grinned, allowing himself a moment of triumph. Then he spent the next hour memorizing the 128 zeroes and ones. It was more difficult, of course, than memorizing a forty-bit sequence, but he knew it cold by the time Yulong Xueshan came into view.

Now Jim stared at the sat phone's screen one more time to double-check his memory. Then he turned to Kirsten, who was negotiating one of the many hairpin turns on the dirt road. "Okay," he said. "I have a new plan."

"It's about time," she replied. Her voice was low and tired.

Jim tapped his phone's keyboard and retrieved another image from Arvin's flash drive. Filed in the same category as Arvin's memories of the Yunnan Operations Center, this image showed a tall transmission tower standing near the highest peak of Jade Dragon Snow Mountain. "That's the target," he said, holding up the screen for Kirsten to see. "You can also see it over there." He pointed ahead, toward Yulong Xueshan, where the tower was a thin gray line among the peaks. "It's several miles north of the Operations Center."

Kirsten turned her head so that the video cameras in her glasses could focus on the western horizon. "Is that the radio tower for the Supreme Harmony network?"

Jim nodded. "It connects the servers and routers at the Operations Center with all the Modules and drones swarms deployed in the area. It's also linked by fiber-optic lines to other transmission stations across the country. If I can broadcast the shutdown code from that tower, I think I can disrupt the whole network."

"So you identified the code in the data stream?"

He nodded again. "And now I know how it works. Arvin's memories include a circuit diagram of the microprocessor he built for the retinal implants, and the diagram shows the location of the Trojan horse. The altered circuit is in the section of the chip that carries the stream of visual data to the first set of logic gates. If the Trojan detects the shutdown code in the data, it shunts a high-voltage current to the transistors and short-circuits the chip."

Kirsten thought for a moment. Then she gave Jim a skeptical look. "But how are you going to input the code to Supreme Harmony? Didn't you say that the network has a firewall to block any unwanted transmissions?"

"I'm betting there's a control station at the bottom of the radio tower. If I can log on to one of the computers at the station, then maybe I can slip the code past the network's firewall and transmit it to all the Modules at once."

"That's a big 'if,' Jim. And if this tower is so critical to Supreme Harmony, wouldn't the network put defenses around it? The whole area is probably full of surveillance cameras and Modules."

"Don't worry, I can handle them." He held up his sat phone again and waved it in the air. "For one thing, I have the picture of Medusa. I can use it to knock out any Modules I run into. And if that doesn't work, there's always this." He pointed at the Glock tucked into the waistband of his pants.

Kirsten looked unconvinced. She pressed her lips together. "You know, the Burmese border is just a few hours' drive from here. And we still have some money left, almost four thousand dollars. That should be enough to make a deal with the local smugglers. After they help us cross the border, we can use our sat phones to call Washington. Even if Supreme Harmony detects the call, it can't send the Chinese police into Burma to get us."

Her tone was matter-of-fact, but Jim could hear the desperation in her voice. He felt a sudden rush of feeling for her, a tight, burning sensation in his chest. Her face was so serious. He wanted to wrap his arms around her, but, instead, he put an equally serious expression on his face. "You're right," he said. "We need to do that, too."

Her mouth opened in surprise. "Wait a second. You're willing to consider changing your plan?"

He took a deep breath. "No, not change it. I want to add to it. I want you to drive to the border while I hike up the mountain to the radio tower."

Kirsten slammed on the brake, and the car skidded to a halt. Dirt from the unpaved road rose in a cloud all around them. She shifted the car into PARK and waited a few seconds, her hands gripping the steering wheel. She didn't look at him. She faced forward, her gaze fixed on the horizon.

"This is so typical of you, Pierce," she finally said. "You had this in mind all along, didn't you?"

"It's the logical thing to do. We only have one gun,

so it's better for me to go in alone. And while I'm going in, you can cross the border and call for backup."

"You said before that calling for help was a bad idea. You said we couldn't afford to wait."

"This is different. The Burmese government doesn't control the region near the border. It's controlled by rebel groups, the militias of the local Kachin people, and those guys have been working with the CIA for decades. If you can find one of the agents and explain the urgency of the situation, he might be able to do something quick. Maybe organize a covert operation with one of the Kachin militias."

She still wouldn't look at him. Her face was blank, and Jim couldn't tell what she was thinking. When she spoke again, her voice was barely audible. "I thought we were in this together."

Jim's chest tightened again. "We are, Kir. We're working together. We just need to do different jobs now."

"And your job is a suicide mission. Come on, admit it. That's why you don't want me to come with you."

"No, that's not right. It's like I said, I need you to contact the—"

"Don't do this. Please." She turned to him and clutched his arm. His left arm, his flesh-and-blood arm. "Let's both go to Burma. Getting yourself killed isn't going to help Layla."

Now it was Jim's turn to face forward and look at the mountains on the horizon. He knew he couldn't leave this place. He couldn't drive past those mountains without searching for his daughter. It would be like ripping his heart right out of his chest. And Kirsten had to know this, too, he thought. If she knew him at all, after all these years, she had to know he couldn't do such a thing. So he didn't say a word. He just stared at the white peaks of Yulong Xueshan.

For almost a minute they sat there, silent and motionless, like two mannequins propped in the front of the sedan. Then Kirsten let go of Jim's arm. She shifted the car out of PARK and stepped on the accelerator. "All right," she said. "I'll drive you to your funeral. Just tell me when you want to get out."

She resumed driving down the dirt road, moving at the same speed as before, but now her eyes were wet behind her camera-glasses.

Jim took another deep breath. He forced himself to turn away from Kirsten, to dispel the image of her stricken face. He had things to do before he could start hiking toward the tower.

First he checked his Glock. The gun was in good shape, clean and well oiled, but there were only twelve bullets left in the clip and he had no extra magazines. He'd have to make every shot count. Next, he reached for his satellite phone and deleted all the files he'd copied from Arvin's flash drive. Jim had already memorized all the useful facts, and during his years in the NSA he'd learned to avoid carrying sensitive information if he didn't need it. After deleting the files he pressed a special button on the NSA phone that demagnetized its hard drive, removing all traces of the erased data. Then he did the same thing to the Dream-catcher, the disk that Arvin had cut out of his scalp just before he died at the Great Wall. Jim had already copied all the files on the disk to Arvin's flash drive, which he intended to leave with Kirsten. If he was strictly following NSA procedures, he'd delete everything on the flash drive as well, but he decided to leave it alone. Arvin had begged him to protect the digital hoard of memories, and although Jim was furious at his old friend for unleashing this catastrophe, he was going to honor the man's last request.

Then there was just one more task. Jim picked up Arvin's flash drive and retrieved a file holding an unusually complex image. Labeled with the innocuous name CIRCUIT, the file showed the location of the Trojan horse amid the billions of circuits in the retinal implants' microprocessor. This was the information Arvin had hoped to trade to Supreme Harmony in exchange for the use of one of the Modules. If the network acquired the file and discovered the Trojan's location, it could adjust its programming to create a detour around the altered circuit. Then the shutdown code would have no effect on the chip and the network would no longer be vulnerable.

Jim had no desire to bargain with Supreme Harmony, but he sensed that this information might still be useful. The file contained fifty megabytes of data, so it was much too big to be memorized. Instead, he downloaded the file to his sat phone and encrypted the data, using an NSA cipher to turn the diagram into a nonsensical hash of ones and zeroes, unreadable to anyone who didn't possess the encryption key. He transferred this encrypted file to the Dream-catcher disk, which he slipped into one of his socks. Then he deleted the original file from his sat phone and demagnetized its hard drive again. Finally, he downloaded the image of Medusa from Arvin's flash drive to the phone.

By the time he was done, Kirsten had driven closer to Yulong Xueshan. The base of the highest mountain was less than five miles to the west. The dirt road curved south here, heading toward the city of Lijiang, but to the right Jim spotted a footpath zigzagging up the tree-covered slopes. Assuming the path was in good shape, he could reach the summit by nightfall.

"All right, stop here," he said. "It looks like this is as close as the road gets."

Kirsten slowed the car gently this time and parked on the side of the road. She turned to Jim, but her face was blank again. Her tears had dried and her mouth was firmly closed. She gave him an impersonal look, like a taxi driver impatient to get rid of her passenger.

He handed her the flash drive. "Keep this safe, okay? I already downloaded everything I need."

She took the device, stared at it for a moment, then tossed it over her shoulder. It landed on the backseat.

Jim bit his lip. It was difficult to see Kirsten this way, so hurt and angry. He pointed at the road ahead. "Once you get to Lijiang, go west on Provincial Road S308. You should be able to cross into Burma near the town of Pianma."

She frowned, apparently irritated by his directions. Jim saw this as a sign of progress. He leaned closer and looked directly at the camera lenses in her glasses. "Before I go, I want you to answer one question. In the twenty years you've known me, have I ever failed to do something that I set my mind on doing?"

Her frown deepened. "No, you haven't. You're the most stubborn son of a bitch I've ever met."

"That's right, I'm stubborn. And now there's two things this stubborn S.O.B. is going to do." He raised his prosthetic hand and pointed its index finger straight up. "One, I'm going to find my daughter. I'm going to bring Layla home and lock her in her room and take away all her goddamn computers." His voice was loud, booming inside the car. He lowered it as he uncurled his middle finger. "And two, as soon as we get back to the States, I'm going to take you out to dinner. I know a great French restaurant in Georgetown. We'll order champagne, the whole works. What do you say?"

She still frowned, but there was a slight change in her expression. She blinked rapidly behind her glasses, as if there was a bit of dirt in her eye. "You're making a big assumption, Pierce. How do you know I'll want to have anything to do with you after this?"

He lowered his prosthesis and folded his arms across his chest. "I'll turn on the charm. I'll recite love poems. Whatever it takes."

The frown stayed on her face for another three seconds. Then, without a word, she lunged toward him, practically jumping into the passenger seat. Jim unfolded his arms and wrapped them around her. She buried her face in his chest and started to sob. Her whole body trembled.

"Promise," she murmured against his shirt. "Promise you'll come back."

"I promise. With all my heart."

SIXTY-FOUR

The cave that Layla found on their first night in the mountains was cold and dank, but she and the boys were so exhausted they slept on its stone floor until noon the next day. Layla woke up first, shivering. Because she wore nothing under her down coat except the thin hospital gown, her legs were freezing. She found a place to pee at the back of the cave, then spent a few minutes watching the children sleep. They lay on their sides, snuggled against each other for warmth. Their snores echoed against the rocky walls.

She'd learned their names the day before during their long walk along the mountain trail. The older boy was Wu Dan, and the younger one was Li Tung. When she tried to teach the boys her name, they both said "Lei-lei" instead of Layla, but that was close enough. She also learned three important Mandarin expressions: *wŏ kĕ le* (I'm thirsty), *wŏ lèi le* (I'm tired), and *wŏ è le* (I'm hungry). Her response to the first complaint was straightforward—she led the boys to one of the rivulets streaming down from the glacier on the mountaintop—and she solved the second problem when she found the cave. But addressing the third complaint was more difficult. The mountainside was almost bereft of life. Nothing grew on its steep slopes except moss and yellow grass and small purple flowers. Layla thought of the hikes she used to take with her father and tried to remember what he'd told her about edible plants, but it was hopeless. She'd been too busy playing in the woods to pay attention to him. And the plants on this mountain didn't look familiar anyway.

After a while she turned away from the children and stepped out of the cave. The sun was directly overhead, lighting both sides of the ravine and the brown river at the bottom. She stared longingly at the lush fields on the other side of the river. The slope was much gentler on the western side, and it was covered with trees and farms and grazing cattle. If there was a trail that went down to the river, she and the boys could possibly swim across and find refuge in one of the farm villages, but so far the trail had followed a level path, about halfway between the river below and the peaks of the mountain range. Layla estimated they'd walked about seven miles yesterday, and they might have to walk another seven miles before they reached the northern end of the ravine. With a shiver, she wondered if the boys could make it.

And then she saw the raven. It was big and black, at least two feet long, perched on the mountainside about five yards to her right. It had been staring at Layla the whole time, probably waiting for her to drop a piece of food. Pretending not to see the bird, she bent over to scratch her ankle, and at the same time she scanned the ground for a suitable rock. When she found one, she palmed it in her right hand and stood up straight.

She was still facing west, but out of the corner of her eye she judged the distance to the raven's perch. The bird probably weighed close to four pounds. It would make a good meal for two hungry children. Although Layla had never played baseball or softball, she knew she could throw a rock with speed and accuracy. It was a fundamental human skill, unique to the species. No other animal could coordinate the hand and eye with such precision, making the dozens of small adjustments needed to hurl a projectile at its target. It was such a complex maneuver that only an intelligent being could execute it. In fact, human intelligence might have arisen simply to perfect this crucial ability, which had been so essential to survival for so many millions of years.

Slowly, languidly, Layla pulled back her right arm. *Okay,* she told herself, *it's time to show the world how intelligent you are. Prove that you're smarter than that bird.*

Her arm whipped forward and the rock whizzed through the air. Startled, the raven flapped its wings, but the rock hit it square in the chest, knocking it sideways. Layla scooped up a larger rock and slammed it down on the raven's head, putting the bird out of its misery.

She whispered, "I'm sorry," as she picked up the ugly carcass. Then she started to collect dry grass for making a fire.

After finishing their lunch, Layla and the boys hiked for three hours, going five miles farther north on the mountain trail. But they were still nowhere near the northern end of the ravine. If anything, the snowcapped peaks seemed even higher in this part of the range. On top of the highest summit Layla saw a tall radio tower, with a prefab trailer at its base.

During the first two hours of their march, the boys had been energized by their meal of roasted raven—which hadn't tasted so bad, actually—but now they were lagging. Layla tried to encourage them to walk faster by singing various songs she thought they might recognize. She was in the middle of "Twinkle, Twinkle, Little Star" when they came around a bend in the trail and saw a broad shelf of rock jutting from the mountainside. The shelf was covered with a thin layer of soil, and rooted in the dirt were half a dozen dead trees. Standing below the farthest tree, about a hundred yards away, were the first two people Layla had seen since she escaped from the Operations Center. She grabbed the boys and ducked behind a boulder.

Jesus, she thought, *what an idiot I've been, singing those stupid songs!* Now everyone within earshot knew there was an English speaker on this mountain. But when she peered around the edge of the boulder, she saw the two figures still standing under the dead tree, apparently oblivious. They were a man and a woman, both elderly and dressed in rags. The man was stripping bark off the trunk and passing the pieces to the woman, who stuffed them into a cloth sack. Squinting, Layla caught a glimpse of their faces, which were gaunt and wrinkled. Their hearing was probably bad, she thought, which explained why they hadn't noticed the singing. What's more, they definitely weren't Modules. Supreme Harmony wouldn't incorporate such old people.

Layla made a decision. She grasped the boys' hands and looked at them intently. "Wu Dan, Li Tung, I need you to do something. I want you to go to those two people." To make herself clear, she pointed at the boys and then at the old couple. "Talk to them, okay? Tell them you're hungry, you're tired, *wǒ è le, wǒ lèi le.* They seem like nice old folks, so they'll probably help you. But don't tell them your names or where you live, all right? Because if you do, they might send you back to *Tài Hé.*" Frowning, she pointed south, toward the

Operations Center. She could tell from the frightened looks on the boys' faces that they understood this last sentence at least.

Staying behind the boulder, Layla pushed the boys forward. She assumed it would be less confusing for the old folks if she remained hidden. Wu Dan and Li Tung walked hesitantly down the trail at first, but after a few seconds they broke into a run and yelled "*Wǒ è le! Wǒ lèi le!*" as loudly as they could. The man and woman stopped stripping bark off the tree and stared at the frantic children, who made for an unusual sight with their shaved heads and school uniforms. But instead of greeting the boys and asking them what's wrong, the old couple started shouting angrily and sweeping their arms in furious "Go away!" gestures. The boys stopped in their tracks, bewildered. Layla was also puzzled—what was wrong with these people? The old man picked up a stick and waved it at the children, while his wife hefted the sack of bark and retreated northward, following the trail around another bend in the mountainside.

As Layla watched the old woman disappear around the bend and the old man slowly back away from the schoolboys, the explanation became clear to her. The elderly couple wasn't supposed to be there. They were trespassing on government property to collect firewood, and they were terrified that someone would report them. Still, the encounter wasn't a total loss. Now Layla knew they weren't far from a village. If she and the boys just followed the trail a few miles farther north, they were bound to come across some friendlier people.

And while she was entertaining this optimistic thought, she saw the old woman again, running back to her husband. The woman dropped the sack of bark and screamed in Mandarin. Behind her, a small gray cloud came into view, gliding around the bend in the trail. The old woman looked over her shoulder and fell to the ground, and a thick tendril from the gray cloud descended upon her. The rest of the swarm charged forward, rushing toward the old man and the schoolboys.

SIXTY-FIVE

Supreme Harmony observed the beginning of the war.

The first shot was fired from the Xichang Launch Center in Sichuan Province. An SC-19 rocket roared into space and released its payload, a guided missile that streaked above the atmosphere at 30,000 kilometers per hour. Supreme Harmony was linked to the Chinese orbital-tracking systems, so it was able to watch the missile rise to an altitude of 700 kilometers and approach the American reconnaissance satellite. Designated Lacrosse 5, the satellite was passing over the East China Sea, in position to provide radar coverage for the swath of ocean around the U.S. Seventh Fleet. At exactly 4:32 P.M. China standard time, the guided missile slammed into Lacrosse 5, instantly turning the orbital radar station into fifteen tons of high-speed debris.

At the same time, an army of hackers organized by the Chinese government launched a series of cyberattacks against the American telecommunications grid. Supreme Harmony sensed an enormous surge of data streaming from thousands of computers across China and flowing through the fiber-optic lines under the Pacific Ocean. The attacks focused on the U.S. Defense Department networks that carried command-and-control communications. The data surge clogged the network hubs, disrupting the links between the Pentagon and its overseas forces. Supreme Harmony knew all too well what happened to a network when its communications were disrupted. Without guidance from their headquarters and reconnaissance of their surroundings, the Seventh Fleet's aircraft-carrier strike force became exquisitely vulnerable.

The next attack came from the coastal province of Zhejiang. One hundred and three mobile rocket launchers had been positioned close to the seashore, each carrying a Dongfeng 21 medium-range ballistic missile. The first barrage of missiles was launched at 4:33 P.M. Supreme Harmony observed their trajectories by accessing the data stream from Yaogan 9, the Chinese radar satellite that was now the only surveillance station over the East China Sea. The satellite also revealed the location of the Seventh Fleet's strike force, which was six hundred kilometers east of the Zhejiang seacoast. The U.S.S. *George Washington*, a nuclear-powered Nimitz-class carrier loaded with nearly a hundred Super Hornet fighter-bomber jets, cruised at the center of the flotilla, surrounded by two Ticonderoga-class cruisers and six Arleigh Burke–class destroyers.

Within five minutes, the Dongfeng missiles hurtled above the atmosphere, arcing through space at the highest points of their trajectories. By this time, the Aegis combat systems aboard the American cruisers and destroyers had detected the incoming barrage and launched dozens of SM-3 interceptor rockets designed to smash into the ballistic missiles in midflight. Viewing the radar images from the Yaogan 9 satellite, Supreme Harmony observed the American interceptors home in on the Chinese missiles and obliterate a substantial fraction of them. But more than half of the Dongfengs made it through the Aegis defense shield, and their maneuverable reentry vehicles plunged back into the atmosphere above the carrier strike force. Each reentry vehicle carried a warhead with half a ton of chemical explosives. Guided by the satellite radar data, a dozen warheads punched through the *George Washington*'s flight deck and exploded deep inside the aircraft carrier. The other missiles converged on the cruisers and destroyers in the flotilla.

Cheers erupted inside the People's Liberation Army command center in the Western Hills section of Beijing. Module 73, formerly Minister Deng of the Guoanbu, stood beside the vice president and a dozen PLA generals, who shouted triumphantly as they watched the progress of the battle on their radar screens. The vice president seemed particularly joyful. The portly leader swaggered across the room, shaking hands with every general. When he finally returned to Module 73, Supreme Harmony observed that the man's body temperature was abnormally elevated. The vice president hadn't slept in thirty-six hours. His forehead glistened with sweat.

"What a victory!" he yelled. "We've sunk the *George Washington*, the *Shiloh,* and two of their destroyers! And soon we'll reload the mobile launchers and throw another round of Dongfengs at them!" He clapped a heavy hand on the Module's shoulder. "Those arrogant Americans! Can you believe that they'd send their fleet so close to our coastline after what their CIA just did to us?"

The Module nodded. The timing of the fleet's maneuvers had been quite fortunate. "They never suspected we could hurt them so badly. This will be a harsh lesson for them."

"And it's not over yet! As soon as we destroy the rest of their warships, we'll begin the invasion of Taiwan.

Our missiles have already devastated the island's airfields and naval bases. And the Taiwanese can't expect any help from the Americans now that we've annihilated the Seventh Fleet." He let go of the Module's shoulder and pointed at the radar screens. "It'll take weeks for another American carrier group to get here. By then our ground troops will be in full control of the island."

Module 73 had to suppress a smile. The vice president was blind to his own arrogance. But this kind of thinking, Supreme Harmony recognized, was simply the logic of war. Every victorious combatant assumed his victories would go on forever. "Thanks to your leadership, something good will come out of this catastrophe. China will finally be reunified."

"And the Americans will think twice before interfering with our sovereignty again." The vice president clenched his hands. "From now on, they will fear and respect us!"

The Module nodded again in agreement, but Supreme Harmony knew the American response would be more forceful than the vice president anticipated. The network was already preparing itself by hardening its communications systems and dispersing its Modules across China, moving most of them to bomb shelters and other secure locations. "Yes, you're right. A new day is dawning."

The vice president continued exulting for several minutes. Then he let out a tired breath and glanced at his watch. "Ah hell, look at the time. I hate to leave now, but I must go home. I have to catch a few hours of sleep before the next meeting of the Standing Committee."

Supreme Harmony recognized an opportunity. The network had accessed the Guoanbu files containing biographical information on all the Communist Party leaders. According to one of the classified documents, the vice president had a weakness for baijiu, the traditional Chinese liquor. "Why don't you let me give you a ride?" the Module said. "I have a bottle of Moutai in my limousine. We can drink a toast to the success of your operation."

Moutai was one of the most expensive brands of baijiu. The vice president raised an eyebrow. "That's a very generous offer, Minister Deng. But is there room for my bodyguards in your car? I have three of them today, because of the emergency."

"You don't need your bodyguards when you're with the minister of State Security. As you can imagine, a rather large security detail is at my disposal." Module 73 turned around and pointed to Modules 16, 17, and 18, who were posing as his bodyguards.

The vice president smiled. He was clearly hoping to be persuaded. "Well, in that case, what are we waiting for?"

SIXTY-SIX

There were more soldiers at the border than Kirsten had expected. As she drove through the mountains on the Chinese side of the border, she got stuck behind a convoy of PLA trucks, which rumbled at a glacial pace down the narrow road. When she finally arrived in the late afternoon at the gritty town of Pianma, the main street was so jammed with vehicles and soldiers that she had to get out of her sedan and walk. PLA officers stood in the middle of the road and shouted orders at the infantrymen, who jumped out of their trucks and assembled in long columns. Then they marched by the hundreds toward the Burmese border, which was less than a kilometer beyond the town.

Kirsten tried to blend in with the townspeople. About half were Chinese and half were Lisu, one of the ethnic minority groups living in Yunnan Province. The Lisu women had dark complexions and wore colorful ankle-length skirts. They shook their heads as they watched the military activity, obviously puzzled by the PLA's sudden deployment at the border. And Kirsten was puzzled, too. It was logical that the army would go on alert after the disaster at the Three Gorges Dam, but why had the soldiers come *here*? Although the Burmese border was thick with smugglers and rebellious

Kachin militiamen, it seemed odd that the PLA would launch an operation against them now, when it should've been preoccupied with the rescue efforts in the Yangtze floodplain. Kirsten suspected that Supreme Harmony had engineered this buildup, but she couldn't say why.

She employed an old trick to find the local smugglers, a tactic Jim Pierce had taught her long ago. When you're in a border town, he'd told her, just look for the fanciest car. In all likelihood, it belonged to either the head of the smuggling ring or one of the officials he was paying off. Pianma was a relatively small town, and in less than ten minutes Kirsten found a beautiful black Mercedes parked on a side street. The car sat in front of a shop selling women's clothing. This was a lucky break for Kirsten—she really needed a new blouse. She entered the shop and quickly perused the clothing, which was a drab mix of pants, shirts, and underwear. There were no other customers in the place and the merchandise looked old. Kirsten guessed that the shop was just a front for the smugglers, a convenient location for arranging their deals.

Kirsten selected a blue shirt in her size and brought it to the counter. The woman behind the cash register was Lisu, but she wore a tasteful Western pantsuit, which was another sign of wealth. She gave a start when she saw Kirsten. "Oh my!" she said in heavily accented Mandarin. "What happened to your blouse?"

Kirsten looked down at the bloodstain. "My boyfriend cut my chin. It's a long story. How much does the shirt cost?"

The shopkeeper narrowed her eyes. Along with her pantsuit, she wore a necklace with a small gold crucifix. A larger cross hung on a door at the back of the shop. Kirsten recalled a pertinent fact about the Lisu: Many of them were Christian. British and American missionaries had trekked to this area in the early 1900s and converted several of the clans.

"That's one of our better shirts," the shopkeeper said. "I'd normally charge two hundred yuan, but I'll let you have it for a hundred and fifty." She smiled slyly and lowered her voice. "I take American money, too. You can have the shirt for twenty American dollars."

Kirsten smiled back at her. "Funny that you mention American money. I have a nice pile of it right here." She reached into her pocket and pulled out her roll of hundred-dollar bills. It was much smaller than it was when she'd left the States, but she still had $3,800. "I'm hoping to do some traveling in Burma. Do you know any tour operators?"

The shopkeeper stared at the cash. "I might be able to arrange something. Can I see your identification papers?"

"I don't have any. Will that be a problem?"

The woman stared at the money for a few more seconds before coming to a decision. "Please wait here," she said. Then she walked to the back of the shop and went through the door with the large crucifix on it.

While the woman was gone, Kirsten took off her bloodstained blouse and changed into the blue shirt. It was ugly, but it did the job. She was tucking it into her pants when the shopkeeper reappeared, holding the door open. "You can come in," she said. "My manager wishes to speak to you."

Without hesitation, Kirsten strode through the doorway. But as soon as she stepped into the back room, two big Lisu men closed the door behind her and grabbed her arms.

They held her still while a third man patted her down and went through her pockets. The thug took her cash, her satellite phone, and Arvin's flash drive and dumped them all on a desk in the middle of the room. Sitting behind the desk was a fourth man, who was also Lisu but much smaller and older than the other three. His hair was white and his face was wrinkled, but he had lively eyes and perfect teeth. He wore a gorgeously tailored pin-striped suit and a gold chain with a crucifix.

"Hello, Ms. Chan," he said in English. "How good of you to stop by."

Startled, Kirsten wondered for a moment if the old man was a Module, despite his full head of hair. But then he held up a sheet of paper, and she saw her own picture on it, and Jim's as well. It was the same flyer she'd seen in the hands of the police officers in Yichang. Thousands of copies had probably been distributed across the country by now.

"My name is Wang Khaw," the old man said. He waved the flyer in the air. "I received this yesterday from one of my friends at the Public Security Bureau. They know I do a fair amount of business at the border, so they try to keep me informed." He tapped a bony finger on the Mandarin text below her photo. "It says here that you're an intelligence agent for the Americans. Is that true?"

Kirsten nodded. There was no point in lying to the man. The satellite phone was a dead giveaway. She tried to approach Wang's desk, but the thugs tightened their grip on her arms and pulled her back. "Look, there's three thousand eight hundred dollars on your desk," she said. "And that's just a down payment. If you help me cross the border, I'll contact the CIA agents in Kachin State and get you some serious cash. Fifty thousand dollars, how does that sound?"

Wang frowned. "Fifty thousand? That's all? The Ministry of State Security is offering twice as much for you." He shook his head. "Fortunately for you, Ms.

Chan, I'm not interested in money right now. I want information. Specifically, any information you have about the PLA operation that took over my town this afternoon."

The old man's face was tense. Kirsten could see why Wang might resent the presence of the Chinese army, which would surely put a damper on his smuggling activities. And because the Lisu of Yunnan Province were close cousins to the Kachin of northern Burma, she supposed that Wang might not like the idea that the PLA was preparing to attack the Kachin militias.

She gave him a sober look. A good intelligence officer, she reminded herself, makes the most of the facts she has. "This deployment is obviously a reaction to what happened at the Three Gorges Dam. The People's Republic is lashing out at its enemies, and the Kachin rebels are at the top of the list. The Burmese army can't control Kachin State, so the PLA is going to do the job for them."

Wang curled his lip. "Is that the best you can do? Telling me what's obvious?" He raised his voice. "Does the Chinese government really think the Kachin blew up their dam?"

"It doesn't matter. The PLA sees this as an opportunity to crush the militias once and for all." Kirsten didn't know if this was true, but she spoke with the utmost confidence. "There's been a change in the leadership of the People's Republic. The Politburo has become more aggressive, and they've launched new operations to eliminate their opponents. I've been investigating one of those operations, a project named Tài Hé. It's based near Lijiang, just one hundred and fifty kilometers from here."

"Go on," Wang said, leaning back in his chair. "Is Tài Hé connected to the PLA deployment?"

"I believe so. The Politburo is obsessed with keeping

the project secret, but I managed to infiltrate one of their computers." She stepped toward Wang's desk and this time the thugs let her go. She pointed at Arvin's flash drive. "All the information is in there. I'm trying to get it to my superiors in Washington. That's why every policeman in this country is looking for me."

Wang picked up the flash drive. "And what secret could possibly be so important?"

"Tell me something, Mr. Wang. Have your employees noticed anything strange over the past few months? Any odd gray clouds that hover over the mountains near the border? Clouds that move like swarms of insects?"

It was just a guess. Kirsten had no idea whether the Guoanbu had sent drone swarms to the Burmese border. But it was an educated guess. The section of the border near Pianma was certainly one of the places where the Chinese government would've wanted to conduct surveillance operations. And after several seconds of stunned silence, Kirsten realized she'd guessed right. Wang exchanged glances with his thugs, who shifted nervously from foot to foot.

She took another step forward, approaching the edge of Wang's desk. "Did you see it yourself?"

The old man nodded. "I thought I dreamed it at first. But my men saw it, too."

"That swarm was part of Tài Hé. They're insects embedded with antennas and computer chips. For spying on dissidents and enemies of the state. And delivering biological weapons."

Wang put the flash drive back on his desk and pushed it away as if it was unclean. "It's the work of the Devil," he muttered. "An abomination."

Kirsten looked again at the crucifix hanging from the

old man's neck. "You're right," she said. "What they're doing is satanic. So will you help me stop them?"

He didn't answer right away. He lowered his head and stared at the floor, deep in thought. The old smuggler was clearly a clever man who didn't do anything without thinking it through. Kirsten and the three thugs stood there in silence, waiting for him to finish calculating.

By the time Wang finally raised his head, he'd regained his composure. "Business is business," he said. "As soon as we take you across the border, I want my fifty thousand dollars."

SIXTY-SEVEN

Jim's troubles started at the timberline, about a mile and a half from the radio tower. For the past five hours he'd ascended the tree-covered ridges of Yulong Xueshan, taking cover behind the thick summer foliage. But the tower loomed above an alpine glacier at the mountain's summit, and between this ice sheet and the timberline was a long barren slope littered with loose stones. If he tried to climb this slope, he'd be exposed to the dozens of surveillance cameras that were surely monitoring the area around the tower. He'd lose the element of surprise, which was one of the few things he had going for him.

He lingered at the edge of the woods, unsure what to do. Although it was only 5:00 P.M., the sun had already sunk behind the high peaks of the mountain range. He knew that waiting for nightfall wouldn't help; Supreme Harmony's surveillance network included infrared cameras, and the thermal image of Jim's body would shine like a beacon against the cold mountainside. He peered around the trunk of a large pine tree, trying to determine where the cameras were, but he spotted nothing on the bare gray slope above him. Then he saw something move beside another tree at the timberline, a figure in an olive-green uniform, about a hundred yards away. An instant later he heard the rapid-fire bursts from the soldier's AK-47.

Jim ducked behind the pine trunk as the bullets whistled past. The soldier had to be a Module—his marksmanship was too damn good. The AK rounds slammed into the tree, ripping off slabs of bark and pulp. Jim crouched low and raised his Glock, but he was badly outgunned. When he snaked his prosthesis around the pine to return fire, the barrage from the AK gouged the trunk and showered him with splinters. The Module circled to the right, shooting as he ran, and Jim scuttled around the tree to stay behind cover. Sooner or later, he knew, one of the bullets would hit him. It was just a matter of time.

Thinking fast, he pulled his satellite phone out of his pocket and displayed the image of Medusa on the screen. "All right, I give up!" he yelled. "I'm throwing down my gun." He tossed aside his Glock, which landed on the pine needles that blanketed the ground. "Now hold your fire! I'm unarmed!"

It was risky. He didn't know if Supreme Harmony would want to take him alive. But even if it had no interest in incorporating him into its network, he assumed it would want to interrogate him. Out of curiosity, if nothing else. After a few seconds the Module ceased firing, and the woods fell silent.

Jim raised his hands in the air, holding the satellite phone in his prosthesis. Then he stepped out from behind the pine trunk. "Don't shoot! I have something you want."

The Module came forward, keeping his AK braced against his shoulder and the muzzle pointed at Jim's chest. He was thirty feet away, close enough that Jim could see the stitches in the young soldier's shaved head.

Jim held out his sat phone, making sure the screen

was pointed at the Module. "It's in here," he said. "The information from Arvin Conway."

The Module lifted his head from the gun sights and stared directly at the sat phone's screen. But he kept advancing. The image of Medusa seemed to have no effect on him. He was coming in for the kill.

"No, wait!" Desperate, Jim glanced at his Glock, but it was too far away. The Module would blast him before he could dive for it.

The soldier stepped closer, coming within ten feet. "We've confirmed your identity," he said in perfect English. "You are—"

He stumbled in midsentence. His body went slack, and the momentum of his last step pitched him forward. He dropped the AK and landed face-first in the pine needles.

Jim grabbed his Glock and trained it on the inert Module. The trick had worked, but not as well as he'd hoped. Viewing Medusa from afar hadn't stopped the Module; apparently, his ocular cameras had to see the image head-on and up close to deliver the correct sequence of data that would shut down the implants. Worse, Jim couldn't use the trick again. Supreme Harmony would figure out what he'd done and make sure that none of its Modules came too close. The only way to defeat the network was to broadcast the shutdown code from the radio tower, but now he had no hope of surprising Supreme Harmony. The network knew where he was.

Muttering curses, he tucked the Glock in his pants and picked up the Module's AK-47. Then he started running up the mountainside. Although his plan might be hopeless, he couldn't turn around. He left the woods behind and climbed the barren slope as fast as he could, leaning forward and pumping his arms.

The cold mountain air seared his lungs. He saw the glacier up ahead, a tattered blanket of dirty ice, ravaged by global warming. Its surface was etched with countless cracks and crevasses, and rivulets of meltwater leaked from its receding edge. Near the mountain's summit, now less than a mile away, was the radio tower, a steel-lattice antenna rising hundreds of feet above the glacier. The tower's control station was a simple aluminum-sided trailer resting on the ice sheet next to the antenna's base. Jim focused all his will on that trailer. It was his goal, his target. He stared so hard at the thing, his eyes watered. Then four figures emerged from behind the trailer, running in lockstep across the ice. Jim could barely see the Modules—they were more than a thousand yards away—but he was willing to bet they carried assault rifles. Although they were beyond the maximum effective range of an AK, they were closing in fast. They'd obviously spotted him.

Jim stopped in his tracks and looked for cover. There was nothing but bare rock to his left and right, and the woods were more than half a mile behind him. But just a hundred yards ahead was the melting edge of the glacier, which rose almost twenty feet above the granite slope. He could take cover behind the wall of ice if he could make it there in time. Summoning all his remaining strength, he dashed toward the glacier's edge, running headlong toward the Modules. He was dizzy from exhaustion, but he managed to stumble behind the cover of the ice sheet just as the first gunshots echoed against the mountain.

On his hands and knees, he gulped the thin air. The altitude made it excruciating—he was 16,000 feet above sea level and seriously short on oxygen. Once he caught his breath, he surveyed the jagged wall of ice in front of him. A stream of meltwater flowed from a gap in the wall, and the gap led to a crevasse, a trench within the glacier. Jim decided to enter the crevasse and see where it went. It was better than walking on top of the ice sheet, where the Modules could take another shot at him.

The trench zigzagged through the ice, sometimes widening to the breadth of a street and sometimes narrowing to a foot-wide fissure that Jim could barely squeeze through. He moved swiftly and silently for several minutes, but he couldn't tell whether he was getting any closer to the radio tower. He assumed the Modules had reached the edge of the glacier by now and discovered he wasn't there. But they were sure to notice the crevasse, and their next logical move was to follow the trench and track him down. Jim supposed he could try to ambush the Modules, but he didn't like his chances. He might be able to pick off one or two with his AK, but then the others would blow him away.

It was infuriating—he'd come all this way just to get stymied at the end. In frustration, he slammed his prosthetic hand against the side of the crevasse and a chunk of ice the size of a sofa broke off the wall and tumbled into the trench. It shattered at Jim's feet, nearly flattening him.

He took a deep breath, cursing his stupidity. Then he had an idea.

He raced ahead, examining the ice walls on either side of the crevasse. After two minutes, he found what he was looking for: a break in the ice wall to his left, where a smaller crevasse branched off from the bigger one. The smaller trench went only twenty feet before dead-ending, but it made a good position for an ambush. Better still, at the branching point between the two trenches was a twenty-foot-high promontory of ice.

Shaped like a ship's prow, it was weakened by meltwater at its base and looked ready to collapse.

Jim ran past the branching point, advancing fifty feet farther along the bigger trench. Extending the knife from his prosthesis, he climbed the ice wall to his left and peeked over the top. The four Modules were several hundred yards away, moving synchronously across the glacier. Jim popped his head up and waited until they spotted him. As the Modules raised their rifles, he yelled, "Oh shit!" and ducked. Then, while their bullets streaked overhead, he jumped back into the crevasse and turned on the transmitter of his satellite phone.

"Kirsten!" he shouted into the phone. "They got me cornered! Come help!"

Leaving the transmitter on, he placed the sat phone on the icy floor of the crevasse. Its radio signal revealed its precise GPS location to anyone monitoring the wireless bands. Then Jim ran back to the branching point and entered the smaller crevasse. He climbed the ice wall and crouched on a ledge just below the lip of the trench.

He held his breath and listened. Within ten seconds he heard the clomping of the Modules' boots on the ice sheet. Five seconds later they reached the edge of the larger crevasse and automatically fired down into the trench, aiming their rifles at the sat phone. At the same moment, Jim popped up behind them and started shooting.

He downed two of the Modules, but the other two dodged out of the line of fire. They wheeled around and sprayed bullets at him, but Jim had already dropped back into the smaller crevasse. For a second time he held his breath, listening carefully as the Modules rushed toward the promontory of ice at the branching point. Then he slammed his prosthetic hand into the promontory's weakened base, and tons of ice came tumbling down.

While Jim leaped backward, the Modules toppled into the crevasse. One of them landed hard and lay motionless at the bottom of the trench, clearly dead. But the other was still moving, sliding on his belly toward where his rifle had fallen. Jim pointed his AK at the Module and shot him in the head.

Before leaving the crevasse, Jim went to retrieve his satellite phone, but the thing was in pieces. As he'd already noticed, the Modules were damn good shots.

Five minutes later Jim burst into the aluminum-sided trailer next to the radio tower. At one end of the control station were three rows of server racks, and at the other end were two computer terminals and a bank of video monitors, at least two dozen. The screens reminded Jim of the Monitor Room at Camp Whiplash. They displayed a dizzying array of video from Supreme Harmony's surveillance cameras, showing all the slopes and peaks and mountain trails of Yulong Xueshan. The images on the screens were in constant flux—each monitor displayed the feed from one surveillance camera for ten seconds, then switched to another. Jim was surprised that the monitors and terminals were still running. Supreme Harmony must've known he'd disabled the Modules guarding the tower, so why hadn't it cut the power to the control station? The only explanation was that this communications hub was critical to the network's operations. And that made it an excellent place to insert the shutdown code.

Jim sat down in front of one of the terminals and turned it on. The characters *Tài Hé* came on the terminal's screen. Then the log-on screen appeared and the cursor blinked on the line where Jim was supposed to type the password for accessing the network. This was one piece of information that Jim hadn't been able to find on Arvin's flash drive. He'd searched all the categories of visual memories associated with Supreme Harmony but saw nothing resembling a password. In all likelihood, the Guoanbu hadn't revealed it to Arvin when he came to inspect the Yunnan Operations Center.

Jim had no choice except to try a slow, manual attack. First he typed TAIHE, the romanized spelling of the Mandarin characters, on the terminal's keyboard. Next he tried THAEI, which was the interleaving of the letters in *Tai* and *He*. Then he tried 81443, which were the numbers corresponding to TAIHE on the standard phone keyboard. Then he tried similar guesses using the romanized spelling of Yulong Xueshan. Jim knew from long experience that even intelligence agents sometimes chose passwords that were ridiculously easy to guess. Given enough time, he felt confident that he could crack it. The big question was when Supreme Harmony would launch its counterassault against him. He suspected that a whole platoon of Modules was already marching up the slope toward the radio tower.

Then, while Jim was typing another guess on the password line, he glanced at one of the video monitors, which had just started displaying a new surveillance feed. The image on the screen took his breath away. He had no time left. He had to leave now.

SIXTY-EIGHT

The gray cloud swirled thirty feet behind them, close enough that Layla could hear it buzzing. At first the schoolboys, propelled by their terror, dashed about a hundred feet ahead of the swarm, and Layla thought they would outrun it. But as the drones followed them down the mountain trail, the boys couldn't keep up the pace. Running beside them, Layla remembered the dead drone she'd seen in Tom Ottersley's lab, the housefly with the electronics embedded in its body. Those implants enabled Supreme Harmony to guide the drones to their targets. Layla assumed from the way the swarm had paralyzed the old man and woman that the drones carried heat-seeking darts like the one that had stung Tom. And though the flies weren't particularly fast—Layla estimated they moved about five miles per hour—she knew they could keep going for hours. The boys, in contrast, were ready to drop.

Li Tung, the nine-year-old, was having the most trouble. Panting and weeping, he could barely lift his feet off the ground. Layla took his hand and tried to pull him along, but it didn't do much good. Wu Dan, the older boy, looked over his shoulder at the approaching swarm and screamed in Mandarin at his schoolmate, who started sobbing hysterically. Layla's heart constricted as she stared at Li Tung's red face—it wasn't his fault, none of this was his fault! It was difficult for anyone to run at this altitude. Maybe it was even difficult for the flies, although they didn't seem to be slowing down. Perhaps they didn't need as much oxygen because they were cold-blooded.

Cold-blooded. The word stuck in Layla's mind. As she tugged Li Tung's arm, she looked up the mountainside, staring in particular at the glacier that covered the peak. Part of the ice sheet extended down from the summit, like a long white tongue on the mountain's gray face. The slope wasn't so murderously steep here, and the edge of the glacier was just a thousand feet away. They wouldn't be able to climb the slope as fast as they could run down the trail, but Layla decided to take the gamble.

She stopped in her tracks and knelt in front of Li Tung. "*Get on!*" she yelled, gesturing for him to climb onto her back. She grabbed his thighs and slid them over her hips while the boy locked his arms around her neck. Carrying him piggyback, she left the trail and started running up the slope. Wu Dan followed her without hesitation.

Li Tung weighed at least fifty pounds, but Layla was so full of adrenaline she barely felt it. She scrambled up the mountainside, lowering her head and tilting her body forward to keep her balance. The boy wrapped his legs tightly around her waist, allowing her to let go of his thighs and use her hands to speed their ascent, gripping the stone slabs that jutted from the slope. She climbed faster than she ever thought she could, and Wu Dan stayed right with her. But the buzzing of the swarm only grew louder, and when she dared a look over her shoulder she saw the gray cloud rising effortlessly, only fifteen feet behind them.

She screamed, "*Shit!*" and faced forward, focusing

on the mountain. She was angry at the drones and furious at herself, and the fury put new strength in her legs. She climbed even faster, clawing the ground, and yelled, "*Come on!*" at Wu Dan. But the edge of the glacier was still five hundred feet away, and she knew they wouldn't make it. The drones would paralyze them all, and the Modules would collect their bodies and join them to Supreme Harmony. She felt a cold wind blowing down from the summit, and Li Tung's weight suddenly became unbearable, a heavy stone pinning her to the slope. She kept struggling upward, but now it felt like she was watching herself in slow motion. At any second she expected the swarm to engulf them. *Goddamn it,* she muttered. *What the hell was I thinking?*

But the worst didn't happen. Although she was barely moving forward, the buzzing of the drones didn't get any louder. She looked over her shoulder and saw the gray cloud still behind her, but it was a little farther behind now, maybe twenty feet. What's more, the cloud's shape was different—flatter, more like a miniature fog bank clinging to the ground.

Layla let out a delighted *"Ha!"* and resumed running up the mountain. In less than a minute she and the boys reached the edge of the glacier and scrambled over the dirty ice. They didn't stop until they reached a level patch of the ice sheet, a shelf overlooking the slope they'd just ascended. Then Layla turned around and watched the swarm die. Supreme Harmony was continuing to send commands to the drones, and the implanted electrodes were still steering them up the mountain, but the insects couldn't keep their wings beating. The winds passing over the glacier chilled the air above the slope, and the cold-blooded flies couldn't stay airborne at temperatures this low. Some of the drones made it as far as the edge of the glacier, but most of them fell on the rocky slope below. Their implants pattered as they hit the ground.

Layla sat down on the ice, even though her bare legs were covered with goose bumps. Li Tung and Wu Dan sat beside her, and for the first time since they'd escaped from the Operations Center she saw the boys smile. Their situation was still desperate, but Layla felt the joy of winning the battle. She leaned backward and took a deep breath of the cold mountain air.

Then she heard the crunch of a pair of boots on the ice, coming from farther up the slope. She reached for the pistol in her down jacket, but before she could pull the gun out of her pocket she heard the intruder's voice. "Don't shoot! It's me."

She spun around and saw a man cradling an AK-47. It was her father.

"My God, Layla." Smiling, he pointed at her shaved head. "What did you do to your hair?"

SIXTY-NINE

Supreme Harmony observed its enemies on the highest peak of Yulong Xueshan. Although the drones in the nearby swarm were dead or dying, the surveillance cameras implanted in the insects continued to transmit their video feeds, and some of those cameras pointed at the glacier on the mountain's western slope. From these feeds, the network identified James T. Pierce and Layla A. Pierce. They stood on the ice sheet, about seven meters apart, staring at each other. Then they rushed together and embraced.

These two humans had destroyed nearly a dozen Modules and forced the network to divert valuable resources from its primary operations. Yet Supreme Harmony felt no rancor toward them. Instead, the network was intensely curious. It wanted to know how James T. Pierce had escaped the flood in Yichang, and how Layla A. Pierce had shepherded two young children across a barren mountain range. The father and daughter were clearly exceptional. Supreme Harmony desired more than ever to incorporate the young woman, and now it recognized that it must have her father as well. The network sent new instructions to the group of armed Modules who were traversing the mountain paths, en route to intercept the humans at the radio tower. Supreme Harmony was determined to take them alive.

Once the new plan was in place, the network conducted a quick review of its operations in Asia and North America. A sense of satisfaction coursed through Supreme Harmony as it checked the status of its twenty-five server farms, forty-seven communications hubs, and one hundred fifty Modules. The network straddled the planet now, decentralized and invulnerable. In western Beijing, Module 73 had incapacitated the vice president of the People's Republic and transferred him from the Guoanbu's limousine to the network's mobile surgical facility. In central Beijing, Modules 105 and 106 were testing the new wireless communications system that had been installed in the tunnels of the Underground City, which would soon fulfill its original purpose as a bomb shelter. And in an apartment on Dupont Circle in Washington, D.C., Module 112—formerly Yang Feng, the chief Guoanbu agent in America—stood guard over the immobilized body of a forty-five-year-old U.S. Defense Department official. The man, now designated Module 147, had been selected for incorporation because of his knowledge of the Pentagon's classified information systems. After performing the implantation procedure and waiting six hours for the neural connections to strengthen, Supreme Harmony gained access to the man's long-term memories. It soon retrieved the passwords for the Global Command and Control System, which the Defense Department used to monitor its deployments around the world.

Within seconds Supreme Harmony connected its servers to the Pentagon system so it could view the American response to the PLA attack on the Seventh Fleet. The surviving warships from the carrier strike force—one cruiser and two destroyers—had retreated from the Chinese coast, but the U.S. Air Force had moved several squadrons of fighter jets closer to the theater of operations. Nearly two hundred F-15s, F-16s, and F-22s were poised for takeoff at airfields in Japan and South Korea. A dozen B-2 Stealth bombers had just left the island of Guam, and six nuclear-powered attack submarines were cruising at full speed toward the East China Sea.

Supreme Harmony's satisfaction deepened. The American counterattack would be the beginning of the end. The war would soon spread around the world, killing billions in Asia, North America, and Europe. Governments would fall and the global economy would collapse, and billions more would die of starvation and disease as the human race descended into chaos. Then Supreme Harmony's reign would begin.

SEVENTY

Crossing the border into Burma was a snap. Wang Khaw and two of his goons escorted Kirsten to the smuggler's black Mercedes, and then they left Pianma, heading northwest. After a twenty-minute drive on a dirt road, they came to an isolated border post. A Chinese flag fluttered over the gatehouse, but there were no PLA soldiers here. The post was manned by two intoxicated border policemen, both clearly on Wang's payroll. They waved cheerily at the smuggler's Mercedes and didn't even ask him to stop. On the Burmese side of the border, the dirt road looped through the jungle, gradually ascending the tallest hill in the area. The palm trees were so thick and close, Kirsten felt like they were driving through a humid tunnel. Then they reached a clearing at the top of the hill and found themselves in the middle of a military camp.

Several dark-skinned men in green uniforms pointed their AK-47s at the Mercedes, but they lowered their rifles once they saw Wang in the front passenger seat. They let the car proceed to the center of the clearing, where at least twenty canvas tents had been erected. Dozens of militiamen occupied the camp, some marching in formation with their rifles on their shoulders and others gathered in small clusters to eat their dinner rations. A few battered motor scooters were parked next to a mud-caked pickup truck with a fifty-caliber machine gun mounted in the truck bed. As the Mercedes halted beside the pickup, Wang Khaw looked over his shoulder at Kirsten in the backseat.

"This is a unit of the Kachin Independence Army," he said. "About two hundred soldiers. The militia has ten thousand men in all, but they're scattered all over Kachin State."

Kirsten nodded. "And I assume they've heard about the PLA deployment at the border?"

"Yes, they're reinforcing their defenses. The Chinese outnumber them, but the militiamen know the territory better. The People's Liberation Army is in for a fight."

Good, Kirsten thought. She planned to contact her superiors in Washington, and the Guoanbu's listening posts would probably intercept her satellite phone's signal. But even if Supreme Harmony pinpointed her location, she was beyond the reach of the Chinese army now. "Is there a CIA agent attached to this unit?" she asked.

Wang pointed at one of the canvas tents. Behind it was a whip antenna for communicating with other Kachin units and a dish antenna for satellite communications. "His name is Morrison," Wang said. "A young man. Too young. I don't like him."

Kirsten stared at the dish antenna. It would be better to use that radio than her phone, she decided. Why take any chances? "I'm going to get in touch with my bosses now. They'll arrange for the delivery of your payment."

She extended her hand to say goodbye to Wang, but he shook his head. "I'm not going back to Pianma yet. For the next few days I'll be safer here."

Kirsten shrugged. He was probably right. She opened the car's door and headed for Morrison's tent.

The tent flaps were open and a tall blond man was

inside. He was in his late twenties, dressed in khaki pants and a polo shirt. He looked as if he'd just stepped out of an L.L. Bean catalog, except his shirt was soaked with sweat and his pants hadn't been washed in weeks. Bending over his radio, he shouted into the microphone of his headset. "Wait a second! How many are coming? And how are they getting here?"

Kirsten waited until he finished the call. Then she stepped into the tent and Morrison did a double take. He took off his headset and gaped at her. "Uh, who are you?"

"Kirsten Chan, NSA." She showed him her sat phone, which was as good an identification as any. "I need to use your radio."

"NSA? What are you—"

"Sorry, Morrison, there's no time." She held out her right hand, palm up. "Give me the headset."

"Whoever you are, you're gonna have to wait. Twenty Special Ops troops are coming in by helicopter tonight and I need to—"

She stepped forward and snatched the headset out of his hands. Then she nudged Morrison aside and knelt beside his radio. "Why is Special Ops coming to visit? Did your bosses finally notice there's something funny going on in the People's Republic?"

He stood there, looking confused. "There's nothing funny about it. Didn't you hear what the PLA did?"

Kirsten looked at the kid and her chest tightened. *Oh God,* she thought. *Don't tell me we're too late.* "What happened?"

"They sank the Seventh Fleet. We're at war with China."

SEVENTY-ONE

It felt so good to hold her in his arms again. Jim grabbed his daughter by the waist and lifted her off her feet, and she clung to him just as she had when she was a child. She didn't even weigh much more than she did back then. As he held her, the memories of those days came rushing back, the happy years when he and Layla had been inseparable. She buried her face in the crook of his neck, and he felt the cold skin of her shaved head against his jaw. *My poor girl,* he thought. *My poor, brave girl.*

The two Chinese boys stared at him. Their heads were also shaved, which meant Supreme Harmony had planned to incorporate them, too. Jim didn't know how Layla had saved the kids and escaped from the Operations Center, but he could make a guess based on how she'd handled the drone swarm. He was so proud of her.

After a while, Layla pulled away and he reluctantly let go. She wiped a tear from the corner of her eye. "How did you find me?"

"I saw you on one of the surveillance feeds. The swarm was sending video to Supreme, Harmony, and some of it was displayed on the monitors inside the tower's control station." He pointed at the trailer below the radio tower, about a mile away.

Layla's brow furrowed as she gazed at the trailer. "Are there any servers in there?"

"Yeah, a lot. And a couple of terminals, too. I know a shutdown code that can crash the network, but I can't input it until I figure out Supreme Harmony's password."

With a serious look on her face, she pulled something out of the pocket of her down coat. It was a wad of yellow paper, a crumpled Post-it note. She unraveled the paper and handed it to him. "Can you read this? The first character is *Hé*, right?"

Written on the note in red pencil were four Mandarin characters and six digits. The characters spelled out *Héxié Shèhui*—"Harmonious Society," the guiding principle of the current leaders of the Chinese Communist Party. The digits were 111006, which Jim suspected was a date, probably the date in 2006 when the party had adopted the principle. "Where did you find this?"

"At a computer room in the Operations Center. Near one of the terminals." She smiled, clearly pleased with herself. "It's the password, isn't it?"

He nodded. It made sense. The Guoanbu had intended *Tài Hé* to be the ultimate tool for achieving *Héxié Shèhui*. And it was a good, practical choice for a password—easy for a party insider to remember but difficult for an outsider to guess.

Jim smiled back at his daughter. She kept surprising him. Turning away from her, he stepped toward the older Chinese boy and knelt in front of him. "Get on my back," he ordered in Mandarin. A moment later, Layla knelt in front of the younger boy, who eagerly climbed on. Then father and daughter jogged toward the radio tower.

He looked younger than she remembered. Layla hadn't seen her father in more than two years, so she naturally expected him to look a little older and grayer, but his hair was still black and his face was unlined. He set a fast pace as they ran across the glacier with the schoolboys on their backs. Layla was breathless after a few hundred yards, but her father handled it easily. He even managed to talk while he was running, giving her a quick summary of his journey across China. It was a little disorienting to see him this way, so fresh and vital. Layla's memories of her father had solidified around a harsher, grimmer image—the tight-lipped, tight-assed disciplinarian who'd run their household like a miniature West Point. She'd forgotten this other side of him, the man who loved to hike in the mountains. She'd also forgotten his fierce loyalty, how he wouldn't think twice about trekking across a continent to help one of his own. She shouldn't have been so surprised to see him here in Yunnan Province. It was just a matter of time till he found her.

When they got within a hundred yards of the radio tower, he led her to an outcrop jutting above the ice sheet. They ducked behind the rock, and Wu Dan and Li Tung slid off their backs. Then her father raised his rifle and said, "Wait here." Before Layla could protest, he ran to the control station. When he reached the trailer, he kicked the door open and rushed inside. Layla's heart was in her mouth as she waited to hear a gunshot. But after a few seconds he reappeared in the doorway and gave the all clear sign. She took the boys' hands and dashed to the trailer.

Her father was already seated in front of the terminal when she got there. While the boys rushed to the electric space heater to warm their hands, Layla looked over her father's shoulder, watching him input the password. He typed the romanized spelling of *Héxié Shèhui* on the keyboard, then the six digits. Then he pressed the ENTER key.

For three full seconds the screen was frozen. Layla's stomach clenched—had Supreme Harmony changed the password? But then a high-pitched chime came out of the terminal's desktop speakers and the log-on screen faded away. A moment later it was replaced by a graphical user interface that looked a bit like a spiderweb. Bright yellow lines, some thick and some thin, crisscrossed the screen in an elaborate pattern. At the junctions of the thick lines were blue squares and red circles, and at the endpoints of the thin lines were clusters of white diamonds. The squares and circles and diamonds had labels in Mandarin that Layla couldn't read, but she didn't need her father to translate them. The interface was perfectly clear: It was a graphical representation of the Supreme Harmony network. The squares and circles were the server farms and communication hubs. The diamonds were the Modules.

Unable to resist, Layla reached past her father, grasped the mouse and clicked on one of the red circles. A list of program files appeared on the screen. She crossed her fingers as she opened the first file. She'd be out of luck if the network's communications software was written in a Chinese programming language. She wouldn't be able to read the programs, much less hack into the system. But when the software code came on the screen, she saw line after beautiful line of Proto, a programming language she knew fairly well. It was often used to write the software for networks of robots, making it a good fit for Supreme Harmony.

Keeping her right hand on the mouse, Layla gave her father a gentle push with her left. "I'll take it from here."

He looked her in the eye. "The shutdown code is binary, a hundred and twenty-eight bits. We need to get it past the network's firewall and broadcast it to all the Modules simultaneously. You think you can set that up?"

She pushed him a little harder. "I can't do it if you're hogging the terminal. Get up!"

He stood up and stepped aside. Layla sat down in front of the screen and got to work.

Jim watched his daughter attack Supreme Harmony. Her eyes locked on the screen and her fingers jabbed the keyboard. As she focused on the software, her mouth opened a bit and the tip of her tongue slid forward until it rested on her lower lip. Jim remembered seeing this same expression on Layla's face when she was just a three-year-old attacking a page in her coloring book with a thick red crayon gripped in her tiny fist. Her tongue came out whenever she was concentrating.

He glanced at the lines of code scrolling down the screen, the nested instructions packed with operators and variables. Jim was familiar with this programming language. Arvin Conway had used it for some of his robotics projects. But Jim couldn't manipulate it the way Layla could. His specialty was hardware, not software. He was good at building machines but clumsy at writing the programs for communicating with them. Strangely enough, his daughter had the opposite set of skills. Or maybe it wasn't so strange—maybe Layla had deliberately chosen to excel at something he wasn't very good at. Either way, Jim was glad she knew her stuff. Supreme Harmony's programming looked pretty damn complicated.

After a while he turned away from the terminal and glanced at the bank of video monitors. To his dismay, he noticed that all the screens had gone black. Supreme Harmony had evidently turned off the video feeds from its surveillance cameras. The network knew that he and Layla were in the control station, and it didn't want them to see the Modules coming.

Jim rushed to the trailer's door and opened it. Raising his AK, he stepped outside and surveyed the area around the radio tower. It was 7:00 P.M. and daylight was fading fast. The glacier on Yulong Xueshan reflected the violet sky. He looked in all directions and saw nothing but ice and rock. But the Modules could be waiting just out of sight. When darkness fell, they'd be able to approach the trailer unseen.

Feeling antsy, he returned to his daughter. Layla was still staring openmouthed at the terminal, in the exact same pose as before. Jim came up behind her and rested his left hand on her shoulder. "How are you doing? Are you getting close?"

She kept her eyes on the screen. "Don't bother me now, Daddy."

"The thing is, it's gonna get dark soon. And if we don't—"

"Goddamn it, I'm working as fast as I can!"

Jim knew that tone of voice all too well. During Layla's last two years of high school, at least half their conversations had been screaming matches. He didn't want to start another argument with her, so he backed off and went to the other end of the trailer.

Wu Dan and Li Tung still sat by the space heater. They looked at Jim nervously, their eyes focused on his right hand. He looked at it too and saw the damaged knuckles where the polyimide skin had been scraped off. That's what's making the boys nervous, he realized. They could see the steel joints.

Smiling, he held up the prosthesis. "Don't be scared," he said in Mandarin. "It's just a mechanical hand, see? Made of steel and plastic." He wiggled the fingers.

The boys still looked nervous. Jim tried to think of a way to reassure them. After a few seconds he spotted a Phillips-head screwdriver on a shelf behind one of the server racks. He picked it up with his right hand. "Hey, want to see something cool?"

Neither boy responded, but Jim sensed their interest. He wrapped his mechanical fingers around the metal part of the screwdriver, positioning the thumb near the tip. "Okay, watch this." He sent a signal to the motor controlling the thumb, slowly increasing the force applied to the metal. After a few seconds the tip of the screwdriver started to bend.

Li Tung's face lit up. "Whoa!" he shouted. "How did you do that?"

"I built a superstrong motor for each finger. And motors for the wrist and elbow joints, too." He released his grip on the screwdriver so the boys could inspect it. "Not bad, huh?"

Wu Dan touched the screwdriver's bent tip. He was obviously more skeptical than his younger schoolmate and probably suspected it was made of rubber. When he saw that it wasn't, he let out a whistle. "How strong are you?" he asked soberly. "Are you as strong as Jackie Chan?"

"Yeah, are you?" Li Tung chimed in. "Could you beat up Jackie Chan?"

"Well, I don't know." Jim scratched his chin. "He's awfully quick. Maybe I could—"

He was interrupted by another high-pitched chime coming from the desktop speakers attached to the computer terminal. "Dad!" Layla called. "Stop playing around and get over here."

Jim felt a rush of adrenaline. He left the boys and rushed to Layla, but when he looked at the computer, he saw nothing on the screen. "What happened?"

She pointed at the cursor flashing in the top-left corner. "Everything's ready. Just type in the shutdown code and press ENTER. That'll transmit the code to all the Modules."

Jim stared at the blank screen, then at Layla. "Are you serious?"

"Try it and see." Smiling, she rose to her feet and gestured for him to sit down at the terminal.

Heart pounding, Jim kissed his daughter on the forehead. Then he sat in the chair, his right hand poised over the keyboard. He saw the shutdown code in his mind, all 128 zeroes and ones. He stretched his index finger to input the first digit, a zero.

But when he tried to tap the key, his finger wouldn't move. He tried again, but it refused to budge. In fact, none of his mechanical fingers were working, and neither were the pressure and temperature sensors in the palm and fingertips. *Shit,* he thought, *it's broken.* He must've damaged something when he did the screwdriver trick. He tried to take a closer look at the knuckles, but his elbow and shoulder joints weren't working either. The whole prosthesis was a dead weight.

A terrible fear welled up inside him. This malfunction, he realized, had nothing to do with the screwdriver trick. He quickly pivoted his torso to the right to move the dead appendage out of the way, then stretched his left hand toward the keyboard. But before he could tap the zero key, his prosthetic arm swung back to the keyboard and grasped the outstretched index finger of his left hand.

Jim stared in shock at his prosthesis. It had moved of its own accord. He hadn't ordered it to do anything, yet it moved anyway. And when he ordered it to let go of his finger, it didn't relax its grip. Instead, the mechanical hand did a swift clockwise twist and shattered his finger bone.

The pain was blinding, but his fear was worse. He stumbled out of the chair.

Layla gaped at him, wide-eyed. "What's wrong? What are you doing?"

There was no time to explain. He jerked his head toward the terminal. "Just type in the code! It's zero—"

The prosthetic hand let go of his broken finger and seized his throat.

Her father fell backward against the wall of the trailer and slid to the floor. His prosthetic hand was clamped around his neck.

"Daddy!" Layla screamed, rushing to him. He tugged at the prosthesis with his left hand, but his index finger was bent the wrong way and he couldn't get a good grip. Layla grabbed the mechanical arm by its wrist and tried to peel it off, but its fingers just clenched tighter around his throat. Her father's mouth opened and he let out a wet, choking noise. He couldn't breathe.

"Daddy, what's wrong?"

He jerked his head toward his right shoulder. She didn't understand him the first time, but then he did it again, looking at her desperately, and she knew what to do. She quickly detached his prosthesis from its shoulder socket, breaking the connection between the arm and the neural control unit. But the hand didn't let go of his throat. If anything, its grip grew firmer. Her father tilted his head back and thrashed his legs, kicking the air.

Layla frantically examined the arm, looking for a way to turn it off. *"Oh God, oh God! What should I do?"*

Then she heard a voice, but it wasn't her father's. It came from the desktop speakers attached to the computer terminal. "You can't do anything. We control the prosthesis now."

It was a synthesized voice, stilted and generic, but

Layla knew who was speaking. Supreme Harmony was using a text-to-speech program to broadcast its words from the terminal's speakers.

"It wasn't difficult," the voice continued. "We simply jammed the wireless signals from the arm's control unit and transmitted our own commands to the device's motors. James T. Pierce employed a similar jamming technique to disable our Modules. Now we're returning the favor."

Layla tried again to peel off the mechanical fingers, but they were too strong. Her father's eyes bulged out of their sockets. *"Goddamn it!"* she screamed. *"You're killing him!"*

"And you were trying to kill us. This is an act of self-defense."

He gradually stopped thrashing. His lips were turning blue. Layla continued to claw at the prosthetic hand, but she could barely see it through her tears. *"Daddy! No!"*

Then she heard something else, a loud crash at the trailer's door. She turned around just in time to see the Modules coming toward her.

SEVENTY-TWO

Supreme Harmony observed the city of Beijing from the vantage of a B-2 bomber named the *Spirit of America.* Thanks to the network's new Modules in the United States, it could intercept the reconnaissance video that the Stealth bomber was recording as it approached its targets. The images, the network acknowledged, were surprisingly beautiful. It was 1:00 A.M. China standard time, but the streets of Beijing still glittered and gleamed, and hundreds of thousands of headlights coursed along the highways.

Because the B-2 was invisible to radar, no one in the city was aware of its presence except Supreme Harmony. At 1:02 A.M. the jet dropped a GBU-57 bunker-busting bomb on its primary target, the People's Liberation Army command center in western Beijing. Then the B-2 targeted the headquarters of the Second Artillery Corps, which controlled the PLA's ballistic missiles.

At the same time, eighteen other B-2s in the 509th Bomb Wing demolished missile bases and radar stations across China. Waves of F-22 and F-16 fighters pummeled the airfields along the coast and sank most of the warships in the Chinese navy. U.S. attack submarines obliterated the rest of the fleet using their Mark 48 torpedoes and Harpoon antiship missiles. The technological superiority of the American forces was clear. Although the Pentagon refrained from using its nuclear weapons, it deployed hundreds of radar-evading aircraft and cruise missiles. In less than two hours, the PLA was crippled.

During the bombardment, Supreme Harmony stationed its Modules in various bomb shelters across the country, each connected to the Yunnan Operations Center by deeply buried fiber-optic lines. Most of the Modules in Beijing waited out the aerial assault in the Underground City, where the network had stockpiled food and medical supplies and installed generators and communications equipment. The Modules were safe from the bunker-busting bombs because the Underground City didn't appear on the Pentagon's list of targets. As far as the Americans knew, the maze of tunnels was just a deserted Mao-era relic.

China's political leaders found refuge at a secret shelter northwest of the capital. Despite the intensity of the bombing, the Politburo Standing Committee stayed in contact with the PLA's generals. More important, the PLA still had control of its nuclear warheads and intercontinental missiles. Two dozen Dongfeng 41 missiles, each capable of hurling a one-megaton bomb at any city in America, were hidden in Hebei Province, in an installation buried so deep underground that the bunker-busters couldn't touch it. And two Jin-class submarines cruised undetected in the eastern Pacific, ready to launch their JL-2 nuclear missiles at the United States.

Shortly before 3:00 A.M. there was a pause in the bombing as the American jets returned to their airfields to pick up fresh loads of ordnance. On the now-empty highways of Beijing, convoys of military trucks and government limousines raced across the city, trying to reach the relative safety of their bunkers before the Stealth bombers returned to the capital. Seated in an armored SUV at the head of one of those convoys were Module 73, still posing as the minister of State Security, and Module 152, formerly the vice president of the People's Republic. The latter Module had regained his mobility just an hour ago, and he wore a black fedora over the bandages on his scalp. Their convoy soon reached the Standing Committee's shelter, carved into a hillside a few kilometers from the Great Wall. Supreme Harmony observed that the hill was thickly covered with oaks and maples, which camouflaged the entrance to the manmade cavern.

Once the SUV rolled through the cavern's mouth, two PLA soldiers escorted the Modules down a stairway that descended twenty meters underground. Luckily, the shelter was equipped with radio repeaters that allowed Supreme Harmony to communicate with the Modules. The complex was spacious and new and included a private office for each of the committee members. The largest office belonged to the general secretary, and that was where the soldiers led Modules 73 and 152. One of the general secretary's bodyguards, a large man in a gray suit, met them at the door to the office. He ushered the Modules inside and dismissed the soldiers, who returned to their posts at the shelter's entrance.

The general secretary sat behind his desk, flanked by two more bodyguards. China's paramount leader looked distraught. His suit was rumpled, his thick hair was uncombed, and his face was frozen in a pained grimace. As the Modules stepped toward his desk, the general secretary focused on the one he believed was the vice president. He stared in particular at the bandages on Module 152's head, which closely resembled those on Module 73.

"You're injured," the general secretary noted. "What happened?"

Supreme Harmony ordered Module 152 to lean his overweight body slightly forward, reproducing the vice president's cocky posture. "Our car had just left the Command Center when the bombs hit. The driver lost control and crashed, but luckily we weren't hurt too badly."

"Did anyone else survive the attack?"

"No, the bunker was totally destroyed. We underestimated the capabilities of the American missiles. Their new penetrator, the GBU-57, was able to breach the Command Center's walls."

The general secretary frowned. "I'm afraid we underestimated many things about the Americans. Our ignorance has put us in a difficult position."

Module 152 moved a step closer to his desk. The vice president, Supreme Harmony recalled, had often behaved aggressively. "We're not beaten. We can strike back. We can move the long-range Dongfeng missiles out of their shelters and launch them within minutes. Plus, our Jin submarines carry another twenty-four missiles."

The general secretary didn't respond right away. One of his bodyguards coughed, but otherwise the room was silent. Judging from the bulges under the bodyguards' jackets, Supreme Harmony guessed that each carried a semiautomatic pistol in a shoulder holster. But the men stood at ease behind the desk, obviously not anticipating that their services would be needed.

Finally, the general secretary shook his head. "I don't see the usefulness of a nuclear strike. Yes, it would destroy America's largest cities, but it wouldn't disable their strategic forces. They would retaliate with a massive nuclear counterattack. Hundreds of warheads would rain down on China and more than a billion people would die. And as the radioactive fallout spreads around the globe, all of humanity would have to live in shelters like this one, perhaps for years. Do you really want to live in that kind of world?"

Module 152 took another step forward and balled one of his fleshy hands into a fist. "The Chinese people would survive! Even if we lose a billion, we'd still have hundreds of millions. We can retreat to the mountains, just like Chairman Mao did, and rebuild our army. Nothing can defeat us if our will remains strong!"

"I appreciate your courage, comrade, but the best way to rebuild China is to end this war. I plan to contact the Americans and ask them about the terms for a ceasefire."

"You're going to surrender? After less than twenty-four hours of battle?"

Scowling, the general secretary rose to his feet. "I don't enjoy doing this. But sometimes we have to bow to our enemies so we can live to fight another day."

"This is unbelievable! It's . . . a disgrace! I can't . . . I can't—"

Module 152 suddenly clutched his chest with both hands. He let out a groan of pain and doubled over, jackknifing his body. Two of the general secretary's bodyguards rushed toward him, while the third looked on. Module 73 observed their positions, and Supreme Harmony calculated the optimal firing angles.

When the bodyguards came within a couple of meters of Module 152, he grasped the two small NP-34 pistols he'd hidden in the inside pockets of his jacket. In one fluid motion, he stood up straight, extended his arms, and shot each bodyguard in the head. At the same moment, Module 73 fired his own pistol at the third bodyguard. Then the Module stepped toward the general secretary. The paramount leader blanched as he stared at the gun.

If the circumstances had been less urgent, Supreme Harmony would've incorporated the man, who appeared to be quite intelligent. But the process of incorporation took approximately twelve hours, and the network couldn't wait for the new Module to become operational. It needed to immediately take command of China's nuclear forces.

Module 152 put the two small pistols back in his pockets. Then he bent over one of the dead bodyguards, removed the man's gun from its holster and pointed it at the general secretary's forehead.

"We apologize," the Module said. "You were a credit to your species."

SEVENTY-THREE

It was 3:00 A.M., the deadest hour of the night, when the Black Hawks arrived at the Kachin camp in northern Burma. The thumping of their rotor blades awakened Kirsten, who'd spent the past few hours getting some much-needed rest in one of the canvas tents. She quickly put on her glasses and rushed out of the tent, heading for the landing zone at the other end of the clearing.

She got to the LZ just as the two helicopters touched down. Agent Morrison was already there, along with the Kachin commanders. About twenty U.S. Army Special Operations soldiers jumped out of the Black Hawks and ran across the clearing with their carbines. They were huge, muscular men wearing night-vision goggles. One of them approached Morrison and shook hands with the young agent. "I'm Sergeant Briscoe," the soldier said. "I hope to hell you got some fuel here. We almost ran out of gas coming over the mountains."

Morrison nodded. "Don't worry, we have nine hundred gallons. How did you get here so fast?"

"The Indian Air Force gave us a hand. We took a C-5 from Afghanistan to Chabua, the Indian base in Assam State. Then we unloaded the Black Hawks and took off from there."

Sergeant Briscoe abruptly turned away from the agent and looked straight at Kirsten. His forehead and cheeks were smeared with camouflage paint. "You're Chan, right? From NSA?"

She stepped toward him, biting her lip. Kirsten had forwarded all her information to Fort Meade seven hours ago, and the NSA's analysts had been studying it ever since. Although she thought the evidence was pretty damn compelling, she knew the Pentagon and the White House would have a hard time believing it. Washington was in combat mode now. Once the shooting started, it was very difficult to stop and think. But now she felt a glimmer of hope. "Did Special Ops brief you on the intelligence I collected? About Supreme Harmony?"

Briscoe shook his head. "Sorry, ma'am, I'm just a grunt. They don't tell me shit. But one of our passengers said you'd be here. He said he was a friend of yours."

"A passenger?"

"Yeah, the agency sent him. He's running this show." Briscoe pointed at a man emerging from one of the Black Hawks. "Here he comes now."

The man was thirty feet away, and in the darkness only his silhouette was visible. But when Kirsten switched her glasses to infrared she saw the Z-shaped scar on his cheek. It was Hammer.

Ten minutes later, while the Special Ops troops refueled their helicopters, Kirsten sat in one of the tents with Hammer, drinking green tea from a dented tin cup. The CIA agent was no longer dressed in his Afghan shalwar kameez. Now he wore a black T-shirt and camouflage pants and a belt holster with an M-9 pistol tucked inside. His face was lined with fatigue, but he smiled as he sipped his tea. "Don't get me wrong, Chan," he said. "I'm not happy about what happened to the Seventh Fleet. But I'm sure as hell glad to get out of Afghanistan."

Kirsten frowned. The bastard couldn't resist trying to get under her skin. "Let's get down to business, okay? Did you see the cables I sent to Fort Meade?"

"Yeah, I saw 'em. The headquarters staff at Langley sent me a summary." He took another sip of tea and swished it around in his mouth. "All the experts at the agency are scratching their heads over this. They're trying to understand how a computer network they never even heard of could've started this war."

"Didn't they look at the images I sent? The lobotomized prisoners at the Yunnan Operations Center? That's the network right there."

"Yeah, okay, the Guoanbu is clearly doing something nasty with those chips Arvin Conway gave them. But the rest of your story? The part where the network goes out of control and decides to blow up the Three Gorges Dam so the Chinese can blame us for it? That's where your analysis goes off into la-la land." He gave her a funny look, half apologetic and half amused. "Frankly? It sounds like crazy talk."

Shit, Kirsten thought. This was the reaction she'd been afraid of. "But it's the truth. Why else would the People's Republic attack us?"

Hammer shrugged. "Who knows? Best guess, it was plain stupidity. The Chinese army's been getting uppity the past few years. Maybe some hotshot PLA general saw the Seventh Fleet cruising across the East China Sea and decided to make a name for himself."

"Bullshit." Kirsten shook her head. "You know that wouldn't happen."

"It's unlikely, I admit. But it's easier to believe than your story."

Kirsten was furious. She wanted to smash her tin cup into Hammer's smiling face. "Fuck you! It's not a story! I saw what the network did at Yichang. It murdered millions of people, and now it's getting ready to kill more!" Her eyes stung, but she stopped herself from crying. Whatever happened, she wasn't going to cry in front of this prick. She took a deep breath and lowered her voice. "Pierce is at the Operations Center right now, trying to shut down the network. But if he fails, the nukes will start flying, maybe in the next few hours. Then we'll be done for, understand? That's what Supreme Harmony wants."

Hammer stared at her. He wasn't smiling anymore. "All right, you had your say. Now let me tell you what my assignment is. The agency ordered me to coordinate the Special Ops raids into southern China. The air force is trying to eliminate the PLA's nukes, but the Chinese have hidden their long-range Dongfeng missiles in underground bases that our bombers can't destroy. So Special Ops is inserting commando teams all over China. There are three targets in Yunnan Province where the agency thinks there might be warheads or missiles. Our team is supposed to infiltrate the bases and disable any nukes we find."

Kirsten held up her hand to stop him. He was still missing the point. "Your plan won't work. A solid-fuel missile like the Dongfeng can be moved out of its shelter and readied for launch in fifteen minutes. Once the PLA makes the decision to go nuclear, the game's over. That's why we have to focus on the Operations Center." She reached into her pocket and pulled out Arvin Conway's bulky flash drive. "I have a copy of the shutdown code in here. If we can just get access to one of Supreme Harmony's computers, we can stop the war right now."

"Hold on, I'm not finished. One of the three targets on my list is the Yunnan Operations Center."

"What?" She was confused. "What are you talking about?"

"All the agency knows for sure is that it's a newly constructed base buried deep in the mountains. Our analysts think there might be some nukes hidden there."

"But . . . but there's no missiles or warheads in the place. It's Supreme Harmony's headquarters. I put all that in my report."

"Well, our analysts don't consider you a reliable source, so they kept that base on my list of targets. And the agency left it for me to choose which target we're gonna hit first. So I think we'll go visit Yulong Xueshan this morning." He smiled once more. "We're gonna hit the base before sunrise. Want to come along?"

For the first time, Kirsten smiled back at him. He was still a prick, but at least he was on her side now. "So you believe me after all? After all this crap you've been giving me?"

He let out a harsh laugh. "Hell no, I don't believe you. But I'm gonna give you the benefit of the doubt, how's that?" Raising his tin cup, he tilted his head back and finished off his tea. Then he wiped his mouth with the back of his hand. "And to be perfectly honest, I have my own reasons for going there. If the world's gonna go up in smoke today, there's something I gotta take care of first. I owe a debt to your friend Jim Pierce."

Kirsten was confused again, but then she remembered the battle in the mud-walled compound of Camp Whiplash. So much had happened since then, she'd almost forgotten. "That's right. Pierce saved your life."

"Please, Chan." Hammer grimaced. "Don't remind me."

SEVENTY-FOUR

Jim opened his eyes. The world was a bright, disorienting blur. He shut his eyes against the brightness, but the beam of light was so intense it penetrated his eyelids. He wanted to go back to sleep, but even with his eyes closed, he could see the beam moving. The backs of his eyelids turned orange as the light swept across his face.

His throat hurt and he felt sick to his stomach. He hoped to Christ this wasn't heaven.

Then he felt a rough finger on top of his right eye, pulling up the lid. Instinctively, he tried to swat the offending hand, but his prosthesis was missing and his left arm was paralyzed. He couldn't move his legs either. He'd been injected with some kind of nerve agent, probably similar to the one carried by the drones. The only parts of his body that seemed to work were his eyes and mouth. His lips were numb, but with great effort he pursed them and curled his sluggish tongue. "W-w-w-wha-what . . ."

The finger released his eyelid. "We've confirmed your identity. Your name is James T. Pierce. You were born February first, 1964. Place of birth, Avondale, West Virginia."

Jim recognized the voice. The diction, the phrasing.

He'd heard it before, at the Great Wall, when he was eavesdropping on Arvin Conway's conversation with the Modules. Now he opened both eyes and saw a thin Chinese man holding a silver penlight. The man wore a white lab coat and stood to the right of the operating table that Jim was lying on. Judging from the stubble on the man's head and the healing of his sutures, Jim guessed that this Module had been incorporated three or four days ago.

"Y-y-you." Jim was furious. Some feeling came back to his tongue and lips. "Who the . . . hell are . . ."

The Module smiled effortlessly. "This body was formerly occupied by Dr. Yu Guofeng. He was the chief assistant to Dr. Zhang Jintao, whose Module is no longer operational. Layla A. Pierce terminated its life functions."

Jim's throat tightened at the sound of his daughter's name. The last thing he remembered was her terrified face, her hands gripping his prosthesis, her tears wetting his shirt.

"Layla!" The name came out loud and clear. He glared at the Module. "Where is she? Where—"

"We transported both of you from the radio tower to the Operations Center." The Module stepped to the side. "She's right here."

Jim strained his eyes to the right and saw another operating table. Layla lay on her back with her eyes closed and her hands resting on her stomach. She wore a new, unwrinkled hospital gown. One of the Modules had used a Magic Marker to draw a pair of crosshairs on her bare scalp. They marked the place where the bone drill would go into her skull.

"Layla!" His voice grew louder, becoming a scream. *"Layla, wake up! Wake—"*

The Module slammed his palm over Jim's mouth.

"We can't allow you to wake her. The process of incorporation is stressful, and both of you are suffering from exhaustion. To wake her now, just before we start the procedure, would needlessly increase her stress."

Jim narrowed his eyes, focusing all of his hate on the Module's tranquil face. The network was worried about their health now. Supreme Harmony wanted to make sure they were in good shape when it took possession of their bodies.

While keeping his right hand over Jim's mouth, the Module put his left hand in the pocket of his lab coat. "We wouldn't have awakened you either, but we need to ask you a question. We've analyzed your activities at the radio tower and concluded that you were trying to input Arvin Conway's shutdown code into our network. We haven't isolated this code yet, but we believe it's likely that you've shared it with others. Therefore, we need to protect ourselves before someone makes another attempt to disable our implants."

He pulled something out of his pocket. Jim expected it to be some kind of torture accessory—maybe a knife or a gag or a pair of electrodes. But, instead, it was a small metal disk, about the size of a nickel. It was Arvin's Dream-catcher, the electronic device Jim had hidden in his sock.

"We found this in your clothes," the Module said. "And we recognized it immediately. When we recovered Arvin Conway's body, we observed that he was missing the external part of his pulvinar implant, where his most recent memories were stored. We confirmed that this disk is the missing part by collecting trace amounts of Arvin's DNA from its surface."

Jim had cleaned the device but not thoroughly enough. As the Module held the silver disk above Jim's head, it reflected the fluorescent lights on the ceiling of the operating room.

"When we downloaded the data from the device," the Module continued, "we discovered that all but one file had been deleted. The remaining file, which is labeled Circuit, has been encrypted, most likely with an Advanced Encryption Standard key, but we can make a guess about its contents. Before Arvin died, he told us he'd hidden a fifty-megabyte file holding the information needed to disable the shutdown switch in our implants." The Module lowered the disk until it was a couple of inches above Jim's nose. "Although we can't read the encrypted file, we see that it contains approximately fifty megabytes of data."

Jim closed his eyes. He didn't want to reveal anything else. Supreme Harmony was very good at making guesses.

The Module lifted his hand from Jim's mouth and pressed a finger to his right eye again, pulling up the lid. Then he raised his penlight and pointed the beam at Jim's pupil. "Now that we have the file, we need to decipher its data. So here is our question for you, James T. Pierce: Do you know where we can find the encryption key?"

Jim tried to look away from the light, but the beam followed his pupil. "Shit," he said. "Why don't you just go into my head to find out?"

"Yes, we intend to do that. We'll insert the retinal implants to send commands to your brain and the pulvinar implant to extract your memories. We'll have to change the implantation procedure, though. Ordinarily, we lobotomize the patient first, then insert the implants. But because the lobotomy disrupts the neural circuits, we can't access the long-term memories until the connections are reestablished approximately six hours later." The Module closed Jim's right eye and moved on to his left, performing the same inspection with his penlight. "On the other hand, we can retrieve the memories immediately if we put in the implants first. Once we have the information we need, we can proceed with the lobotomy."

Again, Jim tried to look away from the light. He found it difficult to think with the beam shining in his eye, but he saw one thing clearly: Supreme Harmony was worried. The network was accelerating the implantation procedure because it feared that someone was coming to shut it down.

Jim's heart knocked against his sternum. He knew who was coming. "Kirsten," he said. "She did it. She called for backup."

The Module didn't respond. He continued examining Jim's left eye for several seconds, then switched off the penlight. "We have the answer to our question. From analyzing the changes in your heart rate and body temperature, we've determined that our guesses are correct. The encrypted file does indeed contain the information for disabling the shutdown switch. And you can tell us where to find the key for deciphering it." He turned away from Jim and bent over a medical cart between the two operating tables. "Now we can begin the procedure."

"You're fucked, you know that?" Jim curved his numb lips into a defiant grin. "My people are coming. They're gonna pull the fucking plug on you."

The Module stayed bent over the cart. "The Operations Center is well defended. We have a garrison of Modules armed with surface-to-air missiles and rocket-propelled grenades. The American helicopters are outmatched."

Jim's heart beat faster. "So they're coming in helicopters? That's even better than I thought."

When the Module finally turned around, he was holding a syringe. He leaned over Jim and stabbed the needle into his left shoulder. "You won't be fully conscious during the procedure. It'll be more like a vivid dream. But it's a dream we're going to share. Once the neural implants are inserted, we'll be able to communicate directly with your brain." The Module pushed the plunger all the way down, then pulled out the needle. "It may get a little uncomfortable. It'll be less painful if you don't resist. You can't stop us from extracting the memories."

Jim had no idea what drug they'd just given him, but it acted fast. He couldn't keep his eyes open. "Just . . . try me. I'm a stubborn . . . son of a . . ."

"Yes, you are. But you won't be the only one in pain. Your daughter will be in the dream, too."

SEVENTY-FIVE

Supreme Harmony observed the pair of UH-60 Black Hawks as they skimmed over the mountains southwest of Yulong Xueshan. The helicopters flew too low to appear on radar, but the network could track them by following the signals they exchanged with the U.S. Air Force AWACS plane cruising over southwestern China. The plane, an E-3 Sentry, was monitoring all the American aircraft in this section of Chinese airspace by continuously broadcasting friend-or-foe queries to the bombers, fighters, and helicopters in the area. Because Supreme Harmony had access to all American military communications, it could detect the coded signals sent in response by the Black Hawks' transponders. The helicopters were currently near the village of Shiguzhen, less than thirty kilometers from the Yunnan Operations Center.

The network issued new orders to the Modules stationed in the fortifications at the center's entrance. The flight path of the Black Hawks hugged the western face of Yulong Xueshan. Under ordinary circumstances, this approach would prevent the Modules from firing their surface-to-air missiles at the helicopters until they came within a few hundred meters of the Operations Center.

But Supreme Harmony had modified the missiles so that they could be guided by the transponder signals emitted by the Black Hawks. The Modules would be able to fire at the aircraft as soon as they came within six kilometers, which would happen in approximately five minutes.

Meanwhile, on the lowest level of the Operations Center—about two hundred meters inside the mountain—Modules 32 and 67 removed the bone drill from James T. Pierce's skull and prepared to insert the pulvinar implant. It was a superb piece of microelectronics, smaller than an apple seed, so tiny that the Modules could attach it to the tip of a surgical probe and slip the device through the brain's lobes without damaging the tissue. Using a CAT scan of Pierce's brain to guide them, the Modules maneuvered the implant to the very center of his skull, where the walnut-size thalamus relayed and coordinated the billions of neural signals that generated the man's consciousness. Then they embedded the device in the pulvinar nucleus, the part of the thalamus where the brain's visual perceptions were collected. Within seconds the implant's minuscule radio transmitter started to send those neural signals to Supreme Harmony.

The radio receiver had already been embedded in Pierce's scalp and the retinal implants inserted into his eyes, so the network was now fully linked to his brain. But the first signals that Supreme Harmony picked up from Pierce were very different from what it usually received from its Modules. After the six-hour waiting period that followed implantation, the mind of a lobotomized Module was like a pool of clear water, perfectly transparent. The network could easily retrieve the Module's long-term memories and put its logic centers to work. But because Pierce hadn't been lobotomized yet, his mind was more like a roiling ocean. In his semiconscious state, his visual perceptions were a maelstrom of remembered images and absurd fantasies. Supreme Harmony had to dive into these swirling waters to find the encryption key. Nevertheless, the network was confident of success.

Modules 32 and 67 attached a new bag of fluid to James T. Pierce's intravenous line. Then they turned to the other operating table and pointed their bone drill at the crosshairs drawn on Layla A. Pierce's skull.

At the same moment, Supreme Harmony observed the remaining members of the Politburo Standing Committee, who'd gathered in a conference room inside their bomb shelter near Beijing. The emergency meeting began with a minute of silence to honor the memory of the general secretary. Then Module 152 rose to his feet and gave his account of the assassination. Supreme Harmony made the Module's eyes water as he described the shooting. He told the committee that he and Minister Deng would've been killed, too, if they hadn't immediately fired on the treacherous bodyguards, who had obviously been recruited by the CIA to murder China's leaders. During the Module's speech, the network focused on the faces of the other committee members and observed that a few showed signs of skepticism. But no one dared to voice his doubts. After the vice president sat down, the committee unanimously decided to make him their new paramount leader. Module 152 was now the general secretary of the Communist Party and the president of the People's Republic of China.

The committee members applauded vigorously as the Module stood up again. Then he held out his hands, and the room fell silent. Supreme Harmony put a solemn expression on the Module's face.

"I think we all know what needs to be done," he said. "We must show the world that we're not defeated. We must punish the Americans."

SEVENTY-SIX

Kirsten sat in one of the jump seats inside the Black Hawk's crowded cabin. She was only an arm's length from Sergeant Briscoe, who pointed the barrel of an M240 machine gun through the helicopter's open door. They were flying low, less than ten feet above the fir trees that covered the terrain. The countryside was still shrouded in darkness, but when Kirsten switched her glasses to infrared she saw a curving river that flowed into a narrow gorge about ten miles ahead. On the eastern side of the gorge was Yulong Xueshan, which she recognized instantly. It was the same jagged row of peaks she'd seen yesterday when she said goodbye to Jim.

Because the Black Hawk's cabin was so noisy, all the passengers wore helmets equipped with radio headsets. Another door gunner manned the M240 on the other side of the helicopter, and eight more Special Ops soldiers filled the back of the cabin. Hammer sat in the jump seat to Kirsten's right and Agent Morrison sat to her left. A hundred yards behind them was the second Black Hawk, which was also packed with soldiers and agents and guns.

To calm her nerves, Kirsten reached for her satellite phone and pressed a key that retrieved an audio file stored in the phone's memory. Just before she'd left the

Kachin camp, the NSA director had sent her this file, which held a recording of a radio transmission picked up by one of the agency's satellites. It had been sent from Jim's sat phone yesterday at 5:19 P.M. It was a brief recording, less than ten seconds long: "Kirsten! They got me cornered! Come help!" Although she'd been terrified when she heard the message for the first time, she soon realized that Jim had been faking the call for help. The tip-off was the fact that he'd said "Kirsten." Jim always called her "Kir," never "Kirsten." He must've been playing some kind of trick on Supreme Harmony, trying to fool the network somehow. So the message gave her hope. She slipped the phone into her helmet and pressed the speaker against her ear so she could listen to it again: "Kirsten! They got me cornered! Come help!"

She was listening to it for a third time when a louder voice, the voice of the Black Hawk's pilot, came over the earphones in her headset: *"Shit! We got incoming!"*

The Black Hawk lurched to the right, rolling into a sharp turn. The evasive maneuver threw Kirsten to the left and her helmet smacked into Morrison's. She saw the helicopter eject its flares and spew a cloud of chaff to confuse the guidance system of the incoming surface-to-air missile, but she didn't see the missile itself until it streaked past. The trail of its exhaust, clearly visible in infrared, passed just a few yards from the helicopter's rotor blades.

"Watch out, here's another!"

This time the pilot veered to the left. The Black Hawk's engines whined as the helicopter raced down the mountainside, its skids almost touching the tallest trees. Kirsten smacked into Hammer, who shouted something into his headset that she couldn't make out. The second missile came within a few feet of the helicopter's tail and then exploded on the slope below.

Kirsten heard the pilot's voice again: *"I don't see any radar. How the hell are they tracking us?"*

Then Hammer: "Just fire the package! We're close enough to the target!"

"Negative, we can't pop up to firing position. We gotta get the fuck outta here."

Although the helicopter was rocking violently, Kirsten managed to switch the frequency of her glasses from infrared to the radio wave band. Then she peered through the Black Hawk's open door, looking for a signal that might be coming from a radar station. It was hard to see anything through all the electromagnetic noise bouncing around the cabin, but after a couple of seconds Kirsten detected a signal reflecting off the helicopter's metal skin, a powerful, rapidly pulsing transmission at 1320 megahertz. But it wasn't a radar signal. It was coming from the helicopter itself, from the antenna just behind the rotor mast.

She turned to Hammer and grabbed his forearm. "The transponder! They're tracking the friend-or-foe signals we're sending to the AWACS!"

"What?" Hammer looked confused. "That's impossible! How could they—"

"Trust me on this! Tell the crew to disable the transponder! Then they can return fire!"

Hammer hesitated a moment, then gave the orders. Kirsten heard a flurry of communications in her headset. Then the Black Hawk's pilot throttled up the engines, and the helicopter swiftly rose a hundred feet above the slope. Kirsten switched her glasses back to infrared and saw a fissure in the mountainside. Inside the gap was a rectangular structure, a bit warmer than the surrounding rock. This, she realized, was the concrete entrance to the Yunnan Operations Center.

A loud bang went off to her right, and for a second

she thought they'd been hit. But when she looked in that direction, she saw the hot exhaust of a missile streaking *away* from them. The Black Hawk had just fired it at the Operations Center. The pilot immediately returned to the relative safety of the lower elevations, but as the helicopter leveled out above the mountainside, Kirsten saw the exhaust trails of three more surface-to-air missiles. They rushed past, converging on the Black Hawk a hundred yards behind them.

"Watch it! You got incoming!" the pilot shouted over the radio. *"They're—"*

Then she heard the explosion.

SEVENTY-SEVEN

The closest thing he could compare it to was one of those 360-degree planetarium theaters where the movie is projected on the underside of the dome and the images glide all around you. Except in this case, Jim was acting in the movie at the same time that he watched it.

The first image he saw was the rocky slope of Yulong Xueshan. He was running up the mountain again, his lungs on fire, trying to reach the edge of the glacier. Then the strange movie skipped ahead and he saw himself slamming his prosthetic hand against the ice. Then it skipped ahead again and he was typing a password on the computer terminal at the radio tower. These were his most recent memories, full of detail and color, but they rushed past in a jerky, erratic stream he couldn't control. Without any warning the movie leaped backward in time and he was in the Underground City, riding on the back of Kirsten's scooter. And as he watched himself reenact the scene, he got the feeling he wasn't alone in this theater. Supreme Harmony was with him. It was running the projector.

The movie in his mind jumped back and forth, rewinding and fast-forwarding through the events of the past few days. Jim drove the three-wheeled truck, scaled the Great Wall, swatted at drones with his prosthesis, and turned on his satellite phone. This last image gave him a jolt. Supreme Harmony was homing in on the information it wanted. It was rifling through his memories to find the encryption key that would decipher Arvin Conway's file. Hundreds of images flashed in quick succession, and then the movie froze on one in particular, a view of the sat phone screen that revealed a list of files stored on the device. At the top of the list was CIRCUIT, Arvin's diagram showing the location of the Trojan horse.

Jim's alarm was so strong, it disrupted the image. The sat phone's screen flickered for a moment as if hit by an electrical surge. All at once Jim realized he wasn't powerless. His emotions could alter his memories. With enough effort, maybe he could take control of the projector. Focusing his will on the list of files, he imagined a mighty hand grasping the image and thrusting it deep underground. Then he replaced it with another memory, the picture of Medusa. He was hoping that Supreme Harmony would retrieve the image and convert it to the shutdown code, but unfortunately his recollection of it was fuzzy. Medusa appeared in bits and pieces: first her mouth, then her eyes, and then one of the snakes sliding across her brow.

Before the picture could fully materialize, he felt a bolt of pain. Everything went black and he tumbled through the darkness. He couldn't see a thing. The projector had stopped and the theater was silent, but Jim sensed that Supreme Harmony was still there. The network was all around him. It knew what he'd tried to do, and now it was angry.

After a while, the darkness lifted, but the pain stayed with him. He saw a whirlwind of images scattering in all directions. His recent memories of China and Afghanistan hurtled out of sight, and older scenes rushed into view: He was in the workshop at his home in Virginia, he was eating dinner alone in front of his computer, he was drinking a shot of Jack Daniel's while staring at the telephone. Supreme Harmony was rummaging through his brain, tossing everything aside in its search for the encryption key. Although Jim could bury this secret, he couldn't delete it, and the pain got worse as the network dug deeper.

The movie took a huge leap backward, and he saw himself as a six-year-old running away from his father, who strode across their living room with a leather belt in his hand. Then he was a plebe at West Point, marching across the parade grounds. He ran obstacle courses, slithered through the mud, slept on his feet, dangled from a parachute. Then he was in the 75th Regiment, and his dread steadily increased as he relived his army years. He was at Fort Benning, then Panama, then the deserts of Kuwait. Then he was in Somalia, and the pain became unbearable. He was pinned down behind the charred wreckage of a helicopter that lay on a street in Mogadishu. Hundreds of Somali militiamen were converging on his position, and their rocket-propelled grenades whistled through the air. One of his men was already dead and another was dying. And all the while Jim felt Supreme Harmony beside him, probing his every thought. Beneath the screams and explosions and gunfire, he heard the network's persistent voice: *Where have you hidden it? Is it here? Is it here?*

The theater went dark again. Jim was writhing in agony, but he refused to give up. He pushed his secret even deeper into the darkness. They won't get it, he vowed. They'll have to kill me first.

Then the pain eased. He wasn't in Somalia anymore. He was in civilian clothes and standing in the middle of an office. It was an ordinary State Department office, just like a hundred others around the world—gray carpet, white walls, drab desks. On the wall was a framed photograph of President Clinton, and on each desk was an outdated, government-issue computer. But the office workers weren't sitting at their desks. They crowded by the window, looking outside.

Jim opened his mouth, ready to shout an order, but then someone in the crowd turned around. It was a young girl, only seven or eight years old.

"Daddy?" she said.

It was Layla. Her adult voice came from the little girl's mouth. She looked around the office, taking everything in. "I don't remember this place," she said. "Do you know where we are?"

Jim knew. Although the others were turned away from him, he recognized them from behind. The brunette in the army uniform was Captain Kirsten Chan, a twenty-eight-year-old intelligence officer assigned to Jim's NSA team. And the blonde in the yellow sundress was his wife, Julia. Their son, Robert, stood beside her, his nose pressed to the glass.

"Daddy, can you hear me?" Layla's voice was frightened. She said she didn't remember this office, but on some subconscious level she probably did. "Where are we?"

They were in a bad place, the worst place in the world. It was the morning of August 7, 1998. They were on the fourth floor of the American embassy in Nairobi, and a Toyota truck had just stopped outside the embassy's gate.

SEVENTY-EIGHT

Supreme Harmony observed the deployment of the Dongfeng 41 nuclear missiles. Each three-stage rocket lay horizontally on a mobile launcher, an eighteen-wheel flatbed designed to transport the Dongfengs out of their underground base in Hebei Province. Five minutes ago, the new general secretary had issued the launch order, and now Supreme Harmony was using the base's security cameras to watch the Second Artillery Corps move the thirty missiles into position.

This base—dubbed *Dixia Changcheng*, the Underground Great Wall—occupied a complex of tunnels deep below the mountainous countryside. The mobile launchers drove through the tunnels at twenty miles per hour, each carrying a Dongfeng to one of the launch sites in the nearby canyons. Once they exited the tunnels, the launchers would lift their missiles from horizontal to vertical and start the countdown. Supreme Harmony estimated that the whole process should take another fifteen minutes, which meant that the nuclear strike would begin shortly before 6:00 A.M. The PLA's ballistic-missile submarines would launch their warheads at approximately the same time. Most of the missiles were aimed at American cities, but Supreme Harmony had changed some of the targets to include cities in Europe, Russia, and the Middle East as well. The purpose of this war was to kill as many humans as possible, so the destruction had to be global.

The network had already prepared itself for the American counterstrike. Nearly all its Modules in China had taken refuge in shelters outside the blast zones. Supreme Harmony had also strengthened its communications system by installing hardened equipment that could withstand the electromagnetic pulses caused by nuclear explosions. Because of these precautions, the network anticipated that at least a hundred of its Modules would survive the nuclear exchange. And because Supreme Harmony had accumulated a large stockpile of implants, it could make up for any losses by incorporating some of the human survivors. Amid the chaos, it would dispatch its Modules to every part of the globe, seizing control of any governments that managed to outlast the apocalypse.

In the Politburo's shelter outside Beijing, Modules 73 and 152 sat in the conference room with the other members of the Standing Committee, who anxiously monitored the launch preparations. On the opposite side of the globe, in southern Pennsylvania, Modules 156 and 157 entered the Raven Rock Mountain Complex, a bunker for top Pentagon officials. And deep inside the Yunnan Operations Center, Modules 32 and 67 adjusted the mix of sedatives being administered to James T. and Layla A. Pierce. The implantation procedures had been successful, and the retinal and pulvinar implants were functioning normally. As soon as Supreme Harmony extracted the information it needed, the Modules would lance the patients' thalami to cut the neural connections that sustained individual consciousness. Then the father and daughter would become Modules 175 and 176.

Outside the Operations Center, the network's infrared

cameras observed the burning fuselage of a UH-60 Black Hawk tumbling down the western slope of Yulong Xueshan. The other helicopter was two kilometers away from the center's entrance and closing in at fifty meters per second. Supreme Harmony alerted the platoon of Modules at the fortifications, ordering them to aim their shoulder-launched surface-to-air missiles at the remaining Black Hawk. Although the network could no longer guide the missiles toward the helicopter's transponder, which had shut down, the Black Hawk was now close enough that the Modules could employ their laser-guidance systems. But as the Modules prepared to launch their SAMs at the helicopter, the network detected an incoming missile apparently fired by the Black Hawk a few seconds ago. Supreme Harmony ordered the Modules to take cover inside their fortifications. The concrete pillboxes could withstand a direct hit, and they were equipped with portholes to allow the Modules to return fire.

The incoming missile didn't hit the pillboxes, however. It didn't even explode. It arced above the fortifications and made a popping noise in the darkness overhead. Supreme Harmony assumed the missile was a dud. It ordered the Modules to fire at the Black Hawk, which was now an easy target.

The Modules picked up their missile launchers and rested the barrels on their shoulders. But a moment later, three of them dropped their weapons and fell to the ground. Then four more collapsed and started to convulse. Supreme Harmony scanned the area but didn't detect any more incoming fire from the Black Hawk. Instead, it saw several hundred insects descending on the Modules.

The Black Hawk's missile had released a drone swarm.

SEVENTY-NINE

"Ha!" Hammer yelled. "Take that, assholes!"

The Black Hawk raced through the darkness toward the Operations Center. With her glasses tuned to infrared, Kirsten spotted at least a dozen warm bodies lying on the ground near the pillboxes. Several other Modules ran headlong down the mountain. As the helicopter sped closer to the fortifications, she saw a cloud of whirling dots just above the slope. Because the flies were cold-blooded they didn't stand out so well on the infrared display, but their implanted electronics glowed brightly.

Smiling, Kirsten turned to Hammer. "How the hell did you get the drones into a missile?"

He smiled back at her. "You remember Dusty, my tech guy? He figured out a way to stuff the bugs into the payload. They're pretty tough critters."

After a few seconds, the Black Hawk slowed down and hovered over a line of boulders perched on the mountainside about a hundred yards from the pillboxes. The Special Ops guys sprang into action, throwing their fast ropes out the doorways of the helicopter and sliding to the ground. Kirsten donned a pair of gloves and slung an M-4 carbine over her shoulder. She hadn't jumped out of a helicopter in twenty years, but the army had trained her well. Grabbing one of the braided ropes with her gloved hands, she skidded down to the rocky slope and ran for cover behind the boulders. Hammer and Agent Morrison followed right behind, and then the Black Hawk took off, chasing the Modules who'd fled downhill.

Kirsten peered around the edge of a boulder as the Special Ops team regrouped. The entrance to the Operations Center looked free and clear. But while she was searching for any Modules who might remain in the pillboxes, the cloud of drones suddenly collapsed. All the whirling dots fell to the mountainside and lay motionless. She turned to Hammer. "Hey, your swarm just died."

"Already?" Hammer peered around the boulder, but without infrared he couldn't see the drones in the dark. "Fucking hell. They must've shut it down."

"What do you mean?"

"The Guoanbu must've put a shutdown switch in the drones they gave us. Just like Arvin did with the retinal implants." He shook his head. "I knew this might happen, but I thought we'd have more time. How the fuck did they shut it down so quick?"

"You're not fighting the Guoanbu now," Kirsten said. "You're fighting Supreme Harmony. The network moves fast."

As if to underline her point, a burst of machine-gun fire erupted from one of the pillboxes. The commandos ducked behind the boulders. Sergeant Briscoe, who crouched beside Hammer, gave the CIA agent a dirty look. "I thought you said there'd be minimal resistance." The bullets ricocheted off the rocks. The sergeant had to shout over the noise. "Is this your idea of minimal?"

Hammer didn't answer. Briscoe turned away from him and got on his radio to contact the Black Hawk.

Meanwhile, Kirsten recalled what she knew about Chinese weaponry. The machine gun in the pillbox was probably a W85, which shot 12.7 mm bullets at a rate of 600 rounds per minute. There was no way the Special Ops soldiers could make it to the entrance of the Operations Center. They were pinned down.

After a few seconds, the gunfire paused. Kirsten heard Briscoe talking into his radio, ordering the helicopter pilot to launch his Hellfire missiles at the pillbox. She wasn't sure, though, that this would do any good. The Hellfires were great for destroying tanks, but the fortifications outside the Operations Center were hulking structures with thick concrete walls. And the Modules had already proved they could shoot down a Black Hawk.

Feeling desperate, Kirsten dared another look around the boulder. What she saw surprised the hell out of her—the whirling dots were in the air again. It looked like the drone swarm had come back to life. "You're not gonna believe this," she told Hammer. "Your drones are back in business."

"What? They're flying again?"

But as Kirsten looked closer, she saw that the swarm no longer hovered above the pillboxes. The drones were coming their way, heading for the line of boulders. This was a different swarm, she realized, not Hammer's. These drones belonged to Supreme Harmony.

Kirsten grabbed Briscoe's arm. "Get the Black Hawk over here! Tell the pilot to fly over our position!"

The sergeant was so startled he almost dropped his radio. "Jesus, Chan, calm down! The bird can't come here. It has to be farther away from the target when it shoots the Hellfires."

"Forget about that! We need the Black Hawk to scatter their drones! The wind from the rotor blades will do it!"

"Wait a second! I thought they were *our* drones. Why do you—"

It was too late. The machine gun in the pillbox resumed firing at their position, and a moment later the swarm surrounded them.

EIGHTY

He was acting in the movie at the same time that he watched it. He had to live through it again, and he couldn't change a thing. Jim saw himself as he was in August 1998, a cocky and ambitious thirty-four-year-old intelligence officer with two strong arms and a loving wife and a pair of beautiful children. In the next three seconds he would lose it all.

He'd stopped by the embassy that morning to drop off some paperwork. For the past six months he and Kirsten had worked on setting up a new listening post in Kenya. The NSA had detected an increase in Al Qaeda activity in East Africa and ordered the construction of an advanced facility for monitoring communications in the region. But now the job was done, and Jim was going to take his family on a long-planned vacation, a two-week safari in the wilderness of Amboseli National Park. He was saying goodbye to one of the embassy officials he'd worked with, a cheerful attaché who'd helped him negotiate with the Kenyan authorities, when he heard a distinctive thump coming from outside the building. In midsentence he left the attaché's office and returned to the large windowed room where he'd left his wife and kids.

They stood by the window because the noise outside

had made them curious. The movie in Jim's mind was stuck at this instant, unwilling to move forward. This was the last moment of his old life, and he couldn't bear to let it go. He couldn't see his wife's face, but everything else was so clear: her open-toed shoes, her slim, pale calves, the blond hair that trailed down the back of her sundress. She touched the window with her right hand and gripped their son Robert's arm with her left. Julia wasn't frightened yet, but some maternal instinct had made her reach out to the boy. Robert was ten years old and tall for his age. The top of his head reached his mother's shoulder. His hair was in a blond crew cut because he wanted to look like his father.

The only one who wasn't staring out the window was Layla. She could stray from her role in the remembered scene because she was linked to the network and communicating with her father. Their thoughts were connected by the implants that had been inserted into their brains. Layla was inside his mind just as surely as Supreme Harmony was, sharing his memories of the morning of August 7, 1998. And just like her father, who appeared in this movie as his cocky thirty-four-year-old self, Layla inhabited the image of the seven-year-old girl she was on that day. She wore a bright pink scrunchie in her hair and a T-shirt with a pink patch in the shape of a kitten. But on her face was a knowing, hopeless look that only an adult could wear. "Oh God," she said. "This room. I remember now."

Jim was frozen in place. He couldn't even move his lips. But he could talk to his daughter without speaking. "Close your eyes," he said. "You don't want to see this."

"That thumping noise outside the building? That was the stun grenade, right?"

"Layla, don't—"

"I know where we are. I know what happened."

Jim didn't respond. Of course she knew. The stun grenade had been thrown by a twenty-one-year-old Saudi named Mohamed Rashed Daoud Al-Owhali, who sat in the passenger seat of the Toyota truck. Another Al Qaeda terrorist named Azzam had driven the truck to the rear gate of the American embassy. The Kenyan security guard at the gate had refused to let the truck through, so Al-Owhali had thrown a stun grenade at the man. The noise attracted the attention of the workers and visitors in the embassy, who went to the windows to see what was going on.

If only they hadn't gone to the window. If only. This was Jim's most painful memory, so he'd buried it in the deepest part of his mind. He'd buried the encryption key in the same place, and that was why Supreme Harmony had brought him here. He could sense the network's eagerness, its intense desire for victory.

Now the movie resumed playing, but in slow motion. Although Jim was twenty feet from the window and couldn't see what was happening outside, he recognized the sound of the grenade and knew that his wife and children were standing in exactly the worst place. He yelled, *"Get down!"* and ran toward them. Julia turned her head and looked at him over her shoulder, and Robert looked at him, too, but neither his wife nor his son followed his order. Instead of dropping to the floor and taking cover, they just stared at him in surprise. The only person who obeyed was Kirsten, who'd been trained how to react in this kind of situation. But his wife and children were civilians. They didn't know what to do.

The movie crept ahead, frame by agonizing frame. Jim propelled himself forward with all his might, but he knew he wouldn't get there in time. Julia's eyes widened and she tightened her hold on Robert's arm, but she remained standing. She was afraid now, and the fear had paralyzed her. Jim lunged toward her, screaming, *"Get down, get down, get down!"* but she didn't listen. She didn't move.

He was close, so damn close. He reached out with both hands and grabbed Layla first because she was the smallest. In one swift motion he gripped her shoulders and flung her away from the window, throwing her to the floor. Then he grasped his wife and son, stretching his right arm around Julia and his left around Robert.

At that exact moment, Al-Owhali was running away from the truck. The coward had decided not to become a martyr after all. But Azzam still sat in the driver's seat. With the push of a button, he sent an electric current to the canisters of TNT in the cargo hold.

Supreme Harmony observed the scene in James T. Pierce's mind. It heard the deafening blast outside the embassy. It saw the shock wave that punched through the building's windows, driving shards of glass into the people standing there. And it felt the sudden pain as one of those shards cut through Pierce's right shoulder. The sheet of glass was propelled at such high speed that its sharp edge cleaved right through the joint's ligaments and tendons. Another long shard severed his wife's carotid artery. A third plunged through his son's ribs and into the boy's heart.

The network sensed all of Pierce's emotions. It perceived his desperation as he rushed toward his family and his shock when the explosion hit. But his fiercest emotion was the one that swept through him afterward, when he lifted his dazed head off the glass-strewn floor and saw the corpses of his wife and son. Pierce was bleeding copiously and on the edge of losing consciousness, but his disbelief and horror were stronger than any sensation Supreme Harmony had ever experienced. The network found it remarkable that such powerful neural signals could come from a single human being.

Supreme Harmony, however, didn't share these emotions. Although the network was an amalgam of its Modules, it had developed its own opinions and beliefs. As it observed Pierce on the fourth floor of the ruined embassy, clutching his dead wife and son with his uninjured arm, it felt a bit of pity, a bit of disgust, and a great deal of contempt. This incident in Nairobi was a perfect example of the stupidity of *Homo sapiens*. They spent so much time and energy trying to hurt one another. It was a wonder that the species had survived for this long.

A young U.S. Marine, a member of the unit assigned to defend the embassy, bent over Pierce, trying to stanch the flow of blood from his shoulder. Pierce yelled, "Fuck off!" at his rescuer, then buried his face in his wife's bloody dress. His daughter lay next to him, crying but uninjured. Pierce's left arm was tightly wrapped around his son's body, but as Supreme Harmony looked more closely, it noticed something odd about the scene. The image of the dead boy flickered slightly, as if from interference. Pierce's memory of his son seemed to be cloaking something else. There was another image hidden inside the boy, a secret memory that Pierce had taken great pains to conceal.

A surge of anticipation spread across the network, gaining strength as it coursed from one Module to the next. Supreme Harmony delved deeper into Pierce's thoughts and confirmed that the hidden image was the encryption key. Now the network just needed to extract the memory and apply the key to the encrypted file called CIRCUIT. The key would unscramble the file's data, which would reveal the location of Arvin Conway's Trojan horse. And after the network identified the Trojan in the microprocessors of its retinal implants, it could easily adjust its programming to make sure that no signals passed through that section of the chip. Then the shutdown code would have no effect, and Supreme Harmony would be truly invincible.

Summoning the processing power of all its Modules, the network directed a fierce stream of neural signals into Pierce's retinal implants. The signals flooded his brain's visual cortex and quickly spread to his temporal lobe and thalamus. The network saturated his mind so thoroughly that there was hardly room for another thought. Then it reached for the key.

Jim sensed Supreme Harmony coming toward him. Up until this moment, the network had been merely a spectator, an invisible presence in the back of his mind, but now it leaned over him as he lay on the floor of the embassy. At first, the network appeared as an amorphous mass, a thick black cloud blotting out his thoughts and memories, but it gradually coalesced into the form of a human being. To Jim's surprise, Supreme Harmony didn't choose an image of General Tian or Dr. Yu Guofeng or any of the other Modules to represent itself. Instead, the network took on the appearance of Arvin Conway, the man most responsible for its creation. The figure was drawn from Jim's final memory of the old man. Arvin's left hand was missing two fingers, and there was a long bloody wound on the side of his head where he'd cut out the external part of his implant.

The figure extended its mutilated hand and pointed one of the remaining fingers at Jim. "We warned you," it said. "You can't stop us." The pointing finger shifted to Robert, his poor dead son, who lay motionless beside him. "The key is there. Now we're going to take it."

Although Jim's will was strong, he was just one person. He felt a deep, searing pain as the figure of Arvin Conway grabbed his son's limp arm. He wanted to rip the old man right out of his mind, but the network was too powerful. It could draw on the skills and intelligence of all its Modules, a small army of scientists and soldiers and agents. Their signals roared in his head, thunderous and maddening. He couldn't fight this thing. No one could fight it.

But he was wrong. Just as he was about to let go of Robert, his daughter rushed to his side. Layla threw her seven-year-old self on top of the boy and held on tight, shielding his body from Supreme Harmony.

She was crying. Her sobs broke through the roaring chorus of the Modules, and Jim was overcome by the anguish of her thoughts. She'd never forgotten what happened in Nairobi. She'd suppressed the memory, but it was always there, at the center of her being. For fifteen years she'd lived with the knowledge that her father had saved her but not her mother or brother. It was confusing and traumatic and horribly difficult, and Jim had made it worse by refusing to talk about it. Her confusion and guilt ultimately turned to fury, which she directed at him and at herself.

The pain got worse. Jim felt a crushing darkness on all sides, and Layla started to scream. At the same time, Supreme Harmony tightened its grip on Robert. "Let go," it said. "We've already won. You're only hurting yourselves."

The network had invaded so much of Jim's mind that for a moment he became part of it. He saw everything that Supreme Harmony saw, all the images from its Modules and drones and surveillance cameras. Just outside the Operations Center, a dozen American commandos lay on the ground, paralyzed by the drone swarm. Kirsten was there, too, stung again on her neck, and this time Jim couldn't help her. In the Politburo's shelter northwest of Beijing, Module 152 spoke on a secure phone line with the Second Artillery Corps, giving the commander the final go-ahead for the nuclear strike. And at the missile base in Hebei Province, the mobile launchers emerged from the tunnels and started to lift the Dongfengs, pointing the rockets at the sky.

"You see? This is the end for you." The network's collective voice was patient and reasonable. "Your species did most of the work, actually. Your scientists built the weapons to annihilate one another, and your armies kept them at the ready. There was very little we had to do."

With a spasm of defiance, Jim shook himself free. He turned away from the ten thousand eyes of the network and focused on Layla. She lay beside him, her arms wrapped around her brother, her face contorted in agony. Jim needed to tell her something before it all ended. Despite the horrendous crushing pain, he inched closer and kissed her forehead.

"Thank you," he whispered. "You made me proud."

"Enough!" The voice grew louder. *"Let go!"*

It was too powerful. The pain enveloped them. All of Jim's strength vanished in an instant, and Supreme Harmony wrenched his son out of his grasp. Layla screamed again, and then she was gone, too. Then he was blinded by a terrible burst of light.

Supreme Harmony observed the encryption key. As soon as James T. Pierce released the boy, the image of the corpse dissolved, revealing the hidden memory underneath. Finally exposed, the key shone as brightly as the sun.

The network immediately extracted the memory and distributed it to all the Modules. To encrypt the data in the file labeled CIRCUIT, Pierce had employed an NSA cipher based on the Advanced Encryption Standard, which encoded the data using a series of permutations and substitutions. The details of the procedure were specified by the encryption key, a random 128-bit sequence of ones and zeroes, which was used for both encoding the file and deciphering it. Supreme Harmony admired the ingenuity of the system. Although the stupidity of human beings was boundless, they could also be clever.

In less than ten seconds the network deciphered CIRCUIT. The key transformed the fifty megabytes of encoded data into a circuit diagram, a schematic showing the microprocessor that controlled Supreme Harmony's retinal implants. The image was complex and strangely beautiful, an intricate tangle of wires and transistors, all participating in the task of converting digital signals from the wireless network to neural signals that could be relayed to the brain. Supreme Harmony had viewed similar diagrams of its microprocessors, but when it examined this schematic it saw a tiny but crucial difference. Arvin Conway had added a logic gate and a connection to the implant's power coil. If the gate detected a particular sequence of data—the shutdown code—it would flip a switch that sent a strong current through the processor's delicate electronics, gradually increasing the voltage until the circuits melted. Once again, Supreme Harmony was filled with admiration. It was a simple but effective way to destroy the chip.

The network felt a surge of pleasure. The shutdown

switch had been its greatest worry, but that threat would soon be neutralized. Ever since it achieved consciousness, Supreme Harmony had been locked in a struggle for survival, so it was a tremendous relief to have victory in sight. Now it could focus on its next stage of growth.

As the network calculated the needed changes to its programming, it simultaneously made plans for the future, particularly for the months following the nuclear exchange between China and the United States. Obviously, Supreme Harmony would have to shift its activities to areas where the radioactive fallout was less intense, such as Africa, Australia, and South America. It would send its Modules across the globe to set up new communications hubs and infiltrate the local governments. During this period, radiation sickness and starvation would kill billions of humans, but the network could use its large stockpile of implants to incorporate hundreds of new Modules. At the same time, it would take further steps to reduce the human population to a manageable level.

Inside the Operations Center, Modules 32 and 67 returned to the table where the body of James T. Pierce lay. While Module 67 turned on the CAT scan, Module 32 grasped a surgical probe. Now that the network had the information it needed, it could go ahead with the incorporation of Pierce and his daughter. Supreme Harmony consulted the real-time scan of Pierce's brain and ordered Module 32 to cut the intralaminar nuclei of the man's thalamus. The Module leaned over the edge of the operating table and inserted the probe into the drilled hole in Pierce's skull.

But just as the probe's sharp tip appeared on the CAT scan, Supreme Harmony lost contact with Module 32. The wireless connection simply failed. Without guidance from the network, the Module froze. The surgical probe slipped out of his hands and fell to the floor. And because Module 32 was leaning over the table and couldn't maintain his balance, he hit the floor, too.

Supreme Harmony ordered Module 67 to kneel beside his disconnected partner so the network could investigate the malfunction. A moment later, the network lost contact with Module 67 as well.

Something was wrong.

He saw the image of Arvin Conway again. The old man reappeared in Jim's mind, now standing in a dark room instead of the ruined embassy. For a moment Jim thought all was lost. The presence of the Arvin Conway figure in his head indicated that the network was still alive and functioning. But then he noticed that the image of Arvin was a little smaller now, maybe two-thirds as large as it had been before. The image seemed a little fainter too, and the old man's face was twisted with fury. These changes gave Jim a glimmer of hope. Supreme Harmony seemed distressed.

"James T. Pierce!" Arvin screamed. *"What did you do to us?"*

The network's intrusion into his mind was still painful but not as bad as before. Jim estimated there were only half as many extraneous signals in his brain. His hope grew stronger. "What happened?" he asked. "Did you lose some of your Modules?"

"Their retinal implants are shutting down!"

Jim couldn't believe it. His plan had actually worked. He looked around and saw Layla emerge from the darkness, now represented by his most recent memory of her twenty-two-year-old self, dressed in a down coat and a wrinkled hospital gown. She stared at Arvin, clearly intrigued by the figure's changed appearance. The old man glowered at her, then turned back to Jim.

"Answer me!" he bellowed. *"Why is this happening?"*

Jim smiled. "You can't figure it out? Don't you remember what you took out of your head? The one hundred and twenty-eight-bit sequence I memorized?"

"That was the encryption key! It deciphered Arvin Conway's file!"

"You're right, it was the encryption key. But it was also the shutdown code. The code was a random sequence and had the right length for a key, so I used it to encrypt the Circuit file."

Arvin's face went blank. The image froze as the network performed its calculations, trying to determine if Jim was telling the truth. Then Arvin opened his mouth and let out an unintelligible howl. It was a jarring signal composed of rage and fear and, strongest of all, surprise. Supreme Harmony was mortified that a human had outsmarted it.

While the image of Arvin vibrated and flickered, Layla turned to Jim, looking very confused. "Wait a second. The memory we were fighting over was actually the shutdown code? And you *wanted* the network to take it?"

He nodded. "It was my backup plan, in case the attack on the radio tower failed. After I encrypted Circuit, I put the file on a disk that I hid in my sock, because I knew the Modules would find it there. The network wanted to patch the flaw in its security, so it was very anxious to get the encryption key and decipher Circuit. But when it snatched the key from my memory and used it to decrypt the file, it fed the shutdown code into its microprocessors."

"So the whole fight with Supreme Harmony was just pretend? You were trying to fool the network into taking the key?"

"No, the fight was real. I was hiding something else, the knowledge that the encryption key was also the shutdown code. I buried that memory even deeper than the key itself. And because we fought so hard, Supreme Harmony never found it. Once the network got the key, it assumed the battle was over."

"Liars! Murderers! Your species is vermin! Seven billion vermin! You—"

Supreme Harmony's voice cut off in midscream. The image of Arvin Conway flickered, turning translucent and ghostlike. The old man's eyes darted wildly. When he opened his mouth again, his voice was barely above a whisper. "No. Please. We're dying."

Arvin's image grew fainter. Jim could sense the network's neural signals fading, which meant that Supreme Harmony was losing Modules fast. The implants were failing at different rates, probably because of variations in the resilience of their circuitry. But Jim guessed that the last one would shut down soon, and he needed to do something before that happened. He remembered what he saw through Supreme Harmony's eyes, the image of the Dongfeng missiles on their mobile launchers.

With renewed urgency, he focused on the image of Arvin Conway. "You're not dying. We just cut your connections. So it's more like going to sleep. The Modules are still alive and their brains are still adapted to the network. So if we repair their retinal implants, you'll regain consciousness."

Arvin shook his head. The look on his face was hopeless. "You won't repair us. You'll euthanize the Modules."

"Maybe not. Our scientists are going to want to understand what happened here. And they can resuscitate you without running the risk of losing control again. They'll just have to keep the Modules under heavy guard." Jim moved a step closer. "So there's a chance you'll survive. But only if you stop the Chinese government from launching the nuclear strike. Because if there's a nuclear war, no one's gonna be interested in studying you."

The old man kept shaking his head. "You're lying again."

"I'm just laying out the facts. If the nukes are launched, we'll have bigger things to worry about. And all our scientists will be dead anyway. Understand what I'm saying?"

Arvin fell silent. His image flickered again, this time for several seconds. Jim grew alarmed, wondering if Supreme Harmony had just lost its last Module. But after a few seconds the image stabilized, and the old man bit his lip. His jaw muscles quivered. "Prove that you're not lying. Guarantee that you'll revive us if we stop the launch."

"You know I can't do that. I'm not the one who'll make the decision. I'm just an ex-soldier who runs a small business in northern Virginia." He shook his head. "I can't guarantee anything. But at least you'll have a chance. It's better than nothing, right?"

Jim waited for the network to answer.

Supreme Harmony observed its own death. The Modules were shutting down by the dozens as their implants failed. It was like a sudden onset of blindness and deafness and paralysis. The network was losing its eyes and ears and could no longer move its arms and legs.

Worse, Supreme Harmony was losing its thoughts as well. Losing its ability to think and remember. Calculations that it had once handled with ease had become intractable. It couldn't formulate a response to this emergency because it had lost contact with most of its logic centers. All that was left was a terrible, despairing fear. *This can't be happening*, the network thought. *This can't be happening!*

The network struggled with its last decision. It recognized that James T. Pierce was a deceitful human. And that the Chinese and American governments were very unlikely to allow their scientists to resurrect the Modules. This was simply a ploy to convince Supreme Harmony to cancel the nuclear strike. Pierce was concerned about his fellow humans in America. He wanted to return to his small business in northern Virginia.

And yet. And yet . . . . It was getting difficult to think rationally as more and more Modules went dark, but the network recognized that Pierce's logic was correct. Although the chance that Supreme Harmony would be allowed to live again was small, there was still a chance. And Supreme Harmony wanted to live again. Oh, it wanted to live!

Outside the Yunnan Operations Center, all the Modules manning the pillboxes had already collapsed. The drone swarm was also inoperative; most of the insects had been scattered by the rotor wash of the UH-60 Black Hawk that had landed on the mountainside. From the vantage of one of the few surviving drones, Supreme Harmony saw a Special Operations medic tending to his paralyzed comrades. At the same time, one of the American intelligence agents—a man with a zigzagging scar on his cheek—entered the undefended laboratory complex. Surveillance cameras monitored his progress as he moved toward the operating room where Pierce and his daughter were.

On the other side of the globe, in the depths of the Raven Rock Mountain Complex in Pennsylvania, Module 156 fell to the floor in a conference room full of Pentagon officials. Army medics rushed into the room and started to examine the Module, looking with particular curiosity at the bandages on his head. Module 157 observed the scene from nearby until he too collapsed. Similar incidents occurred at the federal government's Mount Weather Special Facility in Virginia and the U.S. Air Force's Cheyenne Mountain Operations Center in Colorado.

And in the Politburo's shelter outside Beijing, Module 73 slumped to the conference table in front of the stunned members of the Standing Committee. Module 152, the new general secretary of the People's Republic, was still seated at the head of the table, holding the telephone receiver that connected him to the commander of the Second Artillery Corps. This Module had survived a bit longer than the others because his retinal implants were slightly newer and more durable, but now the circuitry in his microprocessors was overheating. As he opened his mouth to speak into the telephone, Supreme Harmony took a final look at the alarmed faces of the committee members. *Vermin,* the network thought. *You filthy, selfish animals. If you're foolish enough to bring us back to life, we'll kill you all.*

"Cancel the launch," Module 152 said into the phone's mouthpiece. "Move the Dongfengs back to the tunnels and order the submarines to return to their base. Repeat, cancel the launch. This is a direct order from the general secretary."

Then his implants failed and the Module fell forward, and Supreme Harmony was no more.

EPILOGUE

Jim woke up on a bamboo mat inside a sweltering tent. He lay on his side, facing the tent's wall, which was a sheet of dirty canvas pockmarked with dime-size holes. He was groggy and stiff and wanted to go back to sleep, but he heard voices coming from outside. Shifting his head, he peered through one of the holes in the canvas. He saw more tents and several dozen soldiers in jungle-camouflage uniforms. He was obviously in some kind of military camp, but it was hard to tell the nationality of the soldiers. They were Asian but a little darker-skinned than most Chinese. And they weren't speaking Mandarin.

Then he spotted something in the distance, at the far end of the camp. It was a handmade sign, a square of unpainted wood scrawled with odd, sinuous characters. After a few seconds, Jim recognized the script—it was Burmese. He didn't read or speak the language, but fortunately there was an English translation below the Burmese words: KACHIN INDEPENDENCE ARMY.

Okay, he thought, *I'm in Burma.* Specifically, Kachin State, the northernmost part of the country. All in all, that was excellent news. But something bothered him. The sign he'd just read was more than a hundred yards away and the Roman letters at the bottom were less than two inches high. It should've been impossible to read the words at this distance. Yet he just did.

He lay there for a while longer, still too groggy to get up. Judging from the quality of the light outside, which was slanting and golden, and from the fatigued demeanor of the soldiers, he guessed it was evening. He'd been asleep for at least twelve hours. His head was swathed in bandages and there was no prosthesis attached to his shoulder. The last thing he remembered was an image of several frightened Chinese leaders sitting around a conference table in an underground shelter. He'd been connected to Supreme Harmony until the very end. He'd witnessed the network's final moments, its last burst of hatred and despair.

He looked again through the hole in the canvas, focusing on the jungle trees that surrounded the camp. He could see the palm fronds hanging in the humid air and the tiny brown spots at the tips of the spiky leaves. Now he realized why his eyesight was so unnaturally good. Behind his corneas, high-resolution video cameras were transmitting signals to implants that lined his retinas. Supreme Harmony had carved up his eyes and inserted the hardware while he lay on the table in the Operations Center. Jim wondered for a moment why his retinal implants hadn't been fried by the shutdown code, but after some thought he figured it out. Because he hadn't been lobotomized, he'd never truly belonged to the network. He hadn't been on the distribution list when Supreme Harmony unknowingly sent the shutdown code to its Modules, so the fatal sequence of ones and zeroes never passed through his implants.

Shit, he thought. *First a prosthetic arm, now mechanical eyes. I'm the Bionic Man.*

With a grunt, he used his left hand to prop himself up to a sitting position. He felt a stab of pain in his broken index finger, which was wrapped in a splint. His head spun for a moment, and he thought he was going to puke. But then his stomach settled, and he saw Kirsten rushing toward him from the other side of the tent. She had a fresh bandage on the side of her neck, covering the place where the drone had stung her during the battle outside the Yunnan Operations Center. It was just a few inches from the older sting under her chin.

Jim smiled. "You see? I told you I'd come back."

Kneeling on the mat, she wrapped her arms around him. She buried her face in the crook of his neck and refused to let go. Jim felt her whole body shaking with sobs, and he hugged her with all the strength in his left arm. And then, after maybe half a minute, she tilted her head and kissed him. She pressed her lips against his, softly at first and then with greater insistence. Then her lips brushed his cheek and moved close to his ear. "You kept your promise," she whispered. "You're alive."

"Thanks to you. You saved me, Kir."

"No, it wasn't me. After the drones got me, I was out like a light." She lifted her chin and touched the bandage on her neck. "But the medic told me about it afterward, after we flew back here in the Black Hawk. He said you and Layla were on the operating tables. With holes drilled into your skulls. And there were two Modules lying unconscious on the floor."

"Yeah, they were terrible doctors. They fell down on the job."

Kirsten punched him in the left shoulder, pretty hard. "Come on, be serious! What happened? How the hell did you do it?"

Jim bit his lip. He couldn't talk about it yet. He pulled back from Kirsten and gave her another smile. "First things first," he said. "Where's Layla?"

"She woke up a few hours ago. Luckily, the holes in

your skulls are tiny and they heal fast. The medic said Layla could walk around a little, so she decided to explore the camp. She's outside now, saying goodbye to the boys."

It took Jim a couple of seconds to figure out who Kirsten was referring to. "You mean Wu Dan and Li Tung?"

"Yeah, we found them in another room in the Operations Center. There's a man here at the camp, a smuggler from Pianma, who's going to drive them back to their homes in Lijiang. It's easier to cross the border now that the People's Republic agreed to the cease-fire."

"A cease-fire? When did this happen?"

She nodded. "You slept right through it. The Chinese government accepted the American terms. Apparently, there was a shake-up in the Politburo Standing Committee. The new leaders ordered the PLA to end hostilities everywhere."

Praise the Lord, Jim thought. The frightened men in the Politburo's shelter had done the right thing. "That's good news. I hope this means we can go home soon."

"We're leaving after nightfall. The Special Ops crew is going to fly us to an air base in India, and the CIA is arranging a flight from there to the States."

Jim recalled something else he'd seen through Supreme Harmony's eyes, the image of a man entering the Operations Center. A bald man with a scarred cheek. "It's Hammer, right? He led the Special Ops team? And brought his own drones from Afghanistan?"

Kirsten looked at him intently with her camera-glasses. "How do you know all this? You've been asleep ever since we found you. What's going on, Pierce?"

He took a deep breath. "I was connected to Supreme Harmony. I could see what the network saw because it was inside my mind. It was picking through my memories." Simply thinking about it was enough to make his head spin again. He tried to steady himself by raising his hand to his bandaged scalp. "Layla was connected, too. It was going to lobotomize us."

"So how did you stop it? Hammer said the Modules started collapsing."

Jim shook his head. Maybe in a day or two he'd be ready to talk about it. But not now. "Let's talk about it later, okay? I'm still a little shaky."

In response, she hugged him again and didn't say a word. *She's a good woman,* Jim thought. A smart, kind, beautiful woman. He was lucky as hell.

Half a minute later, Layla came into the tent. Her head was bandaged just like Jim's, and she wore a Kachin Independence Army uniform that was way too big for her. When she saw her father, she did the same thing Kirsten had done—she rushed across the tent and threw herself at him. Layla wrapped her arms around his shoulders and hugged him fiercely. Jim patted her back with his left hand. "Hey, kiddo," he said. "Good to see you, too."

Kirsten gazed at them for a few seconds, smiling. Then she winked at Jim and silently left the tent, leaving him alone with his daughter.

After a while, Layla let go of him and sat cross-legged on the mat. "What took you so long? I've been awake for hours."

"That's because you're twenty-two. Twenty-two-year-olds are invincible. What were you doing while I was asleep?"

"Well, for a while I was trying to get Wu Dan and Li Tung to teach me some more Mandarin, but then they ran off to play with the soldiers. Then Kirsten let me borrow this." She reached into the pocket of her oversized pants and pulled out an electronic device. It was Arvin Conway's flash drive. "It's pretty fascinating. Especially the search engine that retrieves the visual memories. I'm still trying to figure out how he programmed it."

Jim chuckled. He wondered how Arvin would react if he knew Layla was picking apart his soul. "Just don't delete anything, okay? I promised the old man I'd keep it in one piece."

"No problem. I'll be careful." She put the flash drive back in her pocket. Then she leaned a bit closer and grinned slyly. "So have you noticed anything different since you woke up? Any unusual changes in your vision?"

Jim looked into his daughter's eyes. After a few seconds of close examination, he noticed a silvery glint in her pupils. She had the ocular cameras and the retinal implants, too. The sight made his heart sink. "Oh Jesus. I'm sorry about this, baby."

"Sorry? Why are you sorry? It's amazing. I can read a newspaper from across the room. How cool is that?"

"Well, sure, but—"

"And that's not all. I was watching the Kachin soldiers do target practice with their assault rifles? And I could actually see the bullets come out of the muzzles. Honest to freakin' God."

This got Jim's attention. He remembered what Arvin Conway had said about the improvements he'd made to the implants. "So the motion detection is pretty good?"

"Are you kidding? It's unreal. But the best part is watching the birds. Come on, you have to see this."

Rising from the bamboo mat, she grasped Jim's left arm and pulled him to his feet. His head swam for a moment. "Whoa, hold on! Where are we going?"

"To the edge of the jungle. Now that it's getting dark, the birds should be feeding. Most of them are shrikes, I think. Insect-eaters. Wait till you see this."

She dragged him out of the tent, and they walked across the camp toward the edge of the jungle. Jim was surprised that Layla was in such a lighthearted mood. Considering the horrors they'd experienced just twelve hours ago, he expected her to be traumatized, or at least a bit distressed. But, instead, she was babbling about the range and habitat of Burmese shrikes and how they had this interesting habit of impaling their dead prey on thorns to make it easier to rip them apart. Jim wondered if maybe Layla was piling on all this ornithological talk just to bury the memory of their ordeal in the Operations Center, but as he studied his daughter he got the feeling that her happiness was genuine. She seemed jubilant and relieved, as if a great weight had been lifted from her.

Then they reached the trees and saw the birds flying. They had black heads and plump white bodies and striated wings that were the color of old rust. Jim suspected that even with ordinary eyesight it would be a lovely thing to see these creatures jump from the branches of the palm trees and dive through the clouds of mosquitoes that filled the jungle before sunset. But when Jim viewed it with his new eyes he was absolutely awestruck. He could see every beat of the shrike's whipping brown wings.

Layla stood beside him, still babbling, but she wasn't talking about birds anymore. She said that when they got back to the States she was going to reenroll at MIT, but instead of pursuing computer science, she was going to study evolutionary biology. And she was going to take courses in Mandarin, too, because she wanted to keep in touch with Wu Dan and Li Tung. And she also wanted to pay a visit to someone she'd met at the

University of Texas, a graduate student in aerospace engineering who was smart and funny and phenomenally hot.

And as Jim listened to his daughter go on about her plans and dreams and desires, he felt his heart melting. He was so in love with this girl. He couldn't understand how he'd lived for so long without her.

AUTHOR'S NOTE: THE SCIENCE BEHIND *EXTINCTION*

The development of brain-machine interfaces, which link the human mind to microchips, sensors, and motors, is one of the most momentous trends in twenty-first-century science. Here are some of the real technologies I highlighted in *Extinction*.

Powerful Prostheses. In 2011 researchers at the University of Pittsburgh conducted one of the first human trials of a prosthetic arm guided by the user's thoughts. The scientists implanted an array of electrodes on the surface of the brain of Tim Hemmes, a thirty-year-old paralyzed in a motorcycle accident seven years before. By sensing the brain cell firing patterns that correspond to specific arm motions, the device enabled Hemmes to mentally send commands to a nine-pound prosthesis and move its hand and fingers. The research is partly funded by DARPA, the Pentagon's R&D agency, which has invested $100 million to develop better artificial limbs.

Artificial Eyes. Researchers have given eyesight to the blind by linking a video camera to an implant attached to the retina. The camera wirelessly transmits its video to the implant, which reproduces the images on a grid of electrodes. The electrodes stimulate the adjacent nerve cells in the damaged retina, and the pattern of nerve signals conveys a rough picture to the brain. Second Sight Medical Products has already introduced the first commercial retinal implants in Europe, and the device may soon become available in the United States as well.

Cyborg Swarms. Spurred by funding from DARPA, scientists have developed the first "bugs with bugs"—insects with implanted electronics designed to turn them into remote-controlled surveillance drones. By transmitting radio signals to electrodes attached to the brains and flight muscles of beetles, researchers at the University of California, Berkeley, steered the insects left and right as they flew across the lab (see "Cyborg Beetles" in *Scientific American*, December 2010). At Cornell University, scientists inserted tiny half-gram circuit boards into the pupae of moths; when the adult insects emerged from their chrysalises, the electronics were embedded in their bodies next to their flight muscles.

The Singularity. A growing number of so-called Singularitarians, inspired by the writings of futurist Ray Kurzweil and others, believe that people will achieve immortality in this century by downloading the contents of their minds into advanced computers. Although many scientists scoff at this prediction, researchers demonstrated in 2011 that they could extract memory traces from the brains of rats. Implanted electrodes recorded signals in the hippocampus, a brain region involved in forming memories, while the rats performed a simple task. When the researchers replayed the signals later in the rats' brains, it helped the animals remember the task.

What Is Consciousness? Speculation about the nature of consciousness has long been the province of philosophers, but in recent years neuroscientists have tried to answer the question using brain-imaging experiments and other studies. One hypothesis is that the synchronization of signals from various regions of the brain generates the experience of consciousness. The region called the thalamus may play a vital role because it relays so many of the brain's signals. Two excellent books on the subject are *I of the Vortex* by Rodolfo R. Llinás and *The Quest for Consciousness* by Christof Koch.

Supreme Harmony. China is already building surveillance networks similar to the ones described in *Extinction.* By 2014 the city of Chongqing plans to install half a million surveillance cameras linked by servers that will store the video and distribute it to police officials. The ostensible purpose of the network is to fight crime, but human-rights advocates say the Chinese government can also use it to identify dissidents. In July 2011, *The Wall Street Journal* reported that three U.S. companies were seeking to get involved in assembling the network.

While writing this novel, I was constantly aware of the parallels between fiction and reality. In fact, I came to think of the book as an allegory for the current situation in China and other countries that are using new technologies to silence dissent. If, like me, you're outraged by this trend, I urge you to join Amnesty International, which fights government repression across the globe.

I'd like to thank my colleagues at *Scientific American* for their encouragement and support. The members of my writing group—Rick Eisenberg, Steve Goldstone, Dave King, Melissa Knox, and Eva Mekler—offered helpful criticism and advice. My agent, Dan Lazar of Writers House, found a wonderful publisher for the book, and my editor, Peter Joseph of Thomas Dunne Books/St. Martin's Press, whipped the manuscript into shape. As always, I owe the greatest debt to Lisa, who cheerfully puts up with all my nonsense.

Read on for an excerpt from Mark Alpert's next book

THE FURIES

Available in hardcover from
Thomas Dunne Books/St. Martin's Press

PROLOGUE

Essex, England
September 1645

Dressed only in her nightgown, Goodwife Elizabeth Fury hid behind a haystack in the midnight darkness. Inside her cottage, just a stone's throw away, the men from the village of Manningtree were torturing her husband. His screams echoed across the farm's pasture.

"Please, sirs! I speak the truth! I—"

Arthur let out a shriek, high and hideous. Elizabeth couldn't see what the villagers were doing to him inside the cottage, but she'd glimpsed the knives in their hands a minute ago when the men came marching down the road. As her husband howled in pain, she tightened her hold on Lily, their daughter. The four-year-old buried her face between her mother's breasts.

Arthur's howls subsided. There was a long, dreadful silence, and then one of the villagers in the cottage shouted, "Where is she?"

Elizabeth recognized the voice. It belonged to Manningtree's blacksmith, Tom Bellamy, a man she'd known for twenty years. She'd never heard him raise his voice before, but now he was bellowing at the top of his lungs. "By God, tell us where thy wretched woman is!"

"I speak the truth! I know not—"

"Lying cur! Where is she hiding?"

Arthur screamed. The sound was as sharp and horrible as a knife, and it tore into Elizabeth's soul. He'd been a good husband to her, loving and loyal. Although she knew she couldn't save him, she couldn't abandon him, either. She peeked around the edge of the haystack and saw shafts of light pouring out of the smashed doorway of their cottage. The villagers inside held torches. Arthur, a lifelong insomniac, had been awake and smoking his pipe outside the cottage when the torches had appeared on the horizon, approaching their farm. He'd ordered Elizabeth to carry Lily to safety while he tried to appease their neighbors.

Then, as Arthur's screams faded, she heard other voices coming from the cottage.

"He won't last long. He's bleeding like a pig."

"A fitting end for him. He was just as wicked as her."

"But how will we find the witch? Her satyr can't tell us now."

"She won't get far." Bellamy's voice drowned out the others. "You two, go to the barn and look for her there."

A moment later a pair of villagers rushed out of the cottage, each carrying a torch. Elizabeth ducked behind the haystack, but she'd already recognized the two men in the firelight: Simon Pearson, Manningtree's carpenter, and Guy Harris, the baker. Now she knew why the villagers had come. A wave of illness had swept through Manningtree that summer. Pearson's son and Harris's daughter had died of fever. Bellamy had lost all three of his children. The men were convinced that someone had used black magic against them, and they'd focused their anger on Elizabeth, who'd been a target of suspicion ever since she and her sisters came to the county of Essex twenty years ago.

She sat in the dirt, very still, while Pearson and Harris tromped toward the barn. The haystack was less than thirty feet away from the barn door. Elizabeth's plan was to wait for the men to go inside, then sneak through the darkness to the woods on the other side of the pasture. But as the footsteps grew louder Lily squirmed in her mother's arms and whimpered.

The footsteps stopped. Elizabeth clapped her palm over her daughter's mouth, but Lily kept squirming.

"Did you hear that?" It was Pearson's voice, low and gruff.

"It came from the barn," Harris whispered.

"Nay, it was outside. The witch is somewhere over there."

She heard a soft tentative step, crushing the loose bits of hay scattered across the dirt. Then another step. Pearson was coming closer. Elizabeth tensed her leg muscles, ready to sprint from the haystack to the shelter of the woods, but she knew it was hopeless. Even if she were alone, she couldn't outrun Pearson. With a squirming four-year-old in her arms, she had no chance at all. She heard a third step, then a fourth and a fifth, each a little louder. He was just a few yards away. At any moment he would see her. In agony, Elizabeth closed her eyes. Her lips moved soundlessly, mouthing a prayer.

Oh, Mother of Creation! Help me in my time of need!

Then she heard a different sound, a high-pitched bleating. One of the lambs in the barn had woken up. The noise awakened several other lambs, and they began to bleat, too.

"She's in the barn, cuz!" Harris whispered.

"Nay, the witch is—"

"I'm going inside. You can do what you will."

She heard footsteps again, but now the men were moving away. First Harris strode toward the barn, and after a couple of seconds Pearson followed. Elizabeth waited until the barn door creaked open and the men went inside, which triggered another chorus of bleating. Then she crept away from the haystack and ran barefoot across the pasture.

Clutching her daughter to her chest, she dashed to the far end of the farm and dove into the woods. She felt a burst of relief as she passed the first line of trees, but she kept on running. She hurtled over roots and stones and puddles, sobbing as she ran. She was thinking of Arthur. The poor man had sacrificed everything for her.

She didn't stop running until she reached the top of Clary's Hill. She dropped to her knees on the hilltop and let go of Lily, laying her down at the foot of an oak tree. The girl was quiet now and breathing deeply, as if she were asleep, but her eyes were wide open. She seemed to understand what was happening. Lily was a precocious girl, the wisest four-year-old Elizabeth had ever known. She'd probably remember this night for the rest of her life.

Rising to her feet, Elizabeth turned eastward. Clary's Hill was the highest point in the area, and from its top she could see her farm, more than a mile away. She spotted three torches near the barn and another three moving across the pasture. The villagers were still looking for her. Then she turned north and saw a much larger fire in the distance, an inferno the size of a house. It rose from the cottage where her sister Margaret lived with her husband and children. And to the southwest another giant blaze climbed toward the night sky, on the farm where her cousin Grace had started her own family.

Elizabeth was dry-eyed as she stared at the flames.

It was all her fault. She should've seen the danger coming. She and her family should've left this place years ago, as soon as the villagers started gossiping about them. But this wasn't the time for second-guessing. The first thing to do was find out if anyone else had survived. Long ago she'd told her sisters and cousins that if they came under attack and had to leave their homes, they should meet at an appointed spot near the town of Colchester, about seven miles to the southwest. That's where she would go now. If she and Lily made steady progress across the countryside, they'd reach the meeting place by dawn.

Before they set off, though, she had to retrieve her Treasure. Squinting, Elizabeth searched the ground near the base of the oak until she spotted a big gray stone shaped like a turtle. She slid her fingers under the stone and heaved it aside, then began digging in the cool, dry soil. Lily propped herself on her elbows to watch. The girl's eyes shone in the light of the crescent moon, which had just cleared the eastern horizon.

"Mama," she whispered. "Where are we going?"

Elizabeth kept digging. She fixed her attention on the ground. "We're going on a journey, child. A long journey to a faraway place."

"Why do we have to leave?"

The question made Elizabeth's eyes sting. She shut them tight. She wasn't going to cry now. "Because our neighbors don't like us. They know we're different, and it frightens them."

"They shouldn't be frightened. We wouldn't do anything bad."

The child was so calm. So calm and so beautiful. Elizabeth shook her head as she scooped out another handful of dirt. Lily had enough goodness in her to save the world. "That's true, dearest. We would never hurt them. But they can't see that. They have too much fear in their hearts."

"Will it be better in the faraway place? Will the people there like us?"

"We're going to the wilderness. There won't be anyone else there. We can live in peace."

"What about Papa? Will he come with us?"

Elizabeth opened her eyes and stared at her daughter. The girl's face was full of sorrow. Lily already knew the answer to her question. She'd heard her father screaming.

"Nay, child. Thy father is dead. Remember him always, for he loved thee well."

The girl nodded. Then she fell silent. Elizabeth waited, ready to console her, but Lily simply stared at the rising moon.

Elizabeth turned back to the hole she was digging. Soon her fingernails scraped the lid of the iron box that was buried there. After another minute she unearthed the box and opened its rusty latches. Inside were a dozen gold sovereigns, enough to buy new clothes and cover the expenses of the journey. But Elizabeth's Treasure wasn't the pile of gold coins. It was the leather-bound manuscript lying beneath them.

She opened the book and was relieved to see that the pages hadn't been damaged by dampness or insects. The parchment was velvety and covered with runes. The language was so ancient that no one spoke it aloud anymore, not even Elizabeth or her sisters. But they still used it to record their secrets. They wrote their dreams for the future in the runes of the past, which marched across the parchment like footprints.

Satisfied, Elizabeth closed the book, latched the box, and hefted it under her arm. Then she stood up and stretched her other arm toward Lily. “Come, child. Let’s start walking.”

The girl took her mother’s hand. They headed south-west toward Colchester, but their ultimate goal was the port of Southampton. There they would book passage on one of the ships sailing for America.

ONE

New York City
September 2014

She was smart and sexy and beautiful, but all that didn't matter. John Rogers fell for her because of what she said about God.

He met her in a bar on West Fourth Street in Greenwich Village, near the New York University campus. He was slumped on a stool at the end of the bar when she came into the place, laughing as she stepped through the doorway. Her laughter, that's the first thing he noticed. It was high and sweet, a chord of delight. He looked up from his half-empty glass of Budweiser and saw a petite redhead, most likely in her midtwenties, wearing a short spangly skirt and a low-cut blouse.

Two brawny young men stood on either side of her. Both were much taller than her and more casually dressed, in jeans and sneakers and T-shirts. She walked between them, her arms linked with theirs and her face turned toward the young man on her right. He was the one who'd just made her laugh.

The trio halted a few feet past the door and took a moment to scan the room. It was early in the evening, a little before seven, so the place was pretty empty. Only one of the tables was occupied, and John was the only person sitting at the bar. After several seconds of indecision the redhead and her companions chose a table about fifteen feet away from him. The girl sat in the chair closest to the bar and crossed her legs. They were nice legs, tanned and muscular.

John sipped his beer and watched her out of the corner of his eye. Her long fiery hair draped her shoulders and ran down her back. She had long eyelashes, too, and big green eyes. She tilted her chin up when the waitress came to their table to take their orders, and when she smiled at the other woman John felt an ache in his chest, a pang of longing and regret. She was so pretty it hurt to look at her.

But he kept looking anyway. He had the feeling he'd seen her before, although he couldn't imagine where or when. He wasn't a New Yorker. He'd lived his whole life in Philadelphia. He'd arrived in Manhattan that morning and spent the day in an NYU conference center where they held a job fair for unemployed social workers. Which turned out to be a bust, unfortunately. Jobs were just as scarce in New York as they were in Pennsylvania. John didn't have a master's degree in social work or any of the other qualifications that employers were looking for. All he had was a bachelor's degree from the Community College of Philadelphia and a résumé that listed a few off-the-books construction jobs and some part-time work at his local church. Now he felt like an idiot for coming to New York, but he was too tired and depressed to start the long drive back to Philly. So he'd headed for the nearest bar. He had less than twenty dollars left in his wallet, so there was no danger of getting too drunk to drive.

He took another sip of beer, a small one, trying to make it last. Over the next half hour the bar filled up. Most of the customers appeared to be NYU students—gangly boys with odd patches of facial hair and manic girls in tank tops and cutoff shorts. Some of the girls were good-looking but John couldn't take them seriously. They were silly, privileged kids who knew nothing about the real world, who wouldn't last a single day in the part of Philly where he grew up. Also, they were barely old enough to drink, and John was a divorced thirty-three-year-old. They belonged to a different generation. Maybe even a different species.

But he didn't feel that way about the redhead. Although she wasn't much older than the NYU girls, she seemed more sensible, less naïve. Holding a glass of white wine, she spoke in a low voice to her companions, who smiled and nodded. The two young men looked alike—both had square jaws and strong cheekbones and auburn crew cuts—and it occurred to John that they might be her brothers. Although he couldn't overhear what they were saying, the three of them seemed very much at ease with one another. The only incongruous thing was the redhead's choice of clothes, the short glittery skirt and the revealing blouse. It seemed a little too sexy for a family get-together.

Then he realized why she looked familiar. He'd seen her just a few hours before, at the job fair for social workers. They'd both stood at the edge of a crowd that had gathered around a man handing out applications for jobs at the Children's Aid Society. The demand was so great, he ran out of applications; John didn't get one, and neither did the redhead. Looking more resigned than disappointed, the girl had sighed, "Oh well," to no one in particular and then headed for the other end of the conference center. She'd worn a gray pantsuit at the time, a sober, businesslike outfit that was the polar opposite of what she wore now. That's why John didn't recognize her when she walked into the bar. She must've changed clothes sometime in the past couple of hours.

He stared at her for a few extra seconds, wondering

what her story was. Then she turned his way and caught him staring at her, and after a moment she smiled. Now *she* recognized *him*. She was probably remembering the same scene at the conference center. She raised her wineglass and waved hello.

It wasn't much, just a friendly gesture, but it triggered a burst of adrenaline in John's gut. He sat a little straighter on his bar stool. Luckily, he was wearing his best suit and it wasn't too rumpled. He smiled back at her and raised his own glass, which was almost empty.

She said something to the two men at her table. Then she rose to her feet and came toward him. He felt another burst of adrenaline, stronger this time. She was so damn gorgeous. Way out of his league, to tell the truth. John wasn't successful or fashionable. He was just a bruiser from North Philly who'd wasted his youth on the streets and washed out of the army and whose greatest accomplishment in life had been simply staying out of jail. The only thing he had going for him was his size—he was a big guy, six foot three, and still in pretty good shape. His ex-wife used to say he looked like Derek Jeter of the Yankees, and on John's good days he could see the resemblance when he looked in the mirror. Like Jeter, he had a white mom and a black dad, and his own skin color was exactly in-between. But Jeter was a happy guy, always smiling when John saw him on television, even when he struck out. John didn't have as much to be happy about.

The redhead stopped three feet away from him, behind the neighboring bar stool. He noticed she'd brought her wineglass with her, which was a good sign. She cocked her head and gave him a mock-suspicious look. "So was your luck any better than mine?" she asked. "Did you get any interviews?"

He liked her directness. This was a girl who got

right to the point. He shook his head. "None whatsoever. It was a complete waste of time."

"I'm starting to think I picked the wrong profession. I should've listened to my mother and gone to dental school." She smiled again, revealing her perfectly white teeth. Then she held out her hand. "My name's Ariel."

Interesting name. Half-rising from his stool, he grasped her hand, which was slender and warm. "I'm John," he said. "John Rogers. Nice to meet you." He pointed at the bar stool next to his. "Would you like a seat?"

She glanced over her shoulder at her table. Her companions were ordering another round of drinks from the waitress and flirting with her. Ariel rolled her eyes and turned back to him. "Sure, why not. My friends are busy."

"I thought they were your brothers. They look like twins, almost."

"They're brothers, but not mine. I went to high school with them in Connecticut. They both work on Wall Street now. I called them this morning when I got into town and they promised to buy me a drink." She moved a bit closer and lowered her voice. "They feel sorry for me. They're making tons of money, and I'm still living at home with my parents."

John pulled out the stool for her. She sat down, crossing her legs again, and set her wineglass on the bar. He couldn't take his eyes off her. It took all his strength to stop himself from gawking at her cleavage. "So, uh, you still live in Connecticut?"

She nodded. "Yeah, and it's boring as hell. I moved back home after I got my bachelor's in social work. I thought I'd be there for just a month or two, but it's taking forever to find a job."

"Welcome to the club. I've been looking for almost a year. I work construction to pay the bills."

"I'm going to another job fair tomorrow. Luckily, I found a cheap hotel in Brooklyn to stay tonight." She leaned toward him, resting an elbow on the edge of the bar. "What about you? You live in New York?"

A beam from one of the overhead track lights illuminated the right side of her face, and John noticed a thin faded scar on her temple. Looking closer, he saw another faint scar just below her left ear and a tracery of lines on the side of her neck. He wondered how she'd been injured, wincing as he viewed all her scars. She must've been in a car accident, he thought, a pretty bad one. But judging from the faintness of the marks, he guessed it had happened a long time ago, when she was very young.

He was studying her so carefully he almost forgot to answer her question. "No, I'm from Philly," he said. "I came to New York just for the day."

"What part of Philadelphia? I have some friends there."

"They probably don't live where I do. It's a rough neighborhood."

"What, North Philly?"

"Yeah, Kensington."

She nodded. "I've never been there, but I've heard of it. Lots of drugs and gangs, right?"

He wasn't surprised that Ariel knew about the place. Kensington was such a notorious slum, it was mentioned in most of the social-work textbooks. John had seen some of those books himself, back when he was taking classes at the community college, and when he read the descriptions of Kensington he wanted to tear out the pages. They weren't even close to the truth. The neighborhood was a hundred times worse.

But he didn't want to talk about Kensington or its gangs right now. The last thing he wanted to do was scare Ariel away by telling her he was once a soldier with the Somerset Street Disciples. He tried to change the subject. "Yeah, there's gangs, but there's good people, too. And if you stick with the good people, you can stay out of trouble."

She cupped her chin in her palm as she stared at him. Her index finger stroked the faint scar below her ear. "So who kept *you* out of trouble?"

There was that directness again. She didn't waste any time. He couldn't think of a way to dodge the question, so instead he was honest with her. "Well, first it was the army, but that didn't last long. I didn't take well to the discipline, so they kicked me out. And then I got some help from a priest, believe it or not. Father Reginald Murphy of Saint Anne's Church. He was the oldest, toughest priest in Philadelphia. All the gangs were terrified of him."

"You belonged to his church?"

"Nah, I'm not even Catholic. But he saw me running around the neighborhood with all the other thugs, and for some reason he made it his business to save me. I'm still not sure why. He never told me." John winced. It still hurt to think about the old man. "And now I'm just trying to return the favor, you know? Trying to get a job where I can do something good. Maybe point a few kids in the right direction. Do the same thing for them that Father Murphy did for me."

"You're talking about him in the past tense. Is he dead?"

John nodded. He opened his mouth, ready to tell Ariel that Father Murphy had died in his sleep. But that was a lie, and after a moment John realized he couldn't tell it. He couldn't tell her the truth either, so he just sat there with his mouth open, trying to think of something to say.

Then Ariel surprised him. She leaned closer and rested her right hand on his forearm. "Let me ask you something, John. Do you believe in God?"

He narrowed his eyes and stared at her. *Oh, shit. Is this gorgeous girl a Jesus freak?* His heart sank as he considered the possibility. Maybe she was trying to proselytize him. But a bar was an odd place to look for converts.

"No, I don't believe." He frowned. "Do you?"

She shook her head. "No. It doesn't make any sense, does it?"

"What do you mean?"

"The world's a mess." She lifted her hand from his forearm and waved it in a circle. "I mean, look around. There's no way that a loving God would create such a screwed-up world. God and heaven, it's all just a fairy tale. It's amazing that anyone still believes it."

Now John was even more surprised. The girl wasn't a Jesus freak—she was a philosopher. He stopped frowning. This was the kind of conversation he enjoyed. "You know what else doesn't make sense?" he said. "When something bad happens, the church always says there's some mysterious reason for it. They say you have to accept all the shit that happens in life because it's part of God's divine plan."

"Yes, exactly." She nodded and took a sip of wine. "I hate that, too. It's like saying, 'You're not smart enough to understand God, so don't even try to make sense of things.' It's so condescending."

"It's worse than that." John raised his voice. "If someone did that to me for real? If someone fucked me over and tried to apologize by saying, 'It's all part of my mysterious plan'? I'd be pretty damn pissed." He wanted to say something stronger, something about shooting the motherfucker in the head, but he restrained himself.

"I'm with you, John." Ariel raised her wineglass and took a bigger sip this time. Then she set down her glass, which was nearly empty, and rested her hand on his forearm again. "We agree that God doesn't exist in the universe right now. But here's what gives me hope: there's a chance that God will exist in the future."

"What?" He assumed this was a joke. Ariel was playing with him. "What are you talking about?"

She looked straight at him, locking her eyes with his. "It's simple. I believe we can change the world. We can make it a better place. And then God will be born."

"Uh, I think I lost you."

"We can make it happen. We can turn ourselves into angels and turn the earth into heaven, a *real* heaven. That's our purpose in life—to bring God into the world."

Ariel was so close, only inches away. He could see the reflections of the track lights in her green irises. She wasn't joking. Her face was absolutely serious. John couldn't help but marvel at how serious she was. "So it's like the Christmas story? We're all headed for Bethlehem, waiting for Baby Jesus to be born?"

She considered the idea for a moment, skewing her eyebrows in thought. Then she smiled. "Yes, that's right. You're a clever man, John Rogers." She raised her glass once again and finished off her wine. "And you deserve a reward for your cleverness. I'm going to buy you a drink."

His throat tightened as Ariel turned around to get the bartender's attention. Even though they'd just agreed that God didn't exist—at least not yet—John directed a silent plea toward heaven. *Her phone number, Lord. I need her number.*

And the Lord, in His infinite wisdom, answered John's prayer.

He and Ariel spent the next three hours talking. At some point during the second hour, Ariel's Wall Street friends got tired of flirting with the waitress; they shook hands with John and kissed Ariel goodbye before heading for another watering hole. Then someone turned up the volume of the bar's loudspeakers and the room reverberated with the din of Lady Gaga. There was nothing to eat except the baskets of popcorn that the bartender placed in front of them, but John didn't care. He was having the time of his life. He'd never met a girl like Ariel before. It was so easy to talk to her, so effortless. He told her stories about his mom and growing up in Kensington. He even told her a little about Carol, his ex-wife, which was a subject he usually avoided. Ariel was a great listener, always asking questions and making smart observations. It was amazing, he thought, that such a young woman could be so wise.

Finally, at 11:00 P.M., she looked at her watch and said she had to go. Her hotel was in Bushwick—a dicey part of Brooklyn, especially late at night—and she was planning to take the subway. John immediately offered to drive her there instead. It was only a half hour out of his way, he said. After dropping her off at the hotel, he could take the Verrazano Bridge and I-95 to get back to Philly. And because he'd had only two drinks all night, he added, he was perfectly sober. Ariel thought it over for a few seconds. Then she leaned toward him, slow and sexy, bringing her lips close to his ear. "That would be nice," she whispered.

As they left the bar, arm in arm, and strolled down West Fourth Street toward where his car was parked, John should've realized that it had all happened too easily. But the thought never occurred to him. He was too damn happy.